BROBDINGNAG
Flanflasnic
Lorbrulgrud
Discovered, AD 1703
NORTH AMERICA
Straits of Annian
C Blanco
St Sebastian
NEW ALBION
C Mendocino
Mount St Martin
Pto Sr Francis Drake
P Monterey

Jonathan Swift

Gulliver's Travels

J.S

Jonathan Swift

Gulliver's Travels

Illustrations by Mark Summers

Introduction by J. P. Donleavy

BARNES & NOBLE BOOKS NEW YORK

The text of the Barnes & Noble Deluxe Edition of Jonathan Swift's *Gulliver's Travels* is based upon The Ronald Press Company's 1938 edition of *Gulliver's Travels* edited with notes and commentary by Arthur E. Case.

The maps are based on those in the eighteenth-century editions. Spellings of the place-names have been kept as they appeared in the originals.

Text design by Charles J. Ziga, Ziga Design

Appendices

ISBN 1-56619-784-8, *Deluxe Edition*
ISBN 0-76070-063-X, *Limited Edition*

Printed and bound in the United States of America

MD 9 8 7 6 5 4 3 2 1

ML 9 8 7 6 5 4 3 2 1

Contents

Color Plates

frontispiece, Jonathan Swift

A Voyage to the Swiftian City

VEN NOW, BE IT WINTER OR SUMMER IN DUBLIN, AS the weather moves from the west, the ancient toll of its church bells and the squawk and squeal of its seagulls still echo back and forth under its morning pearl grey heavens and its evening blue-pink tinted skies. The River Liffey which divides Dublin north and south, remains flowing brownly by beneath the Ha'penny Bridge under which the salmon lurk darkly in the water. On the bleak pavements still sit here and there the begrimed faces of this city's faithfully poor with hand and hat held out begging. And by dint of destiny, done with an ancient dignity (for civility is all in this unique city), where the chancers and cads still abound just as they did these hundreds of years past, when Jonathan Swift's pen lampooned the human condition.

This erudite gentleman resided in Dublin when its dead babies were often enough to be seen floating in the River Liffey's waters out to sea. And even as one of the major cities of Europe, its slums were reputed to rival those of Naples. Its tenement streets remained little changed up until the end of the Second World War, and there was still very little in these poverty stricken districts to be seen of pleasure, and much more of deprivation, disease and death. Escape was the tavern and entertainment was but to listen to the connivers with their conundrums, who suffering the same woes and telling and hearing

stories of others' despairs, became anesthetised over their vessels of grog. However, in your better places, there were your intellectuals and wits, each of them cautiously arriving among the assembled, hoping not to be snubbed and armed with their own words available to assail and parry the ridicule always ready to be administered by the company present. Even with Ireland having since Swift's day entered the modern world and undergoing two great revolutions in the past fifty years, and ridding itself of its social sores, much of the old Dublin is still there, and nothing changed in the Irish character.

Swift's satire has, by its own duration and recognition in the rest of the world, become sacred, but in the country where he spent most of his life, his words arising out of Ireland's writhing bowels of begrudgement, still arouse a bemused ire and awe, and his causticity of thought has remained in this country's strange conscience. His bones and epitaph anciently inciting rebellion to oppression and inspiring Ireland, a land long shackled in its own repression and held in another's subjugation, to achieve its sovereignty. But in another way, the native Irish, finally becoming confident of their own destiny, and to whom Swift proposed that you can cook, boil, fry and eat babies, he has been looked upon with less than endearment until now. For the nation has at last come to cease censoring and instead to celebrate its exiled authors. And awakened, too, to the attractiveness Swift has proved to have for tourists who presently pour in their hoards into St. Patrick's Cathedral where they tread, largely indifferent, upon this brilliant satirist's bones resting under its cold floor.

This present edition of *Gulliver's Travels* makes for me a poignant reminder of my now long association with Ireland and Dublin. I never entered St. Patrick's Cathedral till this recent day, but I a thousand times patrolled the by-ways which its steeple surveyed. Following other authors in their footsteps through its dear dirty, shabby streets, so long unloved but which also made this city a never forgotten place. And perhaps more ghosts such as Swift's roam Baile Atha Cliath than any other conurbation on earth, where its inmates carried as they did

their dreams which, daily dismembered, left their souls adrift on its sea of despair. But even so those many who, tail between their legs, retreated, spending years away in foreign parts, always dreamt of return, and in doing so found that their only satisfaction was to be back.

My own arrival in Dublin came when Ireland had been frozen, isolated by the years of the Second World War, with most of its teeming tenements much as they must have been in Swift's time. In my sometimes nightly winter strolls through these slum streets, the front elevations of these houses were a mosaic of poverty, windows shattered and patched like missing eyes. By the cold evening's darkness, the red glow of a votive light to the Virgin Blessed or to Jesus Christ wearing his crown of thorns was the only sign of life to be seen. And passing the long terraces of Georgian mansions, their doorless entrances to the once sumptuous hallways opening to the winds and rain, rats scuttled across debris strewn floors. And descending the steps of one of these houses, one might confront a white coffin of a child borne aloft on someone's shoulders. Such scenes of sorrow in Swift's time must have provoked his sense of injustice cruel and omnipresent and aroused the scatological writings of this monumentally satiric man.

As one progresses towards the River Liffey from St. Patrick's Cathedral and down the grim slope, as it was then, of Winetavern Street, one reaches the ancient hostelry of the Brazen Head, Dublin's oldest inn. It would have been one of the few such places in existence in Swift's time and one to which one can imagine someone of Swift's curious mind going to find in it a redoubt of meditation and solitariness near the river, as it was to Sebastian Dangerfield quaffing bottles of stout who made his way there, as was reflected in *The Ginger Man.*

O the Winetavern Street
    Is the silliest
Of the streets full of fury
    O the very, very best
For this moo from Missouri

But there was an underlying humanity and comraderie to the discomfort and harsh reality of the wretched poverty in Dublin which helped its surviving souls endure and in whom it bred a buoyant defiance to the grimness of its tenements choked by a dozen bodies alive to a room, with malnutrition and tuberculosis providing an ever present death. I learned of such from two of my contemporaries, Ernest Gébler° and Brendan Behan, both writers who knew this world intimately. And of the defiance found in the mouths and minds making words in the pubs, where flowed the thick and sweet "red biddy," a drink that could stupefy the brain to the verge of insanity, or excite it to the extreme of attempting insults in their own homemade language. And if you did so inebriate yourself beyond soundness of mind onwards to death, no better place existed for mourners to mourn or to witness the solemn beauty of your remains tugged by teams of plumed black horses and followed by gleaming broughams bearing the bereaved. And if there were to be seen happy faces galore, be assured no sympathy or commiseration was lacking as they trundled to take your corpse to its final resting place, a glass or two of grog on the way, a ritual unchanged since Swift's day.

But rotund of cheeks, life for Swift would have been vastly different from the hollow-faced cowed and thwarted sea of Catholic poor and should he so choose, he could keep far distant from the lower orders of doubly shrewd connivers, twisters and shysters. For as a member of the dominating Protestant church he would be among those who habitually dined at the great tables in the great mansions of Dublin, where music could be heard as the candles glowed and crinoline swirled and servants ministrated, and the beeves came rare upon their silver platters while crystal goblets of the best of grog were put to lips. And there were many who, aware of the hoards of the hungry abroad

° While most readers are undoubtedly familiar with Behan and his *Borstal Boy,* the work of his contemporary Ernest Gébler is sadly overlooked today. His book *He Had My Heart Scalded* presents a brilliant picture of the Dublin poor before the war. —*JPD*

throughout the city, would take such knowledge as merely an incitement to the appetite.

However the harsh realities of Dublin, which did not mean to be cruel and which solicited compassion, did provide where and when it could. Brendan Behan, one of the few who moved in both these worlds of the well possessed and that of the dispossessed, and was the son of its most bitter environs, often occupied for a shilling an overnight cubicle in the Iveagh Hostel, in Bride Road, merely a stone's throw from Swift's cathedral. Behan, one of Dublin's own, and later famed as poet, novelist and playwright, strode like a king in his unkempt clothes through the thoroughfares that he regarded belonged to him and he frequently talked of and quoted Swift in this Swiftian city. Met on the more fashionable streets, with the tongue of his untied shoes hanging out, he'd shout an appropriate, if not always taken as a flattering greeting, but meant as such to all those familiar he passed. Roaming everywhere he would stop and chat along the streets of Nighttown. Always exuding a universal cheerfulness, he'd know as ancient friends the whores on the quays. Up dark alleys he'd confer with gun men on the run. Greeting the passing stranger arrived anew, whom if they stopped to chat, Behan would mesmerise to follow in his wake either to a pub or the notorious catacombs of Dublin's iconoclasts, there to live the first day of their lives changed forever.

It was Behan who was the one and the only man I have ever heard sing Dublin's praises, reverently loving every inch of this city and who I often heard declaim as he would from his bar stool an irreverent parody of Swift's last will and testament:

> I do hereby vouchsafe to make my last will and testicle. Not having a penny or pot to piss in I nevertheless verily do decree that there be upon the present site where I have placed, what respectable parlance dictates I refer to as my buttocks, an edifice to be erected large enough for the reception of as many incurable

accountants, tax collectors, bailiffs, money lenders, solicitors, barristers, judges, and hangmen and gas meter readers, and other odiferous total bollocks as can be collected at any one time at high noon in off the streets of Dublin and without ponces, whores, eunuchs, hetero and homo sexuals galore or golden balls of malt to keep them in contentment, leave them to suffer indefinitely in their continued middle class repression.

And so, back we should go to the great ancient cathedral of St. Patrick's. As it still stately sits unchanged amid a rapidly changing city. Its massive oak door opening upon its great darkness. To find revealed wolfhounds who lie crouched in their stone rigid integrity and find in the ancient grey gloom more of what is known about this man upon whose grave now march the thousands of tourists. Statues and tablets and monuments proclaim the great deeds of the departed. Words and testimonies of sincere affection carved in the stone or pressed on brass. The brightest, purest, the zealous, candid and bravely bold. None of whom ever stooped to the unworthy. And Swift. A man who loved and was loved. His and Stella's skulls lie together. He who could not be indifferent to suffering and poverty or the children's bodies floating down the Liffey.

And perhaps Swift living was not universally esteemed and perhaps dead not universally lamented. But he is not ignored. His skull upon death split open to examine his brain and later passed around the drawing rooms of Dublin. This city with another ancient church in whose tower has rung Dublin's oldest bells, tolled during stormy weather to remind citizens to pray for those at sea.

J. P. Donleavy
County Westmeath
Ireland
1995

Jonathan Swift

Gulliver's Travels

VOLUME III.

Of the AUTHOR's

WORKS.

CONTAINING,

TRAVELS

INTO SEVERAL

Remote Nations of the WORLD.

In Four PARTS, *viz.*

I. A Voyage to LILLIPUT.

II. A Voyage to BROBDINGNAG.

III. A Voyage to LAPUTA, BALNIBARBI, LUGGNAGG, GLUBBDUBDRIB and JAPAN.

IV. A Voyage to the COUNTRY of the HOUYHNHNMS.

By *LEMUEL GULLIVER*, firſt a Surgeon, and then a CAPTAIN of ſeveral SHIPS.

——— ——— *Retroq;*
Vulgus abhorret ab his.

In this Impreſſion ſeveral Errors in the *London* and *Dublin* Editions are corrected.

DUBLIN:

Printed by and for GEORGE FAULKNER, Printer and Bookſeller, in *Eſſex-Street*, oppoſite to the Bridge. MDCCXXXV.

A letter from Capt. Gulliver to his cousin Sympson

I hope you will be ready to own publicly, whenever you shall be called to it, that by your great and frequent urgency you prevailed on me to publish a very loose and uncorrect account of my travels; with direction to hire some young gentlemen of either university to put them in order, and correct the style, as my cousin Dampier[1] did by my advice, in his book called *A Voyage round the World.* But I do not remember I gave you power to consent, that any thing should be omitted, and much less that any thing should be inserted: therefore, as to the latter, I do here renounce every thing of that kind; particularly a paragraph about her Majesty the late Queen Anne, of most pious and glorious memory; although I did reverence and esteem her more than any of human species. But you, or your interpolator, ought to have considered, that as it was not my inclination, so was it not decent to praise any animal of our composition before my master Houyhnhnm: and besides, the fact was altogether false; for to my knowledge, being in England during some part of her Majesty's reign, she did govern by a chief minister; nay, even by two successively; the first whereof was the Lord of Godolphin, and the second the Lord of Oxford; so that you have made me 'say the thing that was not'. Likewise, in the account of the Academy of Projectors, and several passages of my discourse to my master Houyhnhnm, you have either omitted some material circumstances, or minced or changed them in such a manner, that I do hardly know mine own work. When I formerly hinted to you something of this in a letter, you were pleased to answer, that you were afraid of giving offence; that people in power were very watchful over the press, and apt not only to interpret, but to punish every thing which looked like an *innuendo* (as I think you called it). But pray, how

1. William Dampier, the famous circumnavigator and author. His book had been published in 1697. [The notes to this edition are by Arthur E. Case.]

could that which I spoke so many years ago, and at above five thousand leagues distance, in another reign, be applied to any of the yahoos who now are said to govern the herd; especially at a time when I little thought on or feared the unhappiness of living under them? Have not I the most reason to complain, when I see these very yahoos carried by Houyhnhnms in a vehicle, as if these were brutes, and those the rational creatures? And indeed, to avoid so monstrous and detestable a sight was one principal motive of my retirement hither.

Thus much I thought proper to tell you in relation to yourself, and to the trust I reposed in you.

I do in the next place complain of my own great want of judgment, in being prevailed upon by the intreaties and false reasonings of you and some others, very much against mine own opinion, to suffer my travels to be published. Pray bring to your mind how often I desired you to consider, when you insisted on the motive of *public good;* that the yahoos were a species of animals utterly incapable of amendment by precepts or examples: and so it hath proved; for instead of seeing a full stop put to all abuses and corruptions, at least in this little island, as I had reason to expect: behold, after above six months'[2] warning, I cannot learn that my book hath produced one single effect according to mine intentions: I desired you would let me know by a letter, when party and faction were extinguished; judges learned and upright; pleaders honest and modest, with some tincture of common sense; and Smithfield[3] blazing with pyramids of law-books; the young nobility's education entirely changed; the physicians banished; the female yahoos abounding in virtue, honour, truth, and good sense; courts and levees of great ministers thoroughly weeded and swept; wit, merit, and learning rewarded: all disgracers of the press in prose

2. A slip on Swift's part: the *Travels* had been published a little more than five months before the date of this letter.

3. A district in London, containing many bookshops, about half a mile north of St. Paul's Cathedral.

and verse condemned to eat nothing but their own cotton,[4] and quench their thirst with their own ink. These, and a thousand other reformations, I firmly counted upon by your encouragement; as indeed they were plainly deducible from the precepts delivered in my book. And it must be owned, that seven months were a sufficient time to correct every vice and folly to which yahoos are subject, if their natures had been capable of the least disposition to virtue or wisdom: yet so far have you been from answering mine expectation in any of your letters, that on the contrary you are loading our carrier every week with libels, and keys, and reflections, and memoirs, and second parts; wherein I see myself accused of reflecting upon great statesfolk; of degrading human nature (for so they have still the confidence to style it), and of abusing the female sex. I find likewise, that the writers of those bundles are not agreed among themselves; for some of them will not allow me to be author of mine own travels; and others make me author of books to which I am wholly a stranger.[5]

I find likewise, that your printer hath been so careless as to confound the times, and mistake the dates of my several voyages and returns; neither assigning the true year, or the true month, or day of the month: and I hear the original manuscript is all destroyed, since the publication of my book. Neither have I any copy left: however, I have sent you some corrections, which you may insert, if ever there should be a second edition: and yet I cannot stand to them, but shall leave that matter to my judicious and candid readers, to adjust it as they please.

I hear some of our sea-yahoos find fault with my sea-language, as not proper in many parts, nor now in use.[6] I cannot help it. In my first voyages, while I was young, I was instructed by the oldest mariners,

4. Apparently meaning 'paper', but there is no other recorded use of the word in this sense.

5. A frequent and thoroughly justified complaint of Swift's, although the condition he objected to was a natural result of his practice of publishing anonymously.

6. This is almost certainly a reference to the description of the storm in the second voyage (pp. 98–99).

and learned to speak as they did. But I have since found that the sea-yahoos are apt, like the land ones, to become new-fangled in their words; which the latter change every year, insomuch, as I remember upon each return to mine own country, their old dialect was so altered, that I could hardly understand the new. And I observe, when any yahoo comes from London out of curiosity to visit me at mine own house, we neither of us are able to deliver our conceptions in a manner intelligible to the other.

If the censure of yahoos could any way affect me, I should have great reason to complain, the some of them are so bold as to think my book of travels a mere fiction out of mine own brain, and have gone so far as to drop hints, that the Houyhnhnms and yahoos have no more existence than the inhabitants of Utopia.

Indeed I must confess, that as to the people of Lilliput, Brobdingrag (for so the word should have been spelt, and not erroneously 'Brobdingnag'),[7] and Laputa, I have never yet heard of any yahoo so presumptuous as to dispute their being, or the facts I have related concerning them; because the truth immediately strikes every reader with conviction. And is there less probability in my account of the Houyhnhnms or yahoos, when it is manifest as to the latter, there are so many thousands even in this city, who only differ from their brother brutes in Houyhnhnmland, because they use a sort of a jabber, and do not go naked? I wrote for their amendment, and not their approbation. The united praise of the whole race would be of less consequence to me than the neighing of those two degenerate Houyhnhnms I keep in my stable; because from these, degenerate as they are, I still improve in some virtues, without any mixture of vice.

Do these miserable animals presume to think that I am so far degenerated as to defend my veracity? Yahoo as I am, it is well known through all Houyhnhnmland, that by the instructions and example of

7. It has generally been assumed that this correction is a burlesque of pedantic scholarly accuracy, but in the light of the fact that the other emendations contained in the letter are genuine it is impossible to be sure.

my illustrious master, I was able in the compass of two years (although I confess with the utmost difficulty) to remove that infernal habit of lying, shuffling, deceiving, and equivocating, so deeply rooted in the very souls of all my species; especially the Europeans.

I have other complaints to make upon this vexatious occasion; but I forbear troubling myself or you any further. I must freely confess, that since my last return some corruptions of my yahoo nature have revived in me by conversing with a few of your species, and particularly those of mine own family, by an unavoidable necessity; else I should never have attempted so absurd a project as that of reforming the yahoo race in this kingdom; but I have now done with all such visionary schemes for ever.

April 2, 1727

The Publisher to the Reader

The author of these *Travels,* Mr. Lemuel Gulliver,[1] is my ancient and intimate friend; there is likewise some relation between us by the mother's side. About three years ago Mr. Gulliver, growing weary of the concourse of curious people coming to him at his house in Redriff,[2] made a small purchase of land, with a convenient house, near Newark in Nottinghamshire, his native country; where he now lives retired, yet in good esteem among his neighbours.

Although Mr. Gulliver was born in Nottinghamshire, where his father dwelt, yet I have heard him say, his family came from Oxfordshire; to confirm which, I have observed in the churchyard at Banbury, in that county, several tombs and monuments of the Gullivers.

Before he quitted Redriff, he left the custody of the following papers in my hands, with the liberty to dispose of them as I should think fit. I have carefully perused them three times: the style is very plain and simple; and the only fault I find is, that the author, after the manner of travellers, is a little too circumstantial. There is an air of truth apparent through the whole; and indeed, the author was so distinguished for his veracity, that it became a sort of proverb among his neighbours at Redriff, when any one affirmed a thing, to say, it was as true as if Mr. Gulliver had spoke it.

By the advice of several worthy persons, to whom, with the author's permission, I communicated these papers, I now venture to send them into the world, hoping they may be at least, for some time, a better entertainment to our young noblemen than the common scribbles of politics and party.

1. 'Gulliver' is a genuine English name: Swift probably chose it for his hero because of the suggestion of hoaxing contained in the first syllable. 'Lemuel' may have been selected because it connoted uprightness, conscientousness and self-control: cf. Prov. 31.1–9.
2. A corrupted spelling of Rotherhithe—the name of a district on the Surrey side of the Thames, a short distance below London Bridge, largely given over to maritime interests.

This volume would have been at least twice as large, if I had not made bold to strike out innumerable passages relating to the winds and tides, as well as to the variations and bearings in the several voyages; together with the minute descriptions of the management of the ship in storms, in the style of sailors: likewise the account of the longitudes and latitudes; wherein I have reason to apprehend that Mr. Gulliver may be a little dissatisfied: but I was resolved to fit the work as much as possible to the general capacity of readers. However, if my own ignorance in sea-affairs shall have led me to commit some mistakes, I alone am answerable for them: and if any traveller hath a curiosity to see the whole work at large, as it came from the hand of the author, I shall be ready to gratify him.

As for any further particulars relating to the author, the reader will receive satisfaction from the first pages of the book.

RICHARD SYMPSON[3]

3. The name of Gulliver's fictitious cousin may have been suggested by that of another imaginary character, 'William Symson', the ostensible author of *A New Voyage to the East-Indies* (1715).

Contents

PART FOUR

A Voyage to the Country of the Houyhnhnms

CHAPTER TWELVE 327

The author's veracity. His design in publishing this work. His censure of those travellers who swerve from the truth. The author clears himself from any sinister ends in writing. An objection answered. The method of planting colonies. His native country commended. The right of the crown to those countries described by the author is justified. The difficulty of conquering them. The author takes his last leave of the reader, proposeth his manner of living for the future, gives good advice, and concludes.

PART ONE

A Voyage to Lilliput

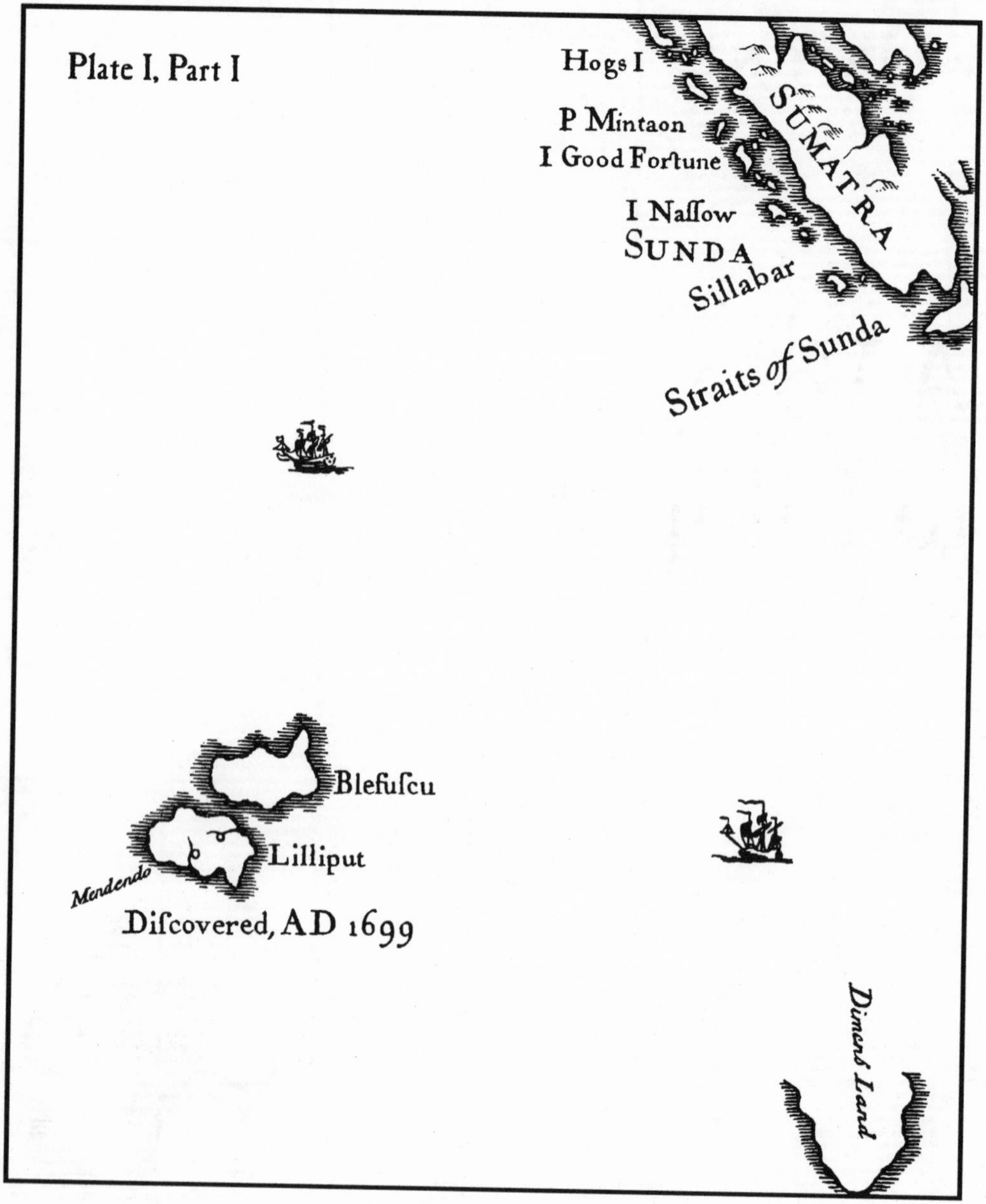

Plate I, Part I

Hogs I
P Mintaon
I Good Fortune
I Naſſow
SUMATRA
SUNDA
Sillabar
Straits of Sunda
Blefuſcu
Lilliput
Mendendo
Diſcovered, AD 1699
Dimens Land

Chapter One

The author gives some account of himself and family: his first inducements to travel. He is shipwrecked, and swims for his life; gets safe on shore in the country of Lilliput: is made a prisoner, and carried up the country.

Y FATHER HAD A SMALL ESTATE IN NOTTINGHAMSHIRE; I was the third of five sons. He sent me to Emanuel College in Cambridge, at fourteen years old, where I resided three years, and applied myself close to my studies: but the charge of maintaining me (although I had a very scanty allowance) being too great for a narrow fortune, I was bound apprentice to Mr. James Bates, an eminent surgeon in London, with whom I continued four years; and my father now and then sending me small sums of money, I laid them out in learning navigation, and other parts of the mathematics, useful to those who intend to travel, as I always believed it would be some time or other my fortune to do. When I left Mr. Bates, I went down to my father; where, by the assistance of him and my uncle John, and some other relations, I got forty pounds, and a promise of thirty pounds a year to maintain me at Leyden:[1] there I studied physic two years and seven months, knowing it would be useful in long voyages.

Soon after my return from Leyden, I was recommended, by my good master Mr. Bates, to be surgeon to the *Swallow,* Captain Abraham Pannell commander; with whom I continued three years and a half, making a voyage or two into the Levant, and some other parts.

1. At this time the most important European center for the study of medicine.

When I came back, I resolved to settle in London, to which Mr. Bates, my master, encouraged me, and by him I was recommended to several patients. I took part of a small house in the Old Jury;[2] and being advised to alter my condition, I married Mrs.[3] Mary Burton, second daughter to Mr. Edmond Burton hosier in Newgate Street, with whom I received four hundred pounds for a portion.

But, my good master Bates dying in two years after, and I having few friends, my business began to fail; for my conscience would not suffer me to imitate the bad practice of too many among my brethren. Having therefore consulted with my wife, and some of my acquaintance, I determined to go again to sea. I was surgeon successively in two ships, and made several voyages, for six years, to the East and West Indies, by which I got some addition to my fortune. My hours of leisure I spent in reading the best authors ancient and modern, being always provided with a good number of books; and when I was ashore, in observing the manners and dispositions of the people, as well as learning their language, wherein I had a great facility by the strength of my memory.

The last of these voyages not proving very fortunate, I grew weary of the sea, and intended to stay at home with my wife and family. I removed from the Old Jury to Fetter Lane,[4] and from thence to Wapping,[5] hoping to get business among the sailors; but it would not turn to account. After three years' expectation that things would mend, I accepted an advantageous offer from Captain William Prichard, master of the *Antelope,* who was making a voyage to the South

2. More accurately 'the Old Jewry', a street near the Guildhall in the east end of the City (old London within the city walls).
3. This title (pronounced 'Mistress') was given to all women of the better class, whether they were married or single.
4. A street in the west end of the City, near the Temple: a respectable middle-class neighborhood, like the Old Jury.
5. A hamlet on the left bank of the Thames, opposite Rotherhithe, and of the same general character.

Sea.[6] We set sail from Bristol May 4th, 1699, and our voyage at first was very prosperous.

It would not be proper, for some reasons, to trouble the reader with the particulars of our adventures in those seas: let it suffice to inform him, that in our passage from thence to the East Indies we were driven by a violent storm to the northeast of Van Diemen's Land.[7] By an observation, we found ourselves in the latitude of 30 degrees 2 minutes south. Twelve of our crew were dead by immoderate labour, and ill food, the rest were in a very weak condition. On the fifth of November, which was the beginning of summer in those parts, the weather being very hazy, the seamen spied a rock, within half a cable's length of the ship; but the wind was so strong, that we were driven directly upon it, and immediately split. Six of the crew, of whom I was one, having let down the boat into the sea, made a shift to get clear of the ship, and the rock. We rowed by my computation about three leagues, till we were able to work no longer, being already spent with labour while we were in the ship. We therefore trusted ourselves to the mercy of the waves, and in about half an hour the boat was overset by a sudden flurry from the north. What became of my companions in the boat, as well as of those who escaped on the rock, or were left in the vessel, I cannot tell; but conclude they were all lost. For my own part, I swam as fortune directed me, and was pushed forward by wind and tide. I often let my legs drop, and could feel no bottom: but when I was almost gone, and able to struggle no longer, I found myself within my depth; and by this time the storm was much abated. The declivity was so small, that I walked near a mile before I got to the shore, which I conjectured was about eight o'clock in the evening. I then advanced forward near half a mile, but could not discover any sign of houses or inhabitants; at least I was in so weak a condition, that I did not observe them. I was extremely tired, and

6. The South Pacific Ocean.
7. This name was applied to both Tasmania and the northwestern part of Australia: apparently Swift refers to the former in this instance.

with that, and the heat of the weather, and about half a pint of brandy that I drank as I left the ship, I found myself much inclined to sleep. I lay down on the grass, which was very short and soft, where I slept sounder than ever I remember to have done in my life, and, as I reckoned, above nine hours; for when I awaked, it was just daylight. I attempted to rise, but was not able to stir: for as I happened to lie on my back, I found my arms and legs were strongly fastened on each side to the ground; and my hair, which was long and thick, tied down in the same manner. I likewise felt several slender ligatures across my body, from my armpits to my thighs. I could only look upwards, the sun began to grow hot, and the light offended my eyes. I heard a confused noise about me, but, in the posture I lay, could see nothing except the sky. In a little time I felt something alive moving on my left leg, which advancing gently forwards over my breast, came almost up to my chin; when, bending my eyes downwards as much as I could, I perceived it to be a human creature not six inches high,[8] with a bow and arrow in his hands, and a quiver at his back. In the mean time, I felt at least forty more of the same kind (as I conjectured) following the first. I was in the utmost astonishment, and roared so loud, that they all ran back in a fright; and some of them, as I was afterwards told, were hurt with the falls they got by leaping from my sides upon the ground. However, they soon returned, and one of them, who ventured so far as to get a full sight of my face, lifting up his hands and eyes by way of admiration,[9] cried out in a shrill, but distinct voice, *'Hekinah degul'*:[10] the others repeated the same words several times, but I then knew not what they meant. I lay all this while, as the reader may believe, in great uneasiness: at length, struggling to get loose, I had the fortune to break the strings and wrench out the pegs that

8. The key to the scale used in this voyage: linear distances are one-twelfth of those in Europe, and square and cubic measurements are in accord.

9. 'Admire' originally meant 'wonder'—not necessarily with approval. The word and its derivatives are commonly used in this sense by Swift.

10. It is impossible to determine the precise meaning of this phrase or of most of the other passages in imaginary languages.

fastened my left arm to the ground; for, by lifting it up to my face, I discovered the methods they had taken to bind me; and, at the same time, with a violent pull, which gave me excessive pain, I a little loosened the strings that tied down my hair on the left side, so that I was just able to turn my head about two inches. But the creatures ran off a second time, before I could seize them; whereupon there was a great shout in a very shrill accent, and after it ceased, I heard one of them cry aloud, '*Tolgo phonac*'; when in an instant I felt above an hundred arrows discharged on my left hand, which pricked me like so many needles; and besides they shot another flight into the air, as we do bombs in Europe, whereof many, I suppose, fell on my body (though I felt them not) and some on my face, which I immediately covered with my left hand. When this shower of arrows was over, I fell a groaning with grief and pain, and then striving again to get loose, they discharged another volley larger than the first, and some of them attempted with spears to stick me in the sides; but, by good luck, I had on me a buff jerkin, which they could not pierce. I thought it the most prudent method to lie still, and my design was to continue so till night, when, my left hand being already loose, I could easily free myself: and as for the inhabitants, I had reason to believe I might be a match for the greatest armies they could bring against me, if they were all of the same size with him that I saw. But fortune disposed otherwise of me. When the people observed I was quiet, they discharged no more arrows: but by the noise I heard I knew their numbers encreased; and about four yards from me, over against my right ear, I heard a knocking for above an hour, like that of people at work; when, turning my head that way, as well as the pegs and strings would permit me, I saw a stage erected about a foot and an half from the ground, capable of holding four of the inhabitants, with two or three ladders to mount it: from whence one of them, who seemed to be a person of quality, made me a long speech, whereof I understood not one syllable. But I should have mentioned, that before the principal person began his oration, he cried out three times, '*Langro dehul san*':

(these words and the former were afterwards repeated and explained to me). Whereupon immediately about fifty of the inhabitants came, and cut the strings that fastened the left side of my head, which gave me the liberty of turning it to the right, and of observing the person and gesture of him that was to speak. He appeared to be of a middle age, and taller than any of the other three who attended him, whereof one was a page that held up his train, and seemed to be somewhat longer than my middle finger; the other two stood one on each side to support him. He acted every part of an orator, and I could observe many periods of threatenings, and others of promises, pity and kindness. I answered in a few words, but in the most submissive manner, lifting up my left hand and both my eyes to the sun, as calling him for a witness; and being almost famished with hunger, having not eaten a morsel for some hours before I left the ship, I found the demands of nature so strong upon me, that I could not forbear showing my impatience (perhaps against the strict rules of decency) by putting my finger frequently on my mouth, to signify that I wanted food. The *hurgo* (for so they call a great lord, as I afterwards learnt) understood me very well. He descended from the stage, and commanded that several ladders should be applied to my sides, on which above an hundred of the inhabitants mounted, and walked towards my mouth, laden with baskets full of meat, which had been provided and sent thither by the King's orders upon the first intelligence he received of me. I observed there was the flesh of several animals, but could not distinguish them by the taste. There were shoulders, legs and loins shaped like those of mutton, and very well dressed, but smaller than the wings of a lark. I eat[11] them by two or three at a mouthful, and took three loaves at a time, about the bigness of musket bullets. They supplied me as they could, showing a thousand marks of wonder and astonishment at my bulk and appetite. I then made another sign that I

11. Pronounced 'et': the preterite form of the verb, now archaic. It is used consistently in *Gulliver's Travels.*

wanted drink. They found by my eating that a small quantity would not suffice me, and being a most ingenious people, they slung up with great dexterity one of their largest hogsheads, then rolled it towards my hand, and beat out the top; I drank it off at a draught, which I might well do, for it did not hold half a pint, and tasted like a small wine of Burgundy, but much more delicious. They brought me a second hogshead, which I drank in the same manner, and made signs for more, but they had none to give me. When I had performed these wonders, they shouted for joy, and danced upon my breast, repeating several times as they did at first, *'Hekinah degul'*. They made me a sign that I should throw down the two hogsheads, but first warned the people below to stand out of the way, crying aloud, *'Borach mivola'*, and when they saw the vessels in the air, there was an universal shout of *'Hekinah degul'*. I confess I was often tempted, while they were passing backwards and forwards on my body, to seize forty or fifty of the first that came in my reach, and dash them against the ground. But the remembrance of what I had felt, which probably might not be the worst they could do, and the promise of honour I made them, for so I interpreted my submissive behaviour, soon drove out these imaginations. Besides, I now considered myself as bound by the laws of hospitality to a people who had treated me with so much expense and magnificence. However, in my thoughts I could not sufficiently wonder at the intrepidity of these diminutive mortals, who durst venture to mount and walk upon my body, while one of my hands was at liberty, without trembling at the very sight of so prodigious a creature as I must appear to them. After some time, when they observed that I made no more demands for meat, there appeared before me a person of high rank from his Imperial Majesty. His Excellency, having mounted on the small of my right leg, advanced forwards up to my face, with about a dozen of his retinue. And producing his credentials under the Signet Royal, which he applied close to my eyes, spoke about ten minutes, without any signs of anger, but with a kind of determinate resolution; often pointing forwards, which, as I after-

wards found, was towards the capital city, about half a mile distant, whither it was agreed by his Majesty in council that I must be conveyed. I answered in few words, but to no purpose, and made a sign with my hand that was loose, putting it to the other (but over his Excellency's head, for fear of hurting him or his train) and then to my own head and body, to signify that I desired my liberty. It appeared that he understood me well enough, for he shook his head by way of disapprobation, and held his hand in a posture to show that I must be carried as a prisoner. However, he made other signs to let me understand that I should have meat and drink enough, and very good treatment. Whereupon I once more thought of attempting to break my bonds, but again, when I felt the smart of their arrows upon my face and hands, which were all in blisters, and many of the darts still sticking in them, and observing likewise that the number of my enemies encreased, I gave tokens to let them know that they might do with me what they pleased. Upon this the *hurgo* and his train withdrew with much civility and cheerful countenances. Soon after I heard a general shout, with frequent repetitions of the words, *'Peplom selan'*, and I felt great numbers of the people on my left side relaxing the cords to such a degree, that I was able to turn upon my right, and to ease myself with making water; which I very plentifully did, to the great astonishment of the people, who conjecturing by my motions what I was going to do, immediately opened to the right and left on that side to avoid the torrent which fell with such noise and violence from me. But before this, they had daubed my face and both my hands with a sort of ointment very pleasant to the smell, which in a few minutes removed all the smart of their arrows. These circumstances, added to the refreshment I had received by their victuals and drink, which were very nourishing, disposed me to sleep. I slept about eight hours, as I was afterwards assured; and it was no wonder, for the physicians, by the Emperor's order, had mingled a sleepy potion in the hogsheads of wine.

It seems that upon the first moment I was discovered sleeping on

the ground after my landing, the Emperor had early notice of it by an express, and determined in council that I should be tied in the manner I have related (which was done in the night while I slept), that plenty of meat and drink should be sent me, and a machine prepared to carry me to the capital city.

This resolution perhaps may appear very bold and dangerous, and I am confident would not be imitated by any prince in Europe on the like occasion; however, in my opinion, it was extremely prudent as well as generous. For supposing these people had endeavoured to kill me with their spears and arrows while I was asleep, I should certainly have awaked with the first sense of smart, which might so far have roused my rage and strength, as to have enabled me to break the strings wherewith I was tied; after which, as they were not able to make resistance, so they could expect no mercy.

These people are most excellent mathematicians, and arrived to a great perfection in mechanics by the countenance and encouragement of the Emperor, who is a renowned patron of learning. This prince hath several machines fixed on wheels for the carriage of trees and other great weights. He often builds his largest men of war, whereof some are nine foot long, in the woods where the timber grows, and has them carried on these engines three or four hundred yards to the sea. Five hundred carpenters and engineers were immediately set at work to prepare the greatest engine they had. It was a frame of wood raised three inches from the ground, about seven foot long and four wide, moving upon twenty-two wheels. The shout I heard was upon the arrival of this engine, which it seems set out in four hours after my landing. It was brought parallel to me as I lay. But the principal difficulty was to raise and place me in this vehicle. Eighty poles, each of one foot high, were erected for this purpose, and very strong cords of the bigness of packthread were fastened by hooks to many bandages, which the workmen had girt round my neck, my hands, my body, and my legs. Nine hundred of the strongest men were employed to draw up these cords by many pulleys fastened on the poles, and

thus, in less than three hours, I was raised and slung into the engine, and there tied fast. All this I was told, for while the whole operation was performing, I lay in a profound sleep, by the force of that soporiferous medicine infused into my liquor. Fifteen hundred of the Emperor's largest horses, each about four inches and an half high, were employed to draw me towards the metropolis, which, as I said, was half a mile distant.

About four hours after we began our journey, I awaked by a very ridiculous accident; for, the carriage being stopped a while to adjust something that was out of order, two or three of the young natives had the curiosity to see how I looked when I was asleep; they climbed up into the engine, and advancing very softly to my face, one of them, an officer in the guards, put the sharp end of his half-pike a good way up into my left nostril, which tickled my nose like a straw, and made me sneeze violently: whereupon they stole off unperceived, and it was three weeks before I knew the cause of my awaking so suddenly. We made a long march the remaining part of that day, and rested at night with five hundred guards on each side of me, half with torches, and half with bows and arrows, ready to shoot me if I should offer to stir. The next morning at sunrise we continued our march, and arrived within two hundred yards of the city gates about noon. The Emperor and all his court came out to meet us, but his great officers would by no means suffer his Majesty to endanger his person by mounting on my body.

At the place where the carriage stopped, there stood an ancient temple, esteemed to be the largest in the whole kingdom, which having been polluted some years before by an unnatural murder, was, according to the zeal of those people, looked on as profane, and therefore had been applied to common uses, and all the ornaments and furniture carried away.[12] In this edifice it was determined I should

12. Probably intended to suggest Westminster Hall, in which Charles I had been tried and condemned to death.

lodge. The great gate fronting to the north was about four foot high, and almost two foot wide, through which I could easily creep. On each side of the gate was a small window not above six inches from the ground: into that on the left side, the King's smiths conveyed fourscore and eleven chains, like those that hang to a lady's watch in Europe, and almost as large, which were locked to my left leg with six and thirty padlocks. Over against this temple, on t'other side of the great highway, at twenty foot distance, there was a turret at least five foot high. Here the Emperor ascended with many principal lords of his court, to have an opportunity of viewing me, as I was told, for I could not see them. It was reckoned that above an hundred thousand inhabitants came out of the town upon the same errand; and in spite of my guards, I believe there could not be fewer than ten thousand, at several times, who mounted upon my body by the help of ladders. But a proclamation was soon issued to forbid it upon pain of death. When the workmen found it was impossible for me to break loose, they cut all the strings that bound me; whereupon I rose up with as melancholy a disposition as ever I had in my life. But the noise and astonishment of the people at seeing me rise and walk are not to be expressed. The chains that held my left leg were about two yards long, and gave me not only the liberty of walking backwards and forwards in a semicircle; but, being fixed within four inches of the gate, allowed me to creep in, and lie at my full length in the temple.

Chapter Two

The Emperor of Lilliput, attended by several of the nobility, come to see the author in his confinement. The Emperor's person and habit described. Learned men appointed to teach the author their language. He gains favour by his mild disposition. His pockets are searched, and his sword and pistols taken from him.

HEN I FOUND MYSELF ON MY FEET, I LOOKED about me, and must confess I never beheld a more entertaining prospect. The country round appeared like a continued garden, and the inclosed fields, which were generally forty foot square, resembled so many beds of flowers. These fields were intermingled with woods of half a stang,[1] and the tallest trees, as I could judge, appeared to be seven foot high. I viewed the town on my left hand, which looked like the painted scene of a city in a theatre.

I had been for some hours extremely pressed by the necessities of nature; which was no wonder, it being almost two days since I had last disburthened myself. I was under great difficulties between urgency and shame. The best expedient I could think on, was to creep into my house, which I accordingly did; and shutting the gate after me, I went as far as the length of my chain would suffer, and discharged my body of that uneasy load. But this was the only time I was ever guilty of so uncleanly an action; for which I cannot but hope the candid reader will give some allowance, after he hath ma-

1. 'Stang' is a name, obsolescent even in Swift's day, for a quarter of an acre.

turely and impartially considered my case, and the distress I was in. From this time my constant practice was, as soon as I rose, to perform that business in open air, at the full extent of my chain, and due care was taken every morning before company came, that the offensive matter should be carried off in wheelbarrows by two servants appointed for that purpose. I would not have dwelt so long upon a circumstance, that perhaps at first sight may appear not very momentous, if I had not thought it necessary to justify my character in point of cleanliness to the world; which I am told some of my maligners have been pleased, upon this and other occasions, to call in question.

When this adventure was at an end, I came back out of my house, having occasion for fresh air. The Emperor was already descended from the tower, and advancing on horseback towards me, which had like to have cost him dear; for the beast, though very well trained, yet wholly unused to such a sight, which appeared as if a mountain moved before him, reared up on his hinder feet: but that prince, who is an excellent horseman, kept his seat, till his attendants ran in, and held the bridle, while his Majesty had time to dismount. When he alighted, he surveyed me round with great admiration, but kept without the length of my chain. He ordered his cooks and butlers, who were already prepared, to give me victuals and drink, which they pushed forward in a sort of vehicles upon wheels till I could reach them. I took those vehicles, and soon emptied them all; twenty of them were filled with meat, and ten with liquor; each of the former afforded me two or three good mouthfuls, and I emptied the liquor of ten vessels, which was contained in earthen vials, into one vehicle, drinking it off at a draught, and so I did with the rest. The Empress, and young princes of the blood, of both sexes, attended by many ladies, sate at some distance in their chairs;[2] but upon the accident that happened to the Emperor's horse, they alighted, and came near his person, which I am now going

2. Sedan chairs.

to describe.[3] He is taller, by almost the breadth of my nail, than any of his court, which alone is enough to strike an awe into the beholders. His features are strong and masculine, with an Austrian lip and arched nose, his complexion olive, his countenance erect, his body and limbs well proportioned, all his motions graceful, and his deportment majestic. He was then past his prime, being twenty-eight years and three quarters old, of which he had reigned about seven, in great felicity, and generally victorious. For the better convenience of beholding him, I lay on my side, so that my face was parallel to his, and he stood but three yards off: however, I have had him since many times in my hand, and therefore cannot be deceived in the description. His dress was very plain and simple, and the fashion of it between the Asiatic and the European; but he had on his head a light helmet of gold, adorned with jewels, and a plume on the crest. He held his sword drawn in his hand, to defend himself, if I should happen to break loose; it was almost three inches long, the hilt and scabbard were gold enriched with diamonds. His voice was shrill, but very clear and articulate, and I could distinctly hear it when I stood up. The ladies and courtiers were all most magnificently clad, so that the spot they stood upon seemed to resemble a petticoat spread on the ground, embroidered with figures of gold and silver. His Imperial Majesty spoke often to me, and I returned answers, but neither of us could understand a syllable. There were several of his priests and lawyers present (as I conjectured by their habits) who were commanded to address themselves to me, and I spoke to them in as many languages as I had the least smattering of, which were High and Low Dutch,[4] Latin, French, Spanish, Italian, and Lingua Franca;[5] but all to no purpose. After about two hours the court retired, and I was left with a strong guard, to prevent the impertinence, and probably the

3. The Emperor represents George I, although much of the description of his physical and mental characteristics is inconsistent with the facts. Swift is either indulging in irony, or taking precautions against possible prosecution, or both. The Empress stands, in the political allegory, not for George's queen, but for his predecessor, Queen Anne.
4. 'High Dutch' equals German: 'Low Dutch' equals Dutch.
5. A commercial language or jargon used by traders in the eastern Mediterranean.

malice of the rabble, who were very impatient to crowd about me as near as they durst, and some of them had the impudence to shoot their arrows at me as I sate on the ground by the door of my house, whereof one very narrowly missed my left eye. But the colonel ordered six of the ringleaders to be seized, and thought no punishment so proper as to deliver them bound into my hands, which some of his soldiers accordingly did, pushing them forwards with the butt-ends of their pikes into my reach; I took them all in my right hand, put five of them into my coat-pocket, and as to the sixth, I made a countenance as if I would eat him alive. The poor man squalled terribly, and the colonel and his officers were in much pain, especially when they saw me take out my penknife: but I soon put them out of fear; for, looking mildly, and immediately cutting the strings he was bound with, I set him gently on the ground, and away he ran; I treated the rest in the same manner, taking them one by one out of my pocket, and I observed both the soldiers and people were highly obliged at this mark of my clemency, which was represented very much to my advantage at court.

Towards night I got with some difficulty into my house, where I lay on the ground, and continued to do so about a fortnight; during which time the Emperor gave orders to have a bed prepared for me. Six hundred beds of the common measure were brought in carriages, and worked up in my house; an hundred and fifty of their beds sewn together made up the breadth and length, and these were four double, which however kept me but very indifferently from the hardness of the floor, that was of smooth stone. By the same computation they provided me with sheets, blankets, and coverlets, tolerable enough for one who had been so long enured to hardships as I.

As the news of my arrival spread through the kingdom, it brought prodigious numbers of rich, idle, and curious people to see me; so that the villages were almost emptied, and great neglect of tillage and household affairs must have ensued, if his Imperial Majesty had not provided by several proclamations and orders of state against this inconveniency. He directed that those who had already beheld me should

return home, and not presume to come within fifty yards of my house without licence from court: whereby the secretaries of state got considerable fees.

In the mean time, the Emperor held frequent councils to debate what course should be taken with me; and I was afterwards assured by a particular friend, a person of great quality, who was looked upon to be as much in the secret as any, that the court was under many difficulties concerning me. They apprehended my breaking loose, that my diet would be very expensive, and might cause a famine. Sometimes they determined to starve me, or at least to shoot me in the face and hands with poisoned arrows, which would soon dispatch me: but again they considered, that the stench of so large a carcase might produce a plague in the metropolis, and probably spread through the whole kingdom.[6] In the midst of these consultations, several officers of the army went to the door of the great council-chamber; and two of them being admitted, gave an account of my behaviour to the six criminals above-mentioned, which made so favourable an impression in the breast of his Majesty and the whole board in my behalf, that an imperial commission was issued out, obliging all the villages nine hundred yards round the city to deliver in every morning six beeves, forty sheep, and other victuals for my sustenance; together with a proportionable quantity of bread, and wine, and other liquors: for the due payment of which his Majesty gave assignments upon his treasury. For this prince lives chiefly upon his own demesnes, seldom except upon great occasions raising any subsidies upon his subjects, who are bound to attend him in his wars at their own expense. An establishment was also made of six hundred persons to be my domestics, who had board-wages[7] allowed for their maintenance, and tents built for them very conveniently on each side of my

6. Possibly a reference to the attitude of the dominant Whig faction in the cabinet of 1708 toward the Tory minority led by Robert Harley, Secretary of State, who became Swift's great friend and patron when the latter transferred his allegiance from the Whigs to the Tories. In the political allegory which underlies the narrative in this voyage Gulliver is a composite figure standing for the Tory leaders, Harley and Henry St. John.
7. Wages including a sum for food.

door. It was likewise ordered, that three hundred tailors should make me a suit of clothes after the fashion of the country: that six of his Majesty's greatest scholars should be employed to instruct me in their language: and, lastly, that the Emperor's horses, and those of the nobility and troops of guards, should be frequently exercised in my sight, to accustom themselves to me. All these orders were duly put in execution, and in about three weeks I made a great progress in learning their language; during which time the Emperor frequently honoured me with his visits, and was pleased to assist my masters in teaching me. We began already to converse together in some sort; and the first words I learnt were to express my desire that he would please to give me my liberty, which I every day repeated on my knees. His answer, as I could apprehend it, was, that this must be a work of time, not to be thought on without the advice of his council, and that first I must *'lumos kelmin pesso desmar lon emposo'*; that is, swear a peace with him and his kingdom. However, that I should be used with all kindness, and he advised me to acquire, by my patience, and discreet behaviour, the good opinion of himself and his subjects. He desired I would not take it ill, if he gave orders to certain proper officers to search me; for probably I might carry about me several weapons, which must needs be dangerous things, if they answered the bulk of so prodigious a person. I said, his Majesty should be satisfied, for I was ready to strip myself, and turn up my pockets before him.[8] This I delivered part in words, and part in signs. He replied, that by the laws of the kingdom I must be searched by two of his officers; that he knew this could not be done without my consent and assistance; that he had so good an opinion of my generosity and justice, as to trust their persons in my hands: that whatever they took from me should be returned when I left the country, or paid for at the rate which I would set upon them. I took up the two officers in my

8. A committee of Whig lords conducted a lengthy investigation into the activities of William Gregg, a clerk in Harley's office, who was guilty of treasonable correspondence with France, but nothing implicating Harley was discovered. Queen Anne favored Harley throughout this period.

hands, put them first into my coat-pockets, and then into every other pocket about me, except my two fobs, and another secret pocket I had no mind should be searched, wherein I had some little necessaries that were of no consequence to any but myself. In one of my fobs there was a silver watch, and in the other a small quantity of gold in a purse. These gentlemen, having pen, ink, and paper about them, made an exact inventory of every thing they saw; and when they had done, desired I would set them down, that they might deliver it to the Emperor. This inventory I afterwards translated into English, and is word for word as follows.

Imprimis, In the right coat-pocket of the Great Man-Mountain (for so I interpret the words *'Quinbus Flestrin'*) after the strictest search, we found only one great piece of coarse cloth, large enough to be a foot-cloth for your Majesty's chief room of state. In the left pocket, we saw a huge silver chest, with a cover of the same metal, which we the searchers were not able to lift. We desired it should be opened, and one of us, stepping into it, found himself up to the mid leg in a sort of dust, some part whereof, flying up to our faces, set us both a sneezing for several times together. In his right waistcoat-pocket, we found a prodigious bundle of white thin substances, folded one over another, about the bigness of three men, tied with a strong cable, and marked with black figures; which we humbly conceive to be writings, every letter almost half as large as the palm of our hands. In the left, there was a sort of engine, from the back of which were extended twenty long poles, resembling the palisados before your Majesty's court; wherewith we conjecture the Man-Mountain combs his head, for we did not always trouble him with questions, because we found it a great difficulty to make him understand us. In the large pocket on the right side of his middle cover (so I translate the word *'ranfu-lo',* by which they meant my breeches) we saw a hollow pillar of iron, about the length of a man, fastened to a strong piece of timber, larger than the pillar; and upon one side of the pillar were huge pieces of iron sticking out, cut into strange figures, which we know not what to make of. In the left pocket, another engine of the same kind. In the smaller pocket on the right side, were several round flat pieces of white and red metal, of different bulk; some of the white, which seemed to be silver, were so large and heavy, that my comrade and I could hardly lift them. In the left pocket were two black pillars irregularly shaped: we could not, without difficulty, reach the top of them as we stood at the bottom of his pocket. One of them was covered, and seemed all of a piece: but at the upper end of the other, there appeared a white round substance, about twice the bigness of our heads. Within each of these was inclosed a prodigious plate of steel; which, by our orders, we obliged him to show us, because we apprehended they might be dangerous engines. He took them out of their cases, and told us, that in his own country his practice was to shave his beard with one of these, and to cut his meat with the other. There were two pockets which we could not enter: these he called his fobs; they were two large slits cut into the top of his middle cover, but squeezed close by the pressure of his belly. Out of the right fob hung a great silver chain, with a wonderful kind of engine at the bottom. We directed him to draw out whatever was fastened to that chain; which appeared to be a globe, half silver, and half of some transparent metal: for on the transparent side we saw certain strange figures circularly drawn, and thought we could touch them, till we found our fingers stopped by that lucid substance. He put this engine to our ears, which made an incessant noise like that of a watermill. And we conjecture it is either some unknown animal, or the god that he worships: but we are more inclined to the latter opinion, because he assured us (if we understood him right, for he expressed himself very imperfectly), that he seldom did any thing without consulting it. He called it his oracle, and said it pointed out the time for every action of his life. From the left fob he took out a net almost large enough for a fisherman, but contrived to open and shut like a purse, and served him for the same use: we found therein several massy pieces of yellow metal, which, if they be real gold, must be of immense value.

Having thus, in obedience to your Majesty's commands, diligently searched all his pockets, we observed a girdle about his waist made of the hide of some prodigious animal; from which, on the left side, hung a sword of the length of five men, and on the right, a bag or pouch divided into two cells, each cell capable of holding three of your Majesty's subjects. In one of these cells were several globes or balls of a most ponderous metal, about the bigness of our heads, and required a strong hand to lift them: the other cell contained a heap of certain black grains, but of no great bulk or weight, for we could hold above fifty of them in the palms of our hands.

This is an exact inventory of what we found about the body of the Man-Mountain, who used us with great civility, and due respect to your Majesty's commission. Signed and sealed on the fourth day of the eighty-ninth moon of your Majesty's auspicious reign.

Clefren Frelock, Marsi Frelock

When this inventory was read over to the Emperor, he directed me, although in very gentle terms, to deliver up the several particulars. He first called for my scimitar, which I took out, scabbard and all. In the mean time he ordered three thousand of his choicest troops (who then attended him) to surround me at a distance, with their bows and arrows just ready to discharge: but I did not observe it, for my eyes were wholly fixed upon his Majesty. He then desired me to draw my scimitar, which, although it had got some rust by the sea-water, was in most parts exceeding bright. I did so, and immediately all the troops gave a shout between terror and surprise; for the sun shone clear, and the reflection dazzled their eyes as I waved the scimitar to and fro in my hand. His Majesty, who is a most magnanimous prince, was less daunted than I could expect; he ordered me to return it into the scabbard, and cast it on the ground as gently as I could, about six foot from the end of my chain. The next thing he demanded was one of the hollow iron pillars, by which he meant my pocket-pistols. I drew it out, and at his desire, as well as I could, expressed to him the use of it; and charging it only with powder, which by the closeness of my pouch happened to scape wetting in the sea (an inconvenience against which all prudent mariners take special care to provide), I first cautioned the Emperor not to be afraid, and then I let it off in the air. The astonishment here was much greater than at the sight of my scimitar. Hundreds fell down as if they had been struck dead; and even the Emperor, although he stood his ground, could not recover himself in some time. I delivered up both my pistols in the same manner as I had done my scimitar, and then my pouch of powder and bullets; begging him that the former might be kept from the fire, for it would kindle with the smallest spark, and blow up his imperial palace into the air. I likewise delivered up my watch, which the Emperor was very curious to see, and commanded two of his tallest yeomen of the guards to bear it on a pole upon their shoulders, as draymen in England do a barrel of ale. He was amazed at the continual noise it made, and the motion of the minute-hand, which he could easily discern; for their sight is much more acute than ours: and asked the opinions of his learned men about him, which were various and remote, as the reader may well imagine without my repeating; although indeed I could not very perfectly understand them. I then gave up my silver and copper money, my purse with nine large pieces of gold, and some smaller ones; my knife and razor, my comb and silver snuff-box, my handkerchief and journal book. My scimitar, pistols, and pouch, were conveyed in carriages to his Majesty's stores; but the rest of my goods were returned me.

I had, as I before observed, one private pocket which escaped their search, wherein there was a pair of spectacles (which I sometimes use for the weakness of my eyes), a pocket-perspective, and several other little conveniencies; which, being of no consequence to the Emperor, I did not think myself bound in honour to discover, and I apprehended they might be lost or spoiled if I ventured them out of my possession.

Chapter Three

The author diverts the Emperor and his nobility of both sexes, in a very uncommon manner. The diversions of the court of Lilliput described. The author hath his liberty granted him, upon certain conditions.

Y GENTLENESS AND GOOD BEHAVIOUR HAD gained so far on the Emperor and his court, and indeed upon the army and people in general, that I began to conceive hopes of getting my liberty in a short time.[1] I took all possible methods to cultivate this favourable disposition. The natives came by degrees to be less apprehensive of any danger from me. I would sometimes lie down, and let five or six of them dance on my hand. And at last the boys and girls would venture to come and play at hide and seek in my hair. I had now made a good progress in understanding and speaking their language. The Emperor had a mind one day to entertain me with several of the country shows, wherein they exceed all nations I have known, both for dexterity and magnificence. I was diverted with none so much as that of the rope-dancers, performed upon a slender white thread, extended about two foot, and twelve inches from the ground. Upon which I shall desire liberty, with the reader's patience, to enlarge a little.

This diversion is only practised by those persons who are candidates for great employments, and high favour, at court. They are trained in this art from their youth, and are not always of noble birth, or liberal

1. During 1710 the Tories gained steadily on the Whigs.

education. When a great office is vacant either by death or disgrace (which often happens) five or six of those candidates petition the Emperor to entertain his Majesty and the court with a dance on the rope, and whoever jumps the highest without falling, succeeds in the office. Very often the chief ministers themselves are commanded to show their skill, and to convince the Emperor that they have not lost their faculty. Flimnap,[2] the Treasurer, is allowed to cut a caper on the strait rope, at least an inch higher than any other lord in the whole empire. I have seen him do the summerset several times together upon a trencher fixed on the rope, which is no thicker than a common packthread in England. My friend Reldresal,[3] Principal Secretary for Private Affairs, is, in my opinion, if I am not partial, the second after the Treasurer; the rest of the great officers are much upon a par.

These diversions are often attended with fatal accidents, whereof great numbers are on record. I myself have seen two or three candidates break a limb. But the danger is much greater when the ministers themselves are commanded to show their dexterity; for by contending to excel themselves and their fellows, they strain so far, that there is hardly one of them who hath not received a fall, and some of them two or three. I was assured that a year or two before my arrival, Flimnap would have infallibly broke his neck, if one of the King's cushions, that accidentally lay on the ground, had not weakened the force of his fall.[4]

There is likewise another diversion, which is only shown before the Emperor and Empress, and first minister, upon particular occasions. The Emperor lays on a table three fine silken threads of six inches

2. This name appears to be compounded from 'flim-flam' and 'nap' (or 'nab'), meaning 'cheat' and 'steal'. It undoubtedly designates Walpole, the Whig politician, who rose to be first minister under George I, and who was as famous for his frank policy of political bribery as for his ability to retain power in times of great uncertainty.

3. Charles, Viscount Townshend, who became Secretary of State under George I, and who was Walpole's chief ally for a long period.

4. The Duchess of Kendal, one of the King's mistresses, assisted Walpole to regain his position and power after his resignation in 1717.

long. One is blue, the other red, and the third green.[5] These threads are proposed as prizes for those persons whom the Emperor hath a mind to distinguish by a peculiar mark of his favour. The ceremony is performed in his Majesty's great chamber of state, where the candidates are to undergo a trial of dexterity very different from the former, and such as I have not observed the least resemblance of in any other country of the old or the new world. The Emperor holds a stick in his hands, both ends parallel to the horizon, while the candidates, advancing one by one, sometimes leap over the stick, sometimes creep under it backwards and forwards several times, according as the stick is advanced or depressed. Sometimes the Emperor holds one end of the stick, and his first minister the other; sometimes the minister has it entirely to himself. Whoever performs his part with most agility, and holds out the longest in leaping and creeping, is rewarded with the blue-coloured silk; the red is given to the next, and the green to the third, which they all wear girt twice round about the middle; and you see few great persons about this court who are not adorned with one of these girdles.

The horses of the army, and those of the royal stables, having been daily led before me, were no longer shy, but would come up to my very feet without starting. The riders would leap them over my hand as I held it on the ground, and one of the Emperor's huntsmen, upon a large courser, took my foot, shoe and all; which was indeed a prodigious leap. I had the good fortune to divert the Emperor one day after a very extraordinary manner. I desired he would order several sticks of two foot high, and the thickness of an ordinary cane, to be brought me; whereupon his Majesty commanded the master of his woods to give directions accordingly, and the next morning six woodmen arrived with as many carriages, drawn by eight horses to each. I took nine of these sticks, and fixing them firmly in the ground in a

5. These are the colors of the ribbons of the orders of the Garter, the Bath, and the Thistle.

quadrangular figure, two foot and an half square, I took four other sticks, and tied them parallel at each corner, about two foot from the ground; then I fastened my handkerchief to the nine sticks that stood erect, and extended it on all sides till it was as tight as the top of a drum; and the four parallel sticks, rising about five inches higher than the handkerchief, served as ledges on each side. When I had finished my work, I desired the Emperor to let a troop of his best horse, twenty-four in number, come and exercise upon this plain. His Majesty approved of the proposal, and I took them up one by one in my hands, ready mounted and armed, with the proper officers to exercise them. As soon as they got into order, they divided into two parties, performed mock skirmishes, discharged blunt arrows, drew their swords, fled and pursued, attacked and retired, and in short discovered the best military discipline I ever beheld. The parallel sticks secured them and their horses from falling over the stage; and the Emperor was so much delighted, that he ordered this entertainment to be repeated several days, and once was pleased to be lifted up, and give the word of command; and, with great difficulty, persuaded even the Empress herself to let me hold her in her close chair[6] within two yards of the stage, from whence she was able to take a full view of the whole performance. It was my good fortune that no ill accident happened in these entertainments, only once a fiery horse that belonged to one of the captains pawing with his hoof struck a hole in my handkerchief, and his foot slipping, he overthrew his rider and himself; but I immediately relieved them both, and covering the hole with one hand, I set down the troop with the other, in the same manner as I took them up. The horse that fell was strained in the left shoulder, but the rider got no hurt, and I repaired my handkerchief as well as I could; however, I would not trust to the strength of it any more in such dangerous enterprises.

About two or three days before I was set at liberty, as I was enter-

6. Enclosed sedan chair.

taining the court with these kind of feats, there arrived an express to inform his Majesty that some of his subjects, riding near the place where I was first taken up, had seen a great black substance lying on the ground, very oddly shaped, extending its edges round as wide as his Majesty's bed-chamber, and rising up in the middle as high as a man; that it was no living creature, as they at first apprehended, for it lay on the grass without motion, and some of them had walked round it several times: that by mounting upon each others' shoulders, they had got to the top, which was flat and even, and stamping upon it they found it was hollow within; that they humbly conceived it might be some thing belonging to the Man-Mountain, and if his Majesty pleased, they would undertake to bring it with only five horses. I presently knew what they meant, and was glad at heart to receive this intelligence. It seems upon my first reaching the shore after our shipwreck, I was in such confusion, that before I came to the place where I went to sleep, my hat, which I had fastened with a string to my head while I was rowing, and had stuck on all the time I was swimming, fell off after I came to land; the string, as I conjecture, breaking by some accident which I never observed, but thought my hat had been lost at sea. I intreated his Imperial Majesty to give orders it might be brought to me as soon as possible, describing to him the use and the nature of it: and the next day the waggoners arrived with it, but not in a very good condition; they had bored two holes in the brim, within an inch and half of the edge, and fastened two hooks in the holes; these hooks were tied by a long cord to the harness, and thus my hat was dragged along for above half an English mile: but the ground in that country being extremely smooth and level, it received less damage than I expected.

Two days after this adventure, the Emperor having ordered that part of his army which quarters in and about his metropolis to be in a readiness, took a fancy of diverting himself in a very singular manner. He desired I would stand like a colossus, with my legs as far asunder as I conveniently could. He then commanded his general (who was an old experienced leader, and a great patron of mine) to draw up the troops in close order, and march them under me, the foot by twenty-four in a breast, and the horse by sixteen, with drums beating, colours flying, and pikes advanced. This body consisted of three thousand foot, and a thousand horse. His Majesty gave orders, upon pain of death, that every soldier in his march should observe the strictest decency with regard to my person; which, however, could not prevent some of the younger officers from turning up their eyes as they passed under me. And, to confess the truth, my breeches were at that time in so ill a condition, that they afforded some opportunities for laughter and admiration.

I had sent so many memorials and petitions for my liberty, that his Majesty at length mentioned the matter, first in the cabinet, and then in a full council; where it was opposed by none, except Skyresh Bolgolam, who was pleased, without any provocation, to be my mortal enemy.[7] But it was carried against him by the whole board, and confirmed by the Emperor. That minister was *Galbet,* or Admiral of the Realm, very much in his master's confidence, and a person well versed in affairs, but of a morose and sour complexion.[8] However, he was at length persuaded to comply; but prevailed that the articles and conditions upon which I should be set free, and to which I must swear, should be drawn up by himself.[9] These articles were brought to me by Skyresh Bolgolam in person, attended by two under-secretaries, and several persons of distinction. After they were read, I was demanded to swear to the performance of them; first in the manner of my own

7. The Earl of Nottingham, a 'high' Tory, hostile to Harley because the latter had succeeded him in office in 1704.

8. The Earl's political nickname was 'Dismal'.

9. When Harley and his supporters came into power late in 1710 Nottingham attempted to embarrass them and restrict their freedom of activity: he carried, in the House of Lords, an amendment to the royal address, stipulating that no peace with France would be acceptable which left Spain and the Indies in the possession of any branch of the House of Bourbon. The implication of the amendment was that the ministry could not be trusted to negotiate a peace which would safeguard England.

country, and afterwards in the method prescribed by their laws; which was to hold my right foot in my left hand, to place the middle finger of my right hand on the crown of my head, and my thumb on the tip of my right ear. But because the reader may perhaps be curious to have some idea of the style and manner of expression peculiar to that people, as well as to know the articles upon which I recovered my liberty, I have made a translation of the whole instrument word for word, as near as I was able, which I here offer to the public.

Golbasto Momaren Evlame Gurdilo Shefin Mully Ully Gue, most mighty Emperor of Lilliput,[10] delight and terror of the universe, whose dominions extend five thousand *blustrugs* (about twelve miles in circumference) to the extremities of the globe; monarch of all monarchs, taller than the sons of men; whose feet press down to the center, and whose head strikes against the sun: at whose nod the princes of the earth shake their knees; pleasant as the spring, comfortable as the summer, fruitful as autumn, dreadful as winter. His most sublime Majesty proposeth to the Man-Mountain, lately arrived to our celestial dominions, the following articles, which by a solemn oath he shall be obliged to perform.

First, The Man-Mountain shall not depart from our dominions, without our licence under our great seal.

2d, He shall not presume to come into our metropolis, without our express order; at which time the inhabitants shall have two hours' warning to keep within their doors.

3d, The said Man-Mountain shall confine his walks to our principal high roads, and not offer to walk or lie down in a meadow or field of corn.[11]

4th, As he walks the said roads, he shall take the utmost care not to trample upon the bodies of any of our loving subjects, their horses, or

10. Professor Henry Morley suggested that the name 'Lilliput' was compounded from 'lilli', an infantile pronunciation of 'little', and 'put', a term of contempt.
11. Grain in general.

avoid the censure of vanity, I shall not repeat, he added, that he hoped I should prove a useful servant, and well deserve all the favours he had already conferred upon me, or might do for the future.[13]

The reader may please to observe, that in the last article for the recovery of my liberty, the Emperor stipulates to allow me a quantity of meat and drink sufficient for the support of 1728 Lilliputians. Some time after, asking a friend at court how they came to fix on that determinate number, he told me, that his Majesty's mathematicians, having taken the height of my body by the help of a quadrant, and finding it to exceed theirs in the proportion of twelve to one, they concluded from the similarity of their bodies, that mine must contain at least 1728 of theirs, and consequently would require as much food as was necessary to support that number of Lilliputians. By which the reader may conceive an idea of the ingenuity of that people, as well as the prudent and exact œconomy of so great a prince.

13. At the end of 1710, to the delight of Queen Anne, Harley and his supporters obtained complete control of the government, Harley becoming Chancellor of the Exchequer (in effect Prime Minister), and St. John Secretary of State.

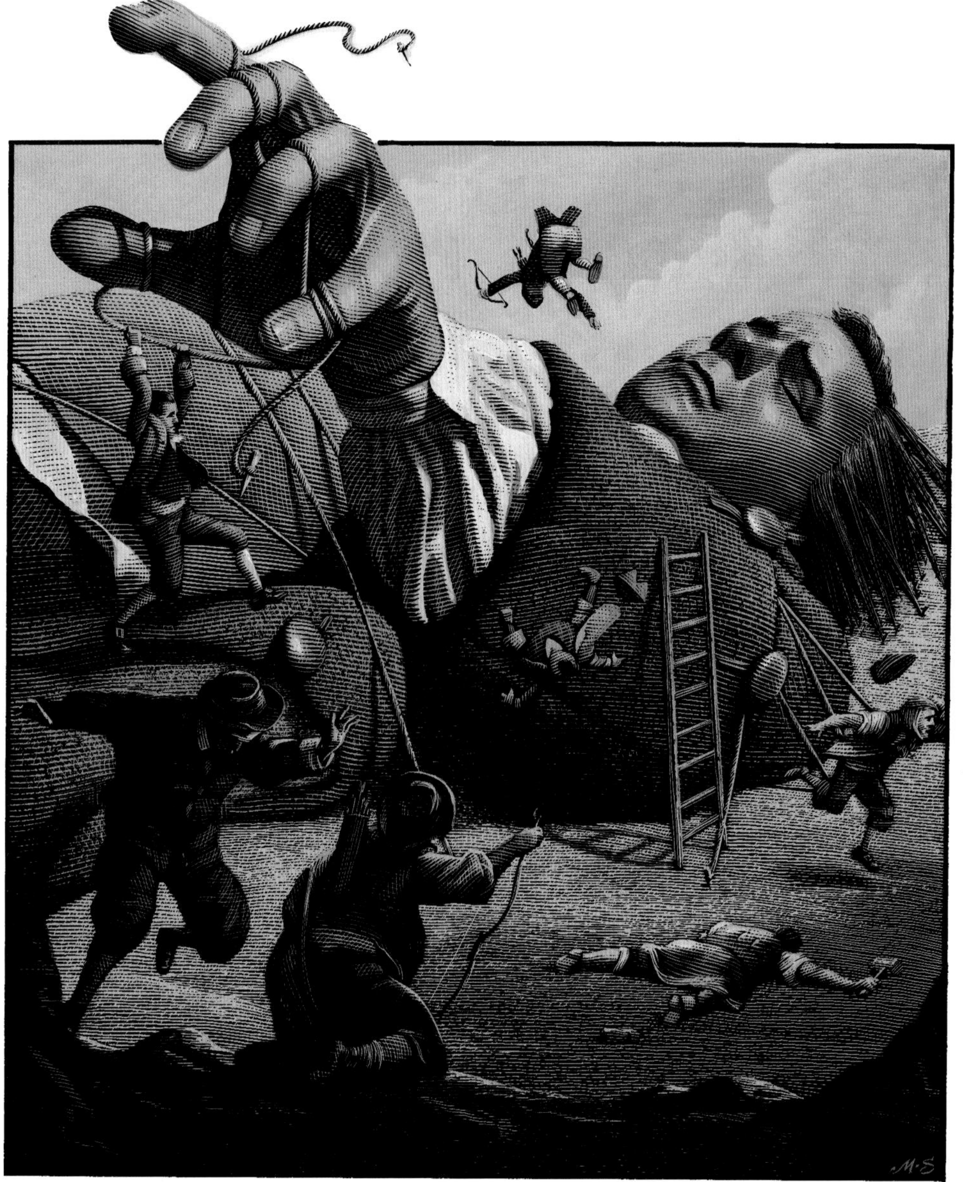

[S]truggling to get loose, I had the fortune to break the strings and wrench out the pegs that fastened my left arm...
PAGES 26-27

carriages, nor take any of our said subjects into his h their own consent.

5th, If an express requires extraordinary dispatc Mountain shall be obliged to carry in his pocket the m horse a six days' journey once in every moon, and r messenger back (if so required) safe to our Imperial P

6th, He shall be our ally against our enemies in Blefuscu, and do his utmost to destroy their fleet, whi paring to invade us.

7th, That the said Man-Mountain shall, at his times aiding and assisting to our workmen, in helping to rais stones, towards covering the wall of the principal park, royal buildings.

8th, That the said Man-Mountain shall, in two mo liver in an exact survey of the circumference of our d computation of his own paces round the coast.

Lastly, That upon his solemn oath to observe all the the said Man-Mountain shall have a daily allowance drink sufficient for the support of 1728 of our subjects, w to our Royal Person, and other marks of our favour. palace at Belfaborac the twelfth day of the ninety-first reign.

I swore and subscribed to these articles with great che content,[12] although some of them were not so honoura have wished; which proceeded wholly from the malic Bolgolam the High Admiral: whereupon my chains were unlocked, and I was at full liberty; the Emperor himself me the honour to be by at the whole ceremony. I made edgements by prostrating myself at his Majesty's feet: manded me to rise; and after many gracious expressio

12. The Tory government decided to ignore the hostile intent of Notti ment, and did not oppose it.

Chapter Four

Mildendo, the metropolis of Lilliput, described, together with the Emperor's palace. A conversation between the author and a principal secretary, concerning the affairs of that empire. The author's offers to serve the Emperor in his wars.

HE FIRST REQUEST I MADE AFTER I HAD OBTAINED my liberty, was, that I might have licence to see Mildendo,[1] the metropolis; which the Emperor easily granted me, but with a special charge to do no hurt, either to the inhabitants, or their houses. The people had notice by proclamation of my design to visit the town. The wall which encompassed it is two foot and an half high, and at least eleven inches broad, so that a coach and horses may be driven very safely round it; and it is flanked with strong towers at ten foot distance. I stepped over the great western gate, and passed very gently, and sideling[2] through the two principal streets, only in my short waistcoat, for fear of damaging the roofs and eaves of the houses with the skirts of my coat. I walked with the utmost circumspection, to avoid treading on any stragglers, that might remain in the streets, although the orders were very strict, that all people should keep in their houses, at their own peril. The garret windows and tops of houses were so crowded with spectators, that I thought in all my travels I had not seen a more populous place. The city is an exact square, each side of the wall being five hundred foot long. The two great streets, which run cross and divide it into four quarters,

1. Mildendo stands for London, but is physically unlike the English capital.
2. Sidelong.

are five foot wide. The lanes and alleys, which I could not enter, but only viewed them as I passed, are from twelve to eighteen inches. The town is capable of holding five hundred thousand souls. The houses are from three to five stories. The shops and markets well provided.

The Emperor's palace is in the center of the city, where the two great streets meet. It is inclosed by a wall of two foot high, and twenty foot distant from the buildings. I had his Majesty's permission to step over this wall; and the space being so wide between that and the palace, I could easily view it on every side. The outward court is a square of forty foot, and includes two other courts: in the inmost are the royal apartments, which I was very desirous to see, but found it extremely difficult; for the great gates, from one square into another, were but eighteen inches high, and seven inches wide. Now the buildings of the outer court were at least five foot high, and it was impossible for me to stride over them, without infinite damage to the pile, though the walls were strongly built of hewn stone, and four inches thick. At the same time the Emperor had a great desire that I should see the magnificence of his palace; but this I was not able to do till three days after, which I spent in cutting down with my knife some of the largest trees in the royal park, about an hundred yards distant from the city. Of these trees I made two stools, each about three foot high, and strong enough to bear my weight. The people having received notice a second time, I went again through the city to the palace, with my two stools in my hands. When I came to the side of the outer court, I stood upon one stool, and took the other in my hand: this I lifted over the roof, and gently set it down on the space between the first and second court, which was eight foot wide. I then stepped over the buildings very conveniently from one stool to the other, and drew up the first after me with a hooked stick. By this contrivance I got into the inmost court; and lying down upon my side, I applied my face to the windows of the middle stories, which were left open on purpose, and discovered the most splendid apartments that can be imagined. There I saw the Empress, and the young princes in their several lodgings, with their chief attendants about them. Her Imperial Majesty was pleased to smile very graciously upon me, and gave me out of the window her hand to kiss.

But I shall not anticipate the reader with farther descriptions of this kind, because I reserve them for a greater work, which is now almost ready for the press, containing a general description of this empire, from its first erection, through a long series of princes, with a particular account of their wars and politics, laws, learning, and religion; their plants and animals, their peculiar manners and customs, with other matters very curious and useful; my chief design at present being only to relate such events and transactions as happened to the public, or to myself, during a residence of about nine months in that empire.

One morning, about a fortnight after I had obtained my liberty, Reldresal, Principal Secretary (as they style him) of Private Affairs, came to my house, attended only by one servant.[3] He ordered his coach to wait at a distance, and desired I would give him an hour's audience; which I readily consented to, on account of his quality, and personal merits, as well as the many good offices he had done me during my solicitations at court. I offered to lie down, that he might the more conveniently reach my ear; but he chose rather to let me hold him in my hand during our conversation. He began with compliments on my liberty, said he might pretend to some merit in it; but, however, added, that if it had not been for the present situation of things at court, perhaps I might not have obtained it so soon. 'For', said he, 'as flourishing a condition as we may appear to be in to foreigners, we labour under two mighty evils; a violent faction at home, and the danger of an invasion by a most potent enemy from abroad. As to the first, you are to understand, that for above seventy moons past, there have been two struggling parties in the empire,

3. This visit is merely an expository device, without any allegorical counterpart.

under the names of *"Tramecksan"*, and *"Slamecksan"*,[4] from the high and low heels on their shoes, by which they distinguish themselves. It is alleged indeed, that the high heels are most agreeable to our ancient constitution: but however this be, his Majesty hath determined to make use of only low heels in the administration of the government and all offices in the gift of the crown, as you cannot but observe; and particularly, that his Majesty's imperial heels are lower at least by a *drurr* than any of his court;[5] (*"drurr"* is a measure about the fourteenth part of an inch). The animosities between these two parties run so high, that they will neither eat nor drink, nor talk with each other. We compute the *Tramecksan,* or High-Heels, to exceed us in number; but the power is wholly on our side. We apprehend his Imperial Highness, the heir to the crown, to have some tendency towards the High-Heels; at least we can plainly discover one of his heels higher than the other, which gives him a hobble in his gait.[6] Now, in the midst of these intestine disquiets, we are threatened with an invasion from the island of Blefuscu,[7] which is the other great empire of the universe, almost as large and powerful as this of his Majesty. For as to what we have heard you affirm, that there are other kingdoms and states in the world, inhabited by human creatures as large as yourself, our philosophers are in much doubt, and would rather conjecture that you dropped from the moon, or one of the stars; because it is certain, that an hundred mortals of your bulk would, in a short time, destroy all the fruits and cattle of his Majesty's dominions. Besides, our histories of six thousand moons make no mention of any other regions, than the two great empires of Lilliput and Blefuscu. Which two mighty powers have, as I was going to tell you, been engaged in a most obstinate war for six and thirty moons past. It

4. The Tories, or high-church party, and the Whigs, or low-church party.
5. George I favored the Whigs, who were in power throughout his reign.
6. The Prince of Wales (later George II) attempted during his father's reign to cultivate the friendship of both parties.
7. France, England's chief opponent in the War of the Spanish Succession, 1701–1713.

began upon the following occasion. It is allowed on all hands, that the primitive way of breaking eggs before we eat them, was upon the larger end: but his present Majesty's grandfather, while he was a boy, going to eat an egg, and breaking it according to the ancient practice, happened to cut one of his fingers.[8] Whereupon the Emperor his father[9] published an edict, commanding all his subjects, upon great penalties, to break the smaller end of their eggs. The people so highly resented this law, that our histories tell us there have been six rebellions raised on that account; wherein one emperor[10] lost his life, and another[11] his crown. These civil commotions were constantly fomented by the monarchs of Blefuscu; and when they were quelled, the exiles always fled for refuge to that empire. It is computed, that eleven thousand persons have, at several times, suffered death, rather than submit to break their eggs at the smaller end. Many hundred large volumes have been published upon this controversy: but the books of the Big-Endians have been long forbidden, and the whole party rendered incapable by law of holding employments. During the course of these troubles, the emperors of Blefuscu did frequently expostulate by their ambassadors, accusing us of making a schism in religion, by offending against a fundamental doctrine of our great prophet Lustrog, in the fifty-fourth chapter of the *Brundecral* (which is their Alcoran). This, however, is thought to be a mere strain upon the text: for the words are these; "That all true believers shall break their eggs at the convenient end": and which is the convenient end, seems, in my humble opinion, to be left to every man's conscience, or at least in the

8. Elizabeth, according to the canons of the Roman Catholic Church, was illegitimate, and consequently incapable of inheriting the crown.

9. Henry VIII. The edict represents Henry's denial of papal authority, and his proclamation of himself as head of the Church of England. What follows is an allegory of the subsequent disputes between Protestantism and Catholicism in England. The egg is probably a symbol of the Eucharist.

10. Charles I. One cause of his overthrow was his support of the principles of Archbishop Laud, which savored of Catholicism.

11. James II, an avowed Roman Catholic.

power of the chief magistrate to determine. Now the Big-Endian exiles have found so much credit in the Emperor of Blefuscu's court, and so much private assistance and encouragement from their party here at home, that a bloody war hath been carried on between the two empires for six and thirty moons with various success;[12] during which time we have lost forty capital ships, and a much greater number of smaller vessels, together with thirty thousand of our best seamen and soldiers; and the damage received by the enemy is reckoned to be somewhat greater than ours. However, they have now equipped a numerous fleet, and are just preparing to make a descent upon us; and his Imperial Majesty, placing great confidence in your valour and strength, hath commanded me to lay this account of his affairs before you'.

I desired the Secretary to present my humble duty to the Emperor, and to let him know, that I thought it would not become me, who was a foreigner, to interfere with parties;[13] but I was ready, with the hazard of my life, to defend his person and state against all invaders.

12. The allies in the War of the Spanish Succession were fighting to keep a balance of power between Catholic and Protestant monarchies.
13. A hint to George I that he, a foreigner, should not meddle in English politics.

Chapter Five

The author, by an extraordinary stratagem prevents an invasion. A high title of honour is conferred upon him. Ambassadors arrive from the Emperor of Blefuscu, and sue for peace. The Empress's apartment on fire by an accident; the author instrumental in saving the rest of the palace.

HE EMPIRE OF BLEFUSCU IS AN ISLAND SITUATED to the north-northeast side of Lilliput, from whence it is parted only by a channel of eight hundred yards wide. I had not yet seen it, and upon this notice of an intended invasion, I avoided appearing on that side of the coast, for fear of being discovered by some of the enemy's ships, who had received no intelligence of me, all intercourse between the two empires having been strictly forbidden during the war, upon pain of death, and an embargo laid by our Emperor upon all vessels whatsoever. I communicated to his Majesty a project I had formed of seizing the enemy's whole fleet; which, as our scouts assured us, lay at anchor in the harbour ready to sail with the first fair wind. I consulted the most experienced seamen upon the depth of the channel, which they had often plumbed, who told me, that in the middle at high water it was seventy *glumgluffs* deep, which is about six foot of European measure; and the rest of it fifty *glumgluffs* at most. I walked towards the northeast coast over against Blefuscu, and lying down behind a hillock, took out my small pocket perspective-glass, and viewed the enemy's fleet at anchor, consisting of about fifty men-of-war, and a great number of transports: I then came back to my house, and gave order (for which I had a warrant) for a great quantity of the strongest cable and bars of iron. The cable was about as thick as packthread, and the bars of the length and size of a knitting-needle. I trebled the cable to make it stronger, and for the same reason I twisted three of the iron bars together, binding the extremities into an hook. Having thus fixed fifty hooks to as many cables, I went back to the northeast coast, and putting off my coat, shoes, and stockings, walked into the sea in my leathern jerkin, about half an hour before high water. I waded with what haste I could, and swam in the middle about thirty yards till I felt ground; I arrived at the fleet in less than half an hour. The enemy was so frighted when they saw me, that they leaped out of their ships, and swam to shore, where there could not be fewer than thirty thousand souls. I then took my tackling, and fastening a hook to the hole at the prow of each, I tied all the cords together at the end. While I was thus employed, the enemy discharged several thousand arrows, many of which stuck in my hands and face; and besides the excessive smart, gave me much disturbance in my work. My greatest apprehension was for my eyes, which I should have infallibly lost, if I had not suddenly thought of an expedient. I kept among other little necessaries a pair of spectacles in a private pocket, which, as I observed before, had scaped the Emperor's searchers. These I took out and fastened as strongly as I could upon my nose, and thus armed went on boldly with my work in spite of the enemy's arrows, many of which struck against the glasses of my spectacles, but without any other effect, further than a little to discompose them. I had now fastened all the hooks, and taking the knot in my hand, began to pull; but not a ship would stir, for they were all too fast held by their anchors, so that the boldest part of my enterprise remained. I therefore let go the cord, and leaving the hooks fixed to the ships, I resolutely cut with my knife the cables that fastened the anchors, receiving above two hundred shots in my face and hands; then I took up the knotted end of the cables to which my hooks were tied, and with great ease drew fifty of the enemy's largest men-of-war after me.

The Blefuscudians, who had not the least imagination of what I intended, were at first confounded with astonishment. They had seen me cut the cables, and thought my design was only to let the ships run adrift, or fall foul on each other: but when they perceived the whole fleet moving in order, and saw me pulling at the end, they set up such a scream of grief and despair, that it is almost impossible to describe or conceive. When I had got out of danger, I stopped a while to pick out the arrows that stuck in my hands and face, and rubbed on some of the same ointment that was given me at my first arrival, as I have formerly mentioned. I then took off my spectacles, and waiting about an hour till the tide was a little fallen, I waded through the middle with my cargo, and arrived safe at the royal port of Lilliput.[1]

The Emperor and his whole court stood on the shore expecting[2] the issue of this great adventure. They saw the ships move forward in a large half-moon, but could not discern me, who was up to my breast in water. When I advanced to the middle of the channel, they were yet more in pain, because I was under water to my neck. The Emperor concluded me to be drowned, and that the enemy's fleet was approaching in a hostile manner: but he was soon eased of his fears, for, the channel growing shallower every step I made, I came in a short time within hearing, and holding up the end of the cable by which the fleet was fastened, I cried in a loud voice, 'Long live the most puissant Emperor of Lilliput!' This great prince received me at my landing with all possible encomiums, and created me a *nardac*[3] upon the spot, which is the highest title of honour among them.

1. The Tory ministry claimed the credit for having brought the war to a successful conclusion. Swift symbolized this by a naval victory partly because Marlborough, the great military hero of the war, was a Whig; and partly because the Tories laid stress upon the fact that the demolition of the French port of Dunkirk, provided for by the treaty of peace, guaranteed the continuance of English naval supremacy.
2. Awaiting.
3. Harley was created Earl of Oxford and Mortimer in 1711, and St. John Viscount Bolingbroke in 1712.

His Majesty desired I would take some other opportunity of bringing all the rest of his enemy's ships into his ports. And so unmeasureable is the ambition of princes, that he seemed to think of nothing less than reducing the whole empire of Blefuscu into a province, and governing it by a viceroy; of destroying the Big-Endian exiles, and compelling that people to break the smaller end of their eggs, by which he would remain the sole monarch of the whole world. But I endeavoured to divert him from this design, by many arguments drawn from the topics of policy as well as justice: and I plainly protested, that I would never be an instrument of bringing a free and brave people into slavery. And when the matter was debated in council, the wisest part of the ministry were of my opinion.[4]

This open bold declaration of mine was so opposite to the schemes and politics of his Imperial Majesty, that he could never forgive it; he mentioned it in a very artful manner at council, where I was told that some of the wisest appeared, at least, by their silence, to be of my opinion; but others, who were my secret enemies, could not forbear some expressions, which by a side-wind reflected on me. And from this time began an intrigue between his Majesty and a junto of ministers maliciously bent against me, which broke out in less than two months, and had like to have ended in my utter destruction. Of so little weight are the greatest services to princes, when put into the balance with a refusal to gratify their passions.

About three weeks after this exploit, there arrived a solemn embassy from Blefuscu, with humble offers of a peace; which was soon concluded upon conditions very advantageous to our Emperor,[5] wherewith I shall not trouble the reader. There were six ambassadors, with a train of about five hundred persons, and their entry was very magnificent, suitable to the grandeur of their master, and the importance of their business. When their treaty was finished, wherein I did them

4. The Whigs accused the Tories of granting France too early and too favorable a peace.
5. The Peace of Utrecht was concluded in 1713, after two years of negotiation.

several good offices by the credit I now had, or at least appeared to have at court, their Excellencies, who were privately told how much I had been their friend, made me a visit in form. They began with many compliments upon my valour and generosity, invited me to that kingdom in the Emperor[6] their master's name, and desired me to show them some proofs of my prodigious strength, of which they had heard so many wonders; wherein I readily obliged them, but shall not trouble the reader with the particulars.

When I had for some time entertained their Excellencies to their infinite satisfaction and surprise, I desired they would do me the honour to present my most humble respects to the Emperor their master, the renown of whose virtues had so justly filled the whole world with admiration, and whose royal person I resolved to attend before I returned to my own country: accordingly, the next time I had the honour to see our Emperor, I desired his general licence to wait on the Blefuscudian monarch, which he was pleased to grant me, as I could plainly perceive, in a very cold manner; but could not guess the reason, till I had a whisper from a certain person, that Flimnap and Bolgolam had represented my intercourse with those ambassadors as a mark of disaffection, from which I am sure my heart was wholly free.[7] And this was the first time I began to conceive some imperfect idea of courts and ministers.

It is to be observed, that these ambassadors spoke to me by an interpreter, the languages of both empires differing as much from each other as any two in Europe, and each nation priding itself upon the antiquity, beauty, and energy of their own tongues, with an avowed contempt for that of their neighbour; yet our Emperor, standing upon the advantage he had got by the seizure of their fleet, obliged them to deliver their credentials, and make their speech, in

6. Louis XIV.

7. The Tories carried on secret negotiations with the French prior to the peace, and were accused by the Whigs of having revealed to the enemy their confidential instructions.

the Lilliputian tongue. And it must be confessed, that from the great intercourse of trade and commerce between both realms, from the continual reception of exiles, which is mutual among them, and from the custom in each empire to send their young nobility and richer gentry to the other, in order to polish themselves, by seeing the world, and understanding men and manners; there are few persons of distinction, or merchants, or seamen, who dwell in the maritime parts, but what can hold conversation in both tongues; as I found some weeks after, when I went to pay my respects to the Emperor of Blefuscu, which in the midst of great misfortunes, through the malice of my enemies, proved a very happy adventure to me, as I shall relate in its proper place.

The reader may remember, that when I signed those articles upon which I recovered my liberty, there were some which I disliked upon account of their being too servile, neither could any thing but an extreme necessity have forced me to submit. But being now a *nardac,* of the highest rank in that empire, such offices were looked upon as below my dignity, and the Emperor (to do him justice) never once mentioned them to me.[8] However, it was not long before I had an opportunity of doing his Majesty, at least as I then thought, a most signal service. I was alarmed at midnight with the cries of many hundred people at my door; by which being suddenly awaked, I was in some kind of terror. I heard the word *'burglum'* repeated incessantly: several of the Emperor's court, making their way through the crowd, intreated me to come immediately to the palace, where her Imperial Majesty's apartment was on fire, by the carelessness of a maid of honour, who fell asleep while she was reading a romance. I got up in an instant; and orders being given to clear the way before me, and it being likewise a moonshine night, I made a shift to get to

8. That is to say, after Harley and St. John had been raised to the peerage and universally accepted as the responsible heads of the ministry, they regarded themselves as released from the restrictions that Nottingham had tried to impose upon their actions, and Queen Anne concurred in this view.

the palace without trampling on any of the people. I found they had already applied ladders to the walls of the apartment, and were well provided with buckets, but the water was at some distance. These buckets were about the size of a large thimble, and the poor people supplied me with them as fast as they could; but the flame was so violent that they did little good. I might easily have stifled it with my coat, which I unfortunately left behind me for haste, and came away only in my leathern jerkin. The case seemed wholly desperate and deplorable, and this magnificent palace would have infallibly been burnt down to the ground, if, by a presence of mind, unusual to me, I had not suddenly thought of an expedient. I had the evening before drank plentifully of a most delicious wine, called *glimigrim* (the Blefuscudians call it *flunec,* but ours is esteemed the better sort), which is very diuretic. By the luckiest chance in the world, I had not discharged myself of any part of it. The heat I had contracted by coming very near the flames, and by my labouring to quench them, made the wine begin to operate by urine; which I voided in such a quantity, and applied so well to the proper places, that in three minutes the fire was wholly extinguished, and the rest of that noble pile, which had cost so many ages in erecting, preserved from destruction.[9]

It was now daylight, and I returned to my house, without waiting to congratulate with the Emperor; because, although I had done a very eminent piece of service, yet I could not tell how his Majesty might resent the manner by which I had performed it: for, by the fundamental laws of the realm, it is capital in any person, of what quality soever, to make water within the precincts of the palace. But I was a little comforted by a message from his Majesty, that he would give orders to the Grand Justiciary for passing my pardon in form; which, how-

9. Gulliver's illegal method of extinguishing the fire presumably stands for the acts of the Tories in opening unauthorized negotiations for a peace with France, which, according to the Tory ministry and their defenders, was vital to the preservation of the realm.

ever, I could not obtain.[10] And I was privately assured, the Empress, conceiving the greatest abhorrence of what I had done, removed to the most distant side of the court, firmly resolved that those buildings should never be repaired for her use; and, in the presence of her chief confidents, could not forbear vowing revenge.[11]

10. George I, in 1716, moved to secure a pardon for Bolingbroke, who had been convicted of treason in the preceding year; Parliament, however, could not be persuaded to this course until 1723, and then granted only a partial pardon.

11. The Empress's indignation at the indecency of Gulliver's action probably represents Queen Anne's resentment of Oxford's disrespectful behavior toward her, which was one of the reasons she gave for dismissing him from office just before her death in 1714.

Chapter Six

Of the inhabitants of Lilliput; their learning, laws, and customs, the manner of educating their children. The author's way of living in that country. His vindication of a great lady.

LTHOUGH I INTEND TO LEAVE THE DESCRIPTION OF this empire to a particular treatise, yet in the mean time I am content to gratify the curious reader with some general ideas. As the common size of the natives is somewhat under six inches high, so there is an exact proportion in all other animals, as well as plants and trees: for instance, the tallest horses and oxen are between four and five inches in height, the sheep an inch and an half, more or less; their geese about the bigness of a sparrow, and so the several gradations downwards, till you come to the smallest, which, to my sight, were almost invisible; but nature hath adapted the eyes of the Lilliputians to all objects proper for their view: they see with great exactness, but at no great distance. And to show the sharpness of their sight towards objects that are near, I have been much pleased observing a cook pulling a lark, which was not so large as a common fly; and a young girl threading an invisible needle with invisible silk. Their tallest trees are about seven foot high; I mean some of those in the great royal park, the tops whereof I could but just reach with my fist clenched. The other vegetables are in the same proportion; but this I leave to the reader's imagination.

I shall say but little at present of their learning, which for many ages hath flourished in all its branches among them: but their manner of writing is very peculiar, being neither from the left to the right, like the Europeans; nor from the right to the left, like the Arabians; nor from up to down, like the Chinese; nor from down to up, like the Cascagians;[1] but aslant from one corner of the paper to the other, like ladies in England.[2]

They bury their dead with their heads directly downwards, because they hold an opinion that in eleven thousand moons they are all to rise again, in which period the earth (which they conceive to be flat) will turn upside down, and by this means they shall, at their resurrection, be found ready standing on their feet.[3] The learned among them confess the absurdity of this doctrine, but the practice still continues, in compliance to the vulgar.

There are some laws and customs in this empire very peculiar, and if they were not so directly contrary to those of my own dear country, I should be tempted to say a little in their justification. It is only to be wished, that they were as well executed. The first I shall mention relates to informers. All crimes against the state are punished here with the utmost severity; but if the person accused maketh his innocence plainly to appear upon his trial, the accuser is immediately put to an ignominious death; and out of his goods or lands, the innocent person is quadruply recompensed for the loss of his time, for the danger he underwent, for the hardship of his imprisonment, and for all the charges he hath been at in making his defence. Or, if that fund be deficient, it is largely supplied by the crown. The Emperor does also confer on him some public mark of his favour, and proclamation is made of his innocence through the whole city.

They look upon fraud as a greater crime than theft, and therefore seldom fail to punish it with death; for they allege, that care and

1. The Cascagians appear to be the invention of Swift.
2. This paragraph Swift borrowed, with alterations, from *A New Voyage to the East-Indies*, by 'William Symson' (1715).
3. By old custom (still widely followed in England) bodies were buried with their feet to the east, toward which they were to hasten at the sound of the last trump.

vigilance, with a very common understanding, may preserve a man's goods from thieves, but honesty has no fence against superior cunning: and since it is necessary that there should be a perpetual intercourse of buying and selling, and dealing upon credit, where fraud is permitted and connived at, or hath no law to punish it, the honest dealer is always undone, and the knave gets the advantage. I remember when I was once interceding with the King for a criminal who had wronged his master of a great sum of money, which he had received by order, and ran away with; and happening to tell his Majesty, by way of extenuation, that it was only a breach of trust; the Emperor thought it monstrous in me to offer, as a defence, the greatest aggravation of the crime: and truly I had little to say in return, farther than the common answer, that different nations had different customs; for, I confess, I was heartily ashamed.[4]

Although we usually call reward and punishment the two hinges upon which all government turns, yet I could never observe this maxim to be put in practice by any nation except that of Lilliput. Whoever can there bring sufficient proof that he hath strictly observed the laws of his country for seventy-three moons, hath a claim to certain privileges, according to his quality and condition of life, with a proportionable sum of money out of a fund appropriated for that use: he likewise acquires the title of *'Snilpall'*, or 'Legal', which is added to his name, but does not descend to his posterity. And these people thought it a prodigious defect of policy among us, when I told them that our laws were enforced only by penalties without any mention of reward. It is upon this account that the image of Justice, in their courts of judicature, is formed with six eyes, two before, as many behind, and on each side one, to signify circumspection; with a bag of gold open in her right hand, and a sword sheathed in her left, to show she is more disposed to reward than to punish.

4. Very few frauds were punishable by the criminal law of England until after the middle of the eighteenth century.

In choosing persons for all employments, they have more regard to good morals than to great abilities; for, since government is necessary to mankind, they believe that the common size of human understandings is fitted to some station or other, and that Providence never intended to make the management of public affairs a mystery, to be comprehended only by a few persons of sublime genius, of which there seldom are three born in an age: but they suppose truth, justice, temperance, and the like, to be in every man's power; the practice of which virtues, assisted by experience and a good intention, would qualify any man for the service of his country, except where a course of study is required. But they thought the want of moral virtues was so far from being supplied by superior endowments of the minds, that employments could never be put into such dangerous hands as those of persons so qualified; and at least, that the mistakes committed by ignorance in a virtuous disposition would never be of such fatal consequence to the public weal, as the practices of a man whose inclinations led him to be corrupt, and had great abilities to manage, and multiply, and defend his corruptions.

In like manner, the disbelief of a divine Providence renders a man uncapable of holding any public station; for since kings avow themselves to be the deputies of Providence, the Lilliputians think nothing can be more absurd than for a prince to employ such men as disown the authority under which he acts.[5]

In relating these and the following laws, I would only be understood to mean the original institutions, and not the most scandalous corruptions into which these people are fallen by the degenerate nature of man. For as to that infamous practice of acquiring great employments by dancing on the ropes, or badges of favour and distinction by leaping over sticks, and creeping under them, the reader is to observe, that they were first introduced by the grandfather of the Emperor now

5. Under the provisions of the Test Acts passed in the reign of Charles II only communicants of the Church of England could hold public office. Swift was among those who strenuously opposed any relaxation of this policy.

reigning,[6] and grew to the present height by the gradual encrease of party and faction.

Ingratitude is among them a capital crime, as we read it to have been in some other countries; for they reason thus, that whoever makes ill returns to his benefactor, must needs be a common enemy to the rest of mankind, from whom he hath received no obligation, and therefore such a man is not fit to live.

Their notions relating to the duties of parents and children differ extremely from ours. For, since the conjunction of male and female is founded upon the great law of nature, in order to propagate and continue the species, the Lilliputians will needs have it, that men and women are joined together like other animals, by the motives of concupiscence; and that their tenderness towards their young proceeds from the like natural principle: for which reason they will never allow, that a child is under any obligation to his father for begetting him, or his mother for bringing him into the world; which, considering the miseries of human life, was neither a benefit in itself, or intended so by his parents, whose thoughts in their love-encounters were otherwise employed. Upon these, and the like reasonings, their opinion is, that parents are the last of all others to be trusted with the education of their own children: and therefore they have in every town public nurseries,[7] where all parents, except cottagers and labourers, are obliged to send their infants of both sexes to be reared and educated when they come to the age of twenty moons, at which time they are supposed to have some rudiments of docility. These schools are of several kinds, suited to different qualities, and to both sexes. They have certain professors well skilled in preparing children for such a condition of life as befits the rank of their parents, and their own capacities as well as inclinations. I shall first say something of the male nurseries, and then of the female.

6. James I was responsible for the widespread sale of honors in his reign.
7. Schools—not necessarily for the very young only.

The nurseries for males of noble or eminent birth are provided with grave and learned professors, and their several deputies. The clothes and food of the children are plain and simple. They are bred up in the principles of honour, justice, courage, modesty, clemency, religion, and love of their country; they are always employed in some business, except in the times of eating and sleeping, which are very short, and two hours for diversions, consisting of bodily exercises. They are dressed by men till four years of age, and then are obliged to dress themselves, although their quality be ever so great; and the women attendants, who are aged proportionably to ours at fifty, perform only the most menial offices. They are never suffered to converse with servants, but go together in small or greater numbers to take their diversions, and always in the presence of a professor, or one of his deputies; whereby they avoid those early bad impressions of folly and vice to which our children are subject. Their parents are suffered to see them only twice a year; the visit is to last but an hour. They are allowed to kiss the child at meeting and parting; but a professor, who always stands by on those occasions, will not suffer them to whisper, or use any fondling expressions, or bring any presents of toys, sweetmeats, and the like.

The pension from each family for the education and entertainment of a child, upon failure of due payment, is levied by the Emperor's officers.

The nurseries for children of ordinary gentlemen, merchants, traders, and handicrafts, are managed proportionably after the same manner; only those designed for trades are put out apprentices at eleven years old, whereas those of persons of quality continue in their nurseries till fifteen, which answers to one and twenty with us: but the confinement is gradually lessened for the last three years.

In the female nurseries, the young girls of quality are educated much like the males, only they are dressed by orderly servants of their own sex, but always in the presence of a professor or deputy, till they

come to dress themselves, which is at five years old. And if it be found that these nurses ever presume to entertain the girls with frightful or foolish stories, or the common follies practiced by chambermaids among us, they are publicly whipped thrice about the city, imprisoned for a year, and banished for life to the most desolate part of the country. Thus the young ladies there are as much ashamed of being cowards and fools as the men, and despise all personal ornaments beyond decency and cleanliness: neither did I perceive any difference in their education, made by their difference of sex, only that the exercises of the females were not altogether so robust, and that some rules were given them relating to domestic life, and a smaller compass of learning was enjoined them: for the maxim is, that among people of quality, a wife should be always a reasonable and agreeable companion, because she cannot always be young. When the girls are twelve years old, which among them is the marriageable age, their parents or guardians take them home, with great expressions of gratitude to the professors, and seldom without tears of the young lady and her companions.

In the nurseries of females of the meaner sort, the children are instructed in all kinds of works proper for their sex, and their several degrees: those intended for apprentices are dismissed at nine years old, the rest are kept to thirteen.

The meaner families who have children at these nurseries are obliged, besides their annual pension, which is as low as possible, to return to the steward of the nursery a small monthly share of their gettings, to be a portion for the child; and therefore all parents are limited in their expenses by the law. For the Lilliputians think nothing can be more unjust, than for people, in subservience to their own appetites, to bring children into the world, and leave the burthen of supporting them on the public. As to persons of quality, they give security to appropriate a certain sum for each child, suitable to their condition; and these funds are always managed with good husbandry, and the most exact justice.

The cottagers and labourers keep their children at home, their business being only to till and cultivate the earth, and therefore their education is of little consequence to the public; but the old and diseased among them are supported by hospitals: for begging is a trade unknown in this kingdom.

And here it may perhaps divert the curious reader, to give some account of my domestic,[8] and my manner of living in this country, during a residence of nine months and thirteen days. Having a head mechanically turned, and being likewise forced by necessity, I had made for myself a table and chair convenient enough, out of the largest trees in the royal park. Two hundred sempstresses were employed to make me shirts, and linen for my bed and table, all of the strongest and coarsest kind they could get; which, however, they were forced to quilt together in several folds, for the thickest was some degrees finer than lawn. Their linen is usually three inches wide, and three foot make a piece. The sempstresses took my measure as I lay on the ground, one standing at my neck, and another at my midleg, with a strong cord extended, that each held by the end, while the third measured the length of the cord with a rule of an inch long. Then they measured my right thumb, and desired no more; for by a mathematical computation, that twice round the thumb is once round the wrist, and so on to the neck and the waist, and by the help of my old shirt, which I displayed on the ground before them for a pattern, they fitted me exactly. Three hundred tailors were employed in the same manner to make me clothes; but they had another contrivance for taking my measure. I kneeled down, and they raised a ladder from the ground to my neck; upon this ladder one of them mounted, and let fall a plumb-line from my collar to the floor, which just answered the length of my coat; but my waist and arms I measured myself. When my clothes were finished, which was done in my house (for the largest of theirs would not be able to hold them) they looked like the patch-

8. Domestic arrangements.

work made by the ladies in England, only that mine were all of a colour.

I had three hundred cooks to dress my victuals, in little convenient huts built about my house, where they and their families lived, and prepared me two dishes apiece. I took up twenty waiters in my hand, and placed them on the table; an hundred more attended below on the ground, some with dishes of meat, and some with barrels of wine, and other liquors, slung on their shoulders; all which the waiters above drew up as I wanted, in a very ingenious manner, by certain cords, as we draw the bucket up a well in Europe. A dish of their meat was a good mouthful, and a barrel of their liquor a reasonable draught. Their mutton yields to ours, but their beef is excellent. I have had a sirloin so large, that I have been forced to make three bits of it; but this is rare. My servants were astonished to see me eat it bones and all, as in our country we do the leg of a lark. Their geese and turkeys I usually eat at a mouthful, and I must confess they far exceed ours. Of their smaller fowl I could take up twenty or thirty at the end of my knife.

One day his Imperial Majesty, being informed of my way of living, desired that himself and his royal consort, with the young princes of the blood of both sexes, might have the happiness (as he was pleased to call it) of dining with me. They came accordingly, and I placed 'em upon chairs of state on my table, just over against me, with their guards about them. Flimnap the Lord High Treasurer attended there likewise, with his white staff;[9] and I observed he often looked on me with a sour countenance, which I would not seem to regard, but eat more than usual, in honour to my dear country, as well as to fill the court with admiration. I have some private reasons to believe, that this visit from his Majesty gave Flimnap an opportunity of doing me ill offices to his master. That minister had always been my secret enemy, though he outwardly caressed me more than was usual to the morose-

9. The symbol of high ministerial office.

ness of his nature. He represented to the Emperor the low condition of his treasury; that he was forced to take up money at great discount; that exchequer bills would not circulate under[10] nine per cent below par; that in short I had cost his Majesty above a million and a half of *sprugs* (their greatest gold coin, about the bigness of a spangle); and upon the whole, that it would be advisable in the Emperor to take the first fair occasion of dismissing me.[11]

I am here obliged to vindicate the reputation of an excellent lady, who was an innocent sufferer upon my account. The Treasurer took a fancy to be jealous of his wife,[12] from the malice of some evil tongues, who informed him that her Grace had taken a violent affection for my person, and the court-scandal ran for some time, that she once came privately to my lodging. This I solemnly declare to be a most infamous falsehood, without any grounds, farther than that her Grace was pleased to treat me with all innocent marks of freedom and friendship. I own she came often to my house, but always publicly, nor ever without three more in the coach, who were usually her sister and young daughter, and some particular acquaintance; but this was common to many other ladies of the court. And I still appeal to my servants round, whether they at any time saw a coach at my door without knowing what persons were in it. On those occasions, when a servant had given me notice, my custom was to go immediately to the door; and, after paying my respects, to take up the coach and two horses very carefully in my hands (for if there were six horses, the postillion always unharnessed four) and place them on a table, where I had fixed a moveable rim quite round, of five inches high, to prevent accidents. And I have often had four coaches and horses at once on my table full of company, while I sate in my chair leaning my face towards them; and when I was engaged with one set, the coachmen

10. At less than.
11. The Whigs complained of the extravagance of the Tory administration.
12. Swift refers, by inversion, to Walpole's complaisance with regard to the widely discussed infidelities of his wife.

would gently drive the others round my table. I have passed many an afternoon very agreeably in these conversations. But I defy the Treasurer, or his two informers (I will name them, and let 'em make their best of it) Clustril and Drunlo, to prove that any person ever came to me *incognito,* except the Secretary Reldresal, who was sent by express command of his Imperial Majesty, as I have before related.[13] I should not have dwelt so long upon this particular, if it had not been a point wherein the reputation of a great lady is so nearly concerned, to say nothing of my own; though I had then the honour to be a *nardac,* which the Treasurer himself is not; for all the world knows he is only a *clumglum,*[14] a title inferior by one degree, as that of a marquis is to a duke in England, although I allow he preceded me in right of his post. These false informations, which I afterwards came to the knowledge of, by an accident not proper to mention, made Flimnap the Treasurer show his lady for some time an ill countenance, and me a worse; and although he were at last undeceived and reconciled to her, yet I lost all credit with him, and found my interest decline very fast with the Emperor himself, who was indeed too much governed by that favourite.

13. The incident of the alleged secret visitors to Gulliver and of the informers who spied upon him are presumably borrowed from the trial of Bishop Atterbury for treason in 1723.
14. Walpole was not raised to the peerage until his final retirement from politics in 1742.

Chapter Seven

The author, being informed of a design to accuse him of high treason, makes his escape to Blefuscu. His reception there.

Before I proceed to give an account of my leaving this kingdom, it may be proper to inform the reader of a private intrigue which had been for two months forming against me.

I had been hitherto all my life a stranger to courts, for which I was unqualified by the meanness of my condition. I had indeed heard and read enough of the dispositions of great princes and ministers; but never expected to have found such terrible effects of them in so remote a country, governed, as I thought, by very different maxims from those in Europe.

When I was just preparing to pay my attendance on the Emperor of Blefuscu, a considerable person at court[1] (to whom I had been very serviceable at a time when he lay under the highest displeasure of his Imperial Majesty) came to my house very privately at night in a close chair, and without sending his name, desired admittance: the chairmen were dismissed; I put the chair, with his Lordship in it, into my coat-pocket; and giving orders to a trusty servant to say I was indisposed and gone to sleep, I fastened the door of my house, placed the chair on the table, according to my usual custom, and sate down by it. After the common salutations were over, observing his Lordship's countenance full of concern, and enquiring into the reason, he desired I would hear him with patience in a matter that highly concerned my

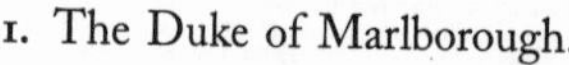
1. The Duke of Marlborough.

honour and my life. His speech was to the following effect, for I took notes of it as soon as he left me.

'You are to know', said he, 'that several committees of council have been lately called in the most private manner on your account:[2] and it is but two days since his Majesty came to a full resolution.

'You are very sensible that Skyresh Bolgolam (*Galbet*, or High Admiral) hath been your mortal enemy almost ever since your arrival. His original reasons I know not, but his hatred is much encreased since your great success against Blefuscu, by which his glory, as Admiral, is obscured. This lord, in conjunction with Flimnap the High Treasurer, whose enmity against you is notorious on account of his lady, Limtoc the General, Lalcon the Chamberlain, and Balmuff the Grand Justiciary,[3] have prepared articles of impeachment against you, for treason, and other capital crimes'.

This preface made me so impatient, being conscious of my own merits and innocence, that I was going to interrupt; when he intreated me to be silent, and thus proceeded.

'Out of gratitude for the favours you have done me, I procured information of the whole proceedings, and a copy of the articles, wherein I venture my head for your service.

'*Articles of Impeachment against Quinbus Flestrin (the Man-Mountain)*

ARTICLE I

Whereas, by a statute made in the reign of his Imperial Majesty Calin Deffar Plune, it is enacted, that whoever shall make water

2. In the summer of 1714, at the time of the death of Queen Anne, the Tories were succeeded in power by the Whigs. A committee of Whigs and 'whimsical' Tories was appointed in 1715 to investigate the activities of the ousted Tory ministry. Upon the report of this committee were based the impeachments of Oxford and Bolingbroke.
3. General Stanhope, Secretary of State for War; the Duke of Devonshire, Lord Steward; Lord Cowper, Lord Chancellor.

within the precincts of the royal palace shall be liable to the pains and penalties of high treason: notwithstanding, the said Quinbus Flestrin, in open breach of the said law, under colour of extinguishing the fire kindled in the apartment of his Majesty's dear imperial consort, did maliciously, traitorously, and devilishly, by discharge of his urine, put out the said fire kindled in the said apartment, lying and being within the precincts of the said royal palace, against the statute in that case provided, etc., against the duty, etc.[4]

ARTICLE II

That the said Quinbus Flestrin, having brought the imperial fleet of Blefuscu into the royal port, and being afterwards commanded by his Imperial Majesty to seize all the other ships of the said empire of Blefuscu, and reduce that empire to a province, to be governed by a viceroy from hence, and to destroy and put to death not only all the Big-Endian exiles, but likewise all the people of that empire who would not immediately forsake the Big-Endian heresy: he, the said Flestrin, like a false traitor against his most Auspicious, Serene, Imperial Majesty, did petition to be excused from the said service, upon pretence of unwillingness to force the consciences, or destroy the liberties and lives of an innocent people.[5]

ARTICLE III

That, whereas certain ambassadors arrived from the court of Blefuscu to sue for peace in his Majesty's court: he the said Flestrin did, like a false traitor, aid, abet, comfort, and divert the said ambassadors, although he knew them to be servants to a prince who was lately an open enemy to his Imperial Majesty, and in open war against his said Majesty.[6]

4. This article corresponds to the charge, in the articles of impeachment against Oxford and Bolingbroke, that the ministers had acted illegally in negotiating peace.
5. This article attacks the mild terms of peace granted to the French.
6. The reference is to the secret understanding between the Tory ministry and the French.

ARTICLE IV

That the said Quinbus Flestrin, contrary to the duty of a faithful subject, is now preparing to make a voyage to the court and empire of Blefuscu, for which he hath received only verbal licence from his Imperial Majesty; and under colour of the said licence, doth falsely and traitorously intend to take the said voyage, and thereby to aid, comfort, and abet the Emperor of Blefuscu, so late an enemy, and in open war with his Imperial Majesty aforesaid.[7]

'There are some other articles, but these are the most important, of which I have read you an abstract.

'In the several debates upon this impeachment, it must be confessed that his Majesty gave many marks of his great lenity, often urging the services you had done him, and endeavouring to extenuate your crimes. The Treasurer and Admiral insisted that you should be put to the most painful and ignominious death, by setting fire on your house at night, and the General was to attend with twenty thousand men armed with poisoned arrows to shoot you on the face and hands. Some of your servants were to have private orders to strew a poisonous juice on your shirts, which would soon make you tear your own flesh, and die in the utmost torture. The General came into the same opinion, so that for a long time there was a majority against you. But his Majesty resolving, if possible, to spare your life, at last brought off the Chamberlain.

'Upon this incident, Reldresal, Principal Secretary for Private Affairs, who always approved himself your true friend,[8] was commanded by the Emperor to deliver his opinion, which he accordingly did; and therein justified the good thoughts you have of him. He allowed your

7. A variation of the charge in the first article, with specific reference to the fact that the royal warrants authorizing the negotiation of the peace were not properly countersigned.

8. When Bolingbroke attempted to obtain pardon for his treason Townshend professed sympathy, but after several years of delay Bolingbroke and his friends came to the conclusion that the Secretary's friendship was feigned.

crimes to be great, but that still there was room for mercy, the most commendable virtue in a prince, and for which his Majesty was so justly celebrated. He said the friendship between you and him was so well known to the world, that perhaps the most honourable board might think him partial: however, in obedience to the command he had received, he would freely offer his sentiments. That if his Majesty, in consideration of your services, and pursuant to his own merciful disposition, would please to spare your life, and only give order to put out both your eyes, he humbly conceived, that by this expedient justice might in some measure be satisfied, and all the world would applaud the lenity of the Emperor, as well as the fair and generous proceedings of those who have the honour to be his counsellors.[9] That the loss of your eyes would be no impediment to your bodily strength, by which you might still be useful to his Majesty. That blindness is an addition to courage, by concealing dangers from us; that the fear you had for your eyes was the greatest difficulty in bringing over the enemy's fleet, and it would be sufficient for you to see by the eyes of the ministers, since the greatest princes do no more.

'This proposal was received with the utmost disapprobation by the whole board. Bolgolam, the Admiral, could not preserve his temper; but rising up in fury, said, he wondered how the Secretary durst presume to give his opinion for preserving the life of a traitor: that the services you had performed were, by all true reasons of state, the great aggravation of your crimes; that you, who were able to extinguish the fire, by discharge of urine in her Majesty's apartment (which he mentioned with horror), might, at another time, raise an inundation by the same means, to drown the whole palace; and the same strength which enabled you to bring over the enemy's fleet might serve, upon the first discontent, to carry it back:[10] that he had good reasons to

9. Bolingbroke's partial pardon, in 1723, did not restore his right to sit in Parliament, and he was therefore condemned to political inactivity.

10. The inveterate enemies of Bolingbroke opposed even his partial pardon, on the ground that if he were allowed to return to England he might foment rebellion.

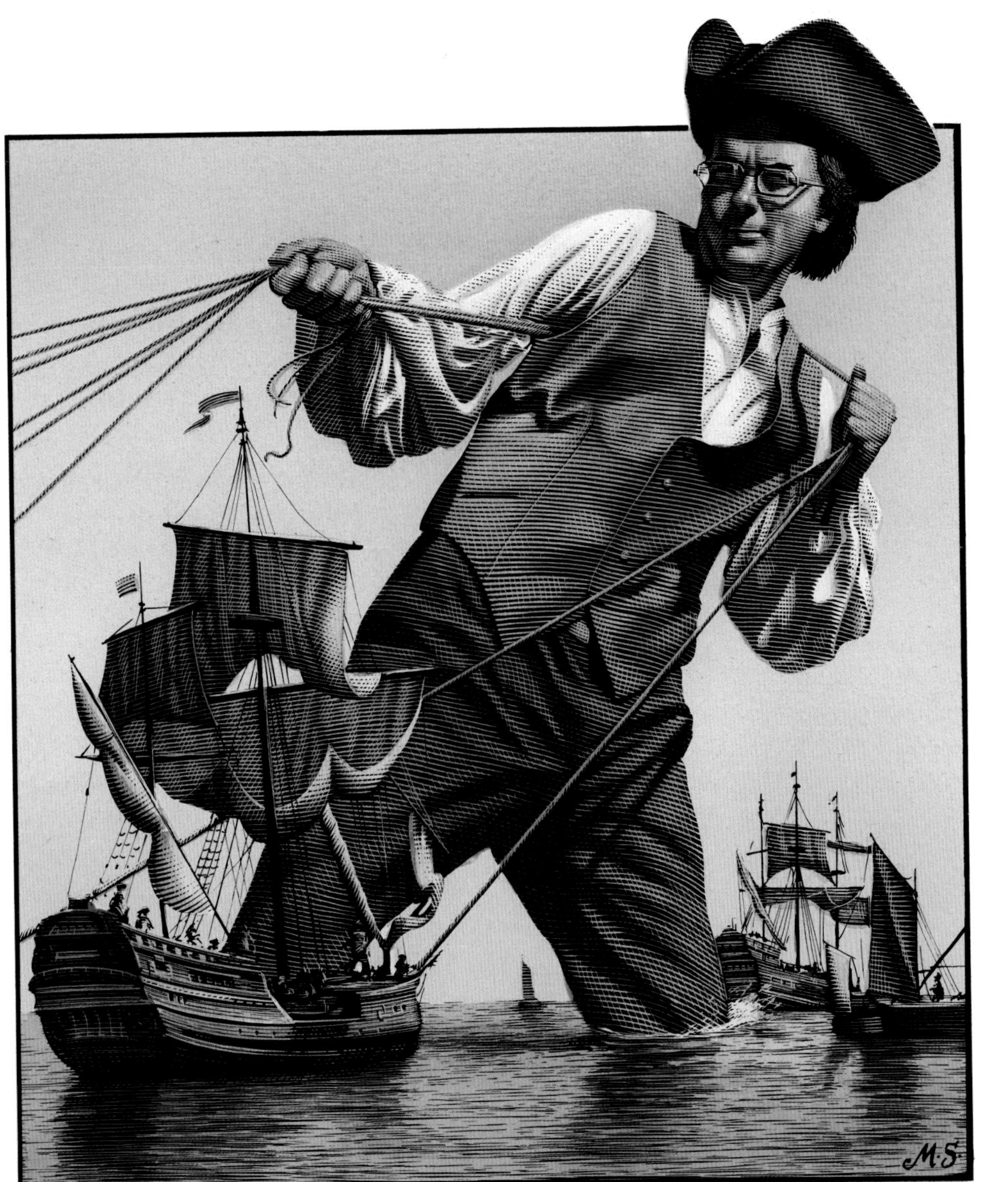
M.S

I had now fastened all the hooks, and taking the knot in my hand, began to pull;...

PAGE 60

think you were a Big-Endian in your heart;[11] and as treason begins in the heart before it appears in overt acts, so he accused you as a traitor on that account, and therefore insisted you should be put to death.

'The Treasurer was of the same opinion; he showed to what straits his Majesty's revenue was reduced by the charge of maintaining you, which would soon grow insupportable: that the Secretary's expedient of putting out your eyes was so far from being a remedy against this evil, it would probably encrease it, as it is manifest from the common practice of blinding some kind of fowl, after which they fed the faster, and grew sooner fat: that his sacred Majesty, and the council, who are your judges, were in their own consciences fully convinced of your guilt, which was a sufficient argument to condemn you to death, without the formal proofs required by the strict letter of the law.[12]

'But his Imperial Majesty, fully determined against capital punishment, was graciously pleased to say, that since the council thought the loss of your eyes too easy a censure, some other may be inflicted hereafter. And your friend the Secretary humbly desiring to be heard again, in answer to what the Treasurer had objected concerning the great charge his Majesty was at in maintaining you, said, that his Excellency, who had the sole disposal of the Emperor's revenue, might easily provide against that evil, by gradually lessening your establishment; by which, for want of sufficient food, you would grow weak and faint, and lose your appetite, and consequently decay and consume in a few months;[13] neither would the stench of your carcass be then so dangerous, when it should become more than half diminished; and immediately upon your death, five or six thousand of his

11. There was no foundation for the suggestion that either Oxford or Bolingbroke was a Roman Catholic.

12. There was great difficulty in collecting evidence to support the charges of treason against the two ministers, and the conviction of Bolingbroke was, in strict law, not well grounded.

13. The suggestion is that the Whigs planned first to render Oxford and Bolingbroke politically impotent, and then to punish them rigorously.

Majesty's subjects might, in two or three days, cut your flesh from your bones, take it away by cart-loads, and bury it in distant parts to prevent infection, leaving the skeleton as a monument of admiration to posterity.

'Thus by the great friendship of the Secretary, the whole affair was compromised. It was strictly enjoined, that the project of starving you by degrees should be kept a secret, but the sentence of putting out your eyes was entered on the books; none dissenting except Bolgolam the Admiral, who, being a creature of the Empress, was perpetually instigated by her Majesty to insist upon your death, she having borne perpetual malice against you, on account of that infamous and illegal method you took to extinguish the fire in her apartment.

'In three days your friend the Secretary will be directed to come to your house, and read before you the articles of impeachment;[14] and then to signify the great lenity and favour of his Majesty and council, whereby you are only condemned to the loss of your eyes, which his Majesty doth not question you will gratefully and humbly submit to; and twenty of his Majesty's surgeons will attend, in order to see the operation well performed, by discharging very sharp-pointed arrows into the balls of your eyes, as you lie on the ground.

'I leave to your prudence what measures you will take; and to avoid suspicion, I must immediately return in as private a manner as I came'.

His Lordship did so, and I remained alone, under many doubts and perplexities of mind.

It was a custom introduced by this prince and his ministry (very different, as I have been assured, from the practices of former times) that after the court had decreed any cruel execution, either to gratify the monarch's resentment, or the malice of a favourite, the Emperor made a speech to his whole council, expressing his great lenity and

14. It was the duty of Townshend, as Secretary of State, to issue the warrants for the arrest of Oxford and Bolingbroke.

tenderness, as qualities known and confessed by all the world.[15] This speech was immediately published through the kingdom; nor did any thing terrify the people so much as those encomiums on his Majesty's mercy; because it was observed, that the more these praises were enlarged and insisted on, the more inhuman was the punishment, and the sufferer more innocent. And as to myself, I must confess, having never been designed for a courtier either by my birth or education, I was so ill a judge of things, that I could not discover the lenity and favour of this sentence, but conceived it (perhaps erroneously) rather to be rigorous than gentle. I sometimes thought of standing my trial, for although I could not deny the facts alleged in the several articles, yet I hoped they would admit of some extenuations. But having in my life perused many state trials, which I ever observed to terminate as the judges thought fit to direct, I durst not rely on so dangerous a decision, in so critical a juncture, and against such powerful enemies. Once I was strongly bent upon resistance, for while I had liberty, the whole strength of that empire could hardly subdue me, and I might easily with stones pelt the metropolis to pieces;[16] but I soon rejected that project with horror, by remembering the oath I had made to the Emperor, the favours I received from him, and the high title of *nardac* he conferred upon me. Neither had I so soon learned the gratitude of courtiers, to persuade myself that his Majesty's present severities acquitted me of all past obligations.

At last I fixed upon a resolution, for which it is probable I may incur some censure, and not unjustly; for I confess I owe the preserving my eyes, and consequently my liberty, to my own great rashness and want of experience: because if I had then known the nature of princes and ministers, which I have since observed in many other courts, and their

15. The House of Lords, in an address to the King at the opening of Parliament in 1716, extolled his 'endearing tenderness and clemency'. Shortly afterward a number of the rebels in the Jacobite uprising of 1715 were executed.
16. A suggestion that Oxford and Bolingbroke, had they really been disloyal to George I, might have raised a successful rebellion against him in 1714.

methods of treating criminals less obnoxious than myself, I should with great alacrity and readiness have submitted to so easy a punishment. But hurried on by the precipitancy of youth, and having his Imperial Majesty's licence to pay my attendance upon the Emperor of Blefuscu, I took this opportunity, before the three days were elapsed, to send a letter to my friend the Secretary, signifying my resolution of setting out that morning for Blefuscu pursuant to the leave I had got; and without waiting for an answer, I went to that side of the island where our fleet lay. I seized a large man-of-war, tied a cable to the prow, and, lifting up the anchors, I stripped myself, put my clothes (together with my coverlet, which I brought under my arm) into the vessel, and drawing it after me between wading and swimming, arrived at the royal port of Blefuscu, where the people had long expected me;[17] they lent me two guides to direct me to the capital city, which is of the same name. I held them in my hands till I came within two hundred yards of the gate, and desired them to signify my arrival to one of the secretaries, and let him know, I there waited his Majesty's commands. I had an answer in about an hour, that his Majesty, attended by the royal family, and great officers of the court, was coming out to receive me. I advanced an hundred yards. The Emperor, and his train, alighted from their horses, the Empress and ladies from their coaches, and I did not perceive they were in any fright or concern. I lay on the ground to kiss his Majesty's and the Empress's hand. I told his Majesty that I was come according to my promise, and with the licence of the Emperor my master, to have the honour of seeing so mighty a monarch, and to offer him any service in my power, consistent with my duty to my own prince; not mentioning a word of my disgrace, because I had hitherto no regular information of it, and might suppose myself wholly ignorant of any such design; neither could I reasonably conceive that the Emperor would

17. Bolingbroke fled to France on the eve of his trial, and was convicted in his absence. Oxford stood his ground, and after two years, by a turn of the political wheel, the charges against him were dropped.

discover[18] the secret while I was out of his power: wherein, however, it soon appeared I was deceived.

I shall not trouble the reader with the particular account of my reception at this court, which was suitable to the generosity of so great a prince; nor of the difficulties I was in for want of a house and bed, being forced to lie on the ground, wrapped up in my coverlet.[19]

18. Disclose.
19. Perhaps a reference to the hardships endured by many of the Jacobite exiles in France.

Chapter Eight

The author, by a lucky accident, finds means to leave Blefuscu, and after some difficulties returns safe to his native country.

HREE DAYS AFTER MY ARRIVAL, WALKING OUT OF curiosity to the northeast coast of the island, I observed, about half a league off, in the sea, somewhat that looked like a boat overturned. I pulled off my shoes and stockings, and wading two or three hundred yards, I found the object to approach nearer by force of the tide, and then plainly saw it to be a real boat, which I supposed might, by some tempest, have been driven from a ship; whereupon I returned immediately towards the city, and desired his Imperial Majesty to lend me twenty of the tallest vessels he had left after the loss of his fleet, and three thousand seamen under the command of his Vice-Admiral. This fleet sailed round, while I went back the shortest way to the coast where I first discovered the boat; I found the tide had driven it still nearer. The seamen were all provided with cordage, which I had beforehand twisted to a sufficient strength. When the ships came up, I stripped myself, and waded till I came within an hundred yards of the boat, after which I was forced to swim till I got up to it. The seamen threw me the end of the cord, which I fastened to a hole in the fore-part of the boat, and the other end to a man-of-war: but I found all my labour to little purpose; for being out of my depth, I was not able to work. In this necessity, I was forced to swim behind, and push the boat forwards as often as I could, with one

of my hands; and the tide favouring me, I advanced so far, that I could just hold up my chin and feel the ground. I rested two or three minutes, and then gave the boat another shove, and so on till the sea was no higher than my armpits; and now the most laborious part being over, I took out my other cables, which were stowed in one of the ships, and fastening them first to the boat, and then to nine of the vessels which attended me; the wind being favourable the seamen towed, and I shoved till we arrived within forty yards of the shore, and waiting till the tide was out, I got dry to the boat, and by the assistance of two thousand men, with ropes and engines, I made a shift to turn it on its bottom, and found it was but little damaged.

I shall not trouble the reader with the difficulties I was under by the help of certain paddles, which cost me ten days making, to get my boat to the royal port of Blefuscu, where a mighty concourse of people appeared upon my arrival, full of wonder at the sight of so prodigious a vessel. I told the Emperor that my good fortune had thrown this boat in my way, to carry me to some place from whence I might return into my native country, and begged his Majesty's orders for getting materials to fit it up, together with his licence to depart; which, after some kind expostulations, he was pleased to grant.

I did very much wonder, in all this time, not to have heard of any express relating to me from our Emperor to the court of Blefuscu. But I was afterwards given privately to understand, that his Imperial Majesty, never imagining I had the least notice of his designs, believed I was only gone to Blefuscu in performance of my promise, according to the licence he had given me, which was well known at our court, and would return in a few days when that ceremony was ended. But he was at last in pain at my long absence; and after consulting with the Treasurer, and the rest of that cabal, a person of quality was dispatched with the copy of the articles against me. This envoy had instructions to represent to the monarch of Blefuscu the great lenity of his master, who was content to punish me no further than with the loss of my eyes; that I had fled from justice, and if I did not return in two hours, I should be deprived of my title of *nardac,* and declared a traitor. The envoy further added, that in order to maintain the peace and amity between both empires, his master expected, that his brother of Blefuscu would give orders to have me sent back to Lilliput, bound hand and foot, to be punished as a traitor.[1]

The Emperor of Blefuscu, having taken three days to consult, returned an answer consisting of many civilities and excuses. He said, that as for sending me bound, his brother knew it was impossible; that although I had deprived him of his fleet, yet he owed great obligations to me for many good offices I had done him in making the peace. That however both their Majesties would soon be made easy; for I had found a prodigious vessel on the shore, able to carry me on the sea, which he had given order to fit up with my own assistance and direction, and he hoped in a few weeks both empires would be freed from so insupportable an incumbrance.

With this answer the envoy returned to Lilliput, and the monarch of Blefuscu related to me all that had passed, offering me at the same time (but under the strictest confidence) his gracious protection, if I would continue in his service; wherein although I believed him sincere, yet I resolved never more to put any confidence in princes or ministers, where I could possibly avoid it; and therefore, with all due acknowledgements for his favourable intentions, I humbly begged to be excused. I told him, that since fortune, whether good or evil, had thrown a vessel in my way, I was resolved to venture myself in the ocean, rather than be an occasion of difference between two such mighty monarchs. Neither did I find the Emperor at all displeased; and I discovered by a certain accident, that he was very glad of my resolution, and so were most of his ministers.

These considerations moved me to hasten my departure somewhat sooner than I intended; to which the court, impatient to have me

1. The English government protested frequently against the harboring of Jacobites by the French.

gone, very readily contributed. Five hundred workmen were employed to make two sails to my boat, according to my directions, by quilting thirteen fold of their strongest linen together. I was at the pains of making ropes and cables, by twisting ten, twenty or thirty of the thickest and strongest of theirs. A great stone that I happened to find, after a long search by the seashore, served me for an anchor. I had the tallow of three hundred cows for greasing my boat, and other uses. I was at incredible pains in cutting down some of the largest timber trees for oars and masts, wherein I was, however, much assisted by his Majesty's ship-carpenters, who helped me in smoothing them, after I had done the rough work.

In about a month, when all was prepared, I sent to receive his Majesty's commands, and to take my leave. The Emperor and royal family came out of the palace; I lay down on my face to kiss his hand, which he very graciously gave me: so did the Empress, and young princes of the blood. His Majesty presented me with fifty purses of two hundred *sprugs* apiece, together with his picture at full length,[2] which I put immediately into one of my gloves, to keep it from being hurt. The ceremonies at my departure were too many to trouble the reader with at this time.

I stored the boat with the carcases of an hundred oxen, and three hundred sheep, with bread and drink proportionable, and as much meat ready dressed as four hundred cooks could provide. I took with me six cows and two bulls alive, with as many ewes and rams, intending to carry them into my own country, and propagate the breed. And to feed them on board, I had a good bundle of hay, and a bag of corn. I would gladly have taken a dozen of the natives, but this was a thing the Emperor would by no means permit; and besides a diligent search into my pockets, his Majesty engaged my honour not to carry away any of his subjects, although with their own consent and desire.

Having thus prepared all things as well as I was able, I set sail on

2. Louis XIV conferred various favors upon Bolingbroke.

the twenty-fourth day of September, 1701, at six in the morning; and when I had gone about four leagues to the northward, the wind being at southeast, at six in the evening, I descried a small island about half a league to the northwest. I advanced forwards, and cast anchor on the lee-side of the island, which seemed to be uninhabited. I then took some refreshment, and went to my rest. I slept well, and I conjecture at least six hours, for I found the day broke in two hours after I awaked. It was a clear night. I eat my breakfast before the sun was up; and heaving anchor, the wind being favourable, I steered the same course that I had done the day before, wherein I was directed by my pocket-compass. My intention was to reach, if possible, one of those islands which I had reason to believe lay to the northeast of Van Diemen's Land. I discovered nothing all that day; but upon the next, about three in the afternoon, when I had by my computation made twenty-four leagues from Blefuscu, I descried a sail steering to the southeast; my course was due east. I hailed her, but could get no answer; yet I found I gained upon her, for the wind slackened. I made all the sail I could, and in half an hour she spied me, then hung out her ancient,[3] and discharged a gun. It is not easy to express the joy I was in upon the unexpected hope of once more seeing my beloved country, and the dear pledges I had left in it. The ship slackened her sails, and I came up with her between five and six in the evening, September 26; but my heart leapt within me to see her English colours. I put my cows and sheep into my coat-pockets, and got on board with all my little cargo of provisions. The vessel was an English merchantman, returning from Japan by the North and South Seas;[4] the captain, Mr. John Biddel of Deptford, a very civil man, and an excellent sailor. We were now in the latitude of 30 degrees south; there were about fifty men in the ship; and here I met an old comrade of mine, one Peter Williams, who gave me a good character to the

3. Flag.
4. The North and South Pacific.

captain. This gentleman treated me with kindness, and desired I would let him know what place I came from last, and whither I was bound; which I did in few words, but he thought I was raving, and that the dangers I underwent had disturbed my head; whereupon I took my black cattle and sheep out of my pocket, which, after great astonishment, clearly convinced him of my veracity. I then showed him the gold given me by the Emperor of Blefuscu, together with his Majesty's picture at full length, and some other rarities of that country. I gave him two purses of two hundred *sprugs* each, and promised, when we arrived in England, to make him a present of a cow and a sheep big with young.

I shall not trouble the reader with a particular account of this voyage, which was very prosperous for the most part. We arrived in the Downs[5] on the 13th of April, 1702. I had only one misfortune, that the rats on board carried away one of my sheep; I found her bones in a hole, picked clean from the flesh. The rest of my cattle I got safe on shore, and set them a grazing in a bowling-green at Greenwich, where the fineness of the grass made them feed very heartily, though I had always feared the contrary; neither could I possibly have preserved them in so long a voyage, if the captain had not allowed me some of his best biscuit, which, rubbed to powder, and mingled with water, was their constant food. The short time I continued in England, I made a considerable profit by showing my cattle to many persons of quality, and others: and before I began my second voyage, I sold them for six hundred pounds. Since my last return, I find the breed is considerably encreased, especially the sheep; which I hope will prove much to the advantage of the woollen manufacture, by the fineness of the fleeces.

I stayed but two months with my wife and family; for my insatiable desire of seeing foreign countries would suffer me to continue no longer. I left fifteen hundred pounds with my wife, and fixed her in a

5. A roadstead on the coast of Kent, about ten miles northeast of Dover.

good house at Redriff. My remaining stock I carried with me, part in money, and part in goods, in hopes to improve my fortunes. My eldest uncle John had left me an estate in land, near Epping, of about thirty pounds a year; and I had a long lease of the Black Bull in Fetter Lane, which yielded me as much more: so that I was not in any danger of leaving my family upon the parish. My son Johnny, named so after his uncle, was at the grammar school, and a towardly[6] child. My daughter Betty (who is now well married, and has children) was then at her needlework. I took leave of my wife, and boy and girl, with tears on both sides, and went on board the *Adventure,* a merchant-ship of three hundred tons, bound for Surat,[7] Captain John Nicholas of Liverpool commander. But my account of this voyage must be referred to the second part of my *Travels.*

The End of the First Part

6. Precocious.
7. In Bombay.

PART TWO

A Voyage to Brobdingnag

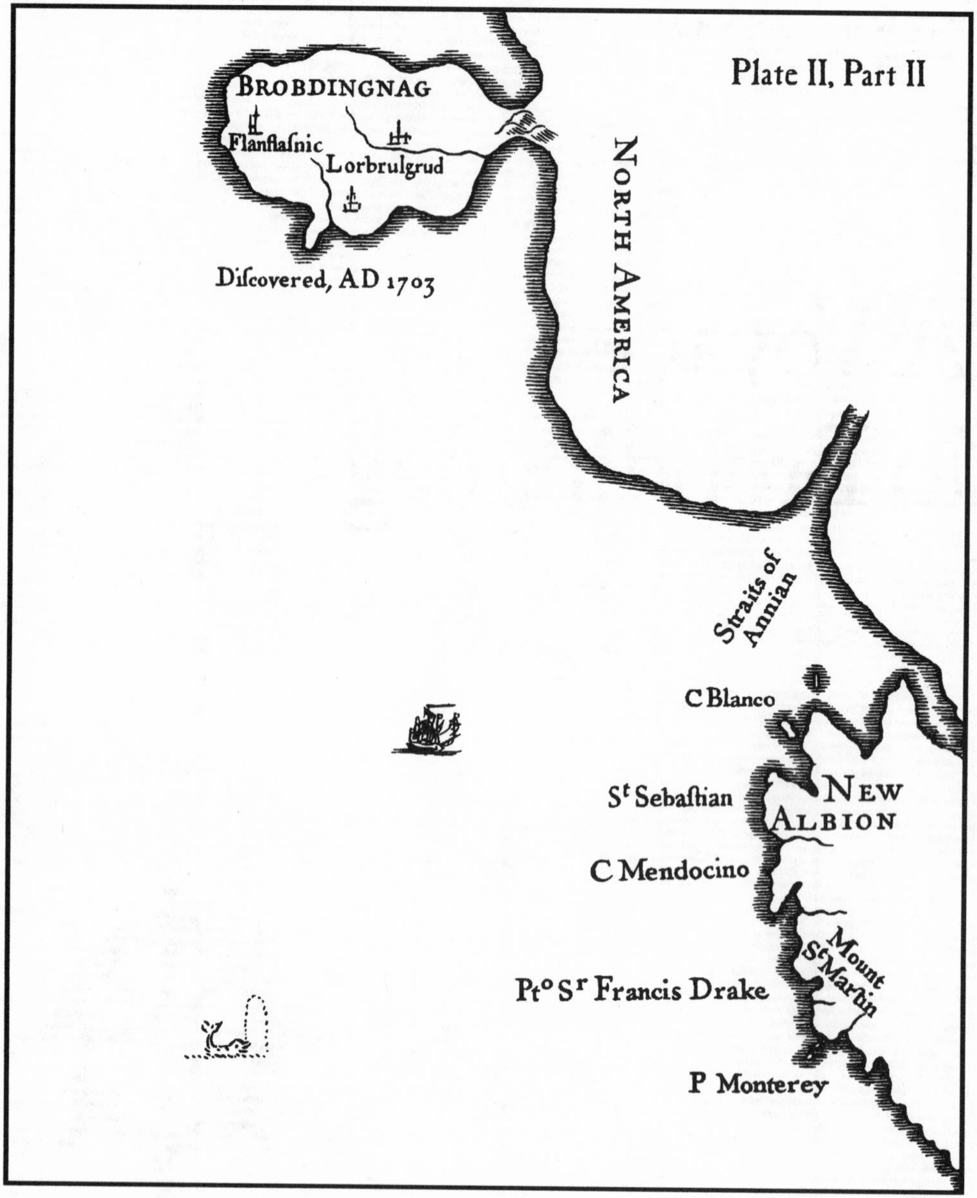

Plate II, Part II

BROBDINGNAG

Flanflaſnic

Lorbrulgrud

Diſcovered, AD 1703

NORTH AMERICA

Straits of Annian

C Blanco

St Sebaſtian

NEW ALBION

C Mendocino

Mount St Martin

Pto Sr Francis Drake

P Monterey

Chapter One

A great storm described, the longboat sent to fetch water, the author goes with it to discover the country. He is left on shore, is seized by one of the natives, and carried to a farmer's house. His reception there, with several accidents that happened there. A description of the inhabitants.

AVING BEEN CONDEMNED BY NATURE AND FORtune to an active and restless life, in two months after my return I again left my native country, and took shipping in the Downs on the 20th day of June, 1702, in the *Adventure,* Capt. John Nicholas, a Cornish man, commander, bound for Surat. We had a very prosperous gale till we arrived at the Cape of Good Hope, where we landed for fresh water, but discovering a leak we unshipped our goods, and wintered[1] there; for the captain falling sick of an ague, we could not leave the Cape till the end of March. We then set sail, and had a good voyage till we passed the Straits of Madagascar; but having got northwards of that island, and to about five degrees south latitude, the winds, which in those seas are observed to blow a constant equal gale between the north and west from the beginning of December to the beginning of May, on the 9th of April began to blow with much greater violence, and more westerly than usual, continuing so for twenty days together, during which time we were driven a little to the east of the Molucca Islands, and about three degrees northwards of the Line, as our captain found

1. Gulliver is using the term loosely, since March is the end of summer in southern latitudes.

by an observation he took the 2nd of May, at which time the wind ceased, and it was a perfect calm, whereat I was not a little rejoiced. But he, being a man well experienced in the navigation of those seas, bid us all prepare against a storm, which accordingly happened the day following: for a southern wind, called the southern monsoon, began to set in.

Finding it was like to overblow,[2] we took in our spritsail, and stood by to hand the foresail; but making foul weather, we looked the guns were all fast, and handed the missen. The ship lay very broad off, so we thought it better spooning before the sea, than trying or hulling. We reefed the foresail and set him, we hauled aft the fore-sheet; the helm was hard a weather. The ship wore bravely. We belayed the fore-downhaul; but the sail was split, and we hauled down the yard, and got the sail into the ship, and unbound all the things clear of it. It was a very fierce storm; the sea broke strange and dangerous. We hauled off upon the lanyard of the whipstaff, and helped the man at helm. We would not get down our topmast, but let all stand, because she scudded before the sea very well, and we knew that the topmast being aloft, the ship was the wholesomer, and made better way through the sea, seeing we had sea-room. When the storm was over, we set foresail and mainsail, and brought the ship to. Then we set the missen, main-topsail and the fore-topsail. Our course was east-northeast, the wind was at southwest. We got the starboard tacks aboard, we cast off our weather-braces and lifts; we set in the lee braces, and hauled forwards by the weather bowlings, and hauled them taut, and belayed them and hauled over the missen tack to windward, and kept her full and by as near as she would lie.

During this storm, which was followed by a strong wind west-southwest, we were carried by my computation about five hundred leagues to the east, so that the oldest sailor on board could not tell in

2. This paragraph is drawn almost verbatim (with the necessary alterations in the verbs) from directions for handling a ship in a storm published in Samuel Sturmy's *Mariners Magazine* (1669).

what part of the world we were. Our provisions held out well, our ship was staunch, and our crew all in good health; but we lay in the utmost distress for water. We thought it best to hold on the same course rather than turn more northerly, which might have brought us to the northwest parts of Great Tartary,[3] and into the frozen sea.

On the 16th day of June, 1703, a boy on the topmast discovered land. On the 17th we came in full view of a great island or continent (for we knew not whether) on the south side whereof was a small neck of land jutting out into the sea, and a creek too shallow to hold a ship of above one hundred tons. We cast anchor within a league of this creek, and our captain sent a dozen of his men well armed in the longboat, with vessels for water if any could be found. I desired his leave to go with them, that I might see the country, and make what discoveries I could. When we came to land we saw no river or spring, nor any sign of inhabitants. Our men therefore wandered on the shore to find out some fresh water near the sea, and I walked alone about a mile on the other side, where I observed the country all barren and rocky. I now began to be weary, and seeing nothing to entertain my curiosity, I returned gently down towards the creek; and the sea being full in my view, I saw our men already got into the boat, and rowing for life to the ship. I was going to hollow after them, although it had been to little purpose, when I observed a huge creature walking after them in the sea, as fast as he could: he waded not much deeper than his knees, and took prodigious strides: but our men had the start of him half a league, and the sea thereabouts being full of sharp pointed rocks, the monster was not able to overtake the boat. This I was afterwards told, for I durst not stay to see the issue of that adventure; but ran as fast as I could the way I first went; and then climbed up a steep hill which gave me some prospect of the country. I found it fully cultivated; but that which first surprised me was the length of the grass, which

3. The old name for an indefinite territory including much of central Asia: here the reference is to Siberia.

in those grounds that seemed to be kept for hay was above twenty foot high.[4]

I fell into a high road, for so I took it to be, though it served to the inhabitants only as a footpath through a field of barley. Here I walked on for some time, but could see little on either side, it being now near harvest, and the corn rising at least forty foot. I was an hour walking to the end of this field, which was fenced in with a hedge of at least one hundred and twenty foot high, and the trees so lofty that I could make no computation of their altitude. There was a stile to pass from this field into the next. It had four steps, and a stone to cross over when you came to the uppermost. It was impossible for me to climb this stile, because every step was six foot high, and the upper stone above twenty. I was endeavouring to find some gap in the hedge, when I discovered one of the inhabitants in the next field advancing towards the stile, of the same size with him whom I saw in the sea pursuing our boat. He appeared as tall as an ordinary spire-steeple, and took about ten yards at every stride, as near as I could guess. I was struck with the utmost fear and astonishment, and ran to hide myself in the corn, from whence I saw him at the top of the stile, looking back into the next field on the right hand, and heard him call in a voice many degrees louder than a speaking-trumpet; but the noise was so high in the air, that at first I certainly thought it was thunder. Whereupon seven monsters like himself came towards him with reaping-hooks in their hands, each hook about the largeness of six scythes. These people were not so well clad as the first, whose servants or labourers they seemed to be. For, upon some words he spoke, they went to reap the corn in the field where I lay. I kept from them at as great a distance as I could, but was forced to move with extreme difficulty, for the stalks of the corn were sometimes not above a foot distant, so that I could hardly squeeze my body betwixt them. How-

4. The scale employed in this voyage is nowhere stated specifically, but it is not difficult to deduce that it is the exact opposite of that used in the first voyage.

ever, I made a shift to go forwards till I came to a part of the field where the corn had been laid by the rain and wind. Here it was impossible for me to advance a step: for the stalks were so interwoven that I could not creep through, and the beards of the fallen ears so strong and pointed that they pierced through my clothes into my flesh. At the same time I heard the reapers not above an hundred yards behind me. Being quite dispirited with toil, and wholly overcome by grief and despair, I lay down between two ridges, and heartily wished I might there end my days. I bemoaned my desolate widow, and fatherless children. I lamented my own folly and wilfulness in attempting a second voyage against the advice of all my friends and relations. In this terrible agitation of mind I could not forbear thinking of Lilliput, whose inhabitants looked upon me as the greatest prodigy that ever appeared in the world: where I was able to draw an imperial fleet in my hand, and perform those other actions which will be recorded for ever in the chronicles of that empire, while posterity shall hardly believe them, although attested by millions. I reflected what a mortification it must prove to me to appear as inconsiderable in this nation as one single Lilliputian would be among us. But this I conceived was to be the least of my misfortunes: for, as human creatures are observed to be more savage and cruel in proportion to their bulk, what could I expect but to be a morsel in the mouth of the first among these enormous barbarians that should happen to seize me? Undoubtedly philosophers are in the right when they tell us, that nothing is great or little otherwise than by comparison. It might have pleased fortune to let the Lilliputians find some nation, where the people were as diminutive with respect to them, as they were to me. And who knows but that even this prodigious race of mortals might be equally overmatched in some distant part of the world, whereof we have yet no discovery?

Scared and confounded as I was, I could not forbear going on with these reflections, when one of the reapers, approaching within ten yards of the ridge where I lay, made me apprehend that with the next

step I should be squashed to death under his foot, or cut in two with his reaping hook. And therefore, when he was again about to move, I screamed as loud as fear could make me. Whereupon the huge creature trod short, and looking round about under him for some time, at last espied me as I lay on the ground. He considered a while with the caution of one who endeavours to lay hold on a small dangerous animal in such a manner that it shall not be able either to scratch or to bite him, as I myself have sometimes done with a weasel in England. At length he ventured to take me up behind by the middle between his fore-finger and thumb, and brought me within three yards of his eyes, that he might behold my shape more perfectly. I guessed his meaning, and my good fortune gave me so much presence of mind, that I resolved not to struggle in the least as he held me in the air above sixty foot from the ground, although he grievously pinched my sides, for fear I should slip through his fingers. All I ventured was to raise my eyes towards the sun, and place my hands together in a supplicating posture, and to speak some words in an humble melancholy tone, suitable to the condition I then was in. For I apprehended every moment that he would dash me against the ground, as we usually do any little hateful animal which we have a mind to destroy. But my good star would have it, that he appeared pleased with my voice and gestures, and began to look upon me as a curiosity, much wondering to hear me pronounce articulate words, although he could not understand them. In the mean time I was not able to forbear groaning and shedding tears, and turning my head towards my sides; letting him know, as well as I could, how cruelly I was hurt by the pressure of his thumb and finger. He seemed to apprehend my meaning; for, lifting up the lappet of his coat, he put me gently into it, and immediately ran along with me to his master, who was a substantial farmer, and the same person I had first seen in the field.

The farmer, having (as I supposed by their talk) received such an account of me as his servant could give him, took a piece of a small straw, about the size of a walking staff, and therewith lifted up the lappets of my coat; which it seems he thought to be some kind of covering that nature had given me. He blew my hairs aside to take a better view of my face. He called his hinds[5] about him, and asked them (as I afterwards learnt) whether they had ever seen in the fields any little creature that resembled me. He then placed me softly on the ground upon all four, but I got immediately up, and walked slowly backwards and forwards, to let those people see I had no intent to run away. They all sate down in a circle about me, the better to observe my motions. I pulled off my hat, and made a low bow towards the farmer. I fell on my knees, and lifted up my hands and eyes, and spoke several words as loud as I could: I took a purse of gold out of my pocket, and humbly presented it to him. He received it on the palm of his hand, then applied it close to his eye, to see what it was, and afterwards turned it several times with the point of a pin (which he took out of his sleeve), but could make nothing of it. Whereupon I made a sign that he should place his hand on the ground. I took the purse, and opening it, poured all the gold into his palm. There were six Spanish pieces of four pistoles each, beside twenty or thirty smaller coins. I saw him wet the tip of his little finger upon his tongue, and take up one of my largest pieces, and then another, but he seemed to be wholly ignorant what they were. He made me a sign to put them again into my purse, and the purse again into my pocket, which after offering to him several times, I thought it best to do.

The farmer by this time was convinced I must be a rational creature. He spoke often to me, but the sound of his voice pierced my ears like that of a watermill, yet his words were articulate enough. I answered as loud as I could, in several languages, and he often laid his ear within two yards of me, but all in vain, for we were wholly unintelligible to each other. He then sent his servants to their work, and taking his handkerchief out of his pocket, he doubled and spread it on his left hand, which he placed flat on the ground, with the palm

5. Laborers.

upwards, making me a sign to step into it, as I could easily do, for it was not above a foot in thickness. I thought it my part to obey, and for fear of falling, laid myself at length upon the handkerchief, with the remainder of which he lapped me up to the head for further security, and in this manner carried me home to his house. There he called his wife, and showed me to her; but she screamed and ran back as women in England do at the sight of a toad or a spider. However, when she had a while seen my behaviour, and how well I observed the signs her husband made, she was soon reconciled, and by degrees grew extremely tender of me.

It was about twelve at noon, and a servant brought in dinner. It was only one substantial dish of meat (fit for the plain condition of an husbandman) in a dish of about four and twenty foot diameter. The company were the farmer and his wife, three children, and an old grandmother: when they were sat down, the farmer placed me at some distance from him on the table, which was thirty foot high from the floor. I was in a terrible fright, and kept as far as I could from the edge for fear of falling. The wife minced a bit of meat, then crumbled some bread on a trencher, and placed it before me. I made her a low bow, took out my knife and fork, and fell to eat, which gave them exceeding delight. The mistress sent her maid for a small dram cup, which held about three gallons, and filled it with drink; I took up the vessel with much difficulty in both hands, and in a most respectful manner drank to her ladyship's health, expressing the words as loud as I could in English, which made the company laugh so heartily, that I was almost deafened with the noise. This liquor tasted like a small cider, and was not unpleasant. Then the master made me a sign to come to his trencher side; but as I walked on the table, being in great surprise all the time, as the indulgent reader will easily conceive and excuse, I happened to stumble against a crust, and fell flat on my face, but received no hurt. I got up immediately, and observing the good people to be in much concern, I took my hat (which I held under my arm out of good manners) and waving it over my head, made three huzzas to show I had got no mischief by my fall. But advancing forwards towards my master (as I shall henceforth call him) his youngest son who sate next him, an arch boy of about ten years old, took me up by the legs, and held me so high in the air, that I trembled every limb; but his father snatched me from him, and at the same time gave him such a box on the left ear, as would have felled an European troop of horse to the earth, ordering him to be taken from the table. But being afraid the boy might owe me a spite, and well remembering how mischievous all children among us naturally are to sparrows, rabbits, young kittens, and puppy dogs, I fell on my knees, and pointing to the boy, made my master to understand, as well as I could, that I desired his son might be pardoned. The father complied, and the lad took his seat again; whereupon I went to him and kissed his hand, which my master took, and made him stroke me gently with it.

In the midst of dinner, my mistress's favourite cat leapt into her lap. I heard a noise behind me like that of a dozen stocking-weavers at work; and turning my head I found it proceeded from the purring of this animal, who seemed to be three times larger than an ox, as I computed by the view of her head, and one of her paws, while her mistress was feeding and stroking her. The fierceness of this creature's countenance altogether discomposed me; though I stood at the further end of the table, above fifty foot off, and although my mistress held her fast for fear she might give a spring, and seize me in her talons. But it happened there was no danger; for the cat took not the least notice of me when my master placed me within three yards of her. And as I have been always told, and found true by experience in my travels, that flying, or discovering fear before a fierce animal, is a certain way to make it pursue or attack you, so I resolved in this dangerous juncture to show no manner of concern. I walked with intrepidity five or six times before the very head of the cat, and came within half a yard of her; whereupon she drew herself back, as if she were more afraid of me: I had less apprehension concerning the dogs,

whereof three or four came into the room, as it is usual in farmers' houses; one of which was a mastiff equal in bulk to four elephants, and a greyhound somewhat taller than the mastiff, but not so large.

When dinner was almost done, the nurse came in with a child of a year old in her arms, who immediately spied me, and began a squall that you might have heard from London Bridge to Chelsea, after the usual oratory of infants, to get me for a play thing. The mother out of pure indulgence took me up, and put me towards the child, who presently seized me by the middle, and got my head in his mouth, where I roared so loud that the urchin was frighted, and let me drop, and I should infallibly have broke my neck if the mother had not held her apron under me. The nurse to quiet her babe made use of a rattle, which was a kind of hollow vessel filled with great stones, and fastened by a cable to the child's waist: but all in vain, so that she was forced to apply the last remedy by giving it suck. I must confess no object ever disgusted me so much as the sight of her monstrous breast, which I cannot tell what to compare with, so as to give the curious reader an idea of its bulk, shape, and colour. It stood prominent six foot, and could not be less than sixteen in circumference. The nipple was about half the bigness of my head, and the hue both of that and the dug so varified with spots, pimples, and freckles, that nothing could appear more nauseous: for I had a near sight of her, she sitting down the more conveniently to give suck, and I standing on the table. This made me reflect upon the fair skins of our English ladies, who appear so beautiful to us, only because they are of our own size, and their defects not to be seen but through a magnifying-glass, where we find by experiment that the smoothest and whitest skins look rough and coarse, and ill coloured.

I remember when I was at Lilliput, the complexions of those diminutive people appeared to me the fairest in the world; and talking upon this subject with a person of learning there, who was an intimate friend of mine, he said that my face appeared much fairer and smoother when he looked on me from the ground, than it did upon a nearer view when I took him up in my hand, and brought him close, which he confessed was at first a very shocking sight. He said he could discover great holes in my skin, that the stumps of my beard were ten times stronger than the bristles of a boar, and my complexion made up of several colours altogether disagreeable: although I must beg leave to say for my self, that I am as fair as most of my sex and country, and very little sunburnt by all my travels. On the other side, discoursing of the ladies in that emperor's court, he used to tell me, one had freckles, another too wide a mouth, a third too large a nose, nothing of which I was able to distinguish. I confess this reflection was obvious enough; which however I could not forbear, lest the reader might think those vast creatures were actually deformed: for I must do them justice to say they are a comely race of people; and particularly the features of my master's countenance, although he were but a farmer, when I beheld him from the height of sixty foot, appeared very well proportioned.

When dinner was done, my master went out to his labourers, and, as I could discover by his voice and gesture, gave his wife a strict charge to take care of me. I was very much tired and disposed to sleep, which my mistress perceiving, she put me on her own bed, and covered me with a clean white handkerchief, but larger and coarser than the mainsail of a man-of-war.

I slept about two hours, and dreamed I was at home with my wife and children, which aggravated my sorrows when I awaked and found myself alone in a vast room, between two and three hundred foot wide, and above two hundred high, lying in a bed twenty yards wide. My mistress was gone about her household affairs, and had locked me in. The bed was eight yards from the floor. Some natural necessities required me to get down; I durst not presume to call, and if I had, it would have been in vain with such a voice as mine at so great a distance from the room where I lay to the kitchen where the family kept. While I was under these circumstances two rats crept up the curtains, and ran smelling backwards and forwards on the bed. One of them came up almost to my face, whereupon I rose in a fright, and drew out my hanger[6] to defend myself. These horrible animals had the boldness to attack me on both sides, and one of them held his fore-feet at my collar; but I had the good fortune to rip up his belly before he could do me any mischief. He fell down at my feet, and the other, seeing the fate of his comrade, made his escape, but not without one good wound on the back, which I gave him as he fled, and made the blood run trickling from him. After this exploit, I walked gently to and fro on the bed, to recover my breath and loss of spirits. These creatures were of the size of a large mastiff, but infinitely more nimble and fierce, so that if I had taken off my belt before I went to sleep, I must have infallibly been torn to pieces and devoured. I measured the tail of the dead rat, and found it to be two yards long wanting an inch; but it went against my stomach to drag the carcass off the bed, where it lay still bleeding; I observed it had yet some life, but with a strong slash cross the neck I thoroughly dispatched it.

Soon after my mistress came into the room, who seeing me all bloody, ran and took me up in her hand. I pointed to the dead rat, smiling and making other signs to show I was not hurt, whereat she was extremely rejoiced, calling the maid to take up the dead rat with a pair of tongs, and throw it out of the window. Then she set me on a table, where I showed her my hanger all bloody, and wiping it on the lappet of my coat, returned it to the scabbard. I was pressed to do more than one thing which another could not do for me, and therefore endeavoured to make my mistress understand that I desired to be set down on the floor; which after she had done, my bashfulness would not suffer me to express myself farther than by pointing to the door, and bowing several times. The good woman with much difficulty at last perceived what I would be at, and taking me up again in her hand, walked into the garden, where she set me down. I went on one side about two hundred yards, and beckoning to her not to look

6. A short sword.

or to follow me, I hid myself between two leaves of sorrel, and there discharged the necessities of nature.

I hope the gentle reader will excuse me for dwelling on these and the like particulars, which, however insignificant they may appear to grovelling vulgar minds, yet will certainly help a philosopher to enlarge his thoughts and imagination, and apply them to the benefit of public as well as private life, which was my sole design in presenting this and other accounts of my travels to the world; wherein I have been chiefly studious of truth, without affecting any ornaments of learning or of style. But the whole scene of this voyage made so strong an impression on my mind, and is so deeply fixed in my memory, that in committing it to paper I did not omit one material circumstance: however, upon a strict review, I blotted out several passages of less moment which were in my first copy, for fear of being censured as tedious and trifling, whereof travellers are often, perhaps not without justice, accused.

Chapter Two

A description of the farmer's daughter. The author carried to a market-town, and then to the metropolis. The particulars of his journey.

Y MISTRESS HAD A DAUGHTER OF NINE YEARS old, a child of forwards parts for her age, very dextrous at her needle, and skilful in dressing her baby.[1] Her mother and she contrived to fit up the baby's cradle for me against night: the cradle was put into a small drawer of a cabinet, and the drawer placed upon a hanging shelf for fear of the rats. This was my bed all the time I stayed with those people, though made more convenient by degrees, as I began to learn their language, and make my wants known. This young girl was so handy, that after I had once or twice pulled off my clothes before her, she was able to dress and undress me, though I never gave her that trouble when she would let me do either myself. She made me seven shirts, and some other linen, of as fine cloth as could be got, which indeed was coarser than sackcloth; and these she constantly washed for me with her own hands. She was likewise my school-mistress to teach me the language: when I pointed to any thing, she told me the name of it in her own tongue, so that in a few days I was able to call for whatever I had a mind to. She was very good-natured, and not above forty foot high, being little for her age. She gave me the name of 'Grildrig', which the family took up, and afterwards the whole kingdom. The word imports

1. Doll.

what the Latins call *'nanunculus',* the Italians *'homunceletino',*[2] and the English *'mannikin'.* To her I chiefly owe my preservation in that country: we never parted while I was there; I called her my *'glumdalclitch',* or 'little nurse': and I should be guilty of great ingratitude if I omitted this honourable mention of her care and affection towards me, which I heartily wish it lay in my power to requite as she deserves, instead of being the innocent but unhappy instrument of her disgrace, as I have too much reason to fear.

It now began to be known and talked of in the neighbourhood, that my master had found a strange animal in the fields, about the bigness of a *splacknuck,* but exactly shaped in every part like a human creature; which it likewise imitated in all its actions; seemed to speak in a little language of its own, had already learned several words of theirs, went erect upon two legs, was tame and gentle, would come when it was called, do whatever it was bid, had the finest limbs in the world, and a complexion fairer than a nobleman's daughter of three years old. Another farmer who lived hard by, and was a particular friend of my master, came on a visit on purpose to enquire into the truth of this story. I was immediately produced, and placed upon a table, where I walked as I was commanded, drew my hanger, put it up again, made my reverence to my master's guest, asked him in his own language how he did, and told him he was welcome, just as my little nurse had instructed me. This man, who was old and dim-sighted, put on his spectacles to behold me better, at which I could not forbear laughing very heartily, for his eyes appeared like the full moon shining into a chamber at two windows. Our people, who discovered the cause of my mirth, bore me company in laughing, at which the old fellow was fool enough to be angry and out of countenance. He had the character of a great miser, and to my misfortune he well deserved it, by the cursed advice he gave my master to show me as a sight upon a market-day in the next town, which was half an hour's riding, about two and

2. Swift appears to have coined the Latin and Italian words.

twenty miles from our house. I guessed there was some mischief contriving, when I observed my master and his friend whispering long together, sometimes pointing at me; and my fears made me fancy that I overheard and understood some of their words. But the next morning Glumdalclitch my little nurse told me the whole matter, which she had cunningly picked out from her mother. The poor girl laid me on her bosom, and fell a weeping with shame and grief. She apprehended some mischief would happen to me from rude vulgar folks, who might squeeze me to death, or break one of my limbs by taking me in their hands. She had also observed how modest I was in my nature, how nicely I regarded my honour, and what an indignity I should conceive it to be exposed for money as a public spectacle to the meanest of the people. She said, her papa and mamma had promised that Grildrig should be hers, but now she found they meant to serve her as they did last year, when they pretended to give her a lamb, and yet, as soon as it was fat, sold it to a butcher. For my own part, I may truly affirm that I was less concerned than my nurse. I had a strong hope, which never left me, that I should one day recover my liberty; and as to the ignominy of being carried about for a monster, I considered myself to be a perfect stranger in the country, and that such a misfortune could never be charged upon me as a reproach if ever I should return to England; since the King of Great Britain himself, in my condition, must have undergone the same distress.[3]

My master, pursuant to the advice of my friend, carried me in a box the next market-day to the neighbouring town, and took along with him his little daughter my nurse upon a pillion behind him. The box was close on every side, with a little door for me to go in and out, and a few gimlet-holes to let in air. The girl had been so careful to put the quilt of her baby's bed into it, for me to lie down on. However, I was

3. This observation, taken in conjunction with Gulliver's remark about being 'a perfect stranger in the country', implies that the native English regarded George I as a freak.

terribly shaken and discomposed in this journey, though it were but of half an hour. For the horse went about forty foot at every step, and trotted so high, that the agitation was equal to the rising and falling of a ship in a great storm, but much more frequent: our journey was somewhat further than from London to St. Albans.[4] My master alighted at an inn which he used to frequent; and after consulting a while with the inn-keeper, and making some necessary preparations, he hired the *grultrud,* or crier, to give notice through the town of a strange creature to be seen at the Sign of the Green Eagle, not so big as a *splacknuck* (an animal in that country very finely shaped, about six foot long) and in every part of the body resembling an human creature, could speak several words, and perform an hundred diverting tricks.

I was placed upon a table in the largest room of the inn, which might be near three hundred foot square. My little nurse stood on a low stool close to the table, to take care of me, and direct what I should do. My master, to avoid a crowd, would suffer only thirty people at a time to see me. I walked about on the table as the girl commanded; she asked me questions as far as she knew my understanding of the language reached, and I answered them as loud as I could. I turned about several times to the company, paid my humble respects, said they were welcome, and used some other speeches I had been taught. I took up a thimble filled with liquor, which Glumdalclitch had given me for a cup, and drank their health. I drew out my hanger, and flourished with it after the manner of fencers in England. My nurse gave me part of a straw, which I exercised as a pike, having learned the art in my youth. I was that day shown to twelve sets of company, and as often forced to go over again with the same fopperies, till I was half dead with weariness and vexation. For those who had seen me made such wonderful reports, that the people were ready to break down the doors to come in. My master for his own interest

4. About twenty miles.

would not suffer any one to touch me except my nurse; and, to prevent danger, benches were set round the table at such a distance as put me out of every body's reach. However, an unlucky school-boy aimed a hazel nut directly at my head, which very narrowly missed me; otherwise, it came with so much violence that it would have infallibly knocked out my brains, for it was almost as large as a small pumpion:[5] but I had the satisfaction to see the young rogue well beaten, and turned out of the room.

My master gave public notice, that he would show me again the next market-day, and in the mean time he prepared a more convenient vehicle for me, which he had reason enough to do; for I was so tired with my first journey, and with entertaining company for eight hours together, that I could hardly stand upon my legs, or speak a word. It was at least three days before I recovered my strength; and that I might have no rest at home, all the neighbouring gentlemen from an hundred miles round, hearing of my fame, came to see me at my master's own house. There could not be fewer than thirty persons with their wives and children (for the country was very populous); and my master demanded the rate of a full room whenever he showed me at home, although it were only to a single family. So that for some time I had but little ease every day of the week (except Wednesday, which is their Sabbath) although I were not carried to the town.

My master, finding how profitable I was like to be, resolved to carry me to the most considerable cities of the kingdom. Having therefore provided himself with all things necessary for a long journey, and settled his affairs at home, he took leave of his wife, and upon the 17th of August, 1703, about two months after my arrival, we set out for the metropolis, situated near the middle of that empire, and about three thousand miles distance from our house: my master made his daughter Glumdalclitch ride behind him. She carried me on her

5. Pumpkin.

M·S

I could not forbear laughing very heartily, for his eyes appeared like the full moon shining into a chamber at two windows.

PAGE III

lap in a box tied about her waist. The girl had lined it on all sides with the softest cloth she could get, well quilted underneath, furnished it with her baby's bed, provided me with linen and other necessaries, and made every thing as convenient as she could. We had no other company but a boy of the house, who rode after us with the luggage.

My master's design was to show me in all the towns by the way, and to step out of the road for fifty or an hundred miles, to any village or person of quality's house where he might expect custom. We made easy journeys of not above seven or eightscore miles a day: for Glumdalclitch, on purpose to spare me, complained she was tired with the trotting of the horse. She often took me out of my box at my own desire, to give me air, and show me the country, but always held me fast by a leading-string. We passed over five or six rivers many degrees broader and deeper than the Nile or the Ganges; and there was hardly a rivulet so small as the Thames at London Bridge. We were ten weeks in our journeys, and I was shown in eighteen large towns, besides many villages and private families.

On the 26th day of October, we arrived at the metropolis, called in their language 'Lorbrulgrud', or 'Pride of the Universe'. My master took a lodging in the principal street of the city, not far from the royal palace, and put out bills in the usual form, containing an exact description of my person and parts. He hired a large room between three and four hundred foot wide. He provided a table sixty foot in diameter, upon which I was to act my part, and palisadoed it round three feet from the edge, and as many high, to prevent my falling over. I was shown ten times a day to the wonder and satisfaction of all people. I could now speak the language tolerably well, and perfectly understood every word that was spoken to me. Besides, I had learnt their alphabet, and could make a shift to explain a sentence here and there; for Glumdalclitch had been my instructor while we were at home, and at leisure hours during our journey. She carried a little book in her

pocket, not much larger than a Sanson's *Atlas*;[6] it was a common treatise for the use of young girls, giving a short account of their religion; out of this she taught me my letters, and interpreted the words.

6. About twenty-five by twenty inches.

Chapter Three

The author sent for to court. The Queen buys him of his master the farmer, and presents him to the King. He disputes with his Majesty's great scholars. An apartment at court provided for the author. He is in high favour with the Queen. He stands up for the honour of his own country. His quarrels with the Queen's dwarf.

THE FREQUENT LABOURS I UNDERWENT EVERY DAY made in a few weeks a very considerable change in my health: the more my master got by me, the more unsatiable he grew. I had quite lost my stomach, and was almost reduced to a skeleton. The farmer observed it, and concluding I soon must die, resolved to make as good a hand of me as he could. While he was thus reasoning and resolving with himself, a *slardral,* or gentleman usher, came from court, commanding my master to carry me immediately thither for the diversion of the Queen and her ladies. Some of the latter had already been to see me, and reported strange things of my beauty, behaviour, and good sense. Her Majesty and those who attended her were beyond measure delighted with my demeanor. I fell on my knees, and begged the honour of kissing her imperial foot; but this gracious princess held out her little finger towards me (after I was set on a table) which I embraced in both my arms, and put the tip of it, with the utmost respect, to my lip. She made me some general questions about my country and my travels, which I answered as distinctly and in as few words as I could. She asked whether I would be content to live at court. I bowed down to the board of the table, and humbly answered that I was my master's slave, but if I were at my own dis-

posal, I should be proud to devote my life to her Majesty's service. She then asked my master whether he were willing to sell me at a good price. He, who apprehended I could not live a month, was ready enough to part with me, and demanded a thousand pieces of gold, which were ordered him on the spot, each piece being about the bigness of eight hundred moidores; but, allowing for the proportion of all things between that country and Europe, and the high price of gold among them, was hardly so great a sum as a thousand guineas would be in England. I then said to the Queen, since I was now her Majesty's most humble creature and vassal, I must beg the favour, that Glumdalclitch, who had always tended me with so much care and kindness, and understood to do it so well, might be admitted into her service, and continue to be my nurse and instructor. Her Majesty agreed to my petition, and easily got the farmer's consent, who was glad enough to have his daughter preferred at court: and the poor girl herself was not able to hide her joy: my late master withdrew, bidding me farewell, and saying he had left me in a good service; to which I replied not a word, only making him a slight bow.

The Queen observed my coldness, and when the farmer was gone out of the apartment, asked me the reason. I made bold to tell her Majesty that I owed no other obligation to my late master, than his not dashing out the brains of a poor harmless creature found by chance in his field; which obligation was amply recompensed by the gain he had made in showing me through half the kingdom, and the price he had now sold me for. That the life I had since led was laborious enough to kill an animal of ten times my strength. That my health was much impaired by the continual drudgery of entertaining the rabble every hour of the day, and that if my master had not thought my life in danger, her Majesty perhaps would not have got so cheap a bargain. But as I was out of all fear of being ill treated under the protection of so great and good an empress, the Ornament of Nature, the Darling of the World, the Delight of her Subjects, the Phœnix of the Creation; so, I hoped, my late master's apprehensions would appear to be groundless, for I already found my spirits to revive by the influence of her most august presence.

This was the sum of my speech, delivered with great improprieties and hesitation; the latter part was altogether framed in the style peculiar to that people, whereof I learned some phrases from Glumdalclitch, while she was carrying me to court.

The Queen, giving great allowance for my defectiveness in speaking, was however surprised at so much wit and good sense in so diminutive an animal. She took me in her own hands, and carried me to the King, who was then retired to his cabinet. His Majesty, a prince of much gravity, and austere countenance, not well observing my shape at first view, asked the Queen after a cold manner, how long it was since she grew fond of a *splacknuck*; for such it seems he took me to be, as I lay upon my breast in her Majesty's right hand. But this princess, who hath an infinite deal of wit and humour, set me gently on my feet upon the scrutore,[1] and commanded me to give his Majesty an account of myself, which I did in a very few words; and Glumdalclitch, who attended at the cabinet door, and could not endure I should be out of her sight, being admitted, confirmed all that had passed from my arrival at her father's house.

The King, although he be as learned a person as any in his dominions, and had been educated in the study of philosophy, and particularly mathematics; yet when he observed my shape exactly, and saw me walk erect, before I began to speak, conceived I might be a piece of clock-work (which is in that country arrived to a very great perfection), contrived by some ingenious artist. But, when he heard my voice, and found what I delivered to be regular and rational, he could not conceal his astonishment. He was by no means satisfied with the relation I gave him of the manner I came into his kingdom, but thought it a story concerted between Glumdalclitch and her father,

1. Escritoire.

who had taught me a set of words to make me sell at a higher price. Upon this imagination he put several other questions to me, and still received rational answers, no otherwise defective than by a foreign accent, and an imperfect knowledge in the language, with some rustic phrases which I had learned at the farmer's house, and did not suit the polite style of a court.

His Majesty sent for three great scholars who were then in their weekly waiting (according to the custom in that country). These gentlemen, after they had a while examined my shape with much nicety, were of different opinions concerning me. They all agreed that I could not be produced according to the regular laws of nature, because I was not framed with a capacity of preserving my life, either by swiftness, or climbing of trees, or digging holes in the earth. They observed by my teeth, which they viewed with great exactness, that I was a carnivorous animal; yet most quadrupeds being an overmatch for me, and field mice, with some others, too nimble, they could not imagine how I should be able to support myself, unless I fed upon snails and other insects, which they offered by many learned arguments to evince that I could not possibly do. One of these virtuosi[2] seemed to think that I might be an embryo, or abortive birth. But this opinion was rejected by the other two, who observed my limbs to be perfect and finished, and that I had lived several years, as it was manifested from my beard, the stumps whereof they plainly discovered through a magnifying-glass. They would not allow me to be a dwarf, because my littleness was beyond all degrees of comparison; for the Queen's favourite dwarf, the smallest ever known in that kingdom, was near thirty foot high. After much debate, they concluded unanimously that I was only *relplum scalcath,* which is interpreted literally, *'lusus naturæ';* a determination exactly agreeable to the modern philosophy of Europe, whose professors, disdaining the old evasion of 'occult causes', whereby the

2. 'Virtuoso', which originally signified 'scholar' or 'expert', had come to connote 'dilettante'.

followers of Aristotle endeavour in vain to disguise their ignorance,[3] have invented this wonderful solution of all difficulties to the unspeakable advancement of human knowledge.

After this decisive conclusion, I intreated to be heard a word or two. I applied myself to the King, and assured his Majesty that I came from a country which abounded with several millions of both sexes, and of my own stature; where the animals, trees, and houses were all in proportion, and where by consequence I might be as able to defend myself, and to find sustenance, as any of his Majesty's subjects could do here; which I took for a full answer to those gentlemen's arguments. To this they only replied with a smile of contempt, saying, that the farmer had instructed me very well in my lesson. The King, who had a much better understanding, dismissing his learned men, sent for the farmer, who by good fortune was not yet gone out of town: having therefore first examined him privately, and then confronted him with me and the young girl, his Majesty began to think that what we told him might possibly be true. He desired the Queen to order that a particular care should be taken of me, and was of opinion, that Glumdalclitch should still continue in her office of tending me, because he observed we had a great affection for each other. A convenient apartment was provided for her at court; she had a sort of governess appointed to take care of her education, a maid to dress her, and two other servants for menial offices; but the care of me was wholly appropriated to herself. The Queen commanded her own cabinet-maker to contrive a box that might serve me for a bed-chamber, after the model that Glumdalclitch and I should agree upon. This man was a most ingenious artist, and according to my directions, in three weeks finished for me a wooden chamber of sixteen foot square, and twelve high, with sash-windows, a door, and two closets, like a London bed-chamber. The board that made the ceiling was to be

3. Swift was contemptuous of medieval Aristotelianism; he had, however, a considerable respect for Aristotle.

lifted up and down by two hinges, to put in a bed ready furnished by her Majesty's upholsterer, which Glumdalclitch took out every day to air, made it with her own hands, and letting it down at night, locked up the roof over me. A nice workman, who was famous for little curiosities, undertook to make me two chairs, with backs and frames, of a substance not unlike ivory, and two tables, with a cabinet to put my things in. The room was quilted on all sides, as well as the floor and the ceiling, to prevent any accident from the carelessness of those who carried me, and to break the force of a jolt when I went in a coach. I desired a lock for my door to prevent rats and mice from coming in: the smith after several attempts made the smallest that was ever seen among them, for I have known a larger at the gate of a gentleman's house in England. I made a shift to keep the key in a pocket of my own, fearing Glumdalclitch might lose it. The Queen likewise ordered the thinnest silks that could be gotten, to make me clothes, not much thicker than an English blanket, very cumbersome till I was accustomed to them. They were after the fashion of the kingdom, partly resembling the Persian, and partly the Chinese, and are a very grave decent habit.

The Queen became so fond of my company, that she could not dine without me. I had a table placed upon the same at which her Majesty eat, just at her left elbow, and a chair to sit on. Glumdalclitch stood upon a stool on the floor, near my table, to assist and take care of me. I had an entire set of silver dishes and plates, and other necessaries, which, in proportion to those of the Queen, were not much bigger than what I have seen of the same kind in a London toy-shop, for the furniture of a baby-house: these my little nurse kept in her pocket, in a silver box, and gave me at meals as I wanted them, always cleaning them herself. No person dined with the Queen but the two princesses royal, the elder sixteen years old, and the younger at that time thirteen and a month. Her Majesty used to put a bit of meat upon one of my dishes, out of which I carved for myself; and her diversion was to see me eat in miniature. For the Queen (who had indeed but a weak stomach) took up at one mouthful as much as a dozen English farmers could eat at a meal, which to me was for some time a very nauseous sight. She would craunch the wing of a lark, bones and all, between her teeth, although it were nine times as large as that of a full-grown turkey; and put a bit of bread in her mouth, as big as two twelvepenny loaves. She drank out of a golden cup, above a hogshead at a draught. Her knives were twice as long as a scythe set straight upon the handle. The spoons, forks, and other instruments were all in the same proportion. I remember when Glumdalclitch carried me out of curiosity to see some of the tables at court, where ten or a dozen of these enormous knives and forks were lifted up together, I thought I had never till then beheld so terrible a sight.

It is the custom that every Wednesday (which, as I have before observed, was their Sabbath) the King and Queen, with the royal issue of both sexes, dine together in the apartment of his Majesty, to whom I was now become a great favourite; and at these times my little chair and table were placed at his left hand before one of the salt-cellars. This prince took a pleasure in conversing with me, enquiring into the manners, religion, laws, government, and learning of Europe, wherein I gave him the best account I was able. His apprehension was so clear, and his judgment so exact, that he made very wise reflections and observations upon all I said. But I confess, that after I had been a little too copious in talking of my own beloved country, of our trade, and wars by sea and land, of our schisms in religion, and parties in the state, the prejudices of his education prevailed so far, that he could not forbear taking me up in his right hand, and stroking me gently with the other, after an hearty fit of laughing, asked me whether I were a Whig or a Tory. Then turning to his first minister, who waited behind him with a white staff, near as tall as the mainmast of the *Royal Sovereign,*[4] he observed how contemptible a thing was human grandeur, which could be mimicked by such diminutive insects as I: 'And

4. One of the largest English ships of the line.

yet', said he, 'I dare engage, these creatures have their titles and distinctions of honour, they contrive little nests and burrows, that they call houses and cities; they make a figure in dress and equipage;[5] they love, they fight, they dispute, they cheat, they betray'. And thus he continued on, while my colour came and went several times, with indignation to hear our noble country, the mistress of arts and arms, the scourge of France, the arbitress of Europe, the seat of virtue, piety, honour, and truth, the pride and envy of the world, so contemptuously treated.

But, as I was not in a condition to resent injuries, so, upon mature thoughts, I began to doubt whether I were injured or no. For, after having been accustomed several months to the sight and converse of this people, and observed every object upon which I cast my eyes to be of proportionable magnitude, the horror I had first conceived from their bulk and aspect was so far worn off, that if I had then beheld a company of English lords and ladies in their finery and birthday clothes,[6] acting their several parts in the most courtly manner of strutting, and bowing, and prating, to say the truth, I should have been strongly tempted to laugh as much at them as this king and his grandees did at me. Neither indeed could I forbear smiling at myself, when the Queen used to place me upon her hand towards a looking-glass, by which both our persons appeared before me in full view together; and there could nothing be more ridiculous than the comparison: so that I really began to imagine myself dwindled many degrees below my usual size.

Nothing angered and mortified me so much as the Queen's dwarf, who being of the lowest stature that was ever in that country (for I verily think he was not full thirty foot high) became insolent at seeing a creature so much beneath him, that he would always affect to swagger and look big as he passed by me in the Queen's antechamber,

5. Retinue.
6. Custom required English courtiers to appear in new clothes on the sovereign's birthday.

while I was standing on some table talking with the lords or ladies of the court, and he seldom failed of a small word or two upon my littleness; against which I could only revenge myself by calling him 'brother', challenging him to wrestle, and such repartees as are usual in the mouths of *court pages.* One day at dinner this malicious little cub was so nettled with something I had said to him, that raising himself upon the frame of her Majesty's chair, he took me up by the middle, as I was sitting down, not thinking any harm, and let me drop into a large silver bowl of cream, and then ran away as fast as he could. I fell over head and ears, and if I had not been a good swimmer, it might have gone very hard with me; for Glumdalclitch in that instant happened to be at the other end of the room, and the Queen was in such a fright that she wanted presence of mind to assist me. But my little nurse ran to my relief, and took me out, after I had swallowed above a quart of cream. I was put to bed; however I received no other damage than the loss of a suit of clothes, which was utterly spoiled. The dwarf was soundly whipped, and as a further punishment, forced to drink up the bowl of cream into which he had thrown me; neither was he ever restored to favour: for, soon after, the Queen bestowed him to a lady of high quality, so that I saw him no more, to my very great satisfaction; for I could not tell to what extremities such a malicious urchin might have carried his resentment.

He had before served me a scurvy trick, which set the Queen a laughing, although at the same time she were heartily vexed, and would have immediately cashiered him, if I had not been so generous as to intercede. Her Majesty had taken a marrow-bone upon her plate, and after knocking out the marrow, placed the bone again in the dish erect as it stood before; the dwarf watching his opportunity, while Glumdalclitch was gone to the sideboard, mounted upon the stool she stood on to take care of me at meals, took me up in both hands, and squeezing my legs together, wedged them into the marrow-bone above my waist, where I stuck for some time, and made a very ridiculous figure. I believe it was near a minute before any one knew what was become of me, for I thought it below me to cry out. But, as princes seldom get their meat hot, my legs were not scalded, only my stockings and breeches in a sad condition. The dwarf at my intreaty had no other punishment than a sound whipping.

I was frequently rallied by the Queen upon account of my fearfulness, and she used to ask me whether the people of my country were as great cowards as myself. The occasion was this. The kingdom is much pestered with flies in summer, and these odious insects, each of them as big as a Dunstable lark, hardly gave me any rest while I sat at dinner, with their continual humming and buzzing about my ears. They would sometimes alight upon my victuals, and leave their loathsome excrement or spawn behind, which to me was very visible, though not to the natives of that country, whose large optics were not so acute as mine in viewing smaller objects. Sometimes they would fix upon my nose or forehead, where they stung me to the quick, smelling very offensively, and I could easily trace that viscous matter, which our naturalists tell us enables those creatures to walk with their feet upwards upon a ceiling. I had much ado to defend myself against these detestable animals, and could not forbear starting when they came on my face. It was the common practice of the dwarf to catch a number of these insects in his hand as school-boys do among us, and let them out suddenly under my nose on purpose to frighten me, and divert the Queen. My remedy was to cut them in pieces with my knife as they flew in the air, wherein my dexterity was much admired.

I remember one morning when Glumdalclitch had set me in my box upon a window, as she usually did in fair days to give me air (for I durst not venture to let the box be hung on a nail out of the window, as we do with cages in England) after I had lifted up one of my sashes, and sat down at my table to eat a piece of sweet cake for my breakfast, above twenty wasps, allured by the smell, came flying into the room, humming louder than the drones of as many bagpipes. Some of them seized my cake, and carried it piecemeal away, others flew about my head and face, confounding me with the noise, and putting me in the utmost terror of their stings. However I had the courage to rise and draw my hanger, and attack them in the air. I dispatched four of them, but the rest got away, and I presently shut my window. These insects were as large as partridges: I took out their stings, found them an inch and an half long, and as sharp as needles. I carefully preserved them all, and having since shown them with some other curiosities in several parts of Europe, upon my return to England I gave three of them to Gresham College,[7] and kept the fourth for myself.

7. The home of the Royal Society of London for Improving Natural Knowledge (generally referred to merely as the Royal Society).

Chapter Four

The country described. A proposal for correcting modern maps. The King's palace, and some account of the metropolis. The author's way of travelling. The chief temple described.

I now intend to give the reader a short description of this country, as far as I travelled in it, which was not above two thousand miles round Lorbrulgrud the metropolis. For the Queen, whom I always attended, never went further when she accompanied the King in his progresses, and there stayed till his Majesty returned from viewing his frontiers. The whole extent of this prince's dominions reacheth about six thousand miles in length, and from three to five in breadth. From whence I cannot but conclude that our geographers of Europe are in a great error, by supposing nothing but sea between Japan and California; for it was ever my opinion, that there must be a balance of earth to counterpoise the great continent of Tartary; and therefore they ought to correct their maps and charts, by joining this vast tract of land to the northwest parts of America, wherein I shall be ready to lend them my assistance.

The kingdom is a peninsula, terminated to the northeast by a ridge of mountains thirty miles high, which are altogether impassable by reason of the volcanoes upon the tops. Neither do the most learned know what sort of mortals inhabit beyond these mountains, or whether they be inhabited at all. On the three other sides it is bounded by the ocean. There is not one seaport in the whole kingdom, and those parts of the coasts into which the rivers issue are so full of pointed rocks, and the sea generally so rough, that there is no venturing with the smallest of their boats, so that these people are wholly excluded from any commerce with the rest of the world. But the large rivers are full of vessels, and abound with excellent fish, for they seldom get any from the sea, because the sea-fish are of the same size with those in Europe, and consequently not worth catching; whereby it is manifest, that nature in the production of plants and animals of so extraordinary a bulk is wholly confined to this continent, of which I leave the reasons to be determined by philosophers. However, now and then they take a whale that happens to be dashed against the rocks, which the common people feed on heartily. These whales I have known so large that a man could hardly carry one upon his shoulders; and sometimes for curiosity they are brought in hampers to Lorbrulgrud: I saw one of them in a dish at the King's table, which passed for a rarity, but I did not observe he was fond of it; for I think indeed the bigness disgusted him, although I have seen one somewhat larger in Greenland.

The country is well inhabited, for it contains fifty-one cities, near an hundred walled towns, and a great number of villages. To satisfy my curious reader, it may be sufficient to describe Lorbrulgrud. This city stands upon almost two equal parts on each side the river that passes through. It contains above eighty thousand houses, and about six hundred thousand inhabitants. It is in length three *glonglungs* (which make about fifty-four English miles) and two and a half in breadth, as I measured it myself in the royal map made by the King's order, which was laid on the ground on purpose for me, and extended an hundred feet; I paced the diameter and circumference several times barefoot, and computing by the scale, measured it pretty exactly.

The King's palace is no regular edifice, but an heap of buildings about seven miles round: the chief rooms are generally two hundred and forty foot high, and broad and long in proportion. A coach was allowed to Glumdalclitch and me, wherein her governess frequently took her out to see the town, or go among the shops; and I was always

of the party, carried in my box; although the girl at my own desire would often take me out, and hold me in her hand, that I might more conveniently view the houses and the people as we passed along the streets. I reckoned our coach to be about a square of Westminster Hall, but not altogether so high;[1] however, I cannot be very exact. One day the governess ordered our coachman to stop at several shops, where the beggars, watching their opportunity, crowded to the sides of the coach, and gave me the most horrible spectacles that ever an European eye beheld. There was a woman with a cancer in her breast, swelled to a monstrous size, full of holes, in two or three of which I could have easily crept, and covered my whole body. There was a fellow with a wen in his neck, larger than five woolpacks, and another with a couple of wooden legs, each about twenty foot high. But the most hateful sight of all was the lice crawling on their clothes. I could see distinctly the limbs of these vermin with my naked eye, much better than those of an European louse through a microscope, and their snouts with which they rooted like swine. They were the first I had ever beheld, and I should have been curious enough to dissect one of them, if I had proper instruments (which I unluckily left behind me in the ship) although indeed the sight was so nauseous, that it perfectly turned my stomach.

Beside the large box in which I was usually carried, the Queen ordered a smaller one to be made for me, of about twelve foot square, and ten high, for the convenience of travelling, because the other was somewhat too large for Glumdalclitch's lap, and cumbersome in the coach; it was made by the same artist, whom I directed in the whole contrivance. This travelling closet was an exact square with a window in the middle of three of the squares, and each window was latticed with iron wire on the outside, to prevent accidents in long journeys. On the fourth side, which had no window, two strong staples were fixed, through which the person that carried me, when I had a mind to be on horseback, put in a leathern belt, and buckled it about his waist. This

1. I.e., about sixty-eight feet square, but less than eighty-five feet in height.

was always the office of some grave trusty servant in whom I could confide, whether I attended the King and Queen in their progresses, or were disposed to see the gardens, or pay a visit to some great lady or minister of state in the court, when Glumdalclitch happened to be out of order: for I soon began to be known and esteemed among the greatest officers, I suppose more upon account of their Majesties' favour than any merit of my own. In journeys, when I was weary of the coach, a servant on horseback would buckle my box, and place it on a cushion before him; and there I had a full prospect of the country on three sides from my three windows. I had in this closet a field-bed and a hammock hung from the ceiling, two chairs and a table, neatly screwed to the floor, to prevent being tossed about by the agitation of the horse or the coach. And having been long used to sea-voyages, those motions, although sometimes very violent, did not much discompose me.

Whenever I had a mind to see the town, it was always in my travelling-closet, which Glumdalclitch held in her lap in a kind of open sedan, after the fashion of the country, borne by four men, and attended by two others in the Queen's livery. The people, who had often heard of me, were very curious to crowd about the sedan, and the girl was complaisant enough to make the bearers stop, and to take me in her hand that I might be more conveniently seen.

I was very desirous to see the chief temple, and particularly the tower belonging to it, which is reckoned the highest in the kingdom. Accordingly one day my nurse carried me thither, but I may truly say I came back disappointed; for the height is not above three thousand foot, and[2] reckoning from the ground to the highest pinnacle top; which, allowing for the difference between the size of those people and us in Europe, is no great matter for admiration, nor at all equal in proportion (if I rightly remember) to Salisbury steeple.[3] But, not to detract from a nation to which during my life I shall acknowledge

2. Even.
3. Four hundred four feet in height.

myself extremely obliged, it must be allowed that whatever this famous tower wants in height is amply made up in beauty and strength. For the walls are near an hundred foot thick, built of hewn stone, whereof each is about forty foot square, and adorned on all sides with statues of gods and emperors cut in marble larger than the life, placed in their several niches. I measured a little finger which had fallen down from one of these statues, and lay unperceived among some rubbish, and found it exactly four foot and an inch in length. Glumdalclitch wrapped it up in a handkerchief, and carried it home in her pocket to keep among other trinkets, of which the girl was very fond, as children at her age usually are.

The King's kitchen is indeed a noble building, vaulted at top, and about six hundred foot high. The great oven is not so wide by ten paces as the cupola at St. Paul's:[4] for I measured the latter on purpose after my return. But if I should describe the kitchen-grate, the prodigious pots and kettles, the joints of meat turning on the spits, with many other particulars, perhaps I should be hardly believed; at least a severe critic would be apt to think I enlarged a little, as travellers are often suspected to do. To avoid which censure, I fear I have run too much into the other extreme; and that if this treatise should happen to be translated into the language of Brobdingnag (which is the general name of that kingdom) and transmitted thither, the King and his people would have reason to complain that I had done them an injury by a false and diminutive representation.

His Majesty seldom keeps above six hundred horses in his stables: they are generally from fifty-four to sixty foot high. But, when he goes abroad on solemn days, he is attended for state by a militia guard of five hundred horse, which indeed I thought was the most splendid sight that could be ever beheld, till I saw part of his army in battalia, whereof I shall find another occasion to speak.

4. The cupola is 108 feet wide.

Chapter Five

Several adventures that happened to the author. The execution of a criminal. The author shows his skill in navigation.

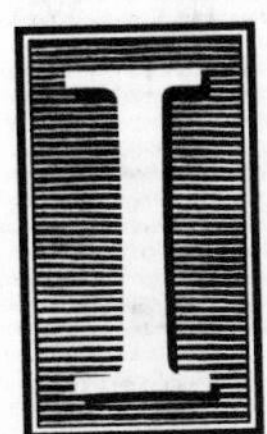

I SHOULD HAVE LIVED HAPPY ENOUGH IN THAT COUNTRY, if my littleness had not exposed me to several ridiculous and troublesome accidents, some of which I shall venture to relate. Glumdalclitch often carried me into the gardens of the court in my smaller box, and would sometimes take me out of it and hold me in her hand, or set me down to walk. I remember, before the dwarf left the Queen, he followed us one day into those gardens, and my nurse having set me down, he and I being close together, near some dwarf apple-trees, I must need show my wit by a silly allusion between him and the trees, which happens to hold in their language as it doth in ours. Whereupon the malicious rogue, watching his opportunity, when I was walking under one of them, shook it directly over my head, by which a dozen apples, each of them near as large as a Bristol barrel, came tumbling about my ears; one of them hit me on the back as I chanced to stoop, and knocked me down flat on my face, but I received no other hurt, and the dwarf was pardoned at my desire, because I had given the provocation.

Another day Glumdalclitch left me on a smooth grass-plot to divert myself while she walked at some distance with her governess. In the mean time there suddenly fell such a violent shower of hail, that I was immediately by the force of it struck to the ground: and when I was down, the hailstones gave me such cruel bangs all over the body, as if I

had been pelted with tennis-balls;[1] however I made a shift to creep on all four, and shelter myself by lying flat on my face on the lee-side of a border of lemon thyme, but so bruised from head to foot that I could not go abroad in ten days. Neither is this at all to be wondered at, because, nature in that country observing the same proportion through all her operations, a hailstone is near eighteen hundred times as large as one in Europe, which I can assert upon experience, having been so curious to weigh and measure them.

But a more dangerous accident happened to me in the same garden, when my little nurse, believing she had put me in a secure place, which I often intreated her to do, that I might enjoy my own thoughts, and having left my box at home to avoid the trouble of carrying it, went to another part of the gardens with her governess and some ladies of her acquaintance. While she was absent and out of hearing, a small white spaniel belonging to one of the chief gardeners, having got by accident into the garden, happened to range near the place where I lay. The dog, following the scent, came directly up, and taking me in his mouth ran straight to his master, wagging his tail, and set me gently on the ground. By good fortune he had been so well taught, that I was carried between his teeth without the least hurt, or even tearing my clothes. But the poor gardener, who knew me well, and had a great kindness for me, was in a terrible fright. He gently took me up in both his hands, and asked me how I did; but I was so amazed and out of breath, that I could not speak a word. In a few minutes I came to myself, and he carried me safe to my little nurse, who by this time had returned to the place where she left me, and was in cruel agonies when I did not appear, nor answer when she called: she severely reprimanded the gardener on account of his dog. But the thing was hushed up, and never known at court; for the girl was afraid of the Queen's anger, and truly as to myself, I thought

1. Not of the modern pneumatic kind, used for lawn tennis, but balls used for the game of court tennis, with interiors composed of closely packed hair or tightly wound cloth.

it would not be for my reputation that such a story should go about.

This accident absolutely determined Glumdalclitch never to trust me abroad for the future out of her sight. I had been long afraid of this resolution, and therefore concealed from her some little unlucky adventures that happened in those times when I was left by myself. Once a kite hovering over the garden made a stoop at me, and if I had not resolutely drawn my hanger, and run under a thick espalier, he would have certainly carried me away in his talons. Another time walking to the top of a fresh mole-hill, I fell to my neck in the hole through which that animal had cast up the earth, and coined some lie not worth remembering, to excuse myself for spoiling my clothes. I likewise broke my right shin against the shell of a snail, which I happened to stumble over, as I was walking alone, and thinking on poor England.

I cannot tell whether I were more pleased or mortified to observe in those solitary walks, that the smaller birds did not appear to be at all afraid of me, but would hop about within a yard distance, looking for worms and other food with as much indifference and security as if no creature at all were near them. I remember, a thrush had the confidence to snatch out of my hand with his bill a piece of cake that Glumdalclitch had just given me for my breakfast. When I attempted to catch any of these birds, they would boldly turn against me, endeavouring to pick my fingers, which I durst not venture within their reach; and then they would turn back unconcerned to hunt for worms or snails, as they did before. But one day I took a thick cudgel, and threw it with all my strength so luckily at a linnet, that I knocked him down, and seizing him by the neck with both my hands, ran with him in triumph to my nurse. However, the bird, who had only been stunned, recovering himself, gave me so many boxes with his wings on both sides of my head and body, though I held him at arm's length, and was out of the reach of his claws, that I was twenty times thinking to let him go. But I was soon relieved by one of our servants, who wrung off the bird's neck, and I had him next day for dinner by the Queen's command. This linnet, as near as I can remember, seemed to be somewhat larger than an English swan.

The maids of honour often invited Glumdalclitch to their apartments, and desired she would bring me along with her, on purpose to have the pleasure of seeing and touching me. They would often strip me naked from top to toe, and lay me at full length in their bosoms; wherewith I was much disgusted; because, to say the truth, a very offensive smell came from their skins; which I do not mention or intend to the disadvantage of those excellent ladies, for whom I have all manner of respect; but I conceive that my sense was more acute in proportion to my littleness, and that those illustrious persons were no more disagreeable to their lovers, or to each other, than people of the same quality are with us in England. And, after all, I found their natural smell was much more supportable than when they used perfumes, under which I immediately swooned away. I cannot forget that an intimate friend of mine in Lilliput took the freedom, in a warm day, when I had used a good deal of exercise, to complain of a strong smell about me, although I am as little faulty that way as most of my sex: but I suppose his faculty of smelling was as nice with regard to me, as mine was to that of this people. Upon this point, I cannot forbear doing justice to the Queen my mistress, and Glumdalclitch my nurse, whose persons were as sweet as those of any lady in England.

That which gave me most uneasiness among these maids of honour, when my nurse carried me to visit them, was to see them use me without any manner of ceremony, like a creature who had no sort of consequence. For they would strip themselves to the skin, and put on their smocks in my presence, while I was placed on their toilet directly before their naked bodies, which, I am sure, to me was very far from being a tempting sight, or from giving me any other emotions than those of horror and disgust. Their skins appeared so coarse and uneven, so variously coloured, when I saw them near, with a mole here and there as broad as a trencher, and hairs hanging from it thicker than packthreads; to say nothing further concerning the rest of their persons. Neither did they at all scruple while I was by to discharge what they had drunk, to the quantity of at least two hogsheads, in a vessel that held above three tuns. The handsomest among these maids of honour, a pleasant frolicsome girl of sixteen, would sometimes set me astride upon one of her nipples, with many other tricks, wherein the reader will excuse me for not being over particular. But I was so much displeased, that I intreated Glumdalclitch to contrive some excuse for not seeing that young lady any more.

One day a young gentleman, who was nephew to my nurse's governess, came and pressed them both to see an execution. It was of a man who had murdered one of that gentleman's intimate acquaintance. Glumdalclitch was prevailed on to be of the company, very much against her inclination, for she was naturally tender-hearted: and as for myself, although I abhorred such kind of spectacles, yet my curiosity tempted me to see something that I thought must be extraordinary. The malefactor was fixed in a chair upon a scaffold erected for the purpose, and his head cut off at a blow with a sword of about forty foot long. The veins and arteries spouted up such a prodigious quantity of blood, and so high in the air, that the great *jet d'eau* at Versailles[2] was not equal for the time it lasted; and the head, when it fell on the scaffold floor, gave such a bounce[3] as made me start, although I were at least half an English mile distant.

The Queen, who often used to hear me talk of my sea-voyages, and took all occasions to divert me when I was melancholy, asked me whether I understood how to handle a sail or an oar, and whether a little exercise of rowing might not be convenient for my health. I answered that I understood both very well. For although my proper

2. The *Bassin de Neptune,* largest of the fountains in the elaborate system of waterworks erected by Louis XIV early in the eighteenth century, threw a stream of water seventy-four feet high.

3. An explosive noise.

employment had been to be surgeon or doctor to the ship, yet often, upon a pinch, I was forced to work like a common mariner. But I could not see how this could be done in their country, where the smallest wherry was equal to a first rate man-of-war among us, and such a boat as I could manage would never live in any of their rivers: her Majesty said, if I would contrive a boat, her own joiner should make it, and she would provide a place for me to sail in. The fellow was an ingenious workman, and by my instructions in ten days finished a pleasure-boat with all its tackling, able conveniently to hold eight Europeans. When it was finished, the Queen was so delighted, that she ran with it in her lap to the King, who ordered it to be put in a cistern full of water, with me in it, by way of trial, where I could not manage my two sculls or little oars for want of room. But the Queen had before contrived another project. She ordered the joiner to make a wooden trough of three hundred foot long, fifty broad, and eight deep; which being well pitched to prevent leaking, was placed on the floor along the wall, in an outer room of the palace. It had a cock near the bottom to let out the water when it began to grow stale, and two servants could easily fill it in half an hour. Here I often used to row for my own diversion, as well as that of the Queen and her ladies, who thought themselves well entertained with my skill and agility. Sometimes I would put up my sail, and then my business was only to steer, while the ladies gave me a gale with their fans; and when they were weary, some of the pages would blow my sail forward with their breath, while I showed my art by steering starboard or larboard as I pleased. When I had done, Glumdalclitch always carried back my boat into her closet, and hung it on a nail to dry.

In this exercise I once met an accident which had like to have cost me my life. For, one of the pages having put my boat into the trough, the governess who attended Glumdalclitch very officiously lifted me up to place me in the boat, but I happened to slip through her fingers, and should have infallibly fallen down forty foot upon the floor if, by the luckiest chance in the world, I had not been stopped by a corking-pin[4] that stuck in the good gentlewoman's stomacher;[5] the head of the pin passed between my shirt and the waistband of my breeches, and thus I was held by the middle in the air till Glumdalclitch ran to my relief.

Another time, one of the servants, whose office it was to fill my trough every third day with fresh water, was so careless to let a huge frog (not perceiving it) slip out of his pail. The frog lay concealed till I was put into my boat, but then seeing a resting place, climbed up, and made it lean so much on one side, that I was forced to balance it with all my weight on the other, to prevent overturning. When the frog was got in, it hopped at once half the length of the boat, and then over my head, backwards and forwards, daubing my face and clothes with its odious slime. The largeness of its features made it appear the most deformed animal that can be conceived. However, I desired Glumdalclitch to let me deal with it alone. I banged it a good while with one of my sculls, and at last forced it to leap out of the boat.

But the greatest danger I ever underwent in that kingdom was from a monkey, who belonged to one of the clerks of the kitchen. Glumdalclitch had locked me up in her closet,[6] while she went somewhere upon business or a visit. The weather being very warm, the closet window was left open, as well as the windows and the door of my bigger box, in which I usually lived, because of its largeness and conveniency. As I sat quietly meditating at my table, I heard something bounce in at the closet window, and skip about from one side to the other; whereat, although I were much alarmed, yet I ventured to look out, but not stirring from my seat; and then I saw this frolicsome animal, frisking and leaping up and down till at last he came to my box, which he seemed to view with great pleasure and curiosity, peeping in at the door and every window. I retreated to the farther corner of my room, or box, but the monkey, looking in at every side, put me

4. A pin of the largest size.
5. An ornamental garment covering the chest.
6. Small private room.

into such a fright, that I wanted presence of mind to conceal myself under the bed, as I might easily have done. After some time spent in peeping, grinning, and chattering, he at last espied me, and reaching one of his paws in at the door, as a cat does when she plays with a mouse, although I often shifted place to avoid him, he at length caught hold of the lappet of my coat (which being made of that country cloth, was very thick and strong) and dragged me out. He took me up in his right fore-foot, and held me as a nurse does a child she is going to suckle, just as I have seen the same sort of creature do with a kitten in Europe: and when I offered to struggle, he squeezed me so hard, that I thought it more prudent to submit. I have good reason to believe that he took me for a young one of his own species, by his often stroking my face very gently with his other paw. In these diversions he was interrupted by a noise at the closet door, as if some body were opening it; whereupon he suddenly leaped up to the window at which he had come in, and thence upon the leads and gutters, walking upon three legs, and holding me in the fourth, till he clambered up to a roof that was next to ours. I heard Glumdalclitch give a shriek at the moment he was carrying me out. The poor girl was almost distracted: that quarter of the palace was all in an uproar; the servants ran for ladders; the monkey was seen by hundreds in the court sitting upon the ridge of a building, holding me like a baby in one of his fore-paws, and feeding me with the other, by cramming into my mouth some victuals he had squeezed out of the bag on one side of his chaps, and patting me when I would not eat; whereat many of the rabble below could not forbear laughing; neither do I think they justly ought to be blamed, for without question the sight was ridiculous enough to every body but myself. Some of the people threw up stones, hoping to drive the monkey down; but this was strictly forbidden, or else very probably my brains had been dashed out.

The ladders were now applied, and mounted by several men, which the monkey observing, and finding himself almost encompassed, not being able to make speed enough with his three legs, let me drop on a ridge tile, and made his escape. Here I sat for some time three hundred yards from the ground, expecting every moment to be blown down by the wind, or to fall by my own giddiness, and come tumbling over and over from the ridge to the eaves. But an honest lad, one of my nurse's footmen, climbed up, and putting me into his breeches pocket, brought me down safe.

I was almost choked with the filthy stuff the monkey had crammed down my throat; but my dear little nurse picked it out of my mouth with a small needle, and then I fell a vomiting, which gave me great relief. Yet I was so weak and bruised in the sides with the squeezes given me by this odious animal, that I was forced to keep my bed a fortnight. The King, Queen, and all the court sent every day to enquire after my health, and her Majesty made me several visits during my sickness. The monkey was killed, and an order made that no such animal should be kept about the palace.

When I attended the King after my recovery, to return him thanks for his favours, he was pleased to rally me a good deal upon this adventure. He asked me what my thoughts and speculations were while I lay in the monkey's paw, how I liked the victuals he gave me, his manner of feeding, and whether the fresh air on the roof had sharpened my stomach. He desired to know what I would have done upon such an occasion in my own country. I told his Majesty, that in Europe we had no monkeys, except such as were brought for curiosities from other places, and so small, that I could deal with a dozen of them together, if they presumed to attack me. And as for that monstrous animal with whom I was so lately engaged (it was indeed as large as an elephant), if my fears had suffered me to think so far as to make use of my hanger (looking fiercely and clapping my hand upon the hilt as I spoke) when he poked his paw into my chamber, perhaps I should have given him such a wound, as would have made him glad to withdraw it with more haste than he put it in. This I delivered in a firm tone, like a person who was jealous lest his courage should be called in question. However, my speech produced nothing else besides a loud laughter, which all the respect due to his Majesty from those about him could not make them contain. This made me reflect how vain an attempt it is for a man to endeavour doing himself honour among those who are out of all degree of equality or comparison with him. And yet I have seen the moral of my own behaviour very frequent in England since my return, where a little contemptible varlet, without the least title to birth, person, wit, or common sense, shall presume to look with importance, and put himself upon a foot with the greatest persons of the kingdom.

I was every day furnishing the court with some ridiculous story; and Glumdalclitch, although she loved me to excess, yet was arch enough to inform the Queen, whenever I committed any folly that she thought would be diverting to her Majesty. The girl, who had been out of order, was carried by her governess to take the air about an hour's distance, or thirty miles from town. They alighted out of the coach near a small footpath in a field, and Glumdalclitch setting down my travelling box, I went out of it to walk. There was a cow-dung in the path, and I must needs try my activity by attempting to leap over it. I took a run, but unfortunately jumped short, and found myself just in the middle up to my knees. I waded through with some difficulty, and one of the footmen wiped me as clean as he could with his handkerchief; for I was filthily bemired, and my nurse confined me to my box till we returned home; where the Queen was soon informed of what had passed, and the footmen spread it about the court, so that all the mirth, for some days, was at my expense.

Chapter Six

Several contrivances of the author to please the King and Queen. He shows his skill in music. The King enquires into the state of Europe, which the author relates to him. The King's observations thereon.

USED TO ATTEND THE KING'S LEVEE ONCE OR TWICE A week, and had often seen him under the barber's hand, which indeed was at first very terrible to behold. For the razor was almost twice as long as an ordinary scythe. His Majesty according to the custom of the country was only shaved twice a week. I once prevailed on the barber to give me some of the suds or lather, out of which I picked forty or fifty of the strongest stumps of hair. I then took a piece of fine wood, and cut it like the back of a comb, making several holes in it at equal distance with as small a needle as I could get from Glumdalclitch. I fixed in the stumps so artificially, scraping and sloping them with my knife towards the points, that I made a very tolerable comb; which was a seasonable supply, my own being so much broken in the teeth, that it was almost useless: neither did I know any artist in that country so nice and exact, as would undertake to make me another.

And this puts me in mind of an amusement wherein I spent many of my leisure hours. I desired the Queen's woman to save for me the combings of her Majesty's hair, whereof in time I got a good quantity, and consulting with my friend the cabinet-maker, who had received general orders to do little jobs for me, I directed him to make two chair-frames, no larger than those I had in my box, and then to bore little holes with a fine awl round those parts where I designed the

backs and seats; through these holes I wove the strongest hairs I could pick out, just after the manner of cane-chairs in England. When they were finished, I made a present of them to her Majesty, who kept them in her cabinet, and used to show them for curiosities, as indeed they were the wonder of every one that beheld them. The Queen would have had me sit upon one of these chairs, but I absolutely refused to obey her, protesting I would rather die a thousand deaths than place a dishonourable part of my body on those precious hairs that once adorned her Majesty's head. Of these hairs (as I had always a mechanical genius) I likewise made a neat little purse about five foot long, with her Majesty's name deciphered in gold letters, which I gave to Glumdalclitch, by the Queen's consent. To say the truth, it was more for show than use, being not of strength to bear the weight of the larger coins, and therefore she kept nothing in it, but some little toys that girls are fond of.

The King, who delighted in music, had frequent consorts[1] at court, to which I was sometimes carried, and set in my box on a table to hear them: but the noise was so great, that I could hardly distinguish the tunes. I am confident that all the drums and trumpets of a royal army, beating and sounding together just at your ears, could not equal it. My practice was to have my box removed from the places where the performers sat, as far as I could, then to shut the doors and windows of it, and draw the window curtains; after which I found their music not disagreeable.

I had learned in my youth to play a little upon the spinet. Glumdalclitch kept one in her chamber, and a master attended twice a week to teach her: I call it a spinet, because it somewhat resembled that instrument, and was played upon in the same manner. A fancy came into my head that I would entertain the King and Queen with an English tune upon this instrument. But this appeared extremely difficult: for the spinet was near sixty foot long, each key being almost a

1. Concerts.

foot wide, so that, with my arms extended, I could not reach to above five keys, and to press them down required a good smart stroke with my fist, which would be too great a labour, and to no purpose. The method I contrived was this. I prepared two round sticks about the bigness of common cudgels; they were thicker at one end than the other, and I covered the thicker ends with a piece of a mouse's skin, that by rapping on them I might neither damage the tops of the keys, nor interrupt the sound. Before the spinet a bench was placed about four foot below the keys, and I was put upon the bench. I ran sideling upon it that way and this, as fast as I could, banging the proper keys with my two sticks, and made a shift to play a jig to the great satisfaction of both their Majesties: but it was the most violent exercise I ever underwent, and yet I could not strike above sixteen keys, nor, consequently, play the bass and treble together, as other artists do; which was a great disadvantage to my performance.

The King, who, as I before observed, was a prince of excellent understanding, would frequently order that I should be brought in my box, and set upon the table in his closet. He would then command me to bring one of my chairs out of the box, and sit down within three yards distance upon the top of the cabinet, which brought me almost to a level with his face. In this manner I had several conversations with him. I one day took the freedom to tell his Majesty, that the contempt he discovered towards Europe, and the rest of the world, did not seem answerable to[2] those excellent qualities of the mind he was master of. That reason did not extend itself with the bulk of the body: on the contrary, we observed in our country that the tallest persons were usually least provided with it. That among other animals, bees and ants had the reputation of more industry, art, and sagacity than many of the larger kinds. And that, as inconsiderable as he took me to be, I hoped I might live to do his Majesty some signal service. The King heard me with attention, and began to conceive a

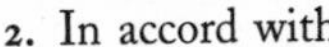

2. In accord with.

much better opinion of me than he had ever before. He desired I would give him as exact an account of the government of England as I possibly could; because, as fond as princes commonly are of their own customs (for so he conjectured of other monarchs by my former discourses), he should be glad to hear of any thing that might deserve imitation.

Imagine with thyself, courteous reader, how often I then wished for the tongue of Demosthenes or Cicero, that might have enabled me to celebrate the praises of my own dear native country in a style equal to its merits and felicity.

I began my discourse by informing his Majesty that our dominions consisted of two islands, which composed three mighty kingdoms under one sovereign, besides our plantations[3] in America. I dwelt long upon the fertility of our soil, and the temperature[4] of our climate. I then spoke at large upon the constitution of an English parliament, partly made up of an illustrious body called the House of Peers, persons of the noblest blood, and of the most ancient and ample patrimonies. I described that extraordinary care always taken of their education in arts and arms, to qualify them for being counsellors born to the king and kingdom, to have a share in the legislature, to be members of the highest court of judicature from whence there could be no appeal; and to be champions always ready for the defence of their prince and country by their valour, conduct, and fidelity. That these were the ornament and bulwark of the kingdom, worthy followers of their most renowned ancestors, whose honour had been the reward of their virtue, from which their posterity were never once known to degenerate. To these were joined several holy persons, as part of that assembly, under the title of bishops, whose peculiar business it is to take care of religion, and of those who instruct the people therein. These were searched and sought out through the whole na-

3. Colonies.
4. Temperateness.

M·S

When the frog was got in, it hopped at once half the length of the boat,... daubing my face and clothes with its odious slime.

PAGE 139

tion, by the prince and his wisest counsellors, among such of the priesthood, as were most deservedly distinguished by the sanctity of their lives, and the depth of their erudition; who were indeed the spiritual fathers of the clergy and the people.

That the other part of the parliament consisted of an assembly called the House of Commons, who were all principal gentlemen, *freely* picked and culled out by the people themselves, for their great abilities, and love of their country, to represent the wisdom of the whole nation. And these two bodies make up the most august assembly in Europe, to whom, in conjunction with the prince, the whole legislature is committed.

I then descended to the courts of justice, over which the judges, those venerable sages and interpreters of the law, presided, for determining the disputed rights and properties of men, as well as for the punishment of vice, and protection of innocence. I mentioned the prudent management of our treasury, the valour and achievements of our forces by sea and land. I computed the number of our people, by reckoning how many millions there might be of each religious sect, or political party among us. I did not omit even our sports and pastimes, or any other particular which I thought might redound to the honour of my country. And I finished all with a brief historical account of affairs and events in England for about an hundred years past.

This conversation was not ended under five audiences, each of several hours, and the King heard the whole with great attention, frequently taking notes of what I spoke, as well as memorandums of several questions he intended to ask me.

When I had put an end to these long discourses, his Majesty in a sixth audience, consulting his notes, proposed many doubts, queries, and objections, upon every article. He asked, what methods were used to cultivate the minds and bodies of our young nobility, and in what kind of business they commonly spent the first and teachable part of their lives. What course was taken to supply that assembly when any noble family became extinct. What qualifications were necessary in those who are to be created new lords: whether the humour of the prince, a sum of money to a court-lady, or a prime minister, or a design of strengthening a party opposite to the public interest, ever happened to be motives in those advancements. What share of knowledge these lords had in the laws of their country, and how they came by it, so as to enable them to decide the properties of their fellow-subjects in the last resort. Whether they were always so free from avarice, partialities, or want, that a bribe, or some other sinister view, could have no place among them. Whether those holy lords I spoke of were always promoted to that rank upon account of their knowledge in religious matters, and the sanctity of their lives; had never been compliers with the times while they were common priests, or slavish prostitute chaplains to some nobleman, whose opinions they continued servilely to follow after they were admitted into that assembly.[5]

He then desired to know what arts were practised in electing those whom I called commoners. Whether a stranger with a strong purse might not influence the vulgar voters to choose him before their own landlord, or the most considerable gentleman in the neighbourhood. How it came to pass, that people were so violently bent upon getting into this assembly, which I allowed to be a great trouble and expense, often to the ruin of their families, without any salary or pension: because this appeared such an exalted strain of virtue and public spirit, that his Majesty seemed to doubt it might possibly not be always sincere: and he desired to know whether such zealous gentlemen could have any views of refunding themselves for the charges and trouble they were at, by sacrificing the public good to the designs of a weak and vicious prince in conjunction with a corrupted ministry. He multiplied his questions, and sifted me thoroughly upon every part of

5. Many of the bishops appointed by the Whigs under George I were of the low-church party, which Swift detested.

this head, proposing numberless enquiries and objections, which I think it not prudent or convenient to repeat.[6]

Upon what I said in relation to our courts of justice, his Majesty desired to be satisfied in several points: and this I was the better able to do, having been formerly almost ruined by a long suit in chancery, which was decreed for me with costs. He asked, what time was usually spent in determining between right and wrong, and what degree of expense. Whether advocates and orators had liberty to plead in causes manifestly known to be unjust, vexatious, or oppressive. Whether party in religion or politics were observed to be of any weight in the scale of justice. Whether those pleading orators were persons educated in the general knowledge of equity, or only in provincial, national, and other local customs. Whether they or their judges had any part in penning those laws which they assumed the liberty of interpreting and glossing upon at their pleasure. Whether they had ever at different times pleaded for and against the same cause, and cited precedents to prove contrary opinions. Whether they were a rich or a poor corporation. Whether they received any pecuniary reward for pleading or delivering their opinions. And particularly whether they were ever admitted as members in the lower senate.

He fell next upon the management of our treasury; and said, he thought my memory had failed me, because I computed our taxes at about five or six millions a year, and when I came to mention the issues, he found they sometimes amounted to more than double; for the notes he had taken were very particular in this point, because he hoped, as he told me, that the knowledge of our conduct might be useful to him, and he could not be deceived in his calculations. But, if what I told him were true, he was still at a loss how a kingdom could run out of its estate like a private person.[7] He asked me, who were our creditors; and where we should find money to pay them. He won-

6. This remark points the application of the preceding sentence to the administration of Walpole.

7. The national debt, as a permanent feature of English fiscal policy, was relatively new, going back only to the reign of William and Mary.

dered to hear me talk of such chargeable and extensive wars; that certainly we must be a quarrelsome people, or live among very bad neighbours, and that our generals must needs be richer than our kings.[8] He asked what business we had out of our own islands, unless upon the score of trade or treaty, or to defend the coasts with our fleet. Above all, he was amazed to hear me talk of a mercenary standing army in the midst of peace, and among a free people.[9] He said if we were governed by our own consent in the persons of our representatives, he could not imagine of whom we were afraid, or against whom we were to fight, and would hear my opinion, whether a private man's house might not better be defended by himself, his children, and family, than by half a dozen rascals picked up at a venture in the streets, for small wages, who might get an hundred times more by cutting their throats.

He laughed at my odd kind of arithmetic (as he was pleased to call it) in reckoning the numbers of our people by a computation drawn from the several sects among us in religion and politics. He said, he knew no reason, why those who entertain opinions prejudicial to the public should be obliged to change, or should not be obliged to conceal them. And as it was tyranny in any government to require the first, so it was weakness not to enforce the second: for a man may be allowed to keep poisons in his closets, but not to vend them about for cordials.

He observed, that among the diversions of our nobility and gentry I had mentioned gaming. He desired to know at what age this entertainment was usually taken up, and when it was laid down. How much of their time it employed; whether it ever went so high as to affect their fortunes. Whether mean vicious people by their dexterity in that art might not arrive at great riches, and sometimes keep our very nobles in dependence, as well as habituate them to vile compan-

8. Tory writers never tired of pointing out that the Duke of Marlborough had made a fortune from his military career.

9. The Tories strenuously opposed bills providing for the establishment of a large standing army, which, they hinted, was intended as an instrument to subvert British liberty.

ions, wholly take them from the improvement of their minds, and force them, by the losses they have received, to learn and practise that infamous dexterity upon others.

He was perfectly astonished with the historical account I gave him of our affairs during the last century, protesting it was only an heap of conspiracies, rebellions, murders, massacres, revolutions, banishments, the very worst effects that avarice, faction, hypocrisy, perfidiousness, cruelty, rage, madness, hatred, envy, lust, malice, or ambition could produce.

His Majesty in another audience was at the pains to recapitulate the sum of all I had spoken, compared the questions he made with the answers I had given; then taking me into his hands, and stroking me gently, delivered himself in these words, which I shall never forget, nor the manner he spoke them in: 'My little friend Grildrig, you have made a most admirable panegyric upon your country. You have clearly proved that ignorance, idleness, and vice are the proper ingredients for qualifying a legislator. That laws are best explained, interpreted, and applied by those whose interest and abilities lie in perverting, confounding, and eluding them. I observe among you some lines of an institution, which in its original might have been tolerable, but these half erased, and the rest wholly blurred and blotted by corruptions. It doth not appear from all you have said, how any one virtue is required towards the procurement of any one station among you, much less that men are ennobled on account of their virtue, that priests are advanced for their piety or learning, soldiers for their conduct or valour, judges for their integrity, senators for the love of their country, or counsellors for their wisdom. As for yourself', continued the King, 'who have spent the greatest part of your life in travelling, I am well disposed to hope you may hitherto have escaped many vices of your country. But, by what I have gathered from your own relation, and the answers I have with much pains wringed and extorted from you, I cannot but conclude the bulk of your natives to be the most pernicious race of little odious vermin that nature ever suffered to crawl upon the surface of the earth'.

Chapter Seven

The author's love of his country. He makes a proposal of much advantage to the King, which is rejected. The King's great ignorance in politics. The learning of that country very imperfect and confined. Their laws, and military affairs, and parties in the state.

OTHING BUT AN EXTREME LOVE OF TRUTH COULD have hindered me from concealing this part of my story. It was in vain to discover my resentments, which were always turned into ridicule; and I was forced to rest with patience while my noble and most beloved country was so injuriously treated. I am heartily sorry as any of my readers can possibly be, that such an occasion was given: but this prince happened to be so curious and inquisitive upon every particular, that it could not consist either with gratitude or good manners to refuse giving him what satisfaction I was able. Yet thus much I may be allowed to say in my own vindication, that I artfully eluded many of his questions, and gave to every point a more favourable turn by many degrees than the strictness of truth would allow. For I have always borne that laudable partiality to my own country, which Dionysius Halicarnassensis[1] with so much justice recommends to an historian. I would hide the frailties and deformities of my political mother, and place her virtues and beauties in the most advantageous light. This was my sincere endeavour in those many

1. Dionysius of Halicarnassus, a Romanized Greek rhetorician of the Augustan Age, stated frankly that he wrote his *Archæologia Romana* to persuade the subjugated Greeks that the virtues of the Romans justified their position of dominance.

discourses I had with that mighty monarch, although it unfortunately failed of success.

But great allowances should be given to a king who lives wholly secluded from the rest of the world, and must therefore be altogether unacquainted with the manners and customs that most prevail in other nations: the want of which knowledge will ever produce many *prejudices,* and a certain *narrowness of thinking,* from which we and the politer countries of Europe are wholly exempted. And it would be hard indeed, if so remote a prince's notions of virtue and vice were to be offered as a standard for all mankind.

To confirm what I have now said, and further to show the miserable effects of a *confined education,* I shall here insert a passage which will hardly obtain belief. In hopes to ingratiate myself farther into his Majesty's favour, I told him of an invention discovered between three and four hundred years ago, to make a certain powder, into an heap of which the smallest spark of fire falling, would kindle the whole in a moment, although it were as big as a mountain, and make it all fly up in the air together, with a noise and agitation greater than thunder. That a proper quantity of this powder rammed into an hollow tube of brass or iron, according to its bigness, would drive a ball of iron or lead with such violence and speed as nothing was able to sustain its force. That the largest balls, thus discharged, would not only destroy whole ranks of an army at once, but batter the strongest walls to the ground, sink down ships, with a thousand men in each, to the bottom of the sea; and when linked together by a chain, would cut through masts and rigging, divide hundreds of bodies in the middle, and lay all waste before them. That we often put this powder into large hollow balls of iron, and discharged them by an engine into some city we were besieging, which would rip up the pavements, tear the houses to pieces, burst and throw splinters on every side, dashing out the brains of all who came near. That I knew the ingredients very well, which were cheap, and common; I understood the manner of compounding them, and could direct his workmen how to make those tubes of a size proportionable to all other things in his Majesty's kingdom, and the largest need not be above an hundred foot long; twenty or thirty of which tubes, charged with the proper quantity of powder and balls, would batter down the walls of the strongest town in his dominions in a few hours, or destroy the whole metropolis, if ever it should pretend to dispute his absolute commands. This I humbly offered to his Majesty as a small tribute of acknowledgement in return of so many marks that I had received of his royal favour and protection.

The King was struck with horror at the description I had given of those terrible engines, and the proposal I had made. He was amazed how so impotent and grovelling an insect as I (these were his expressions) could entertain such inhuman ideas, and in so familiar a manner as to appear wholly unmoved at all the scenes of blood and desolation, which I had painted as the common effects of those destructive machines, whereof he said, some evil genius, enemy to mankind, must have been the first contriver. As for himself, he protested, that although few things delighted him so much as new discoveries in art or in nature, yet he would rather lose half his kingdom than be privy to such a secret, which he commanded me, as I valued my life, never to mention any more.

A strange effect of *narrow principles* and *short views!* that a prince possessed of every quality which procures veneration, love, and esteem; of strong parts, great wisdom, and profound learning, endued with admirable talents for government, and almost adored by his subjects, should from a *nice unnecessary scruple,* whereof in Europe we can have no conception, let slip an opportunity put into his hands, that would have made him absolute master of the lives, the liberties, and the fortunes of his people. Neither do I say this with the least intention to detract from the many virtues of that excellent king, whose character I am sensible will on this account be very much lessened in the opinion of an English reader: but I take this defect among them to have risen from their ignorance, they not having hitherto reduced *politics* into a *science,* as the more acute wits of Europe have done. For

I remember very well, in a discourse one day with the King, when I happened to say there were several thousand books among us written upon the *art of government,* it gave him (directly contrary to my intention) a very mean opinion of our understandings. He professed both to abominate and despise all *mystery, refinement,* and *intrigue,* either in a prince or a minister. He could not tell what I meant by *secrets of state,* where an enemy or some rival nation were not in the case. He confined the knowledge of governing within very *narrow bounds;* to common sense and reason, to justice and lenity, to the speedy determination of civil and criminal causes; with some other obvious topics which are not worth considering. And he gave it for his opinion, that whoever could make two ears of corn, or two blades of grass to grow upon a spot of ground where only one grew before, would deserve better of mankind, and do more essential service to his country, than the whole race of politicians put together.

The learning of this people is very defective, consisting only in morality, history, poetry, and mathematics, wherein they must be allowed to excel. But the last of these is wholly applied to what may be useful in life, to the improvement of agriculture and all mechanical arts; so that among us it would be little esteemed. And as to ideas, entities, abstractions, and transcendentals, I could never drive the least conception into their heads.

No law of that country must exceed in words the number of letters in their alphabet, which consists only in two and twenty. But indeed, few of them extend even to that length. They are expressed in the most plain and simple terms, wherein those people are not mercurial enough to discover above one interpretation. And to write a comment upon any law is a capital crime. As to the decision of civil causes, or proceedings against criminals, their precedents are so few, that they have little reason to boast of any extraordinary skill in either.

They have had the art of printing, as well as the Chinese, time out of mind. But their libraries are not very large; for that of the King's, which is reckoned the biggest, doth not amount to above a thousand

volumes, placed in a gallery of twelve hundred foot long, from whence I had liberty to borrow what books I pleased. The Queen's joiner had contrived in one of Glumdalclitch's rooms a kind of wooden machine five and twenty foot high, formed like a standing ladder; the steps were each fifty foot long. It was indeed a moveable pair of stairs, the lowest end placed at ten foot distance from the wall of the chamber. The book I had a mind to read was put up leaning against the wall. I first mounted to the upper step of the ladder, and turning my face towards the book, began at the top of the page, and so walking to the right and left about eight or ten paces, according to the length of the lines, till I had gotten a little below the level of my eyes, and then descending gradually till I came to the bottom: after which I mounted again, and began the other page in the same manner, and so turned over the leaf, which I could easily do with both my hands, for it was as thick and stiff as a pasteboard, and in the largest folios not above eighteen or twenty foot long.

Their style is clear, masculine, and smooth, but not florid, for they avoid nothing more than multiplying unnecessary words, or using various expressions. I have perused many of their books, especially those in history and morality. Among the rest I was much diverted with a little old treatise, which always lay in Glumdalclitch's bed-chamber, and belonged to her governess, a grave elderly gentle-woman, who dealt in writings of morality and devotion. The book treats of the weakness of human kind, and is in little esteem except among the women and the vulgar. However, I was curious to see what an author of that country could say upon such a subject. This writer went through all the usual topics of European moralists, showing how diminutive, contemptible, and helpless an animal was man in his own nature; how unable to defend himself from the inclemencies of the air, or the fury of wild beasts. How much he was excelled by one creature in strength, by another in speed, by a third in foresight, by a fourth in industry. He added, that nature was degenerated in these latter declining ages of the world, and could now produce only small abortive births in comparison of those in ancient times. He said it was very reasonable to think, not only that the species of men were originally much larger, but also that there must have been giants in former ages, which, as it is asserted by history and tradition, so it hath been confirmed by huge bones and skulls casually dug up in several parts of the kingdom, far exceeding the common dwindled race of man in our days. He argued, that the very laws of nature absolutely required we should have been made, in the beginning, of a size more large and robust, not so liable to destruction from every little accident of a tile falling from an house, or a stone cast from the hand of a boy, or of being drowned in a little brook. From this way of reasoning the author drew several moral applications useful in the conduct of life, but needless here to repeat. For my own part, I could not avoid reflecting how universally this talent was spread of drawing lectures in morality, or indeed rather matter of discontent and repining, from the quarrels we raise with nature. And, I believe, upon a strict enquiry those quarrels might be shown as ill-grounded among us as they are among that people.

As to their military affairs, they boast that the King's army consists of an hundred and seventy-six thousand foot, and thirty-two thousand horse: if that may be called an army which is made up of tradesmen in the several cities, and farmers in the country, whose commanders are only the nobility and gentry without pay or reward. They are indeed perfect enough in their exercises, and under very good discipline, wherein I saw no great merit; for how should it be otherwise, where every farmer is under the command of his own landlord, and every citizen under that of the principal men in his own city, chosen after the manner of Venice by *ballot*?

I have often seen the militia of Lorbrulgrud drawn out to exercise in a great field near the city, of twenty miles square. They were in all not above twenty-five thousand foot, and six thousand horse; but it was impossible for me to compute their number, considering the space of ground they took up. A *cavalier* mounted on a large steed might be

about an hundred foot high. I have seen this whole body of horse upon a word of command draw their swords at once, and brandish them in the air. Imagination can figure nothing so grand, so surprising, and so astonishing. It looked as if ten thousand flashes of lightning were darting at the same time from every quarter of the sky.

I was curious to know how this prince, to whose dominions there is no access from any other country, came to think of armies, or to teach his people the practice of military discipline. But I was soon informed, both by conversation, and reading their histories. For in the course of many ages they have been troubled with the same disease to which the whole race of mankind is subject; the nobility often contending for power, the people for liberty, and the King for absolute dominion. All which, however happily tempered by the laws of the kingdom, have been sometimes violated by each of the three parties, and have once or more occasioned civil wars, the last whereof was happily put an end to by this prince's grandfather by a general composition; and the militia then settled with common consent hath been ever since kept in the strictest duty.

Chapter Eight

The King and Queen make a progress to the frontiers. The author attends them. The manner in which he leaves the country very particularly related. He returns to England.

I HAD ALWAYS A STRONG IMPULSE THAT I SHOULD SOMEtime recover my liberty, though it was impossible to conjecture by what means, or to form any project with the least hope of succeeding. The ship in which I sailed was the first ever known to be driven within sight of that coast, and the King had given strict orders, that if at any time another appeared, it should be taken ashore, and with all its crew and passengers brought in a tumbril[1] to Lorbrulgrud. He was strongly bent to get me a woman of my own size, by whom I might propagate the breed: but I think I should rather have died than undergone the disgrace of leaving a posterity to be kept in cages like tame canary birds, and perhaps in time sold about the kingdom to persons of quality for curiosities. I was indeed treated with much kindness; I was the favourite of a great king and queen, and the delight of the whole court, but it was upon such a foot as ill became the dignity of human kind. I could never forget those domestic pledges I had left behind me. I wanted to be among people with whom I could converse upon even terms, and walk about the streets and fields without fear of being trod to death like a frog or a young puppy. But my deliverance came sooner than I expected, and in a manner not very common: the whole story and circumstances of which I shall faithfully relate.

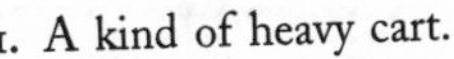

1. A kind of heavy cart.

I had now been two years in this country; and, about the beginning of the third, Glumdalclitch and I attended the King and Queen in a progress to the south coast of the kingdom. I was carried as usual in my travelling-box, which, as I have already described, was a very convenient closet of twelve foot wide. And I had ordered a hammock to be fixed by silken ropes from the four corners at the top, to break the jolts, when a servant carried me before him on horseback, as I sometimes desired, and would often sleep in my hammock while we were upon the road. On the roof of my closet, just over the middle of the hammock, I ordered the joiner to cut out a hole of a foot square to give me air in hot weather as I slept, which hole I shut at pleasure with a board that drew backwards and forwards through a groove.

When we came to our journey's end, the King thought proper to pass a few days at a palace he hath near Flanflasnic, a city within eighteen English miles of the seaside. Glumdalclitch and I were much fatigued; I had gotten a small cold, but the poor girl was so ill as to be confined to her chamber. I longed to see the ocean, which must be the only scene of my escape, if ever it should happen. I pretended to be worse than I really was, and desired leave to take the fresh air of the sea, with a page whom I was very fond of, and who had sometimes been trusted with me. I shall never forget with what unwillingness Glumdalclitch consented, nor the strict charge she gave the page to be careful of me, bursting at the same time into a flood of tears, as if she had some foreboding of what was to happen. The boy took me out in my box about half an hour's walk from the palace towards the rocks on the seashore. I ordered him to set me down, and lifting up one of my sashes, cast many a wistful melancholy look towards the sea. I found myself not very well, and told the page that I had a mind to take a nap in my hammock, which I hoped would do me good. I got in, and the boy shut the window close down to keep out the cold. I soon fell asleep, and all I can conjecture is, that while I slept, the page, thinking no danger could happen, went among the rocks to look for birds' eggs, having before observed him from my window searching about, and picking up one or two in the clefts. Be that as it will, I found myself suddenly awaked with a violent pull upon the ring which was fastened at the top of my box for the conveniency of carriage. I felt my box raised very high in the air, and then borne forwards with prodigious speed. The first jolt had like to have shaken me out of my hammock, but afterwards the motion was easy enough. I called out several times as loud as I could raise my voice, but all to no purpose. I looked towards my windows, and could see nothing but the clouds and sky. I heard a noise just over my head like the clapping of wings, and then began to perceive the woful condition I was in; that some eagle had got the ring of my box in his beak, with an intent to let it fall on a rock like a tortoise in a shell, and then pick out my body and devour it. For the sagacity and smell of this bird enable him to discover his quarry at a great distance, though better concealed than I could be within a two-inch board.

In a little time I observed the noise and flutter of wings to encrease very fast, and my box was tossed up and down like a signpost in a windy day. I heard several bangs or buffets, as I thought, given to the eagle (for such I am certain it must have been that held the ring of my box in his beak) and then all on a sudden felt myself falling perpendicularly down for above a minute, but with such incredible swiftness that I almost lost my breath. My fall was stopped by a terrible squash, that sounded louder to my ears than the cataract of Niagara; after which I was quite in the dark for another minute, and then my box began to rise so high that I could see light from the tops of my windows. I now perceived that I was fallen into the sea. My box, by the weight of my body, the goods that were in, and the broad plates of iron fixed for strength at the four corners of the top and bottom, floated about five foot deep in water. I did then, and do now suppose that the eagle which flew away with my box was pursued by two or three others, and forced to let me drop while he was defending himself against the rest, who hoped to share in the prey. The plates of iron fastened at the bottom of the box (for those were the strongest) preserved the balance while it fell, and hindered it from being broken on the surface of the water. Every joint of it was well grooved, and the door did not move on hinges, but up and down like a sash, which kept my closet so tight that very little water came in. I got with much difficulty out of my hammock, having first ventured to draw back the slip-board on the roof already mentioned, contrived on purpose to let in air, for want of which I found myself almost stifled.

How often did I then wish myself with my dear Glumdalclitch, from whom one single hour had so far divided me! And I may say with truth, that in the midst of my own misfortunes I could not forbear lamenting my poor nurse, the grief she would suffer for my loss, the displeasure of the Queen, and the ruin of her fortune. Perhaps many travellers have not been under greater difficulties and distress than I was at this juncture, expecting every moment to see my box dashed in pieces, or at least overset by the first violent blast, or a rising wave. A breach in one single pane of glass would have been immediate death: nor could any thing have preserved the windows but the strong lettice wires placed on the outside against accidents in travelling. I saw the water ooze in at several crannies, although the leaks were not considerable, and I endeavoured to stop them as well as I could. I was not able to lift up the roof of my closet, which otherwise I certainly should have done, and sate on the top of it, where I might at least preserve myself some hours longer than by being shut up, as I may call it, in the hold. Or, if I escaped these dangers for a day or two, what could I expect but a miserable death of cold and hunger! I was four hours under these circumstances, expecting and indeed wishing every moment to be my last.

I have already told the reader, that there were two strong staples fixed upon that side of my box which had no window, and into which the servant who used to carry me on horseback would put a leathern belt, and buckle it about his waist. Being in this disconsolate state, I heard or at least thought I heard some kind of grating noise on that side of my box where the staples were fixed, and soon after I began to fancy that the box was pulled or towed along in the sea; for I now and then felt a sort of tugging which made the waves rise near the tops of my windows, leaving me almost in the dark. This gave me some faint hopes of relief, although I was not able to imagine how it could be brought about. I ventured to unscrew one of my chairs, which were always fastened to the floor; and having made a hard shift to screw it down again directly under the slipping-board that I had lately opened, I mounted on the chair, and putting my mouth as near as I could to the hole, I called for help in a loud voice, and in all the languages I understood. I then fastened my handkerchief to a stick I usually carried, and thrusting it up the hole, waved it several times in the air, that if any boat or ship were near, the seamen might conjecture some unhappy mortal to be shut up in this box.

I found no effect from all I could do, but plainly perceived my closet to be moved along; and in the space of an hour, or better, that side of the box where the staples were, and had no window, struck against something that was hard. I apprehended it to be a rock, and found myself tossed more than ever. I plainly heard a noise upon the cover of my closet, like that of a cable, and the grating of it as it passed through the ring. I then found myself hoisted up by degrees at least three foot higher than I was before. Whereupon I again thrust up my stick and handkerchief, calling for help till I was almost hoarse. In return to which, I heard a great shout repeated three times, giving me such transports of joy as are not to be conceived but by those who feel them. I now heard a trampling over my head, and some body calling through the hole with a loud voice in the English tongue, 'If there be any body below let them speak'. I answered, I was an Englishman, drawn by ill fortune into the greatest calamity that ever any creature underwent, and begged, by all that was moving, to be delivered out of the dungeon I was in. The voice replied, I was safe, for my box was fastened to their ship; and the carpenter should immediately come, and saw an hole in the cover, large enough to pull me out. I answered, that was needless, and would take up too much time, for there was no more to be done, but let one of the crew put his finger into the ring, and take the box out of the sea into the ship, and so into the captain's cabin. Some of them upon hearing me talk so wildly thought I was mad; others laughed; for indeed it never came into my head that I was now got among people of my own stature and strength. The carpenter came, and in a few minutes sawed a passage about four foot square, then let down a small ladder, upon which I mounted, and from thence was taken into the ship in a very weak condition.

The sailors were all in amazement, and asked me a thousand questions, which I had no inclination to answer. I was equally confounded at the sight of so many pigmies, for such I took them to be, after having so long accustomed my eyes to the monstrous objects I had left. But the captain, Mr. Thomas Wilcocks, an honest worthy Shropshire man, observing I was ready to faint, took me into his cabin, gave me a cordial to comfort me, and made me 'turn in' upon his own bed, advising me to take a little rest, of which I had great need. Before I went to sleep I gave him to understand that I had some valuable furniture in my box, too good to be lost; a fine hammock, an handsome field-bed, two chairs, a table and a cabinet: that my closet was hung on all sides, or rather quilted, with silk and cotton: that if he would let one of the crew bring my closet into his cabin, I would open it there before him, and show him my goods. The captain, hearing me utter these absurdities, concluded I was raving: however (I suppose to pacify me), he promised to give order as I desired, and going upon deck sent some of his men down into my closet, from whence (as I afterwards found) they drew up all my goods, and stripped off the quilting; but the chairs, cabinet, and bedstead, being screwed to the floor, were much damaged by the ignorance of the seamen, who tore them up by force. Then they knocked off some of the boards for the use of the ship, and when they had got all they had a mind for, let the hulk drop into the sea, which, by reason of many breaches made in the bottom and sides, sunk to rights. And indeed I was glad not to have been a spectator of the havoc they made; because I am confident it would have sensibly touched me, by bringing former passages into my mind, which I had rather forget.

I slept some hours, but perpetually disturbed with dreams of the place I had left, and the dangers I had escaped. However, upon waking I found myself much recovered. It was now about eight o'clock at night, and the captain ordered supper immediately, thinking I had already fasted too long. He entertained me with great kindness, observing me not to look wildly, or talk inconsistently; and when we were left alone, desired I would give him a relation of my travels, and by what accident I came to be set adrift in that monstrous wooden chest. He said, that about twelve o'clock at noon, as he was looking through his glass, he spied it at a distance, and thought it was a sail, which he had a mind to make, being not much out of his course, in hopes of buying some biscuit, his own beginning to fall short. That upon coming nearer, and finding his error, he sent out his longboat to discover what I was; that his men came back in a fright, swearing they had seen a swimming house. That he laughed at their folly, and went himself in the boat, ordering his men to take a strong cable along with them. That the weather being calm, he rowed round me several times, observed my windows, and the wire lettices that defended them. That he discovered two staples upon one side, which was all of boards, without any passage for light. He then commanded his men to row up to that side, and fastening a cable to one of the staples, ordered them to tow my chest (as he called it) towards the ship. When it was there, he gave directions to fasten another cable to the ring fixed in the cover, and to raise up my chest with pulleys, which all the sailors were not able to do above two or three foot. He said, they saw my stick and handkerchief thrust out of the hole, and concluded that some unhappy men must be shut up in the cavity. I asked whether he or the crew had seen any prodigious birds in the air about the time he first discovered me. To which he answered, that discoursing this matter with the sailors while I was asleep, one of them said he had 'observed' three eagles flying towards the north, but remarked nothing of their

being larger than the usual size, which I suppose must be imputed to the great height they were at: and he could not guess the reason of my question. I then asked the captain how far he reckoned we might be from land; he said, by the best computation he could make, we were at least an hundred leagues. I assured him, that he must be mistaken by almost half, for I had not left the country from whence I came above two hours before I dropped into the sea. Whereupon he began again to think that my brain was disturbed, of which he gave me a hint, and advised me to go to bed in a cabin he had provided. I assured him I was well refreshed with his good entertainment and company, and as much in my senses as ever I was in my life. He then grew serious, and desired to ask me freely whether I were not troubled in mind by the consciousness of some enormous crime, for which I was punished at the command of some prince, by exposing me in that chest, as great criminals in other countries have been forced to sea in a leaky vessel without provisions: for although he should be sorry to have taken so ill a man into his ship, yet he would engage his word to set me safe on shore in the first port where we arrived. He added, that his suspicions were much encreased by some very absurd speeches I had delivered at first to the sailors, and afterwards to himself, in relation to my closet or chest, as well as by my odd looks and behaviour while I was at supper.

I begged his patience to hear me tell my story, which I faithfully did from the last time I left England to the moment he first discovered me. And, as truth always forceth its way into rational minds, so this honest worthy gentleman, who had some tincture of learning, and very good sense, was immediately convinced of my candor and veracity. But further to confirm all I had said, I intreated him to give order that my cabinet should be brought, of which I had the key in my pocket (for he had already informed me how the seamen disposed of my closet); I opened it in his presence, and showed him the small collection of rarities I made in the country from whence I had been so strangely delivered. There was the comb I had contrived out of the stumps of the King's beard, and another of the same materials, but fixed into a paring of her Majesty's thumb-nail, which served for the back. There was a collection of needles and pins from a foot to half a yard long. Four wasp-stings, like joiners' tacks: some combings of the Queen's hair: a gold ring which one day she made me a present of in a most obliging manner, taking it from her little finger, and throwing it over my head like a collar. I desired the captain would please to accept this ring in return of his civilities, which he absolutely refused. I showed him a corn that I had cut off with my own hand from a maid of honour's toe; it was about the bigness of a Kentish pippin, and grown so hard, that when I returned to England, I got it hollowed into a cup and set in silver. Lastly, I desired him to see the breeches I had then on, which were made of a mouse's skin.

I could force nothing on him but a footman's tooth, which I observed him to examine with great curiosity, and found he had a fancy for it. He received it with abundance of thanks, more than such a trifle could deserve. It was drawn by an unskilful surgeon in a mistake from one of Glumdalclitch's men, who was afflicted with the toothache, but it was as sound as any in his head. I got it cleaned, and put it into my cabinet. It was about a foot long, and four inches in diameter.

The captain was very well satisfied with this plain relation I had given him; and said, he hoped, when we returned to England I would oblige the world by putting it in paper, and making it public. My answer was, that I thought we were already overstocked with books of travels: that nothing could now pass which was not extraordinary, wherein I doubted some authors less consulted truth than their own vanity or interest, or the diversion of ignorant readers. That my story could contain little besides common events, without those ornamental descriptions of strange plants, trees, birds, and other animals, or of the barbarous customs and idolatry of savage people, with which most writers abound. However, I thanked him for his good opinion, and promised to take the matter into my thoughts.

He said he wondered at one thing very much, which was to hear me

speak so loud, asking me whether the King or Queen of that country were thick of hearing. I told him it was what I had been used to for above two years past, and that I admired as much at the voices of him and his men, who seemed to me only to whisper, and yet I could hear them well enough. But when I spoke in that country, it was like a man talking in the street to another looking out from the top of a steeple, unless when I was placed on a table, or held in any person's hand. I told him I had likewise observed another thing, that when I first got into the ship, and the sailors stood all about me, I thought they were the most little contemptible creatures I had ever beheld. For, indeed, while I was in that prince's country, I could never endure to look in a glass after my eyes had been accustomed to such prodigious objects, because the comparison gave me so despicable a conceit of myself. The captain said, that while we were at supper, he observed me to look at every thing with a sort of wonder, and that I often seemed hardly able to contain my laughter, which he knew not well how to take, but imputed it to some disorder in my brain. I answered, it was very true, and I wondered how I could forbear, when I saw his dishes of the size of a silver threepence, a leg of pork hardly a mouthful, a cup not so big as a nutshell: and so I went on, describing the rest of his household-stuff and provisions after the same manner. For although the Queen had ordered a little equipage of all things necessary for me while I was in her service, yet my ideas were wholly taken up with what I saw on every side of me, and I winked at my own littleness as people do at their own faults. The captain understood my raillery very well, and merrily replied with the old English proverb, that he doubted my eyes were bigger than my belly, for he did not observe my stomach so good, although I had fasted all day; and continuing in his mirth, protested he would have gladly given an hundred pounds to have seen my closet in the eagle's bill, and afterwards in its fall from so great an height into the sea; which would certainly have been a most astonishing object, worthy to have the description of it transmitted to future ages: and the comparison of Phæton was so obvious, that he could not forbear applying it, although I did not much admire the conceit.[2]

The captain, having been at Tonquin,[3] was in his return to England driven northeastwards to the latitude of 44 degrees, and of longitude 143. But meeting a trade wind two days after I came on board him, we sailed southwards a long time, and coasting New Holland[4] kept our course west-southwest, and then south-southwest till we doubled the Cape of Good Hope. Our voyage was very prosperous, but I shall not trouble the reader with a journal of it. The captain called in at one or two ports and sent in his longboat for provisions and fresh water, but I never went out of the ship till we came into the Downs, which was on the 3d day of June, 1706, about nine months after my escape. I offered to leave my goods in security for payment of my freight; but the captain protested he would not receive one farthing. We took kind leave of each other, and I made him promise he would come to see me at my house in Redriff. I hired a horse and guide for five shillings, which I borrowed of the captain.

As I was on the road, observing the littleness of the houses, the trees, the cattle, and the people, I began to think myself in Lilliput. I was afraid of trampling on every traveller I met, and often called aloud to have them stand out of the way, so that I had like to have gotten one or two broken heads for my impertinence.

When I came to my own house, for which I was forced to enquire, one of the servants opening the door, I bent down to go in (like a goose under a gate) for fear of striking my head. My wife ran out to embrace me, but I stooped lower than her knees, thinking she could otherwise never be able to reach my mouth. My daughter kneeled to ask me blessing, but I could not see her till she arose, having been so long used to stand with my head and eyes erect to above sixty foot; and then I went to take her up with one hand, by the waist. I looked

2. Turn of thought.
3. Tongking, a district in French Indo-China.
4. Following the coast-line of Australia.

down upon the servants and one or two friends who were in the house, as if they had been pigmies, and I a giant. I told my wife she had been too thrifty, for I found she had starved herself and her daughter to nothing. In short, I behaved myself so unaccountably, that they were all of the captain's opinion when he first saw me, and concluded I had lost my wits. This I mention as an instance of the great power of habit and prejudice.

In a little time I and my family and friends came to a right understanding: but my wife protested I should never go to sea any more; although my evil destiny so ordered that she had not power to hinder me, as the reader may know hereafter. In the mean time I here conclude the second part of my unfortunate voyages.

The End of the Second Part

PART THREE

A Voyage to Laputa, Balnibarbi, Glubbdubdrib, Luggnagg, and Japan

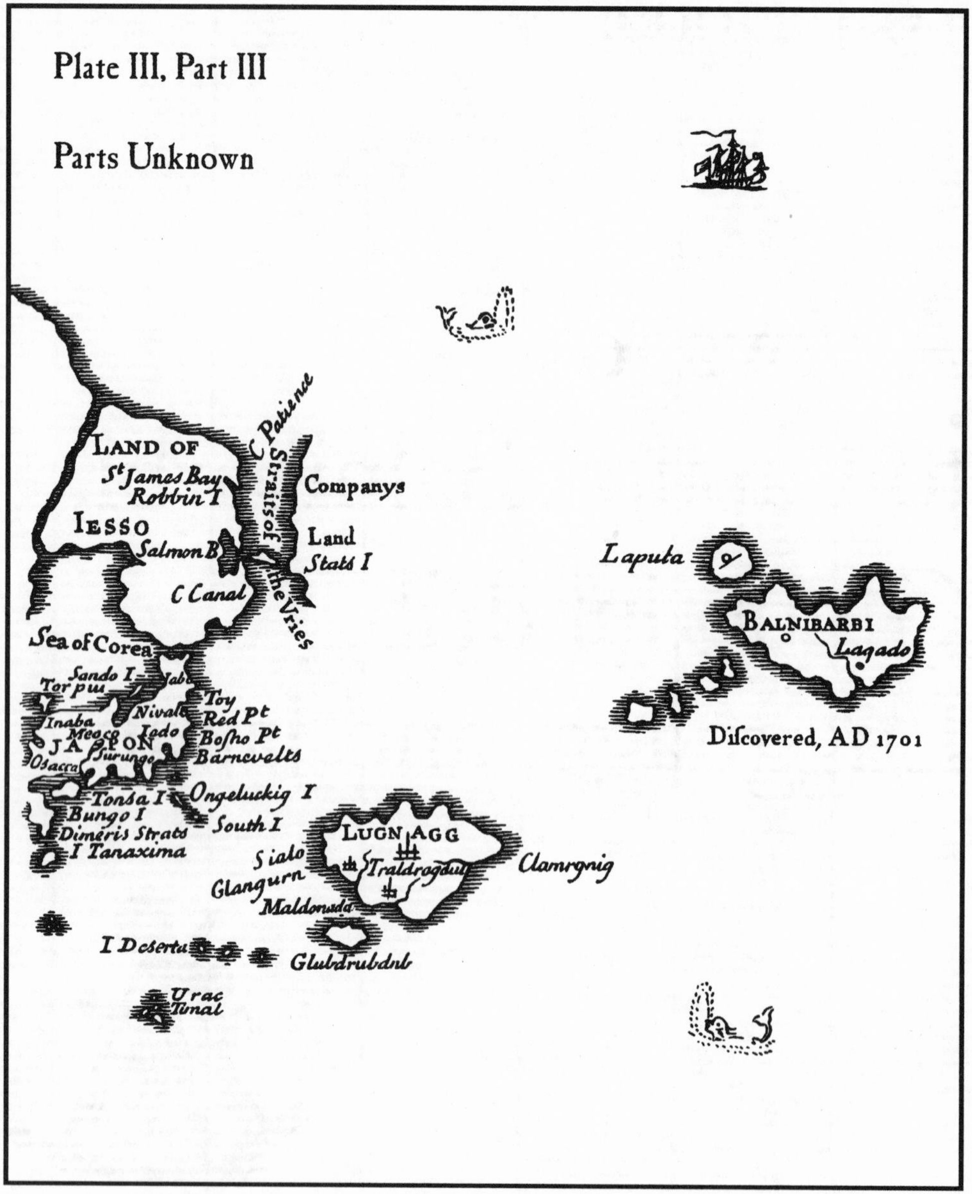

Plate III, Part III

Parts Unknown

Land of
St James Bay
Robbin I
Iesso
Salmon B
C Canal
C Patience
Straits of the Vries
Companys
Land
Stats I
Sea of Corea
Sando I
Torpui
Inaba
Meaco
Nivali
Iedo
Japon
Surungo
Osacca
Toy
Red Pt
Bosho Pt
Barnevalts
Tonsa I
Ongeluckig I
Bungo I
South I
Diméris Strats
I Tanaxima
Laputa
Balnibarbi
Lagado
Discovered, AD 1701
Lugnagg
Traldragdub
Clamrgnig
Sialo
Glangurn
Maldonada
I Deserta
Glubdrubdrib
Urac
Timal

Chapter One

The author sets out on his third voyage; is taken by pirates. The malice of a Dutchman. His arrival at an island. He is received into Laputa.

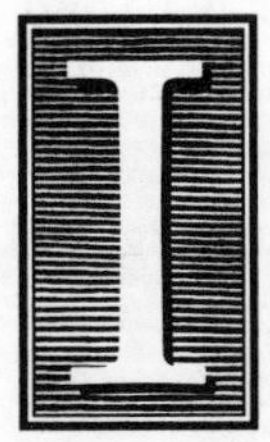

HAD NOT BEEN AT HOME ABOVE TEN DAYS, WHEN Captain William Robinson, a Cornish man, commander of the *Hope-well,* a stout ship of three hundred tons, came to my house. I had formerly been surgeon of another ship where he was master, and a fourth part owner, in a voyage to the Levant; he had always treated me more like a brother than an inferior officer, and hearing of my arrival made me a visit, as I apprehended, only out of friendship, for nothing passed more than what is usual after long absences. But repeating his visits often, expressing his joy to find me in good health, asking whether I were now settled for life, adding that he intended a voyage to the East Indies, in two months, at last he plainly invited me, though with some apologies, to be surgeon of the ship; that I should have another surgeon under me besides our two mates; that my salary should be double to the usual pay; and that having experienced my knowledge in sea-affairs to be at least equal to his, he would enter into any engagement to follow my advice, as much as if I had share in the command.

He said so many other obliging things, and I knew him to be so honest a man, that I could not reject his proposal; the thirst I had of seeing the world, notwithstanding my past misfortunes, continuing as violent as ever. The only difficulty that remained was to persuade my

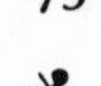

wife, whose consent however I at last obtained, by the prospect of advantage she proposed to her children.

We set out the 5th day of August, 1706, and arrived at Fort St. George[1] the 11th of April, 1708; stayed there three weeks to refresh our crew, many of whom were sick. From thence we went to Tonquin, where the captain resolved to continue some time, because many of the goods he intended to buy were not ready, nor could he expect to be dispatched in some months. Therefore in hopes to defray some of the charges he must be at, he bought a sloop, loaded it with several sorts of goods, wherewith the Tonquinese usually trade to the neighbouring islands, and putting fourteen men on board, whereof three were of the country, he appointed me master of the sloop, and gave me power to traffic for two months, while he transacted his affairs at Tonquin.

We had not sailed above three days, when, a great storm arising, we were driven five days to the north-northeast, and then to the east, after which we had fair weather, but still with a pretty strong gale from the west. Upon the tenth day we were chased by two pirates, who soon overtook us; for my sloop was so deep loaden, that she sailed very slow, neither were we in a condition to defend ourselves.

We were boarded about the same time by both the pirates, who entered furiously at the head of their men, but finding us all prostrate upon our faces (for so I gave order), they pinioned us with strong ropes, and setting a guard upon us, went to search the sloop.

I observed among them a Dutchman, who seemed to be of some authority, though he was not commander of either ship. He knew us by our countenances to be Englishmen, and jabbering to us in his own language, swore we should be tied back to back, and thrown into the sea.[2] I spoke Dutch tolerably well; I told him who we were, and

1. Madras.

2. The commercial rivalry between Holland and England was still bitter, despite their military alliance. Moreover, Swift was prejudiced against the Dutch, who seldom appear to advantage in his writings.

begged him in consideration of our being Christians and Protestants, of neighbouring countries, in strict alliance, that he would move the captains to take some pity on us. This inflamed his rage, he repeated his threatenings, and turning to his companions, spoke with great vehemence, in the Japanese language, as I suppose, often using the word *'Christianos'*.

The largest of the two pirate ships was commanded by a Japanese captain, who spoke a little Dutch, but very imperfectly. He came up to me, and after several questions, which I answered in great humility, he said we should not die. I made the captain a very low bow, and then turning to the Dutchman, said, I was sorry to find more mercy in a heathen, than in a brother Christian. But I had soon reason to repent those foolish words; for that malicious reprobate, having often endeavoured in vain to persuade both the captains that I might be thrown into the sea (which they would not yield to after the promise made me, that I should not die), however prevailed so far as to have a punishment inflicted on me, worse in all human appearance than death itself. My men were sent by an equal division into both the pirate ships, and my sloop new manned. As to myself, it was determined that I should be set adrift in a small canoe, with paddles and a sail, and four days' provisions, which last the Japanese captain was so kind to double out of his own stores, and would permit no man to search me. I got down into the canoe, while the Dutchman, standing upon the deck, loaded me with all the curses and injurious terms his language could afford.

About an hour before we saw the pirates, I had taken an observation, and found we were in the latitude of 46 N. and of longitude 183.[3] When I was at some distance from the pirates, I discovered by my pocket-glass several islands to the southeast. I set up my sail, the wind being fair, with a design to reach the nearest of those islands, which I

3. Longitude was commonly reckoned eastward around the globe: 183° equals 177° west. The position thus indicated is inconsistent with the geographical data given later: the correct position is probably about 19° north, 145° west.

made a shift to do in about three hours. It was all rocky; however I got many birds' eggs, and striking fire I kindled some heath and dry seaweed, by which I roasted my eggs. I eat no other supper, being resolved to spare my provisions as much as I could. I passed the night under the shelter of a rock, strowing some heath under me, and slept pretty well.

The next day I sailed to another island, and thence to a third and fourth, sometimes using my sail, and sometimes my paddles. But not to trouble the reader with a particular account of my distresses, let it suffice that on the 5th day I arrived at the last island in my sight, which lay south-southeast to the former.

This island was at a greater distance than I expected, and I did not reach it in less than five hours. I encompassed it almost round before I could find a convenient place to land in, which was a small creek, about three times the wideness of my canoe. I found the island to be all rocky, only a little intermingled with tufts of grass, and sweet-smelling herbs. I took out my small provisions, and after having refreshed myself, I secured the remainder in a cave, whereof there were great numbers. I gathered plenty of eggs upon the rocks, and got a quantity of dry seaweed, and parched grass, which I designed to kindle the next day, and roast my eggs as well as I could. (For I had about me my flint, steel, match,[4] and burning-glass.) I lay all night in the cave where I had lodged my provisions. My bed was the same dry grass and seaweed which I intended for fuel. I slept very little, for the disquiets of my mind prevailed over my weariness, and kept me awake. I considered how impossible it was to preserve my life, in so desolate a place, and how miserable my end must be. Yet I found myself so listless and desponding, that I had not the heart to rise, and before I could get spirits enough to creep out of my cave, the day was far advanced. I walked a while among the rocks; the sky was perfectly

4. The 'match' of Swift's day was a small piece of wood, cloth, cord, or paper, dipped in sulfur, so that it could be easily lighted by flint and steel.

clear, and the sun so hot, that I was forced to turn my face from it: when all on a sudden it became obscured, as I thought, in a manner very different from what happens by the interposition of a cloud. I turned back, and perceived a vast opaque body between me and the sun, moving forwards towards the island: it seemed to be about two miles high, and hid the sun six or seven minutes, but I did not observe the air to be much colder, or the sky more darkened, than if I had stood under the shade of a mountain. As it approached nearer over the place where I was, it appeared to be a firm substance, the bottom flat, smooth, and shining very bright from the reflection of the sea below. I stood upon a height about two hundred yards from the shore, and saw this vast body descending almost to a parallel with me, at less than an English mile distance. I took out my pocket-perspective, and could plainly discover numbers of people moving up and down the sides of it, which appeared to be sloping, but what those people were doing I was not able to distinguish.

The natural love of life gave me some inward motions of joy, and I was ready to entertain a hope, that this adventure might some way or other help to deliver me from the desolate place and condition I was in. But at the same time the reader can hardly conceive my astonishment, to behold an island in the air, inhabited by men, who were able (as it should seem) to raise, or sink, or put it into a progressive motion, as they pleased. But not being at that time in a disposition to philosophize upon this phænomenon, I rather chose to observe what course the island would take, because it seemed for a while to stand still. Yet soon after it advanced nearer, and I could see the sides of it, encompassed with several gradations of galleries, and stairs, at certain intervals, to descend from one to the other. In the lowest gallery, I beheld some people fishing with long angling rods, and others looking on. I waved my cap (for my hat was long since worn out) and my handkerchief towards the island; and upon its nearer approach, I called and shouted with the utmost strength of my voice; and then looking circumspectly, I beheld a crowd gathered to that side which was most in my view. I found by their pointing towards me and to each other, that they plainly discovered me, although they made no return to my shouting. But I could see four or five men running in great haste up the stairs to the top of the island, who then disappeared. I happened rightly to conjecture, that these were sent for orders to some person in authority upon this occasion.

The number of people encreased, and in less than half an hour the island was moved and raised in such a manner, that the lowest gallery appeared in a parallel of less than an hundred yards' distance from the height where I stood. I then put myself into the most supplicating postures, and spoke in the humblest accent, but received no answer. Those who stood nearest over against me seemed to be persons of distinction, as I supposed by their habit. They conferred earnestly with each other, looking often upon me. At length one of them called out in a clear, polite, smooth dialect, not unlike in sound to the Italian; and therefore I returned an answer in that language, hoping at least that the cadence might be more agreeable to his ears. Although neither of us understood the other, yet my meaning was easily known, for the people saw the distress I was in.

They made signs for me to come down from the rock, and go towards the shore, which I accordingly did; and the flying island being raised to a convenient height, the verge directly over me, a chain was let down from the lowest gallery, with a seat fastened to the bottom, to which I fixed myself, and was drawn up by pulleys.

M·S

But at the same time the reader can hardly conceive my astonishment, to behold an island in the air,...

PAGE 177

CHAPTER TWO

The humours and dispositions of the Laputians described. An account of their learning. Of the King and his court. The author's reception there. The inhabitants subject to fears and disquietudes. An account of the women.

T MY ALIGHTING I WAS SURROUNDED BY A CROWD of people, but those who stood nearest seemed to be of better quality. They beheld me with all the marks and circumstances of wonder, neither indeed was I much in their debt, having never till then seen a race of mortals so singular in their shapes, habits, and countenances. Their heads were all reclined either to the right, or the left; one of their eyes turned inward, and the other directly up to the zenith. Their outward garments were adorned with the figures of suns, moons, and stars, interwoven with those of fiddles, flutes, harps, trumpets, guitars, harpsichords, and many more instruments of music, unknown to us in Europe.[1] I observed here and there many in the habits of servants, with a blown bladder fastened like a flail to the end of a short stick, which they carried in their hands. In each bladder was a small quantity of dried pease or little pebbles (as I was afterwards informed). With these bladders they now and then flapped the mouths and ears of those who stood near them, of which practice I could not then conceive the meaning; it seems, the minds of these people are so taken up with intense speculations, that they neither can

1. These people represent the Englishmen of George I's reign who were interested in abstract science (especially astronomy and higher mathematics) and in the theory of music.

speak, nor attend to the discourses of others, without being roused by some external taction upon the organs of speech and hearing; for which reason those persons who are able to afford it always keep a flapper (the original is *'climenole'*) in their family, as one of their domestics, nor ever walk abroad or make visits without him. And the business of this officer is, when two, three, or more persons are in company, gently to strike with his bladder the mouth of him who is to speak, and the right ear of him or them to whom the speaker addresseth himself. This flapper is likewise employed diligently to attend his master in his walks, and upon occasion to give him a soft flap on his eyes, because he is always so wrapped up in cogitation, that he is in manifest danger of falling down every precipice, and bouncing his head against every post, and in the streets, of justling others or being justled himself into the kennel.[2]

It was necessary to give the reader this information, without which he would be at the same loss with me, to understand the proceedings of these people, as they conducted me up the stairs, to the top of the island, and from thence to the royal palace. While we were ascending, they forgot several times what they were about, and left me to myself, till their memories were again roused by their flappers; for they appeared altogether unmoved by the sight of my foreign habit and countenance, and by the shouts of the vulgar, whose thoughts and minds were more disengaged.

At last we entered the palace, and proceeded into the chamber of presence, where I saw the King[3] seated on his throne, attended on each side by persons of prime quality. Before the throne was a large table filled with globes and spheres, and mathematical instruments of all kinds. His Majesty took not the least notice of us, although our entrance was not without sufficient noise, by the concourse of all

2. Gutter.

3. George I. Having come to England from Hanover at the age of fifty-four, he spoke only broken English, and naturally had no interest in English literature: he patronized music and, less extensively, science, of which, however, he had little personal knowledge.

persons belonging to the court. But he was then deep in a problem, and we attended at least an hour, before he could solve it. There stood by him, on each side, a young page, with flaps in their hands, and when they saw he was at leisure, one of them gently struck his mouth, and the other his right ear, at which he started like one awaked on the sudden, and looking towards me, and the company I was in, recollected the occasion of our coming, whereof he had been informed before. He spoke some words, whereupon immediately a young man with a flap came up to my side, and flapped me gently on the right ear; but I made signs as well as I could, that I had no occasion for such an instrument; which as I afterwards found gave his Majesty and the whole court a very mean opinion of my understanding. The King, as far as I could conjecture, asked me several questions, and I addressed myself to him in all the languages I had. When it was found that I could neither understand nor be understood, I was conducted by the King's order to an apartment in his palace (this prince being distinguished above all his predecessors for his hospitality to strangers),[4] where two servants were appointed to attend me. My dinner was brought, and four persons of quality, whom I remembered to have seen very near the King's person, did me the honour to dine with me. We had two courses, of three dishes each. In the first course there was a shoulder of mutton, cut into an æquilateral triangle, a piece of beef into a rhomboides, and a pudding into a cycloid. The second course was two ducks, trussed up into the form of fiddles; sausages and puddings resembling flutes and hautboys,[5] and a breast of veal in the shape of a harp. The servants cut our bread into cones, cylinders, parallelograms, and several other mathematical figures.

While we were at dinner, I made bold to ask the names of several things in their language, and those noble persons, by the assistance of

4. The English resented George's appointments of numerous Hanoverian favorites to posts of honor and profit in England.

5. Oboes.

their flappers, delighted to give me answers, hoping to raise my admiration of their great abilities, if I could be brought to converse with them. I was soon able to call for bread and drink, or whatever else I wanted.

After dinner my company withdrew, and a person was sent to me by the King's order, attended by a flapper. He brought with him pen, ink, and paper, and three or four books, giving me to understand by signs, that he was sent to teach me the language. We sat together four hours, in which time I wrote down a great number of words in columns, with the translations over against them. I likewise made a shift to learn several short sentences. For my tutor would order one of my servants to fetch something, to turn about, to make a bow, to sit, or stand, or walk and the like. Then I took down the sentence in writing. He showed me also in one of his books the figures of the sun, moon, and stars, the zodiac, the tropics, and polar circles, together with the denominations of many figures of planes and solids. He gave me the names and descriptions of all the musical instruments, and the general terms of art in playing on each of them. After he had left me, I placed all my words with their interpretations in alphabetical order. And thus in a few days, by the help of a very faithful memory, I got some insight into their language.

The[6] word which I interpret the 'Flying' or 'Floating Island' is in the original *'Laputa'*, whereof I could never learn the true etymology. *'Lap'* in the old obsolete language signifieth 'high', and *'untuh'* 'a governor', from which they say by corruption was derived *'Laputa'*, from *'lapuntuh'*. But I do not approve of this derivation, which seems to be a little strained. I ventured to offer to the learned among them a conjecture of my own, that *'Laputa'* was *quasi 'lap outed'*; *'lap'* signifying properly 'the dancing of the sunbeams in the sea', and *'outed'* 'a wing', which however I shall not obtrude, but submit to the judicious reader.

6. This paragraph satirizes contemporary philology.

Those to whom the King had entrusted me, observing how ill I was clad, ordered a tailor to come next morning, and take my measure for a suit of clothes. This operator did his office after a different manner from those of his trade in Europe. He first took my altitude by a quadrant, and then, with rule and compasses, described the dimensions and outlines of my whole body, all which he entered upon paper, and in six days brought my clothes very ill made, and quite out of shape, by happening to mistake a figure in the calculation.[7] But my comfort was, that I observed such accidents very frequent and little regarded.

During my confinement for want of clothes, and by an indisposition that held me some days longer, I much enlarged my dictionary; and when I went next to court, was able to understand many things the King spoke, and to return him some kind of answers. His Majesty had given orders that the island should move northeast and by east, to the vertical point over Lagado,[8] the metropolis of the whole kingdom below upon the firm earth. It was about ninety leagues distant, and our voyage lasted four days and an half. I was not in the least sensible of the progressive motion made in the air by the island. On the second morning about eleven o'clock, the King himself in person, attended by his nobility, courtiers, and officers, having prepared all their musical instruments, played on them for three hours without intermission, so that I was quite stunned with the noise; neither could I possibly guess the meaning till my tutor informed me. He said that the people of their island had their ears adapted to hear the music of the spheres, which always played at certain periods, and the court was now prepared to bear their part in what ever instrument they most excelled.

7. This incident has generally been held to refer to an error in a scientific paper by Sir Isaac Newton, caused by the printer's adding a cipher to the number expressing the distance between the sun and the earth. Swift disliked Newton because the latter had supported the English government in the dispute with Ireland concerning Wood's coinage.
8. London.

In our journey towards Lagado, the capital city, his Majesty ordered that the island should stop over certain towns and villages, from whence he might receive the petitions of his subjects. And to this purpose several packthreads were let down with small weights at the bottom. On these packthreads the people strung their petitions, which mounted up directly like the scraps of paper fastened by school-boys at the end of the string that holds their kite. Sometimes we received wine and victuals from below, which were drawn up by pulleys.

The knowledge I had in mathematics gave me great assistance in acquiring their phraseology, which depended much upon that science and music; and in the latter I was not unskilled. Their ideas are perpetually conversant in lines and figures. If they would, for example, praise the beauty of a woman or any other animal, they describe it by rhombs, circles, parallelograms, ellipses, and other geometrical terms, or by words of art drawn from music, needless here to repeat. I observed in the King's kitchen all sorts of mathematical and musical instruments, after the figures of which they cut up the joints that were served to his Majesty's table.

Their houses are very ill built, the walls bevil, without one right angle in any apartment, and this defect ariseth from the contempt they bear to practical geometry, which they despise as vulgar and mechanic, those instructions they give being too refined for the intellectuals of their workmen, which occasions perpetual mistakes. And although they are dextrous enough upon a piece of paper in the management of the rule, the pencil, and the divider, yet in the common actions and behaviour of life I have not seen a more clumsy, awkward, and unhandy people, nor so slow and perplexed in their conceptions upon all other subjects, except those of mathematics and music. They are very bad reasoners, and vehemently given to opposition, unless when they happen to be of the right opinion, which is seldom their case. Imagination, fancy, and invention, they are wholly strangers to, nor have any words in their language by which those ideas can be expressed; the whole compass of their thoughts and mind being shut up within the two forementioned sciences.

Most of them, and especially those who deal in the astronomical part, have great faith in judicial astrology, although they are ashamed to own it publicly.[9] But what I chiefly admired, and thought altogether unaccountable, was the strong disposition I observed in them towards news and politics, perpetually enquiring into public affairs, giving their judgments in matters of state, and passionately disputing every inch of a party opinion. I have indeed observed the same disposition among most of the mathematicians I have known in Europe, although I could never discover the least analogy between the two sciences; unless those people suppose, that because the smallest circle hath as many degrees as the largest, therefore the regulation and management of the world require no more abilities than the handling and turning of a globe. But I rather take this quality to spring from a very common infirmity of human nature, inclining us to be more curious[10] and conceited in matters where we have least concern, and for which we are least adapted either by study or nature.

These people are under continual disquietudes, never enjoying a minute's peace of mind; and their disturbances proceed from causes which very little affect the rest of mortals. Their apprehensions arise from several changes they dread in the celestial bodies. For instance; that the earth, by the continual approaches of the sun towards it, must in course of time be absorbed or swallowed up. That the face of the sun will by degrees be encrusted with its own effluvia, and give no more light to the world. That the earth very narrowly escaped a brush from the tail of the last comet, which would have infallibly reduced it to ashes; and that the next, which they have calculated for one and thirty years hence, will probably destroy us. For, if in its perihelion it

9. Possibly a reference to Edmond Halley, the astronomer, who had thought it necessary, in predicting the solar eclipse of 1715, to assure the public that the event had no astrological significance, and had thereby drawn some ridicule upon himself.
10. Painstaking.

should approach within a certain degree of the sun (as by their calculations they have reason to dread), it will conceive a degree of heat ten thousand times more intense than that of red-hot glowing iron; and in its absence from the sun, carry a blazing tail ten hundred thousand and fourteen miles long; through which if the earth should pass at the distance of one hundred thousand miles from the nucleus or main body of the comet, it must in its passage be set on fire, and reduced to ashes. That the sun daily spending its rays without any nutriment to supply them, will at last be wholly consumed and annihilated; which must be attended with the destruction of this earth, and of all the planets that receive their light from it.[11]

They are so perpetually alarmed with the apprehensions of these and the like impending dangers, that they can neither sleep quietly in their beds, nor have any relish for the common pleasures or amusements of life. When they meet an acquaintance in the morning, the first question is about the sun's health, how he looked at his setting and rising, and what hopes they have to avoid the stroke of the approaching comet. This conversation they are apt to run into with the same temper that boys discover, in delighting to hear terrible stories of sprites and hobgoblins, which they greedily listen to, and dare not go to bed for fear.

The women of the island have abundance of vivacity; they contemn their husbands, and are exceedingly fond of strangers, whereof there is always a considerable number from the continent below, attending at court, either upon affairs of the several towns and corporations, or their own particular occasions, but are much despised, because they want the same endowments. Among these the ladies choose their gallants: but the vexation is, that they act with too much ease and security, for the husband is always so rapt in speculation, that the mistress and lover may proceed to the greatest familiarities before his

11. Several astronomers in England had discussed the possibility of an astronomical catastrophe involving the earth.

face, if he be but provided with paper and implements, and without his flapper at his side.

The wives and daughters lament their confinement to the island, although I think it the most delicious spot of ground in the world; and although they live here in the greatest plenty and magnificence, and are allowed to do whatever they please, they long to see the world, and take the diversions of the metropolis, which they are not allowed to do without a particular licence from the King; and this is not easy to be obtained, because the people of quality have found by frequent experience how hard it is to persuade their women to return from below. I was told[12] that a great court lady, who had several children, is married to the prime minister, the richest subject in the kingdom, a very graceful person, extremely fond of her, and lives in the finest palace of the island, went down to Lagado, on the pretence of health, there hid herself for several months, till the King sent a warrant to search for her, and she was found in an obscure eating house all in rags, having pawned her clothes to maintain an old deformed footman, who beat her every day, and in whose company she was taken much against her will. And although her husband received her with all possible kindness, and without the least reproach, she soon after contrived to steal down again with all her jewels, to the same gallant, and hath not been heard of since.

This may perhaps pass with the reader rather for an European or English story, than for one of a country so remote. But he may please to consider, that the caprices of womankind are not limited by any climate or nation, and that they are much more uniform than can be easily imagined.

In about a month's time I had made a tolerable proficiency in their language, and was able to answer most of the King's questions, when I had the honour to attend him. His Majesty discovered not the least

12. The story that follows is another reference to the infidelities of Lady Walpole. The real purpose of the allusion, of course, is the jest at Walpole: Swift points it by making the patient husband the prime minister of Laputa.

curiosity to enquire into the laws, government, history, religion, or manners of the countries where I had been, but confined his questions to the state of mathematics, and received the account I gave him with great contempt and indifference, though often roused by his flapper on each side.

Chapter Three

A phænomenon solved by modern philosophy and astronomy. The Laputians' great improvements in the latter. The King's method of suppressing insurrections.

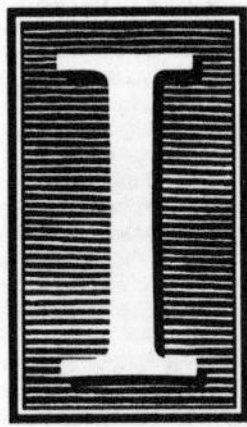

DESIRED LEAVE OF THIS PRINCE TO SEE THE CURIOSITIES of the island, which he was graciously pleased to grant, and ordered my tutor to attend me. I chiefly wanted to know to what cause in art or in nature it owed its several motions, whereof I will now give a philosophical account to the reader.[1]

The Flying or Floating Island is exactly circular, its diameter 7,837 yards, or about four miles and an half, and consequently contains ten thousand acres. It is three hundred yards thick. The bottom or under surface, which appears to those who view it from below, is one even regular plate of adamant, shooting up to the height of about two hundred yards. Above it lie the several minerals in their usual order, and over all is a coat of rich mould ten or twelve foot deep. The declivity of the upper surface, from the circumference to the center, is the natural cause why all the dews and rains which fall upon the island are conveyed in small rivulets towards the middle, where they are emptied into four large basons, each of about half a mile in circuit, and two hundred yards distant from the center. From these basons the water is continually exhaled by the sun in the day time, which effectually prevents their overflowing. Besides, as it is in the power of the

1. The account which follows is a parody of the learned papers published in the transactions of the Royal Society.

monarch to raise the island above the region of clouds and vapours, he can prevent the falling of dews and rains when ever he pleases. For the highest clouds cannot rise above two miles, as naturalists agree, at least they were never known to do in that country.

At the center of the island there is a chasm about fifty yards in diameter, from whence the astronomers descend into a large dome, which is therefore called *'Flandona Gagnole'*,[2] or the 'Astronomer's Cave', situated at the depth of an hundred yards beneath the upper surface of the adamant. In this cave are twenty lamps continually burning, which from the reflection of the adamant cast a strong light into every part. The place is stored with great variety of sextants, quadrants, telescopes, astrolabes, and other astronomical instruments. But the greatest curiosity, upon which the fate of the island depends, is a loadstone of a prodigious size, in shape resembling a weaver's shuttle. It is in length six yards, and in the thickest part at least three yards over. This magnet is sustained by a very strong axle of adamant passing through its middle, upon which it plays, and is poised so exactly that the weakest hand can turn it. It is hooped round with an hollow cylinder of adamant, four foot deep, as many thick, and twelve yards in diameter, placed horizontally, and supported by eight adamantine feet, each six yards high. In the middle of the concave side there is a groove twelve inches deep, in which the extremities of the axle are lodged, and turned round as there is occasion.

The stone cannot be moved from its place by any force, because the hoop and its feet are one continued piece with that body of adamant which constitutes the bottom of the island.

By means of this loadstone, the island is made to rise and fall, and move from one place to another. For, with respect to that part of the earth over which the monarch presides, the stone is endued at one of its sides with an attractive power, and at the other with a repulsive.

2. Possibly intended to suggest Flamsteed House, the first building of the Royal Observatory in Greenwich.

Upon placing the magnet erect with its attracting end towards the earth, the island descends; but when the repelling extremity points downwards, the island mounts directly upwards. When the position of the stone is oblique, the motion of the island is so too. For in this magnet the forces always act in lines parallel to its direction.

By this oblique motion the island is conveyed to different parts of the monarch's dominions. To explain the manner of its progress, let *A B* represent a line drawn cross the dominions of Balnibarbi, let the line *c d* represent the loadstone, of which let *d* be the repelling end, and *c* the attracting end, the island being over *C*; let the stone be placed in the position *c d* with its repelling end downwards; then the island will be driven upwards obliquely towards *D*. When it is arrived at *D*, let the stone be turned upon its axle till its attracting end points towards *E*, and then the island will be carried obliquely towards *E*; where if the stone be again turned upon its axle till it stands in the position *E F*, with its repelling point downwards, the island will rise obliquely towards *F*, where by directing the attracting end towards *G*, the island may be carried to *G*, and from *G* to *H*, by turning the stone, so as to make its repelling extremity point directly downwards. And thus by changing the situation of the stone as often as there is occasion, the island is made to rise and fall by turns in an oblique direction, and by those alternate risings and fallings (the obliquity being not considerable) is conveyed from one part of the dominions to the other.

But it must be observed, that this island cannot move beyond the extent of the dominions below, nor can it rise above the height of four miles. For which the astronomers (who have written large systems concerning the stone) assign the following reason: that the magnetic virtue does not extend beyond the distance of four miles, and that the mineral which acts upon the stone in the bowels of the earth, and in the sea about six leagues distant from the shore, is not diffused through the whole globe, but terminated with the limits of the King's dominions; and it was easy, from the great advantage of such a supe-

Plate IV, Part III

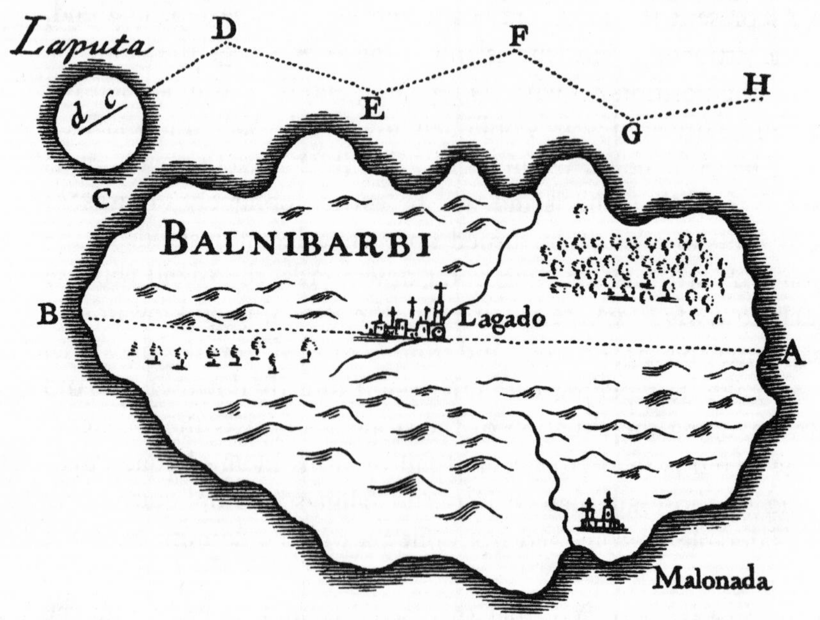

rior situation, for a prince to bring under his obedience whatever country lay within the attraction of that magnet.[3]

When the stone is put parallel to the plane of the horizon, the island standeth still; for in that case, the extremities of it, being at equal distance from the earth, act with equal force, the one in drawing downwards, the other in pushing upwards, and consequently no motion can ensue.

This loadstone is under the care of certain astronomers, who from time to time give it such positions as the monarch directs. They spend the greatest part of their lives in observing the celestial bodies, which they do by the assistance of glasses far excelling ours in goodness. For although their largest telescopes do not exceed three feet, they magnify much more than those of an hundred yards among us, and at the same time show the stars with greater clearness. This advantage hath enabled them to extend their discoveries much farther than our astronomers in Europe; for they have made a catalogue of ten thousand fixed stars, whereas the largest of ours do not contain above one third part of that number.[4] They have likewise discovered two lesser stars, or 'satellites', which revolve about Mars, whereof the innermost is distant from the center of the primary planet exactly three of his diameters, and the outermost five; the former revolves in the space of ten hours, and the latter in twenty-one and an half; so that the squares of their periodical times are very near in the same proportion with the cubes of their distance from the center of Mars, which evidently shows them to be governed by the same law of gravitation, that influences the other heavenly bodies.[5]

They have observed ninety-three different comets, and settled their periods with great exactness. If this be true (and they affirm it with

3. Laputa represents the English court and cabinet, the dominions below the kingdoms of Great Britain and Ireland.

4. The British catalogue of 2,935 fixed stars had been published in 1725 after prolonged controversy in the scientific world. It was chiefly the work of Flamsteed.

5. Oddly enough, Swift guessed with considerable accuracy about these satellites, which were not observed until 1877.

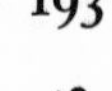

great confidence) it is much to be wished that their observations were made public, whereby the theory of comets, which at present is very lame and defective, might be brought to the same perfection with other parts of astronomy.[6]

The King would be the most absolute prince in the universe, if he could but prevail on a ministry to join with him; but these having their estates below on the continent, and considering that the office of a favourite hath a very uncertain tenure, would never consent to the enslaving their country.

If any town should engage in rebellion or mutiny, fall into violent factions, or refuse to pay the usual tribute, the King hath two methods of reducing them to obedience. The first and the mildest course is by keeping the island hovering over such a town, and the lands about it, whereby he can deprive them of the benefit of the sun and the rain, and consequently afflict the inhabitants with dearth and diseases. And if the crime deserve it, they are at the same time pelted from above with great stones, against which they have no defence but by creeping into cellars or caves, while the roofs of their houses are beaten to pieces. But if they still continue obstinate, or offer to raise insurrections, he proceeds to the last remedy, by letting the island drop directly upon their heads, which makes a universal destruction both of houses and men. However, this is an extremity to which the prince is seldom driven, neither indeed is he willing to put it in execution, nor dare his ministers advise him to an action which, as it would render them odious to the people, so it would be a great damage to their own estates, which lie all below, for the island is the King's demesne.

But there is still indeed a more weighty reason, why the kings of this country have been always averse from executing so terrible an action, unless upon the utmost necessity. For if the town intended to

6. The researches of Halley and others into the periodicity of comets had aroused great interest: Halley's theories were not verified, however, until the return, in 1759, of the comet that now bears his name.

be destroyed should have in it any tall rocks,[7] as it generally falls out in the larger cities, a situation probably chosen at first with a view to prevent such a catastrophe; or if it abound in high spires[8] or pillars of stone,[9] a sudden fall might endanger the bottom or under surface of the island, which although it consist, as I have said, of one entire adamant two hundred yards thick, might happen to crack by too great a shock, or burst by approaching too near the fires from the houses below, as the backs both of iron and stone will often do in our chimneys.[10] Of all this the people are well apprised, and understand how far to carry their obstinacy, where their liberty or property is concerned. And the King, when he is highest provoked, and most determined to press a city to rubbish, orders the island to descend with great gentleness, out of a pretence of tenderness to his people, but indeed for fear of breaking the adamantine bottom; in which case it is the opinion of all their philosophers, that the loadstone could no longer hold it up, and the whole mass would fall to the ground.

About three years before my arrival among them, while the King was in his progress over his dominions, there happened an extraordinary accident which had like to have put a period to the fate of that monarchy, at least as it is now instituted. Lindalino, the second city in the kingdom,[11] was the first his Majesty visited in his progress. Three days after his departure, the inhabitants, who had often complained of great oppressions, shut the town gates, seized on the governor, and with incredible speed and labour erected four large towers,[12] one at every corner of the city (which is an exact square), equal in height to a

7. Possibly representing powerful hereditary peers.
8. Eminent churchmen.
9. Perhaps influential 'self-made' men.
10. The adamantine bottom may stand for the British constitution, or for the monarchy.
11. Dublin. What follows is an allegorical account of the Irish resistance, in 1722–24, against the introduction into the country of copper coins manufactured by an English ironmonger named Wood. This man had bought the privilege from a mistress of George I, to whom it had been given by a political deal.
12. Perhaps the Grand Jury, the Irish Privy Council, and the two Houses of the Irish Parliament are to be understood.

strong pointed rock that stands directly in the center of the city.[13] Upon the top of each tower, as well as upon the rock, they fixed a great loadstone, and in case their design should fail, they had provided a vast quantity of the most combustible fuel, hoping to burst therewith the adamantine bottom of the island, if the loadstone project should miscarry.

It was eight months before the King had perfect notice that the Lindalinians were in rebellion.[14] He then commanded that the island should be wafted over the city. The people were unanimous, and had laid in store of provisions, and a great river runs through the middle of the town. The King hovered over them several days to deprive them of the sun and the rain. He ordered many packthreads to be let down, yet not a person offered to send up a petition, but instead thereof, very bold demands, the redress of all their grievances, great immunities, the choice of their own governor, and other the like exorbitances. Upon which his Majesty commanded all the inhabitants of the island to cast great stones from the lower gallery into the town; but the citizens had provided against this mischief by conveying their persons and effects into the four towers, and other strong buildings, and vaults underground.

The King being now determined to reduce this proud people, ordered that the island should descend gently within forty yards of the top of the towers and rock. This was accordingly done; but the officers employed in that work found the descent much speedier than usual, and by turning the loadstone could not without great difficulty keep it in a firm position, but found the island inclining to fall. They sent the King immediate intelligence of this astonishing event and begged his Majesty's permission to raise the island higher; the King consented, a

13. The Irish Church, headed by the Archbishop and Swift, opposed Wood's patent. Swift was by far the most vigorous antagonist: his anonymous *Drapier's Letters,* rightly regarded as the most effective weapons of the Irish cause, made him the honored champion of the country until his death.

14. The implication is that George's ministers did not always keep him informed about state affairs.

general council was called, and the officers of the loadstone ordered to attend. One of the oldest and expertest among them obtained leave to try an experiment. He took a strong line of an hundred yards, and the island being raised over the town above the attracting power they had felt, he fastened a piece of adamant to the end of his line which had in it a mixture of iron mineral, of the same nature with that whereof the bottom or lower surface of the island is composed, and from the lower gallery let it down slowly towards the top of the towers. The adamant was not descended four yards, before the officer felt it drawn so strongly downwards, that he could hardly pull it back.[15] He then threw down several small pieces of adamant, and observed that they were all violently attracted by the top of the tower. The same experiment was made on the other three towers, and on the rock with the same effect.[16]

This incident broke entirely the King's measures and (to dwell no longer on other circumstances) he was forced to give the town their own conditions.[17]

I was assured by a great minister, that if the island had descended so near the town as not to be able to raise itself, the citizens were determined to fix it for ever, to kill the King and all his servants, and entirely change the government.

By a fundamental law of this realm, neither the King nor either of his two elder sons are permitted to leave the island, nor the Queen, till she is past child-bearing.[18]

15. The Grand Jury of Dublin, despite extraordinary pressure, not only refused to indict anyone who had been concerned with the *Drapier's Letters,* but made official declarations against Wood's coins and those who urged their acceptance.

16. None of the groups opposed to the coins wavered, although threatened with severe penalties.

17. The government eventually gave up the project, canceled the patent, and reimbursed Wood.

18. In 1716 George I secured the repeal of the clause in the Act of Settlement which forbade the king to leave England without the consent of Parliament. He made frequent and prolonged visits to Hanover, his other kingdom, during his reign of thirteen years over England.

CHAPTER FOUR

The author leaves Laputa, is conveyed to Balnibarbi, arrives at the metropolis. A description of the metropolis and the country adjoining. The author hospitably received by a great lord. His conversation with that lord.

LTHOUGH I CANNOT SAY THAT I WAS ILL TREATED in this island, yet I must confess I thought myself too much neglected, not without some degree of contempt. For neither prince nor people appeared to be curious in any part of knowledge, except mathematics and music, wherein I was far their inferior, and upon that account very little regarded.

On the other side, after having seen all the curiosities of the island, I was very desirous to leave it, being heartily weary of those people. They were indeed excellent in two sciences for which I have great esteem, and wherein I am not unversed, but at the same time so abstracted and involved in speculation that I never met with such disagreeable companions. I conversed only with women, tradesmen, flappers, and court-pages, during two months of my abode there, by which at last I rendered myself extremely contemptible, yet these were the only people from whom I could ever receive a reasonable answer.

I had obtained by hard study a good degree of knowledge in their language; I was weary of being confined to an island where I received so little countenance, and resolved to leave it with the first opportunity.

There was a great lord at court,[1] nearly related to the King, and for

1. The Prince of Wales.

that reason alone used with respect. He was universally reckoned the most ignorant and stupid person among them. He had performed many eminent services for the crown, had great natural and acquired parts, adorned with integrity and honour, but so ill an ear for music, that his detractors reported he had been often known to beat time in the wrong place; neither could his tutors without extreme difficulty teach him to demonstrate the most easy proposition in the mathematics.[2] He was pleased to show me many marks of favour, often did me the honour of a visit, desired to be informed in the affairs of Europe, the laws and customs, the manners and learning of the several countries where I had travelled. He listened to me with great attention, and made very wise observations on all I spoke. He had two flappers attending him for state, but never made use of them except at court, and in visits of ceremony, and would always command them to withdraw when we were alone together.

I intreated this illustrious person to intercede in my behalf with his Majesty for leave to depart, which he accordingly did, as he was pleased to tell me, with regret: for indeed he had made me several offers very advantageous, which however I refused with expressions of the highest acknowledgement.

On the 16th day of February, I took leave of his Majesty and the court. The King made me a present to the value of about two hundred pounds English, and my protector his kinsman as much more, together with a letter of recommendation to a friend of his in Lagado, the metropolis; the island being then hovering over a mountain about two miles from it, I was let down from the lowest gallery, in the same manner as I had been taken up.

The continent, as far as it is subject to the monarch of the Flying Island, passes under the general name of Balnibarbi, and the metropolis, as I said before, is called Lagado. I felt some little satisfaction in

2. The Prince was outspoken in his contempt for academic learning, and appears to have patronized music only when he could annoy his father by doing so, as in the case of the famous feud between Händel and Buononcini.

finding myself on firm ground. I walked to the city without any concern, being clad like one of the natives, and sufficiently instructed to converse with them. I soon found out the person's house to whom I was recommended, presented my letter from his friend the grandee in the island, and was received with much kindness. This great lord, whose name was Munodi,[3] ordered me an apartment in his own house, where I continued during my stay, and was entertained in a most hospitable manner.

The next morning after my arrival he took me in his chariot to see the town, which is about half the bigness of London, but the houses very strangely built, and most of them out of repair. The people in the streets walked fast, looked wild, their eyes fixed, and were generally in rags. We passed through one of the town gates, and went about three miles into the country, where I saw many labourers working with several sorts of tools in the ground, but was not able to conjecture what they were about, neither did I observe any expectation either of corn or grass, although the soil appeared to be excellent. I could not forbear admiring at these odd appearances both in town and country, and I made bold to desire my conductor, that he would be pleased to explain to me what could be meant by so many busy heads, hands, and faces, both in the streets and the fields, because I did not discover any good effects they produced; but on the contrary, I never knew a soil so unhappily cultivated, houses so ill contrived and so ruinous, or a people whose countenances and habit expressed so much misery and want.[4]

This Lord Munodi was a person of the first rank, and had been some years Governor of Lagado, but by a cabal of ministers was discharged for insufficiency. However, the King treated him with ten-

3. The Earl of Oxford. The name appears to be compounded from 'mundum odi' ('I hate the world'): if so, it refers to Oxford's retirement into the country and his abstention from public life, after his trial for treason was abandoned in 1717.

4. This picture is Swift's prophetic vision of the future of England in the event of a long continuation of the wave of interest in 'projects' (inventions) and speculation which swept England in the reign of George I.

derness, as a well-meaning man, but of a low contemptible understanding.

When I gave that free censure of the country and its inhabitants, he made no further answer than by telling me that I had not been long enough among them to form a judgment, and that the different nations of the world had different customs, with other common topics to the same purpose. But when we returned to his palace, he asked me how I liked the building, what absurdities I observed, and what quarrel I had with the dress or looks of his domestics. This he might safely do, because every thing about him was magnificent, regular, and polite. I answered that his Excellency's prudence, quality, and fortune had exempted him from those defects which folly and beggary had produced in others. He said if I would go with him to his country house, about twenty miles distant, where his estate lay, there would be more leisure for this kind of conversation. I told his Excellency that I was entirely at his disposal, and accordingly we set out next morning.

During our journey, he made me observe the several methods used by farmers in managing their lands, which to me were wholly unaccountable, for, except in some very few places, I could not discover one ear of corn or blade of grass. But in three hours travelling the scene was wholly altered; we came into a most beautiful country; farmers' houses at small distances, neatly built, the fields inclosed, containing vineyards, corn-grounds, and meadows. Neither do I remember to have seen a more delightful prospect. His Excellency observed my countenance to clear up; he told me with a sigh, that there his estate began, and would continue the same till we should come to his house.[5] That his countrymen ridiculed and despised him for managing his affairs no better, and for setting so ill an example to the kingdom, which however was followed by very few, such as were old and wilful, and weak like himself.

5. Munodi's estate represents England as it might flourish under a government committed to a conservative fiscal policy.

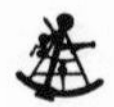

We came at length to the house, which was indeed a noble structure, built according to the best rules of ancient architecture. The fountains, gardens, walks, avenues, and groves were all disposed with exact judgment and taste. I gave due praises to every thing I saw, whereof his Excellency took not the least notice till after supper, when, there being no third companion, he told me with a very melancholy air, that he doubted he must throw down his houses in town and country, to rebuild them after the present mode, destroy all his plantations, and cast others in such a form as modern usage required, and give the same directions to all his tenants, unless he would submit to incur the censure of pride, singularity, affectation, ignorance, caprice, and perhaps encrease his Majesty's displeasure.

That the admiration I appeared to be under would cease or diminish when he had informed me of some particulars, which probably I never heard of at court, the people there being too much taken up in their own speculations to have regard to what passed here below.

The sum of his discourse was to this effect. That about forty years ago, certain persons went up to Laputa either upon business or diversion, and after five months continuance came back with a very little smattering in mathematics, but full of volatile spirits acquired in that airy region. That these persons upon their return began to dislike the management of every thing below, and fell into schemes of putting all arts, sciences, languages, and mechanics upon a new foot. To this end they procured a royal patent for erecting an academy of PROJECTORS[6] in Lagado; and the humour prevailed so strongly among the people, that there is not a town of any consequence in the kingdom without such an academy. In these colleges the professors contrive new rules and methods of agriculture and building, and new instruments and tools for all trades and manufactures, whereby, as they undertake, one man shall do the work of ten; a palace may be built in a week, of materials so durable as to last for ever without repairing. All the fruits

6. The Royal Society of London, founded in 1660.

of the earth shall come to maturity at whatever season we think fit to choose, and encrease an hundred fold more than they do at present, with innumerable other happy proposals. The only inconvenience is, that none of these projects are yet brought to perfection, and in the mean time the whole country lies miserably waste, the houses in ruins, and the people without food or clothes. By all which, instead of being discouraged, they are fifty times more violently bent upon prosecuting their schemes, driven equally on by hope and despair; that as for himself, being not of an enterprising spirit, he was content to go on in the old forms, to live in the houses his ancestors had built, and act as they did in every part of life without innovation. That some few other persons of quality and gentry had done the same, but were looked on with an eye of contempt and ill will, as enemies to art, ignorant, and ill commonwealth's-men, preferring their own ease and sloth before the general improvement of their country.

His Lordship added, that he would not by any further particulars prevent[7] the pleasure I should certainly take in viewing the Grand Academy, whither he was resolved I should go. He only desired me to observe a ruined building upon the side of a mountain about three miles distant, of which he gave me this account. That he had a very convenient mill within half a mile of his house, turned by a current from a large river, and sufficient for his own family as well as a great number of his tenants.[8] That about seven years ago a club of those projectors came to him with proposals to destroy this mill, and build another on the side of that mountain, on the long ridge whereof a long canal must be cut for a repository of water, to be conveyed up by pipes and engines to supply the mill: because the wind and air upon a height agitated the water, and thereby made it fitter for motion: and because the water descending down a declivity would turn the mill

7. Anticipate.

8. The mill is the old English system of providing revenue from taxes sufficient to defray current expenses without incurring a national debt. The 'family' is England, and the 'tenants' are England's allies in the War of the Spanish Succession.

with half the current of a river whose course is more upon a level.[9] He said, that being then not very well with the court, and pressed by many of his friends, he complied with the proposal; and after employing an hundred men for two years, the work miscarried, the projectors went off, laying the blame entirely upon him, railing at him ever since, and putting others upon the same experiment, with equal assurance of success, as well as equal disappointment.

In a few days we came back to town, and his Excellency, considering the bad character he had in the Academy, would not go with me himself, but recommended me to a friend of his to bear me company thither. My Lord was pleased to represent me as a great admirer of projects, and a person of much curiosity and easy belief, which indeed was not without truth, for I had myself been a sort of projector in my younger days.[10]

9. The new mill is the South Sea Company, a highly speculative venture chartered during Oxford's administration, largely upon the advice of Daniel Defoe. It assumed a large part of the national debt: after frantic public speculation in its shares it collapsed in 1720 (the 'South Sea Bubble' year).

10. Possibly a disillusioned comment by Swift on the optimistic desires of reforming the world which he cherished in his youth.

Chapter Five

The author permitted to see the Grand Academy of Lagado. The Academy largely described. The arts wherein the professors employ themselves.

his Academy is not an entire single building, but a continuation of several houses on both sides of a street, which growing waste was purchased and applied to that use.

I was received very kindly by the Warden, and went for many days to the Academy. Every room hath in it one or more projectors, and I believe I could not be in fewer than five hundred rooms.[1]

The first man I saw was of a meager aspect, with sooty hands and face, his hair and beard long, ragged and singed in several places. His clothes, shirt, and skin were all of the same colour. He had been eight years upon a project for extracting sunbeams out of cucumbers, which were to be put into vials hermetically sealed, and let out to warm the air in raw inclement summers. He told me, he did not doubt in eight years more he should be able to supply the Governor's gardens with sunshine at a reasonable rate; but he complained that his stock was low, and intreated me to give him something as an encouragement to ingenuity, especially since this had been a very dear season for cucumbers. I made him a small present, for my Lord had furnished me with

1. Many of the experiments carried on in the Grand Academy are intended to satirize both the activities of contemporary scientists and the impractical political and economic schemes of the Whig administration.

money on purpose, because he knew their practice of begging from all who go to see them.

I went into another chamber, but was ready to hasten back, being almost overcome with an horrible stink. My conductor pressed me forward, conjuring me in a whisper to give no offence, which would be highly resented, and therefore I durst not so much as stop my nose. The projector of this cell was the most ancient student of the Academy. His face and beard were of a pale yellow; his hands and clothes daubed over with filth. When I was presented to him, he gave me a very close embrace (a compliment I could well have excused). His employment from his first coming into the Academy was an operation to reduce human excrement to its original food, by separating the several parts, removing the tincture which it receives from the gall, making the odour exhale, and scumming off the saliva. He had a weekly allowance from the society of a vessel filled with human ordure, about the bigness of a Bristol barrel.

I saw another at work to calcine ice into gunpowder, who likewise showed me a treatise he had written concerning the malleability of fire, which he intended to publish.

There was a most ingenious architect who had contrived a new method for building houses, by beginning at the roof and working downwards to the foundation, which he justified to me by the like practice of those two prudent insects, the bee and the spider.

There was a man born blind, who had several apprentices in his own condition: their employment was to mix colours for painters, which their master taught them to distinguish by feeling and smelling. It was indeed my misfortune to find them at that time not very perfect in their lessons, and the professor himself happened to be generally mistaken: this artist is much encouraged and esteemed by the whole fraternity.

In another apartment I was highly pleased with a projector, who had found a device of plowing the ground with hogs, to save the charges of plows, cattle, and labour. The method is this: in an acre of

ground you bury, at six inches distance, and eight deep, a quantity of acorns, dates, chestnuts, and other mast or vegetables whereof these animals are fondest: then you drive six hundred or more of them into the field, where in a few days they will root up the whole ground in search of their food, and make it fit for sowing, at the same time manuring it with their dung; it is true upon experiment they found the charge and trouble very great, and they had little or no crop. However, it is not doubted that this invention may be capable of great improvement.

I went into another room, where the walls and ceiling were all hung round with cobwebs, except a narrow passage for the artist to go in and out. At my entrance he called aloud to me not to disturb his webs. He lamented the fatal mistake the world had been so long in of using silkworms, while we had such plenty of domestic insects, who infinitely excelled the former, because they understood how to weave as well as spin. And he proposed farther, that by employing spiders the charge of dyeing silks should be wholly saved, whereof I was fully convinced when he showed me a vast number of flies most beautifully coloured, wherewith he fed his spiders, assuring us that the webs would take a tincture from them; and as he had them of all hues, he hoped to fit every body's fancy, as soon as he could find proper food for the flies, of certain gums, oils, and other glutinous matter, to give a strength and consistence to the threads.

There was an astronomer who had undertaken to place a sundial upon the great weathercock on the town-house, by adjusting the annual and diurnal motions of the earth and sun, so as to answer and coincide with all accidental turnings by the wind.

I was complaining of a small fit of the colic, upon which my conductor led me into a room, where a great physician resided, who was famous for curing that disease by contrary operations from the same instrument. He had a large pair of bellows with a long slender muzzle of ivory. This he conveyed eight inches up the anus, and drawing in the wind, he affirmed he could make the guts as lank as a dried

bladder. But when the disease was more stubborn and violent, he let in the muzzle while the bellows were full of wind, which he discharged into the body of the patient, then withdrew the instrument to replenish it, clapping his thumb strongly against the orifice of the fundament; and this being repeated three or four times, the adventitious wind would rush out, bringing the noxious along with it (like water put into a pump) and the patient recover. I saw him try both experiments upon a dog, but could not discern any effect from the former. After the latter, the animal was ready to burst, and made so violent a discharge, as was very offensive to me and my companion. The dog died on the spot, and we left the doctor endeavouring to recover him by the same operation.

I visited many other apartments, but shall not trouble my reader with all the curiosities I observed, being studious of brevity.

I had hitherto seen only one side of the Academy, the other being appropriated to the advancers of speculative learning, of whom I shall say something when I have mentioned one illustrious person more, who is called among them 'the universal artist'. He told us he had been thirty years employing his thoughts for the improvement of human life. He had two large rooms full of wonderful curiosities, and fifty men at work. Some were condensing air into a dry tangible substance, by extracting the nitre, and letting the aqueous or fluid particles percolate; others softening marble for pillows and pincushions; others petrifying the hoofs of a living horse to preserve them from foundering. The artist himself was at that time busy upon two great designs; the first, to sow land with chaff, wherein he affirmed the true seminal virtue to be contained, as he demonstrated by several experiments which I was not skilful enough to comprehend. The other was, by a certain composition of gums, minerals, and vegetables outwardly applied, to prevent the growth of wool upon two young lambs; and he hoped in a reasonable time to propagate the breed of naked sheep all over the kingdom.

We crossed a walk to the other part of the Academy, where, as I have already said, the projectors in speculative learning resided.

The first professor I saw was in a very large room, with forty pupils about him. After salutation, observing me to look earnestly upon a frame, which took up the greatest part of both the length and breadth of the room, he said perhaps I might wonder to see him employed in a project for improving speculative knowledge by practical and mechanical operations. But the world would soon be sensible of its usefulness, and he flattered himself that a more noble exalted thought never sprung in any other man's head. Every one knows how laborious the usual method is of attaining to arts and sciences; whereas by his contrivance the most ignorant person at a reasonable charge, and with a little bodily labour, may write books in philosophy, poetry, politics, law, mathematics, and theology, without the least assistance from genius or study. He then led me to the frame, about the sides whereof all his pupils stood in ranks. It was twenty foot square, placed in the middle of the room. The superficies was composed of several bits of wood, about the bigness of a die, but some larger than others. They were all linked together by slender wires. These bits of wood were covered on every square with papers pasted on them, and on these papers were written all the words of their language in their several moods, tenses, and declensions, but without any order. The professor then desired me to observe, for he was going to set his engine at work. The pupils at his command took each of them hold of an iron handle, whereof there were forty fixed round the edges of the frame, and giving them a sudden turn, the whole disposition of the words was entirely changed. He then commanded six and thirty of the lads to read the several lines softly as they appeared upon the frame; and where they found three or four words together that might make part of a sentence, they dictated to the four remaining boys who were scribes. This work was repeated three or four times, and at every turn the engine was so contrived, that the words shifted into new places, as the square bits of wood moved upside down.

Six hours a day the young students were employed in this labour, and the professor showed me several volumes in large folio already collected, of broken sentences, which he intended to piece together, and out of those rich materials to give the world a complete body of all arts and sciences; which however might be still improved, and much expedited, if the public would raise a fund for making and employing five hundred such frames in Lagado, and oblige the managers to contribute in common their several collections.

He assured me, that this invention had employed all his thoughts from his youth, that he had emptied the whole vocabulary into his frame, and made the strictest computation of the general proportion there is in books between the numbers of particles, nouns, and verbs, and other parts of speech.

I made my humblest acknowledgement to this illustrious person for his great communicativeness, and promised if ever I had the good fortune to return to my native country, that I would do him justice, as the sole inventor of this wonderful machine; the form and contrivance of which I desired leave to delineate upon paper as in the figure here annexed. I told him, although it were the custom of our learned in Europe to steal inventions from each other, who had thereby at least this advantage, that it became a controversy which was the right owner, yet I would take such caution, that he should have the honour entire without a rival.

We next went to the school of languages, where three professors sate in consultation upon improving that of their own country.

The first project was to shorten discourse by cutting polysyllables into one, and leaving out verbs and participles, because in reality all things imaginable are but nouns.

The other project was a scheme for entirely abolishing all words whatsoever; and this was urged as a great advantage in point of health as well as brevity. For it is plain, that every word we speak is in some degree a diminution of our lungs by corrosion, and consequently contributes to the shortening of our lives. An expedient was therefore

Plate V, Part III

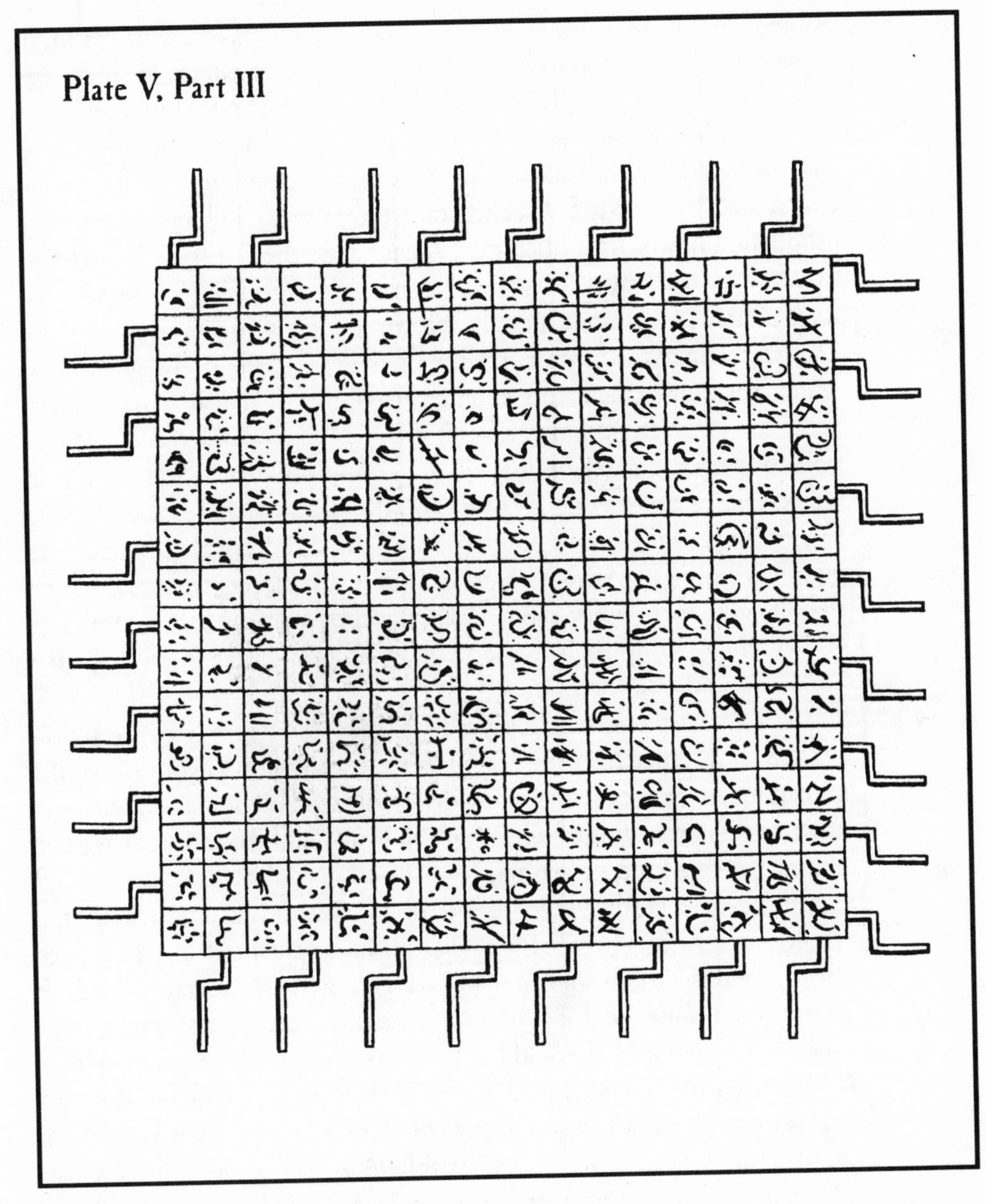

offered, that since words are only names for *things,* it would be more convenient for all men to carry about them such *things* as were necessary to express the particular business they are to discourse on. And this invention would certainly have taken place, to the great ease as well as health of the subject, if the women in conjunction with the vulgar and illiterate had not threatened to raise a rebellion, unless they might be allowed the liberty to speak with their tongues, after the manner of their ancestors; such constant irreconcilable enemies to science are the common people. However, many of the most learned and wise adhere to the new scheme of expressing themselves by *things,* which hath only this inconvenience attending it, that if a man's business be very great, and of various kinds, he must be obliged in proportion to carry a greater bundle of *things* upon his back, unless he can afford one or two strong servants to attend him. I have often beheld two of those sages almost sinking under the weight of their packs, like peddlers among us; who when they met in the streets would lay down their loads, open their sacks and hold conversation for an hour together; then put up their implements, help each other to resume their burthens, and take their leave.

But for short conversations a man may carry implements in his pockets and under his arms, enough to supply him, and in his house he cannot be at a loss; therefore the room where company meet who practise this art is full of all *things* ready at hand, requisite to furnish matter for this kind of artificial converse.

Another great advantage proposed by this invention was that it would serve as an universal language to be understood in all civilised nations, whose goods and utensils are generally of the same kind, or nearly resembling, so that their uses might easily be comprehended. And thus ambassadors would be qualified to treat with foreign princes or ministers of state to whose tongues they were utter strangers.

I was at the mathematical school, where the master taught his pupils after a method scarce imaginable to us in Europe. The proposition and demonstration were fairly written on a thin wafer, with ink composed of a cephalic tincture. This the student was to swallow upon a fasting stomach, and for three days following eat nothing but bread and water. As the wafer digested, the tincture mounted to his brain, bearing the proposition along with it. But the success hath not hitherto been answerable, partly by some error in the *quantum* or composition, and partly by the perverseness of lads, to whom this bolus is so nauseous that they generally steal aside, and discharge it upwards before it can operate; neither have they been yet persuaded to use so long an abstinence as the prescription requires.

Chapter Six

A further account of the Academy. The author proposes some improvements, which are honourably received.

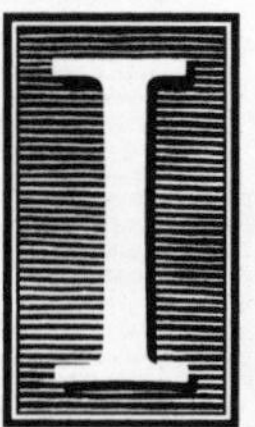

N THE SCHOOL OF POLITICAL PROJECTORS I WAS BUT ILL entertained, the professors appearing in my judgment wholly out of their senses, which is a scene that never fails to make me melancholy. These unhappy people were proposing schemes for persuading monarchs to choose favourites upon the score of their wisdom, capacity, and virtue; of teaching ministers to consult the public good; of rewarding merit, great abilities and eminent services; of instructing princes to know their true interest by placing it on the same foundation with that of their people: of choosing for employments persons qualified to exercise them; with many other wild impossible chimæras, that never entered before into the heart of man to conceive, and confirmed in me the old observation, that there is nothing so extravagant and irrational which some philosophers have not maintained for truth.

But, however, I shall so far do justice to this part of the Academy, as to acknowledge that all of them were not so visionary. There was a most ingenious doctor who seemed to be perfectly versed in the whole nature and system of government. This illustrious person had very usefully employed his studies in finding out effectual remedies for all diseases and corruptions, to which the several kinds of public administration are subject by the vices or infirmities of those who govern, as well as by the licentiousness of those who are to obey. For instance:

whereas all writers and reasoners have agreed, that there is a strict universal resemblance between the natural and the political body; can there be any thing more evident, than that the health of both must be preserved, and the diseases cured, by the same prescriptions? It is allowed that senates and great councils are often troubled with redundant, ebullient, and other peccant humours, with many diseases of the head, and more of the heart; with strong convulsions, with grievous contractions of the nerves and sinews in both hands, but especially the right; with spleen, flatus, vertigos, and deliriums; with scrofulous tumours full of fœtid purulent matter; with sour frothy ructations, with canine[1] appetites and crudeness of digestion, besides many others needless to mention. This doctor therefore proposed, that upon the meeting of a senate, certain physicians should attend at the three first days of their sitting, and, at the close of each day's debate, feel the pulses of every senator; after which, having maturely considered, and consulted upon the nature of the several maladies, and the methods of cure, they should on the fourth day return to the senate house, attended by their apothecaries stored with proper medicines, and before the members sate, administer to each of them lenitives, aperitives, abstersives, corrosives, restringents, palliatives, laxatives, cephalalgics, icterics, apophlegmatics, acoustics, as their several cases required; and according as these medicines should operate, repeat, alter, or omit them at the next meeting.

This project could not be of any great expense to the public, and would, in my poor opinion, be of much use for the dispatch of business in these countries where senates have any share in the legislative power, beget unanimity, shorten debates, open a few mouths which are now closed, and close many more which are now open; curb the petulancy of the young, and correct the positiveness of the old; rouse the stupid, and damp the pert.

Again, because it is a general complaint that the favourites of

1. Morbidly voracious.

princes are troubled with short and weak memories, the same doctor proposed, that whoever attended a first minister, after having told his business with the utmost brevity, and in the plainest words, should at his departure give the said minister a tweak by the nose, or a kick in the belly, or tread on his corns, or lug him thrice by both ears, or run a pin into his breech, or pinch his arm black and blue, to prevent forgetfulness: and at every levee day repeat the same operation, till the business were done or absolutely refused.

He likewise directed, that every senator in the great council of a nation, after he had delivered his opinion, and argued in the defence of it, should be obliged to give his vote directly contrary; because if that were done, the result would infallibly terminate in the good of the public.

When parties in a state are violent, he offered a wonderful contrivance to reconcile them. The method is this. You take an hundred leaders of each party, you dispose them into couples of such whose heads are nearest of a size; then let two nice operators saw off the *occiput* of each couple at the same time, in such a manner that the brain may be equally divided. Let the *occiputs* thus cut off be interchanged, applying each to the head of his opposite party-man. It seems indeed to be a work that requireth some exactness, but the professor assured us, that if it were dextrously performed the cure would be infallible. For he argued thus; that the two half brains being left to debate the matter between themselves within the space of one skull, would soon come to a good understanding, and produce that moderation, as well as regularity of thinking, so much to be wished for in the heads of those who imagine they came into the world only to watch and govern its motion: and as to the difference of brains in quantity or quality, among those who are directors in faction, the doctor assured us from his own knowledge, that it was a perfect trifle.

I heard a very warm debate between two professors, about the most commodious and effectual ways and means of raising money without grieving the subject. The first affirmed the justest method would be to lay a certain tax upon vices and folly, and the sum fixed upon every man to be rated after the fairest manner by a jury of his neighbours. The second was of an opinion directly contrary, to tax those qualities of body and mind for which men chiefly value themselves, the rate to be more or less according to the degrees of excelling, the decision whereof should be left entirely to their own breast. The highest tax was upon men who are the greatest favourites of the other sex, and the assessments according to the number and natures of the favours they have received; for which they are allowed to be their own vouchers. Wit, valour, and politeness were likewise proposed to be largely taxed, and collected in the same manner, by every person's giving his own word for the quantum of what he possessed. But as to honour, justice, wisdom, and learning, they should not be taxed at all, because they are qualifications of so singular a kind, that no man will either allow them in his neighbour, or value them in himself.

The women were proposed to be taxed according to their beauty and skill in dressing, wherein they had the same privilege with the men, to be determined by their own judgment. But constancy, chastity, good sense, and good nature were not rated, because they would not bear the charge of collecting.

To keep senators in the interest of the crown, it was proposed that the members should raffle for employments, every man first taking an oath, and giving security that he would vote for the court, whether he won or no, after which the losers had in their turn the liberty of raffling upon the next vacancy. Thus hope and expectation would be kept alive, none would complain of broken promises, but impute their disappointments wholly to Fortune, whose shoulders are broader and stronger than those of a ministry.

Another professor showed me a large paper of instructions for discovering plots and conspiracies against the government. He advised great statesmen to examine into the diet of all suspected persons; their times of eating; upon which side they lay in bed; with which hand they wiped their posteriors; to take a strict view of their excrements,

and from the colour, the odour, the taste, the consistence, the crudeness or maturity of digestion, form a judgment of their thoughts and designs. Because men are never so serious, thoughtful, and intent, as when they are at stool, which he found by frequent experiment: for in such conjunctures, when he used merely as a trial to consider which was the best way of murdering the King, his ordure would have a tincture of green, but quite different when he thought only of raising an insurrection or burning the metropolis.[2]

The whole discourse was written with great acuteness, containing many observations both curious and useful for politicians, but as I conceived not altogether complete. This I ventured to tell the author, and offered if he pleased to supply him with some additions. He received my proposition with more compliance than is usual among writers, especially those of the projecting species, professing he would be glad to receive farther information.

I told him, that in the kingdom of Tribnia, by the natives called Langden,[3] where I had sojourned some time in my travels, the bulk of the people consist in a manner wholly of discoverers, witnesses, informers, accusers, prosecutors, evidences, swearers, together with their several subservient and subaltern instruments, all under the colours and conduct of ministers of state and their deputies. The plots in that kingdom are usually the workmanship of those persons who desire to raise their own characters of profound politicians, to restore new vigor to a crazy administration, to stifle or divert general discontents, to fill their pockets with forfeitures, and raise or sink the opinion of public credit, as either shall best answer their private advantage. It is first agreed and settled among them what suspected persons shall be accused of a plot: then effectual care is taken to secure all their letters and papers, and put the criminals in chains. These papers are delivered to a set of artists, very dextrous in finding out the mysterious

2. Probably a reference to the trial of Bishop Atterbury, in 1723, for Jacobite plotting. Part of the evidence consisted of papers found in the Bishop's close-stool.
3. Anagrams of 'Britain' and 'England'.

meanings of words, syllables, and letters.[4] For instance, they can discover a close-stool to signify a privy council, a flock of geese a senate, a lame dog an invader,[5] a codshead[6] a ———, the plague a standing army, a buzzard a prime minister, the gout a high priest, a gibbet a secretary of state, a chamber-pot a committee of grandees, a sieve a court lady, a broom a revolution, a mousetrap an employment, a bottomless pit the treasury, a sink the court, a cap and bells a favourite, a broken reed a court of justice, an empty tun a general, a running sore the administration.

When this method fails, they have two others more effectual, which the learned among them call acrostics and anagrams. First they can decipher all initial letters into political meanings. Thus N. shall signify a plot, B. a regiment of horse, L. a fleet at sea. Or secondly by transposing the letters of the alphabet in any suspected paper, they can discover the deepest designs of a discontented party. So, for example, if I should say in a letter to a friend, 'Our brother Tom has just got the piles', a skilful decipherer would discover that the same letters which compose that sentence may be analysed into the following words: 'Resist; a plot is brought home; The Tour'.[7] And this is the anagrammatic method.

The professor made me great acknowledgements for communicating these observations, and promised to make honourable mention of me in his treatise.

I saw nothing in this country that could invite me to a longer continuance, and began to think of returning home to England.

4. In the Atterbury trial experts testified as to the probable meaning of numerous letters alleged to have been written in a secret code.

5. It was asserted that Atterbury's lame dog, Harlequin, mentioned frequently in his correspondence, stood for the Pretender.

6. A blockhead. The dash which follows should undoubtedly be replaced by the word 'king'.

7. 'La Tour' was a pseudonym adopted by Bolingbroke while he was exiled in France as a Jacobite conspirator.

Chapter Seven

The author leaves Lagado, arrives at Maldonada. No ship ready. He takes a short voyage to Glubbdubdrib. His reception by the Governor.

HE CONTINENT OF WHICH THIS KINGDOM IS A PART extends itself, as I have reason to believe, eastward to that unknown tract of America, westward of California and north to the Pacific Ocean, which is not above a hundred and fifty miles from Lagado, where there is a good port and much commerce with the great island of Luggnagg, situated to the northwest about 29 degrees north latitude, and 140 longitude. This island of Luggnagg stands southeastwards of Japan, about an hundred leagues distant. There is a strict alliance between the Japanese Emperor and the King of Luggnagg, which affords frequent opportunities of sailing from one island to the other. I determined therefore to direct my course this way in order to my return to Europe. I hired two mules with a guide to show me the way, and carry my small baggage. I took leave of my noble protector, who had shown me so much favour, and made me a generous present at my departure.

My journey was without any accident or adventure worth relating. When I arrived at the port of Maldonada (for so it is called) there was no ship in the harbour bound for Luggnagg, nor like to be in some time. The town is about as large as Portsmouth. I soon fell into some acquaintance, and was very hospitably received. A gentleman of distinction said to me, that since the ships bound for Luggnagg could

not be ready in less than a month, it might be no disagreeable amusement for me to take a trip to the little island of Glubbdubdrib, about five leagues off to the southwest. He offered himself and a friend to accompany me, and that I should be provided with a small convenient barque for the voyage.

'Glubbdubdrib', as nearly as I can interpret the word, signifies 'The Island of *Sorcerers*' or *'Magicians'*. It is about one third as large as the Isle of Wight, and extremely fruitful: it is governed by the head of a certain tribe, who are all magicians. This tribe marries only among each other, and the eldest in succession is prince or governor. He hath a noble palace and a park of about three thousand acres, surrounded by a wall of hewn stone twenty foot high. In this park are several smaller inclosures for cattle, corn, and gardening.

The Governor and his family are served and attended by domestics of a kind somewhat unusual. By his skill in necromancy, he hath a power of calling whom he pleaseth from the dead, and commanding their service for twenty-four hours, but no longer; nor can he call the same persons up again in less than three months, except upon very extraordinary occasions.

When we arrived at the island, which was about eleven in the morning, one of the gentlemen who accompanied me went to the Governor, and desired admittance for a stranger, who came on purpose to have the honour of attending on his Highness. This was immediately granted, and we all three entered the gate of the palace between two rows of guards, armed and dressed after a very antic[1] manner, and something in their countenances that made my flesh creep with a horror I cannot express. We passed through several apartments between servants of the same sort, ranked on each side as before, till we came to the chamber of presence, where, after three profound obeisances, and a few general questions, we were permitted to sit on three stools near the lowest step of his Highness's throne. He

1. Fantastic.

understood the language of Balnibarbi, although it were different from that of his island. He desired me to give him some account of my travels; and to let me see that I should be treated without ceremony, he dismissed all his attendants with a turn of his finger, at which to my great astonishment they vanished in an instant, like visions in a dream, when we awake on a sudden. I could not recover myself in some time, till the Governor assured me that I should receive no hurt; and observing my two companions to be under no concern, who had been often entertained in the same manner, I began to take courage, and relate to his Highness a short history of my several adventures, yet not without some hesitation, and frequently looking behind me to the place where I had seen those domestic spectres. I had the honour to dine with the Governor, where a new set of ghosts served up the meat, and waited at table. I now observed myself to be less terrified than I had been in the morning. I stayed till sunset, but humbly desired his Highness to excuse me for not accepting his invitation of lodging in the palace. My two friends and I lay at a private house in the town adjoining, which is the capital of this little island; and the next morning we returned to pay our duty to the Governor, as he was pleased to command us.

After this manner we continued in the island for ten days, most part of every day with the Governor, and at night in our lodging. I soon grew so familiarized to the sight of spirits, that after the third or fourth time they gave me no emotion at all; or if I had any apprehensions left, my curiosity prevailed over them. For his Highness the Governor ordered me to call up whatever persons I would choose to name, and in whatever numbers among all the dead from the beginning of the world to the present time, and command them to answer any questions I should think fit to ask; with this condition, that my questions must be confined within the compass of the times they lived in. And one thing I might depend upon, that they would certainly tell me truth, for lying was a talent of no use in the lower world.

I made my humble acknowledgements to his Highness for so great a favour. We were in a chamber, from whence there was a fair prospect into the park. And because my first inclination was to be entertained with scenes of pomp and magnificence, I desired to see Alexander the Great, at the head of his army just after the battle of Arbela, which upon a motion of the Governor's finger immediately appeared in a large field under the window, where we stood. Alexander was called up into the room: it was with great difficulty that I understood his Greek, and had but little of my own. He assured me upon his honour that he was not poisoned, but died of a fever by excessive drinking.

Next I saw Hannibal passing the Alps, who told me he had not a drop of vinegar in his camp.[2]

I saw Cæsar and Pompey at the head of their troops, just ready to engage. I saw the former in his last great triumph. I desired that the Senate of Rome might appear before me in one large chamber, and a modern representative[3] in counterview in another. The first seemed to be an assembly of heroes and demigods; the other a knot of pedlars, pickpockets, highwaymen, and bullies.

The Governor at my request gave the sign for Cæsar and Brutus to advance towards us. I was struck with a profound veneration at the sight of Brutus, and could easily discover the most consummate virtue, the greatest intrepidity and firmness of mind, the truest love of his country, and general benevolence for mankind in every lineament of his countenance. I observed with much pleasure that these two persons were in good intelligence with each other, and Cæsar freely confessed to me, that the greatest actions of his own life were not equal by many degrees to the glory of taking it away. I had the honour to have much conversation with Brutus; and was told, that his ancestor Junius, Socrates, Epaminondas, Cato the younger, Sir Thomas

2. Hannibal removed a rock which impeded the advance of his army by heating it and saturating it with vinegar, after which it was easily cut.

3. The British Parliament.

More and himself were perpetually together: a *sextumvirate* to which all the ages of the world cannot add a seventh.[4]

It would be tedious to trouble the reader with relating what vast numbers of illustrious persons were called up, to gratify that insatiable desire I had to see the world in every period of antiquity placed before me. I chiefly fed my eyes with beholding the destroyers of tyrants and usurpers, and the restorers of liberty to oppressed and injured nations. But it is impossible to express the satisfaction I received in my own mind, after such a manner as to make it a suitable entertainment to the reader.

4. The common virtue of these six men was devotion to duty and the dictates of conscience in the face of grave difficulties. Most of them had also resisted tyrannical oppression.

Chapter Eight

A further account of Glubbdubdrib. Ancient and modern history corrected.

HAVING A DESIRE TO SEE THOSE ANCIENTS WHO were most renowned for wit and learning, I set apart one day on purpose. I proposed that Homer and Aristotle might appear at the head of all their commentators; but these were so numerous that some hundreds were forced to attend in the court and outward rooms of the palace. I knew and could distinguish those two heroes at first sight, not only from the crowd, but from each other. Homer was the taller and comelier person of the two, walked very erect for one of his age, and his eyes were the most quick and piercing I ever beheld. Aristotle stooped much, and made use of a staff. His visage was meager, his hair lank and thin, and his voice hollow. I soon discovered that both of them were perfect strangers to the rest of the company, and had never seen or heard of them before. And I had a whisper from a ghost, who shall be nameless,[1] that these commentators always kept in the most distant quarters from their principals in the lower world, through a consciousness of shame and guilt, because they had so horribly misrepresented the meaning of

1. Perhaps Swift's old patron, Sir William Temple, whose views concerning classical literature Swift had defended in *The Battle of the Books.*

those authors to posterity. I introduced Didymus and Eustathius[2] to Homer, and prevailed on him to treat them better than perhaps they deserved, for he soon found they wanted a genius to enter into the spirit of a poet. But Aristotle was out of all patience with the account I gave him of Scotus[3] and Ramus,[4] as I presented them to him, and he asked them whether the rest of the tribe were as great dunces as themselves.

I then desired the Governor to call up Descartes and Gassendi, with whom I prevailed to explain their systems to Aristotle. This great philosopher freely acknowledged his own mistakes in natural philosophy, because he proceeded in many things upon conjecture, as all men must do; and he found, that Gassendi, who had made the doctrine of Epicurus as palatable as he could, and the *'vortices'* of Descartes, were equally exploded.[5] He predicted the same fate to 'attraction',[6] whereof the present learned are such zealous asserters. He said, that new systems of nature were but new fashions, which would vary in every age; and even those who pretend to demonstrate them from mathematical principles would flourish but a short period of time, and be out of vogue when that was determined.[7]

I spent five days in conversing with many others of the ancient learned. I saw most of the first Roman emperors. I prevailed on the Governor to call up Eliogabalus's[8] cooks to dress us a dinner, but they

2. Commentators upon Homer, belonging respectively to the Age of Augustus and to the twelfth century.

3. Duns Scotus, a thirteenth-century exponent of medieval Aristotelianism.

4. Pierre de la Ramée, a sixteenth-century humanist and an opponent of medieval Aristotelianism. Swift's meaning is that Aristotle has been misinterpreted by both friends and foes.

5. René Descartes and Pierre Gassendi were both early seventeenth-century French philosophers and scientists. The latter, in his *Syntagma Philosophicum,* defended the Epicurean system of physics; the former propounded the theory that all natural motions are in some way circular.

6. Sir Isaac Newton's theory of gravitation.

7. Concluded.

8. Emperor of Rome in the third century: famous as a gourmand.

could not show us much of their skill, for want of materials. A helot of Agesilaus[9] made us a dish of Spartan broth, but I was not able to get down a second spoonful.

The two gentlemen who conducted me to the island were pressed by their private affairs to return in three days, which I employed in seeing some of the modern dead who had made the greatest figure for two or three hundred years past in our own and other countries of Europe; and having been always a great admirer of old illustrious families, I desired the Governor would call up a dozen or two of kings with their ancestors in order for eight or nine generations. But my disappointment was grievous and unexpected. For instead of a long train with royal diadems, I saw in one family, two fiddlers, three spruce courtiers, and an Italian prelate. In another, a barber, an abbot, and two cardinals. I have too great a veneration for crowned heads to dwell any longer on so nice a subject. But as to counts, marquesses, dukes, earls, and the like, I was not so scrupulous. And I confess it was not without some pleasure that I found myself able to trace the particular features, by which certain families are distinguished, up to their originals. I could plainly discover from whence one family derives a long chin, why a second hath abounded with knaves for two generations, and fools for two more; why a third happened to be crack-brained, and a fourth to be sharpers. Whence it came what Polydore Virgil[10] says of a certain great house, '*Nec vir fortis, nec fœmina casta*'. How cruelty, falsehood, and cowardice grew to be characteristics by which certain families are distinguished as much as by their coat of arms. Who first brought the pox into a noble house, which hath lineally descended in scrofulous tumours to their posterity. Neither could I wonder at all this, when I saw such an interruption of

9. King of Sparta in the fourth century B.C.
10. An Italian churchman who resided in England in the early part of the sixteenth century: best known as the author of a history of England, composed in Latin. The quotation ('Not a man of them was brave, not a woman chaste') has not been found in his works.

lineages by pages, lackeys, valets, coachmen, gamesters, captains, and pickpockets.

I was chiefly disgusted with modern history. For having strictly examined all the persons of greatest name in the courts of princes for an hundred years past, I found how the world had been misled by prostitute writers, to ascribe the greatest exploits in war to cowards, the wisest counsel to fools, sincerity to flatterers, Roman virtue to betrayers of their country, piety to atheists, chastity to sodomites, truth to informers. How many innocent and excellent persons had been condemned to death or banishment, by the practising of great ministers upon the corruption of judges, and the malice of factions. How many villains had been exalted to the highest places of trust, power, dignity, and profit: how great a share in the motions and events of courts, councils, and senates might be challenged by bawds, whores, pimps, parasites, and buffoons: how low an opinion I had of human wisdom and integrity, when I was truly informed of the springs and motives of great enterprises and revolutions in the world, and of the contemptible accidents to which they owed their success.

Here I discovered the roguery and ignorance of those who pretend to write 'anecdotes', or secret history, who send so many kings to their graves with a cup of poison; will repeat the discourse between a prince and chief minister, where no witness was by; unlock the thoughts and cabinets of ambassadors and secretaries of state, and have the perpetual misfortune to be mistaken. Here I discovered the secret causes of many great events that have surprised the world, how a whore can govern the back-stairs, the back-stairs a council, and the council a senate. A general confessed in my presence, that he got a victory purely by the force of cowardice and ill conduct: and an admiral that for want of proper intelligence, he beat the enemy to whom he intended to betray the fleet. Three kings protested to me, that in their whole reigns they did never once prefer any person of merit, unless by mistake or treachery of some minister in whom they confided: neither would they do it if they were to live again; and they showed with great strength of reason, that the royal throne could not be supported without corruption, because that positive, confident, restive temper, which virtue infused into man, was a perpetual clog to public business.

I had the curiosity to enquire in a particular manner, by what method great numbers had procured to themselves high titles of honour, and prodigious estates; and I confined my enquiry to a very modern period: however, without grating upon present times, because I would be sure to give no offence even to foreigners (for I hope the reader need not be told that I do not in the least intend my own country in what I say upon this occasion) a great number of persons concerned were called up, and upon a very slight examination, discovered such a scene of infamy, that I cannot reflect upon it without some seriousness. Perjury, oppression, subornation, fraud, pandarism, and the like 'infirmities', were amongst the most excusable arts they had to mention, and for these I gave, as it was reasonable, great allowance. But when some confessed they owed their greatness and wealth to sodomy or incest, others to the prostituting of their own wives and daughters; others to the betraying their country or their prince; some to poisoning, more to the perverting of justice in order to destroy the innocent: I hope I may be pardoned if these discoveries inclined me a little to abate of that profound veneration which I am naturally apt to pay to persons of high rank, who ought to be treated with the utmost respect due to their sublime dignity, by us their inferiors.

I had often read of some great services done to princes and states, and desired to see the persons by whom those services were performed. Upon enquiry I was told that their names were to be found on no record, except a few of them whom history hath represented as the vilest rogues and traitors. As to the rest, I had never once heard of them. They all appeared with dejected looks, and in the meanest habit, most of them telling me they died in poverty and disgrace, and the rest on a scaffold or a gibbet.

Among the rest there was one person whose case appeared a little singular. He had a youth about eighteen years old standing by his side. He told me he had for many years been commander of a ship, and in the sea-fight at Actium had the good fortune to break through the enemy's great line of battle, sink three of their capital ships, and take a fourth, which was the sole cause of Antony's flight, and of the victory that ensued; that the youth standing by him, his only son, was killed in the action. He added, that upon the confidence of some merit, this war being at an end, he went to Rome, and solicited at the court of Augustus to be preferred to a greater ship, whose commander had been killed; but without any regard to his pretensions, it was given to a youth who had never seen the sea, the son of Libertina, who waited on one of the Emperor's mistresses. Returning back to his own vessels, he was charged with neglect of duty, and the ship given to a favourite page of Publicola the Vice-Admiral; whereupon he retired to a poor farm, at a great distance from Rome, and there ended his life.[11] I was so curious to know the truth of this story, that I desired Agrippa might be called, who was admiral in that fight. He appeared and confirmed the whole account, but with much more advantage to the captain, whose modesty had extenuated or concealed a great part of his merit.

I was surprised to find corruption grown so high and so quick in that empire, by the force of luxury so lately introduced, which made me less wonder at many parallel cases in other countries, where vices of all kinds have reigned so much longer, and where the whole praise as well as pillage hath been engrossed by the chief commander, who perhaps had the least title to either.

As every person called up made exactly the same appearance he had done in the world, it gave me melancholy reflections to observe how much the race of human kind was degenerate among us, within these hundred years past. How the pox under all its consequences and de-

11. This incident may be an allegory of the treatment of the Earl of Peterborough by the Whigs.

nominations had altered every lineament of an English countenance, shortened the size of bodies, unbraced the nerves, relaxed the sinews and muscles, introduced a sallow complexion, and rendered the flesh loose and 'rancid'.

I descended so low as to desire that some English yeomen[12] of the old stamp might be summoned to appear, once so famous for the simplicity of their manners, diet, and dress, for justice in their dealings, for their true spirit of liberty, for their valour and love of their country. Neither could I be wholly unmoved after comparing the living with the dead, when I considered how all these pure native virtues were prostituted for a piece of money by their grandchildren, who in selling their votes, and managing at elections, have acquired every vice and corruption that can possibly be learned in a court.

12. Independent farmers—the substantial middle class of the country districts.

Chapter Nine

The author's return to Maldonada; sails to the kingdom of Luggnagg. The author confined. He is sent for to court. The manner of his admittance. The King's great lenity to his subjects.

HE DAY OF OUR DEPARTURE BEING COME, I TOOK leave of his Highness the Governor of Glubbdubdrib, and returned with my two companions to Maldonada, where after a fortnight's waiting, a ship was ready to sail for Luggnagg. The two gentlemen and some others were so generous and kind as to furnish me with provisions, and see me on board. I was a month in this voyage. We had one violent storm, and were under a necessity of steering westward to get into the trade wind, which holds for above sixty leagues. On the 21st of April, 1709, we sailed in the river Clumegnig, which is a seaport town, at the southeast point of Luggnagg. We cast anchor within a league of the town, and made a signal for a pilot. Two of them came on board in less than half an hour, by whom we were guided between certain shoals and rocks, which are very dangerous in the passage, to a large basin, where a fleet may ride in safety within a cable's length of the town wall.

Some of our sailors, whether out of treachery or inadvertence, had informed the pilots that I was a stranger and a great traveller, whereof these gave notice to a custom-house officer, by whom I was examined very strictly upon my landing. This officer spoke to me in the language of Balnibarbi, which by the force of much commerce is generally understood in that town, especially by seamen, and those

employed in the customs. I gave him a short account of some particulars, and made my story as plausible and consistent as I could; but I thought it necessary to disguise my country, and call myself an Hollander, because my intentions were for Japan, and I knew the Dutch were the only Europeans permitted to enter into that kingdom. I therefore told the officer, that having been shipwrecked on the coast of Balnibarbi, and cast on a rock, I was received up into Laputa, or the Flying Island (of which he had often heard), and was now endeavouring to get to Japan, from whence I might find a convenience of returning to my own country. The officer said I must be confined till he could receive orders from court, for which he would write immediately, and hoped to receive an answer in a fortnight. I was carried to a convenient lodging, with a sentry placed at the door; however I had the liberty of a large garden, and was treated with humanity enough, being maintained all the time at the King's charge. I was visited by several persons, chiefly out of curiosity, because it was reported that I came from countries very remote of which they had never heard.

I hired a young man who came in the same ship to be an interpreter; he was a native of Luggnagg, but had lived some years at Maldonada, and was a perfect master of both languages. By his assistance I was able to hold a conversation with those who came to visit me; but this consisted only of their questions, and my answers.

The dispatch came from court about the time we expected. It contained a warrant for conducting me and my retinue to Traldragdubh or Trildrogdrib, for it is pronounced both ways as near as I can remember, by a party of ten horse. All my retinue was that poor lad for an interpreter, whom I persuaded into my service, and at my humble request, we had each of us a mule to ride on. A messenger was dispatched half a day's journey before us, to give the King notice of my approach, and to desire that his Majesty would please to appoint a day and hour, when it would be his gracious pleasure that I might have the honour to 'lick the dust before his footstool'. This is the

court style, and I found it to be more than matter of form. For upon my admittance two days after my arrival, I was commanded to crawl on my belly, and lick the floor as I advanced; but on account of my being a stranger, care was taken to have it swept so clean that the dust was not offensive. However, this was a peculiar grace, not allowed to any but persons of the highest rank, when they desire an admittance. Nay, sometimes the floor is strewed with dust on purpose, when the person to be admitted happens to have powerful enemies at court. And I have seen a great lord with his mouth so crammed, that when he had crept to the proper distance from the throne, he was not able to speak a word. Neither is there any remedy, because it is capital for those who receive an audience to spit or wipe their mouths in his Majesty's presence. There is indeed another custom, which I cannot altogether approve of. When the King hath a mind to put any of his nobles to death in a gentle indulgent manner, he commands to have the floor strowed with a certain brown powder, of a deadly composition, which being licked up infallibly kills him in twenty-four hours. But in justice to this prince's great clemency, and the care he hath of his subjects' lives (wherein it were much to be wished that the monarchs of Europe would imitate him) it must be mentioned for his honour, that strict orders are given to have the infected parts of the floor well washed after every such execution, which if his domestics neglect, they are in danger of incurring his royal displeasure. I myself heard him give directions, that one of his pages should be whipped, whose turn it was to give notice about washing the floor after an execution, but maliciously had omitted it, by which neglect a young lord of great hopes coming to an audience, was unfortunately poisoned, although the King at that time had no design against his life. But this good prince was so gracious as to forgive the poor page his whipping, upon promise that he would do so no more, without special orders.

To return from this digression; when I had crept within four yards of the throne, I raised myself gently upon my knees, and then striking

my forehead seven times on the ground, I pronounced the following words, as they had been taught me the night before, '*Ickpling gloffthrobb squutserumm blhiop mlashnalt, zwin tnodbalkguffh slhiophad gurdlubh asht*'. This is the compliment established by the laws of the land for all persons admitted to the King's presence. It may be rendered into English thus: 'May your Cœlestial Majesty outlive the sun, eleven moons and an half'. To this the King returned some answer, which although I could not understand, yet I replied as I had been directed: '*Fluft drin yalerick dwuldom prastrad mirpush*', which properly signifies, 'My tongue is in the mouth of my friend', and by this expression was meant that I desired leave to bring my interpreter; whereupon the young man already mentioned was accordingly introduced, by whose intervention I answered as many questions as his Majesty could put in above an hour. I spoke in the Balnibarbian tongue, and my interpreter delivered my meaning in that of Luggnagg.

The King was much delighted with my company, and ordered his *bliffmarklub* or high chamberlain to appoint a lodging in the court for me and my interpreter, with a daily allowance for my table, and a large purse of gold for my common expenses.

I stayed three months in this country out of perfect obedience to his Majesty, who was pleased highly to favour me, and made me very honourable offers. But I thought it more consistent with prudence and justice to pass the remainder of my days with my wife and family.

Chapter Ten

The Luggnaggians commended. A particular description of the struldbruggs, with many conversations between the author and some eminent persons upon that subject.

The Luggnaggians are a polite and generous people, and although they are not without some share of that pride which is peculiar to all *eastern* countries, yet they show themselves courteous to strangers, especially such who are countenanced by the court. I had many acquaintance among persons of the best fashion, and being always attended by my interpreter, the conversation we had was not disagreeable.

One day in much good company I was asked by a person of quality, whether I had seen any of their struldbruggs or 'immortals'. I said I had not, and desired he would explain to me what he meant by such an appellation applied to a mortal creature. He told me, that sometimes, though very rarely, a child happened to be born in a family with a red circular spot in the forehead, directly over the left eyebrow, which was an infallible mark that it should never die. The spot, as he described it, was about the compass of a silver threepence, but in the course of time grew larger, and changed its colour; for at twelve years old it became green, so continued till five and twenty, then turned to a deep blue; at five and forty it grew coal black, and as large as an English shilling, but never admitted any farther alteration. He said these births were so rare, that he did not believe there could be above eleven hundred struldbruggs of both sexes in the whole kingdom, of

which he computed about fifty in the metropolis, and among the rest a young girl born about three years ago. That these productions were not peculiar to any family, but a mere effect of chance, and the children of the struldbruggs themselves were equally mortal with the rest of the people.

I freely own myself to have been struck with inexpressible delight upon hearing this account: and the person who gave it me happening to understand the Balnibarbian language, which I spoke very well, I could not forbear breaking out into expressions perhaps a little too extravagant. I cried out as in a rapture: 'Happy nation where every child hath at least a chance for being immortal! Happy people who enjoy so many living examples of ancient virtue, and have masters ready to instruct them in the wisdom of all former ages! But happiest beyond all comparison are those excellent struldbruggs, who born exempt from that universal calamity of human nature, have their minds free and disingaged, without the weight and depression of spirits caused by the continual apprehension of death'. I discovered my admiration that I had not observed any of these illustrious persons at court, the black spot on the forehead being so remarkable a distinction, that I could not have easily overlooked it and it was impossible that his Majesty, a most judicious prince, should not provide himself with a good number of such wise and able counsellors. Yet perhaps the virtue of those reverend sages was too strict for the corrupt and libertine manners of a court. And we often find by experience that young men are too opinionative and volatile to be guided by the sober dictates of their seniors. However, since the King was pleased to allow me access to his royal person, I was resolved upon the very first occasion to deliver my opinion to him on this matter freely, and at large by the help of my interpreter; and whether he would please to take my advice or no, yet in one thing I was determined, that his Majesty having frequently offered me an establishment in this country, I would with great thankfulness accept the favour, and pass my life here in the

conversation of those superior beings the struldbruggs, if they would please to admit me.

The gentleman to whom I addressed my discourse, because (as I have already observed) he spoke the language of Balnibarbi, said to me with a sort of a smile, which usually ariseth from pity to the ignorant, that he was glad of any occasion to keep me among them, and desired my permission to explain to the company what I had spoke. He did so, and they talked together for some time in their own language, whereof I understood not a syllable, neither could I observe by their countenances what impression my discourse had made on them. After a short silence the same person told me, that his friends and mine (so he thought fit to express himself) were very much pleased with the judicious remarks I had made on the great happiness and advantages of immortal life, and they were desirous to know in a particular manner, what scheme of living I should have formed to myself, if it had fallen to my lot to have been born a struldbrugg.

I answered, it was easy to be eloquent on so copious and delightful a subject, especially to me who have been often apt to amuse myself with visions of what I should do if I were a king, a general, or a great lord; and upon this very case I had frequently run over the whole system how I should employ myself and pass the time if I were sure to live for ever.

That if it had been my good fortune to come into the world a struldbrugg, as soon as I could discover my own happiness by understanding the difference between life and death, I would first resolve by all arts and methods whatsoever to procure myself riches. In the pursuit of which by thrift and management, I might reasonably expect in about two hundred years to be the wealthiest man in the kingdom. In the second place, I would from my earliest youth apply myself to the study of arts and sciences, by which I should arrive in time to excel all others in learning. Lastly, I would carefully record every action and event of consequence that happened in the public, impartially draw the characters of the several successions of princes, and great ministers of state, with my own observations on every point. I would exactly set down the several changes in customs, language, fashions of dress, diet, and diversions. By all which acquirements, I should be a living treasury of knowledge and wisdom, and certainly become the oracle of the nation.

I would never marry after threescore, but live in an hospitable manner, yet still on the saving side. I would entertain myself in forming and directing the minds of hopeful young men, by convincing them from my own remembrance, experience, and observation, fortified by numerous examples, of the usefulness of virtue in public and private life. But my choice and constant companions should be a set of my own immortal brotherhood, among whom I would elect a dozen from the most ancient down to my own contemporaries. Where any of these wanted fortunes, I would provide them with convenient lodges round my own estate, and have some of them always at my table, only mingling a few of the most valuable among you mortals, whom length of time would harden me to lose with little or no reluctance, and treat your posterity after the same manner, just as a man diverts himself with the annual succession of pinks and tulips in his garden, without regretting the loss of those which withered the preceding year.

These struldbruggs and I would mutually communicate our observations and memorials through the course of time, remark the several gradations by which corruption steals into the world, and oppose it in every step, by giving perpetual warning and instruction to mankind; which, added to the strong influence of our own example, would probably prevent that continual degeneracy of human nature so justly complained of in all ages.

Add to all this, the pleasure of seeing the various revolutions of states and empires, the changes in the lower and upper world, ancient cities in ruins, and obscure villages become the seats of kings. Famous rivers lessening into shallow brooks, the ocean leaving one coast dry, and overwhelming another; the discovery of many countries yet unknown. Barbarity overrunning the politest nations, and the most bar-

barous become civilised. I should then see the discovery of the *longitude*,[1] the *perpetual motion*, the *universal medicine*, and many other great inventions brought to the utmost perfection.

What wonderful discoveries should we make in astronomy, by outliving and confirming our own predictions, by observing the progress and returns of comets, with the changes of motion in the sun, moon, and stars.

I enlarged upon many other topics which the natural desire of endless life and sublunary happiness could easily furnish me with. When I had ended, and the sum of my discourse had been interpreted as before to the rest of the company, there was a good deal of talk among them in the language of the country, not without some laughter at my expense. At last the same gentleman who had been my interpreter said, he was desired by the rest to set me right in a few mistakes, which I had fallen into through the common imbecility of human nature, and upon that allowance was less answerable for them. That this breed of struldbruggs was peculiar to their country, for there were no such people either in Balnibarbi or Japan, where he had the honour to be ambassador from his Majesty, and found the natives in both those kingdoms very hard to believe that the fact was possible, and it appeared from my astonishment when he first mentioned the matter to me, that I received it as a thing wholly new, and scarcely to be credited. That in the two kingdoms above mentioned, where during his residence he had conversed very much, he observed long life to be the universal desire and wish of mankind. That whoever had one foot in the grave was sure to hold back the other as strongly as he could. That the oldest had still hopes of living one day longer, and looked on death as the greatest evil, from which nature always prompted him to retreat; only in this island of Luggnagg the appetite for living was not

1. A large prize offered by Parliament for the discovery of a method of determining the longitude at sea was still standing at the time when the *Travels* were published. Swift classes the project with two famous chimeras.

so eager, from the continual example of the struldbruggs before their eyes.

That the system of living contrived by me was unreasonable and unjust, because it supposed a perpetuity of youth, health, and vigour, which no man could be so foolish to hope, however extravagant he may be in his wishes. That the question therefore was not whether a man would choose to be always in the prime of youth, attended with prosperity and health, but how he would pass a perpetual life under all the usual disadvantages which old age brings along with it. For although few men will avow their desires of being immortal upon such hard conditions, yet in the two kingdoms before-mentioned of Balnibarbi and Japan, he observed that every man desired to put off death for some time longer, let it approach ever so late, and he rarely heard of any man who died willingly, except he were incited by the extremity of grief or torture. And he appealed to me whether in those countries I had travelled, as well as my own, I had not observed the same general disposition.

After this preface he gave me a particular account of the struldbruggs among them. He said they commonly acted like mortals, till about thirty years old, after which by degrees they grew melancholy and dejected, encreasing in both till they came to fourscore. This he learned from their own confession; for otherwise there not being above two or three of that species born in an age, they were too few to form a general observation by. When they came to fourscore years, which is reckoned the extremity of living in this country, they had not only all the follies and infirmities of other old men, but many more which arose from the dreadful prospects of never dying. They were not only opinionative, peevish, covetous, morose, vain, talkative, but uncapable of friendship, and dead to all natural affection, which never descended below their grandchildren. Envy and impotent desires are their prevailing passions. But those objects against which their envy seems principally directed, are the vices of the younger sort, and the deaths of the old. By reflecting on the former, they find themselves cut off from all possibility of pleasure; and whenever they see a funeral, they lament and repine that others are gone to an harbour of rest, to which they themselves never can hope to arrive. They have no remembrance of any thing but what they learned and observed in their youth and middle age, and even that is very imperfect. And for the truth or particulars of any fact, it is safer to depend on common traditions than upon their best recollections. The least miserable among them appear to be those who turn to dotage and entirely lose their memories; these meet with more pity and assistance, because they want many bad qualities which abound in others.

If a struldbrugg happen to marry one of his own kind, the marriage is dissolved of course by the courtesy of the kingdom, as soon as the younger of the two comes to be fourscore. For the law thinks it a reasonable indulgence, that those who are condemned without any fault of their own to a perpetual continuance in the world, should not have their misery doubled by the load of a wife.

As soon as they have completed the term of eighty years, they are looked on as dead in law; their heirs immediately succeed to their estates, only a small pittance is reserved for their support, and the poor ones are maintained at the public charge. After that period they are held incapable of any employment of trust or profit, they cannot purchase lands or take leases, neither are they allowed to be witnesses in any cause, either civil or criminal, not even for the decision of meers and bounds.

At ninety they lose their teeth and hair, they have at that age no distinction of taste, but eat and drink whatever they can get, without relish or appetite. The diseases they were subject to still continue without encreasing or diminishing. In talking they forget the common appellation of things, and the names of persons, even of those who are their nearest friends and relations. For the same reason they never can amuse themselves with reading, because their memory will not serve to carry them from the beginning of a sentence to the end; and by this

[W]hen I had crept within four yards of the throne,
I raised myself gently upon my knees,...

PAGE 234

defect they are deprived of the only entertainment whereof they might otherwise be capable.

The language of this country being always upon the flux, the struldbruggs of one age do not understand those of another, neither are they able after two hundred years to hold any conversation (farther than by a few general words) with their neighbours the mortals, and thus they lie under the disadvantage of living like foreigners in their own country.

This was the account given me of the struldbruggs, as near as I can remember. I afterwards saw five or six of different ages, the youngest not above two hundred years old, who were brought to me at several times by some of my friends; but although they were told that I was a great traveller, and had seen all the world, they had not the least curiosity to ask me a question; only desired I would give them *slumskudask,* or a token of remembrance, which is a modest way of begging, to avoid the law that strictly forbids it, because they are provided for by the public, although indeed with a very scanty allowance.

They are despised and hated by all sorts of people; when one of them is born, it is reckoned ominous, and their birth is recorded very particularly; so that you may know their age by consulting the registry, which however hath not been kept above a thousand years past, or at least hath been destroyed by time or public disturbances. But the usual way of computing how old they are, is by asking them what kings or great persons they can remember, and then consulting history, for infallibly the last prince in their mind did not begin his reign after they were fourscore years old.

They were the most mortifying sight I ever beheld, and the women more horrible than the men. Besides the usual deformities in extreme old age, they acquired an additional ghastliness in proportion to their number of years, which is not to be described, and among half a dozen I soon distinguished which was the eldest, although there was not above a century or two between them.

The reader will easily believe, that from what I had heard and seen, my keen appetite for perpetuity of life was much abated. I grew heartily ashamed of the pleasing visions I had formed, and thought no tyrant could invent a death into which I would not run with pleasure from such a life. The King heard of all that had passed between me and my friends upon this occasion, and rallied me very pleasantly, wishing I would send a couple of struldbruggs to my own country, to arm our people against the fear of death; but this it seems is forbidden by the fundamental laws of the kingdom, or else I should have been well content with the trouble and expense of transporting them.

I could not but agree that the laws of this kingdom, relating to the struldbruggs, were founded upon the strongest reasons, and such as any other country would be under the necessity of enacting in the like circumstances. Otherwise, as avarice is the necessary consequent of old age, those immortals would in time become proprietors of the whole nation, and engross the civil power, which, for want of abilities to manage, must end in the ruin of the public.

Chapter Eleven

The author leaves Luggnagg, and sails to Japan. From thence he returns in a Dutch ship to Amsterdam, and from Amsterdam to England.

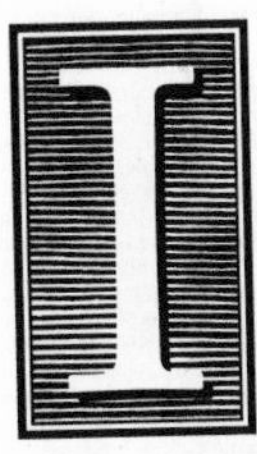 THOUGHT THIS ACCOUNT OF THE STRULDBRUGGS MIGHT be some entertainment to the reader, because it seems to be a little out of the common way, at least, I do not remember to have met the like in any book of travels that hath come to my hands: and if I am deceived, my excuse must be, that it is necessary for travellers who describe the same country very often to agree in dwelling on the same particulars, without deserving the censure of having borrowed or transcribed from those who wrote before them.

There is indeed a perpetual commerce between this kingdom and the great empire of Japan, and it is very probable that the Japanese authors may have given some account of the struldbruggs; but my stay in Japan was so short, and I was so intirely a stranger to that language, that I was not qualified to make any enquiries. But I hope the Dutch upon this notice will be curious and able enough to supply my defects.

His Majesty having often pressed me to accept some employment in his court, and finding me absolutely determined to return to my native country, was pleased to give me his licence to depart, and honoured me with a letter of recommendation under his own hand to the Emperor of Japan. He likewise presented me with four hundred forty-four large pieces of gold (this nation delighting in even num-

bers) and a red diamond which I sold in England for eleven hundred pounds.

On the sixth day of May, 1709, I took a solemn leave of his Majesty, and all my friends. This prince was so gracious as to order a guard to conduct me to Glanguenstald, which is a royal port to the southwest part of the island. In six days I found a vessel ready to carry me to Japan, and spent fifteen days in the voyage. We landed at a small port-town called Xamoschi, situated on the southeast part of Japan; the town lies on the western point where there is a narrow strait, leading northward into a long arm of the sea, upon the northwest part of which Yedo, the metropolis stands.[1] At landing I showed the custom-house officers my letter from the King of Luggnagg to his Imperial Majesty. They knew the seal perfectly well; it was as broad as the palm of my hand. The impression was, *a king lifting up a lame beggar from the earth.* The magistrates of the town, hearing of my letter, received me as a public minister; they provided me with carriages and servants, and bore my charges[2] to Yedo, where I was admitted to an audience, and delivered my letter, which was opened with great ceremony, and explained to the Emperor by an interpreter, who then gave me notice by his Majesty's order, that I should signify my request, and whatever it were, it should be granted for the sake of his royal brother of Luggnagg. This interpreter was a person employed to transact affairs with the Hollanders; he soon conjectured by my countenance that I was an European, and therefore repeated his Majesty's commands in Low Dutch, which he spoke perfectly well. I answered (as I had before determined) that I was a Dutch merchant, shipwrecked in a very remote country, from whence I travelled by sea and land to Luggnagg, and then took shipping for Japan, where I knew my coun-

1. Xamoschi has not been found on any map, but there is a village called Kamoi in the approximate location which Swift describes, i.e., on the western point of the narrow passage leading into Tokyo Bay. Uraga, the old port of entry for Tokyo (Yedo) is little more than a mile distant.
2. Paid my expenses.

trymen often traded, and with some of these I hoped to get an opportunity of returning into Europe: I therefore most humbly intreated his royal favour to give order, that I should be conducted in safety to Nangasac:[3] to this I added another petition, that for the sake of my patron the King of Luggnagg, his Majesty would condescend to excuse my performing the ceremony imposed on my countrymen of *trampling upon the crucifix*,[4] because I had been thrown into his kingdom by my misfortunes, without any intention of trading. When this latter petition was interpreted to the Emperor, he seemed a little surprised, and said he believed I was the first of my countrymen who ever made any scruple in this point, and that he began to doubt whether I was a real Hollander or no; but rather suspected I must be a Christian. However, for the reasons I had offered, but chiefly to gratify the King of Luggnagg, by an uncommon mark of his favour, he would comply with the 'singularity' of my humour; but the affair must be managed with dexterity, and his officers should be commanded to let me pass as it were by forgetfulness. For he assured me, that if the secret should be discovered by my countrymen, the Dutch, they would cut my throat in the voyage. I returned my thanks by the interpreter for so unusual a favour, and some troops being at that time on their march to Nangasac, the commanding officer had orders to convey me safe thither, with particular instructions about the business of the *crucifix*.

On the 9th day of June, 1709, I arrived at Nangasac, after a very long and troublesome journey. I soon fell into company of some Dutch sailors belonging to the *Amboyna* of Amsterdam, a stout ship of 450 tons. I had lived long in Holland, pursuing my studies at Leyden, and I spoke Dutch well. The seamen soon knew from whence I came last; they were curious to enquire into my voyages and course of life. I made up a story as short and probable as I could, but

3. Nagasaki.
4. Japanese suspected of being Christians were compelled to perform this rite, but it is doubtful whether it was imposed upon foreigners.

concealed the greatest part. I knew many persons in Holland, I was able to invent names for my parents, whom I pretended to be obscure people in the province of Gelderland. I would have given the captain (one Theodorus Vangrult) what he pleased to ask for my voyage to Holland; but understanding I was a surgeon, he was contented to take half the usual rate, on condition that I would serve him in the way of my calling. Before we took shipping, I was often asked by some of the crew, whether I had performed the ceremony above-mentioned. I evaded the question by general answers, that I had satisfied the Emperor and court in all particulars. However, a malicious rogue of a skipper[5] went to an officer, and pointing to me, told him, I had not yet *trampled on the crucifix*: but the other, who had received instructions to let me pass, gave the rascal twenty strokes on the shoulders with a bamboo, after which I was no more troubled with such questions.

Nothing happened worth mentioning in this voyage. We sailed with a fair wind to the Cape of Good Hope, where we stayed only to take in fresh water. On the 6th of April we arrived safely at Amsterdam, having lost only three men by sickness in the voyage, and a fourth who fell from the foremast into the sea, not far from the coast of Guinea. From Amsterdam I soon after set sail for England in a small vessel belonging to that city.

On the 10th of April, 1710, we put in at the Downs. I landed the next morning, and saw once more my native country after an absence of three years and eight months complete. I went straight to Redriff, where I arrived the same day at two in the afternoon, and found my wife and family in good health.

THE END OF THE THIRD PART

5. Apparently used here in the less ordinary sense of 'common sailor'. The word is of Dutch origin, and is applied to another Dutch seaman in the fourth voyage (p. 323).

PART FOUR

A Voyage to the Country of the Houyhnhnms

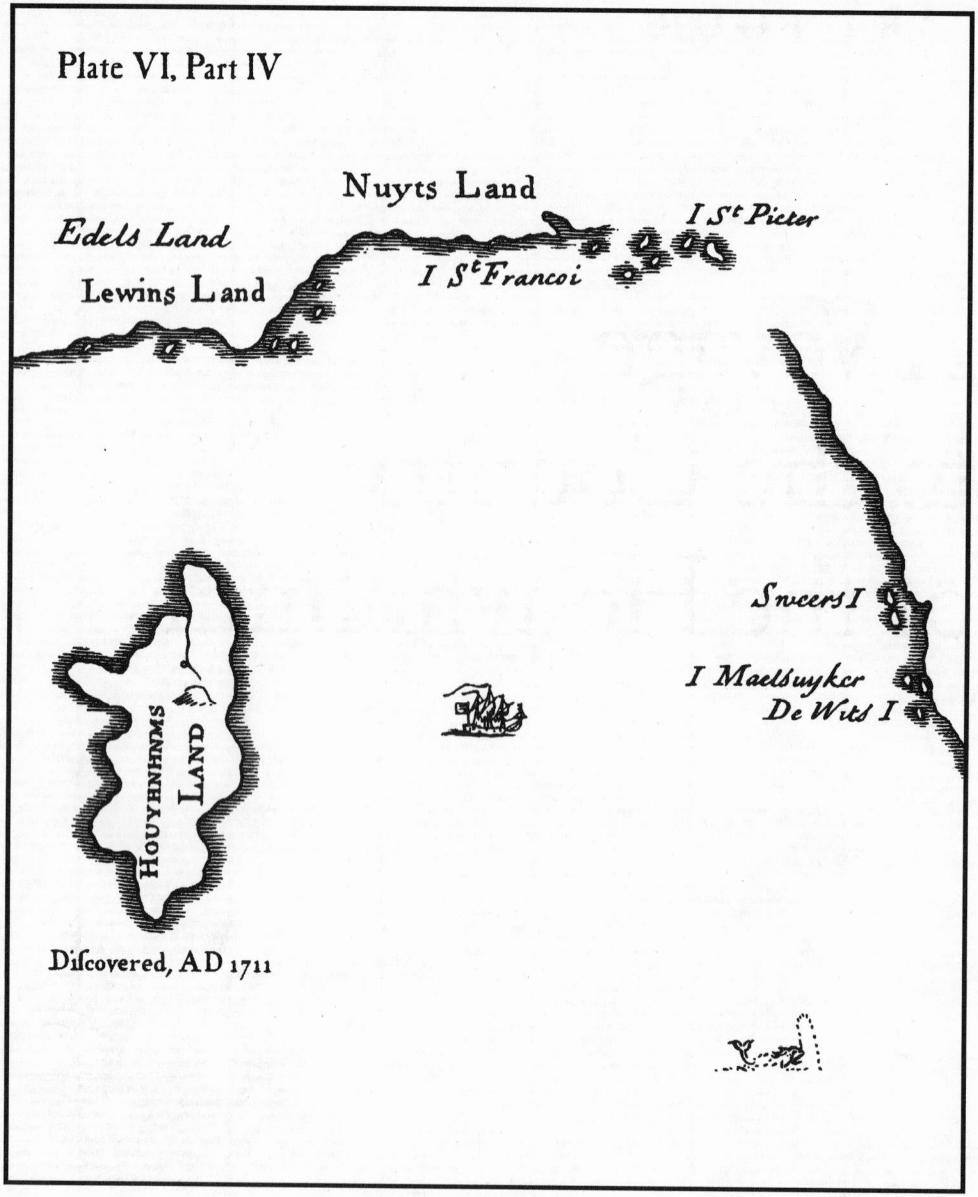

Plate VI, Part IV

Nuyts Land

Edels Land

I St Picter

Lewins Land

I St Francoi

Sneers I

I Maelsuyker

De Wits I

Houyhnhnms Land

Discovered, AD 1711

Chapter One

The author sets out as captain of a ship. His men conspire against him, confine him a long time to his cabin, set him on shore in an unknown land. He travels up in the country. The yahoos, a strange sort of animal, described. The author meets two Houyhnhnms.

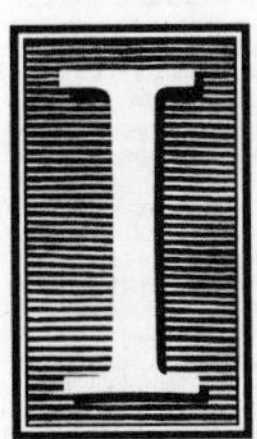

I CONTINUED AT HOME WITH MY WIFE AND CHILDREN about four months in a very happy condition, if I could have learned the lesson of knowing when I was well. I left my poor wife big with child, and accepted an advantageous offer made me to be captain of the *Adventure,* a stout merchantman of 350 tons: for I understood navigation well, and being grown weary of a surgeon's employment at sea, which however I could exercise upon occasion, I took a skilful young man of that calling, one Robert Purefoy, into my ship. We set sail from Portsmouth upon the second day of August, 1710; on the fourteenth, we met with Captain Pocock of Bristol, at Tenariff,[1] who was going to the bay of Campechy,[2] to cut logwood. On the sixteenth, he was parted from us by a storm; I heard since my return that his ship foundered, and none escaped, but one cabin-boy. He was an honest man, and a good sailor, but a little too positive in his own opinions, which was the cause of his destruction, as it hath been of several others. For if he had followed my advice, he might have been safe at home with his family at this time, as well as myself.

I had several men died in my ship of calentures,[3] so that I was

1. Teneriffe, the largest of the Canary Islands.
2. In the Gulf of Mexico.
3. Sunstrokes or tropical fevers.

forced to get recruits out of Barbadoes, and the Leeward Islands, where I touched by the direction of the merchants who employed me, which I had soon too much cause to repent; for I found afterwards that most of them had been buccaneers. I had fifty hands on board, and my orders were, that I should trade with the Indians, in the South Sea, and make what discoveries I could. These rogues whom I had picked up debauched my other men, and they all formed a conspiracy to seize the ship and secure me; which they did one morning, rushing into my cabin, and binding me hand and foot, threatening to throw me overboard, if I offered to stir. I told them, I was their prisoner, and would submit. This they made me swear to do, and then they unbound me, only fastening one of my legs with a chain near my bed, and placed a sentry at my door with his piece charged, who was commanded to shoot me dead, if I attempted my liberty. They sent me down victuals and drink, and took the government of the ship to themselves. Their design was to turn pirates, and plunder the Spaniards, which they could not do, till they got more men. But first they resolved to sell the goods in the ship, and then go to Madagascar for recruits, several among them having died since my confinement. They sailed many weeks, and traded with the Indians, but I knew not what course they took, being kept a close prisoner in my cabin, and expecting nothing less than to be murdered, as they often threatened me.

Upon the ninth day of May, 1711, one James Welch came down to my cabin; and said he had orders from the captain to set me ashore. I expostulated with him, but in vain; neither would he so much as tell me who their new captain was. They forced me into the longboat, letting me put on my best suit of clothes, which were as good as new, and a small bundle of linen, but no arms except my hanger; and they were so civil as not to search my pockets, into which I conveyed what money I had, with some other little necessaries. They rowed about a league, and then set me down on a strand. I desired them to tell me what country it was. They all swore, they knew no more than myself, but said, that the captain (as they called him) was resolved, after they had sold the lading, to get rid of me in the first place where they could discover land. They pushed off immediately, advising me to make haste, for fear of being overtaken by the tide, and so bade me farewell.

In this desolate condition I advanced forwards, and soon got upon firm ground, where I sate down on a bank to rest myself, and consider what I had best to do. When I was a little refreshed I went up into the country, resolving to deliver myself to the first savages I should meet, and purchase my life from them by some bracelets, glass rings, and other toys, which sailors usually provide themselves with in those voyages, and whereof I had some about me: the land was divided by long rows of trees, not regularly planted, but naturally growing; there was great plenty of grass, and several fields of oats. I walked very circumspectly for fear of being surprised, or suddenly shot with an arrow from behind or on either side. I fell into a beaten road, where I saw many tracks of human feet, and some of cows, but most of horses. At last I beheld several animals in a field, and one or two of the same kind sitting in trees. Their shape was very singular, and deformed, which a little discomposed me, so that I lay down behind a thicket to observe them better. Some of them coming forward near the place where I lay, gave me an opportunity of distinctly marking their form. Their heads and breasts were covered with a thick hair, some frizzled and others lank; they had beards like goats, and a long ridge of hair down their backs, and the foreparts of their legs and feet, but the rest of their bodies were bare, so that I might see their skins, which were of a brown buff colour. They had no tails, nor any hair at all on their buttocks, except about the anus; which, I presume, nature had placed there to defend them as they sate on the ground; for this posture they used, as well as lying down, and often stood on their hind feet. They climbed high trees, as nimbly as a squirrel, for they had strong extended claws before and behind, terminating in sharp points, and hooked. They would often spring, and bound, and leap with prodigious agility. The females were not so large as the males; they had long lank hair on their heads, but none on their faces, nor any thing more than a sort of down on the rest of their bodies, except about the anus, and pudenda. Their dugs hung between their fore-feet, and often reached almost to the ground as they walked. The hair of both sexes was of several colours, brown, red, black, and yellow. Upon the whole, I never beheld in all my travels so disagreeable an animal, nor one against which I naturally conceived so strong antipathy. So that thinking I had seen enough, full of contempt and aversion, I got up and pursued the beaten road, hoping it might direct me to the cabin of some Indian. I had not gone far when I met one of these creatures full in my way, and coming up directly to me. The ugly monster, when he saw me, distorted several ways every feature of his visage, and stared as at an object he had never seen before; then approaching nearer, lifted up his fore-paw, whether out of curiosity or mischief, I could not tell. But I drew my hanger, and gave him a good blow with the flat side of it, for I durst not strike him with the edge, fearing the inhabitants might be provoked against me, if they should come to know that I had killed or maimed any of their cattle. When the beast felt the smart, he drew back, and roared so loud, that a herd of at least forty came flocking about me from the next field, howling and making odious faces; but I ran to the body of a tree, and leaning my back against it, kept them off, by waving my hanger. Several of this cursed brood getting hold of the branches behind leapt up in the tree, from whence they began to discharge their excrements on my head: however, I escaped pretty well, by sticking close to the stem of the tree, but was almost stifled with the filth, which fell about me on every side.

In the midst of this distress, I observed them all to run away on a sudden as fast as they could, at which I ventured to leave the tree, and pursue the road, wondering what it was that could put them into this fright. But looking on my left hand, I saw a horse walking softly in the field: which my persecutors having sooner discovered, was the cause of their flight. The horse started a little when he came near me, but soon recovering himself, looked full in my face with manifest tokens of wonder: he viewed my hands and feet, walking round me several times. I would have pursued my journey, but he placed himself directly in the way, yet looking with a very mild aspect, never offering the least violence. We stood gazing at each other for some time; at last I took the boldness to reach my hand towards his neck, with a design to stroke it, using the common style and whistle of jockeys when they are going to handle a strange horse. But this animal, seeming to receive my civilities with disdain, shook his head, and bent his brows, softly raising up his right fore-foot to remove my hand. Then he neighed three or four times, but in so different a cadence, that I almost began to think he was speaking to himself in some language of his own.

While he and I were thus employed, another horse came up; who applying himself to the first in a very formal manner, they gently struck each other's right hoof before, neighing several times by turns, and varying the sound, which seemed to be almost articulate. They went some paces off, as if it were to confer together, walking side by side, backwards and forwards, like persons deliberating upon some affair of weight, but often turning their eyes towards me, as it were to watch that I might not escape. I was amazed to see such actions and behaviour in brute beasts, and concluded with myself, that if the inhabitants of this country were endued with a proportionable degree of reason, they must needs be the wisest people upon earth. This thought gave me so much comfort, that I resolved to go forwards until I could discover some house or village, or meet with any of the natives, leaving the two horses to discourse together as they pleased. But the first, who was a dapple grey, observing me to steal off, neighed after me in so expressive a tone, that I fancied myself to understand what he meant; whereupon I turned back, and came near him, to expect his farther commands. But concealing my fear as much as I could, for I began to be in some pain, how this adventure might terminate; and the reader will easily believe I did not much like my present situation.

The two horses came up close to me, looking with great earnestness upon my face and hands. The grey steed rubbed my hat all round with his right fore-hoof, and discomposed it so much, that I was forced to adjust it better, by taking it off, and settling it again; whereat both he and his companion (who was a brown bay) appeared to be much surprised; the latter felt the lappet of my coat, and finding it to hang loose about me, they both looked with new signs of wonder. He stroked my right hand, seeming to admire the softness, and colour; but he squeezed it so hard between his hoof and his pastern, that I was forced to roar; after which they both touched me with all possible tenderness. They were under great perplexity about my shoes and stockings, which they felt very often, neighing to each other, and using various gestures, not unlike those of a philosopher, when he would attempt to solve some new and difficult phænomenon.

Upon the whole, the behaviour of these animals was so orderly and rational, so acute and judicious, that I at last concluded, they must needs be magicians, who had thus metamorphosed themselves upon some design, and seeing a stranger in the way, were resolved to divert themselves with him; or perhaps were really amazed at the sight of a man so very different in habit, feature, and complexion from those who might probably live in so remote a climate. Upon the strength of this reasoning, I ventured to address them in the following manner: 'Gentlemen, if you be conjurers, as I have good cause to believe, you can understand any language; therefore I make bold to let your Worships know, that I am a poor distressed English man, driven by his misfortunes upon your coast, and I intreat one of you, to let me ride upon his back, as if he were a real horse, to some house or village, where I can be relieved. In return of which favour, I will make you a present of this knife and bracelet' (taking them out of my pocket). The two creatures stood silent while I spoke, seeming to listen with great attention; and when I had ended, they neighed frequently towards each other, as if they were engaged in serious conversation. I plainly observed, that their language expressed the passions very well, and the words might with little pains be resolved into an alphabet more easily than the Chinese.

I could frequently distinguish the word *'yahoo'*, which was repeated by each of them several times; and although it was impossible for me to conjecture what it meant, yet while the two horses were busy in conversation, I endeavoured to practise this word upon my tongue; and as soon as they were silent, I boldly pronounced *'yahoo'*[4] in a loud voice, imitating, at the same time, as near as I could, the neighing of a horse; at which they were both visibly surprised, and the grey repeated the same word twice, as if he meant to teach me the right accent, wherein I spoke after him as well as I could, and found myself perceivably to improve every time, though very far from any degree of perfection. Then the bay tried me with a second word, much harder to be pronounced; but reducing it to the English orthography, may be spelt thus, *'Houyhnhnm'*.[5] I did not succeed in this so well as the former, but after two or three farther trials, I had better fortune; and they both appeared amazed at my capacity.

After some farther discourse, which I then conjectured might relate to me, the two friends took their leaves, with the same compliment of striking each other's hoof; and the grey made me signs that I should walk before him, wherein I thought it prudent to comply, till I could find a better director. When I offered to slacken my pace, he would cry *'Hhuun, hhuun'*; I guessed his meaning, and gave him to understand, as well as I could, that I was weary, and not able to walk faster; upon which he would stand a while to let me rest.

4. Morley suggested that 'yahoo' was compounded from two expressions of disgust, 'yah' and 'ugh' (or 'hoo'), common in the eighteenth century.

5. This word is an obvious imitation of the whinny of a horse.

Chapter Two

The author conducted by a Houyhnhnm to his house. The house described. The author's reception. The food of the Houyhnhnms. The author in distress for want of meat, is at last relieved. His manner of feeding in this country.

HAVING TRAVELLED ABOUT THREE MILES, WE CAME to a long kind of building, made of timber stuck in the ground, and wattled across; the roof was low, and covered with straw. I now began to be a little comforted, and took out some toys, which travellers usually carry for presents to the savage Indians of America and other parts, in hopes the people of the house would be thereby encouraged to receive me kindly. The horse made me a sign to go in first; it was a large room with a smooth clay floor, and a rack and manger extending the whole length on one side. There were three nags, and two mares, not eating, but some of them sitting down upon their hams, which I very much wondered at; but wondered more to see the rest employed in domestic business. They seemed but ordinary cattle; however, this confirmed my first opinion, that a people who could so far civilise brute animals must needs excel in wisdom all the nations of the world. The grey came in just after, and thereby prevented any ill treatment which the others might have given me. He neighed to them several times in a style of authority, and received answers.

Beyond this room there were three others, reaching the length of the house, to which you passed through three doors, opposite to each other, in the manner of a vista; we went through the second room towards the third; here the grey walked in first, beckoning me to attend.[1] I waited in the second room, and got ready my presents for the master and mistress of the house: they were two knives, three bracelets of false pearl, a small looking-glass, and a bead necklace. The horse neighed three or four times, and I waited to hear some answers in a human voice, but I observed no other returns than in the same dialect, only one or two a little shriller than his. I began to think that this house must belong to some person of great note among them, because there appeared so much ceremony before I could gain admittance. But that a man of quality should be served all by horses was beyond my comprehension. I feared my brain was disturbed by my sufferings and misfortunes: I roused myself, and looked about me in the room where I was left alone; this was furnished like the first, only after a more elegant manner. I rubbed my eyes often, but the same objects still occurred. I pinched my arms and sides, to awake myself, hoping I might be in a dream. I then absolutely concluded, that all these appearances could be nothing else but necromancy and magic. But I had no time to pursue these reflections; for the grey horse came to the door, and made me a sign to follow him into the third room, where I saw a very comely mare, together with a colt and foal,[2] sitting on their haunches, upon mats of straw, not unartfully made, and perfectly neat and clean.

The mare, soon after my entrance, rose from her mat, and coming up close, after having nicely observed my hands and face, gave me a most contemptuous look; then turning to the horse, I heard the word *'yahoo'* often repeated betwixt them; the meaning of which word I could not then comprehend, although it were the first I had learned to pronounce; but I was soon better informed, to my everlasting mortification: for the horse beckoning to me with his head, and repeating the word *'Hhuun, hhuun'*, as he did upon the road, which I understood

1. Wait without.
2. Swift evidently intends to differentiate between male and female by these words: they do not ordinarily bear the meanings implied.

was to attend him, led me out into a kind of court, where was another building at some distance from the house. Here we entered, and I saw three of these detestable creatures, whom I first met after my landing, feeding upon roots, and the flesh of some animals, which I afterwards found to be that of asses and dogs, and now and then a cow dead by accident or disease. They were all tied by the neck with strong withes, fastened to a beam; they held their food between the claws of their fore-feet, and tore it with their teeth.

The master horse ordered a sorrel nag, one of his servants, to untie the largest of these animals, and take him into the yard. The beast and I were brought close together, and our countenances diligently compared, both by master and servant, who thereupon repeated several times the word *'yahoo'*. My horror and astonishment are not to be described, when I observed, in this abominable animal, a perfect human figure; the face of it indeed was flat and broad, the nose depressed, the lips large, and the mouth wide. But these differences are common to all savage nations, where the lineaments of the countenance are distorted by the natives suffering their infants to lie grovelling on the earth, or by carrying them on their backs, nuzzling with their face against the mother's shoulders. The fore-feet of the yahoo differed from my hands in nothing else but the length of the nails, the coarseness and brownness of the palms, and the hairiness on the backs. There was the same resemblance between our feet, with the same differences, which I knew very well, though the horses did not, because of my shoes and stockings; the same in every part of our bodies, except as to hairiness and colour, which I have already described.

The great difficulty that seemed to stick with the two horses, was to see the rest of my body so very different from that of a yahoo, for which I was obliged to my clothes, whereof they had no conception: the sorrel nag offered me a root, which he held (after their manner, as we shall describe in its proper place) between his hoof and pastern; I took it in my hand, and having smelt it, returned it to him again as civilly as I could. He brought out of the yahoo's kennel a piece of ass's flesh, but it smelt so offensively, that I turned from it with loathing: he then threw it to the yahoo, by whom it was greedily devoured. He afterwards showed me a wisp of hay, and a fetlock full of oats; but I shook my head, to signify, that neither of these were food for me. And indeed, I now apprehended, that I must absolutely starve, if I did not get to some of my own species: for as to those filthy yahoos, although there were few greater lovers of mankind, at that time, than myself, yet I confess I never saw any sensitive being so detestable on all accounts; and the more I came near them, the more hateful they grew, while I stayed in that country. This the master horse observed by my behaviour, and therefore sent the yahoo back to his kennel. He then put his fore-hoof to his mouth, at which I was much surprised, although he did it with ease, and with a motion that appeared perfectly natural, and made other signs to know what I would eat; but I could not return him such an answer as he was able to apprehend; and if he had understood me, I did not see how it was possible to contrive any way for finding myself nourishment. While we were thus engaged, I observed a cow passing by, whereupon I pointed to her, and expressed a desire to let me go and milk her. This had its effect; for he led me back into the house, and ordered a mare-servant to open a room, where a good store of milk lay in earthen and wooden vessels, after a very orderly and cleanly manner. She gave me a large bowl full, of which I drank very heartily, and found myself well refreshed.

About noon I saw coming towards the house a kind of vehicle drawn like a sledge by four yahoos. There was in it an old steed, who seemed to be of quality; he alighted with his hind feet forward, having by accident got a hurt in his left fore-foot. He came to dine with our horse, who received him with great civility. They dined in the best room, and had oats boiled in milk for the second course, which the old horse eat warm, but the rest cold. Their mangers were placed circular in the middle of the room, and divided into several partitions, round which they sate on their haunches upon bosses of straw. In the middle was a large rack with angles answering to every partition of the manger. So that each horse and mare eat their own hay, and their own mash of oats and milk, with much decency and regularity. The behaviour of the young colt and foal appeared very modest, and that of the master and mistress extremely cheerful and complaisant to their guest. The grey ordered me to stand by him, and much discourse passed between him and his friend concerning me, as I found by the stranger's often looking on me, and the frequent repetition of the word *'yahoo'*.

I happened to wear my gloves, which the master grey observing, seemed perplexed, discovering signs of wonder what I had done to my fore-feet; he put his hoof three or four times to them, as if he would signify, that I should reduce them to their former shape, which I presently did, pulling off both my gloves, and putting them into my pocket. This occasioned farther talk, and I saw the company was pleased with my behaviour, whereof I soon found the good effects. I was ordered to speak the few words I understood, and while they were at dinner, the master taught me the names for oats, milk, fire, water, and some others; which I could readily pronounce after him, having from my youth a great facility in learning languages.

When dinner was done, the master horse took me aside, and by signs and words made me understand the concern that he was in, that I had nothing to eat. Oats in their tongue are called *'hlunnh'*. This word I pronounced two or three times; for although I had refused them at first, yet upon second thoughts, I considered that I could contrive to make of them a kind of bread, which might be sufficient with milk to keep me alive, till I could make my escape to some other country, and to creatures of my own species. The horse immediately ordered a white mare-servant of his family to bring me a good quantity of oats in a sort of wooden tray. These I heated before the fire as well as I could, and rubbed them till the husks came off, which I made a shift to winnow from the grain; I ground and beat them between two stones, then took water, and made them into a paste or cake, which I toasted at the fire, and eat warm with milk. It was at first a very insipid diet, though common enough in many parts of Europe, but grew tolerable by time; and having been often reduced to hard fare in my life, this was not the first experiment I had made how easily nature is satisfied. And I cannot but observe, that I never had one hour's sickness, while I stayed in this island. 'Tis true, I some times made a shift to catch a rabbit, or bird, by springes[3] made of yahoos' hairs, and I often gathered wholesome herbs, which I boiled, or eat as salads with my bread, and now and then, for a rarity, I made a little butter, and drank the whey. I was at first at a great loss for salt; but custom soon reconciled the want of it; and I am confident that the frequent use of salt among us is an effect of luxury, and was first introduced only as a provocative to drink; except where it is necessary for preserving of flesh in long voyages, or in places remote from great markets. For we observe no animal to be fond of it but man:[4] and as to myself, when I left this country, it was a great while before I could endure the taste of it in any thing that I eat.

This is enough to say upon the subject of my diet, wherewith other travellers fill their books, as if the readers were personally concerned whether we fared well or ill. However, it was necessary to mention this matter, lest the world should think it impossible that I could find sustenance for three years in such a country, and among such inhabitants.

When it grew towards evening, the master horse ordered a place for me to lodge in; it was but six yards from the house, and separated from the stable of the yahoos. Here I got some straw, and covering myself with my own clothes, slept very sound. But I was in a short time better accommodated, as the reader shall know hereafter, when I come to treat more particularly about my way of living.

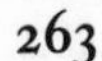

3. Snares.
4. A very inaccurate statement, as Scott observed: many animals, including horses, are extremely fond of salt.

Chapter Three

The author studious to learn the language, the Houyhnhnm his master assists in teaching him. The language described. Several Houyhnhnms of quality come out of curiosity to see the author. He gives his master a short account of his voyage.

Y PRINCIPAL ENDEAVOUR WAS TO LEARN THE language, which my master (for so I shall henceforth call him) and his children, and every servant of his house were desirous to teach me. For they looked upon it as a prodigy that a brute animal should discover such marks of a rational creature. I pointed to every thing, and enquired the name of it, which I wrote down in my journal-book when I was alone, and corrected my bad accent, by desiring those of the family to pronounce it often. In this employment, a sorrel nag, one of the under servants, was very ready to assist me.

In speaking, they pronounce through the nose and throat, and their language approaches nearest to the High Dutch or German, of any I know in Europe; but is much more graceful and significant. The Emperor Charles V made almost the same observation, when he said, that if he were to speak to his horse, it should be in High Dutch.[1]

The curiosity and impatience of my master were so great, that he spent many hours of his leisure to instruct me. He was convinced (as he afterwards told me) that I must be a yahoo, but my teachableness,

1. The original epigram was hardly complimentary either to horses or to the German language: Charles is supposed to have said that he would address his God in Spanish, his mistress in Italian, and his horse in German.

civility, and cleanliness astonished him; which were qualities altogether so opposite to those animals. He was most perplexed about my clothes, reasoning sometimes with himself, whether they were a part of my body; for I never pulled them off till the family were asleep, and got them on before they waked in the morning. My master was eager to learn from whence I came, how I acquired those appearances of reason which I discovered in all my actions, and to know my story from my own mouth, which he hoped he should soon do by the great proficiency I made in learning and pronouncing their words and sentences. To help my memory, I formed all I learned into the English alphabet, and writ the words down with the translations. This last, after some time, I ventured to do in my master's presence. It cost me much trouble to explain to him what I was doing; for the inhabitants have not the least idea of books or literature.

In about ten weeks time I was able to understand most of his questions, and in three months could give him some tolerable answers. He was extremely curious to know from what part of the country I came, and how I was taught to imitate a rational creature, because the yahoos (whom he saw I exactly resembled in my head, hands, and face, that were only visible), with some appearance of cunning, and the strongest disposition to mischief, were observed to be the most unteachable of all brutes. I answered, that I came over the sea, from a far place, with many others of my own kind, in a great hollow vessel made of the bodies of trees. That my companions forced me to land on this coast, and then left me to shift for myself. It was with some difficulty, and by the help of many signs, that I brought him to understand me. He replied, that I must needs be mistaken, or that I 'said the thing which was not'. (For they have no word in their language to express lying or falsehood.) He knew it was impossible that there could be a country beyond the sea, or that a parcel of brutes could move a wooden vessel whither they pleased upon water. He was sure no Houyhnhnm alive could make such a vessel, nor would trust yahoos to manage it.

The word *'Houyhnhnm'*, in their tongue, signifies 'a horse', and in its etymology, 'the perfection of nature'. I told my master, that I was at a loss for expression, but would improve as fast as I could; and hoped in a short time I should be able to tell him wonders: he was pleased to direct his own mare, his colt and foal, and the servants of the family to take all opportunities of instructing me, and every day for two or three hours he was at the same pains himself: several horses and mares of quality in the neighbourhood came often to our house upon the report spread of a wonderful yahoo, that could speak like a Houyhnhnm, and seemed in his words and actions to discover some glimmerings of reason. These delighted to converse with me; they put many questions, and received such answers as I was able to return. By all these advantages, I made so great a progress, that in five months from my arrival I understood whatever was spoke, and could express myself tolerably well.

The Houyhnhnms who came to visit my master, out of a design of seeing and talking with me, could hardly believe me to be a right yahoo, because my body had a different covering from others of my kind. They were astonished to observe me without the usual hair or skin except on my head, face, and hands; but I discovered that secret to my master, upon an accident, which happened about a fortnight before.

I have already told the reader, that every night, when the family were gone to bed, it was my custom to strip and cover myself with my clothes: it happened one morning early, that my master sent for me, by the sorrel nag, who was his valet; when he came, I was fast asleep, my clothes fallen off on one side, and my shirt above my waist. I awaked at the noise he made, and observed him to deliver his message in some disorder; after which he went to my master, and in a great fright gave him a very confused account of what he had seen: this I presently discovered; for going, as soon as I was dressed, to pay my attendance upon his Honour, he asked me the meaning of what his servant had reported, that I was not the same thing when I slept as I appeared to be at other times; that his valet assured him, some part of me was white, some yellow, at least not so white, and some brown.

I had hitherto concealed the secret of my dress, in order to distinguish myself as much as possible from that cursed race of yahoos; but now I found it in vain to do so any longer. Besides, I considered that my clothes and shoes would soon wear out, which already were in a declining condition, and must be supplied by some contrivance from the hides of yahoos or other brutes; whereby the whole secret would be known: I therefore told my master, that in the country from whence I came those of my kind always covered their bodies with the hairs of certain animals prepared by art, as well for decency, as to avoid the inclemencies of air both hot and cold; of which, as to my own person, I would give him immediate conviction, if he pleased to command me; only desiring his excuse, if I did not expose those parts that nature taught us to conceal. He said my discourse was all very strange, but especially the last part; for he could not understand why nature should teach us to conceal what nature had given. That neither himself nor family were ashamed of any parts of their bodies; but however I might do as I pleased. Whereupon, I first unbuttoned my coat, and pulled it off. I did the same with my waistcoat; I drew off my shoes, stockings, and breeches. I let my shirt down to my waist, and drew up the bottom, fastening it like a girdle about my middle to hide my nakedness.

My master observed the whole performance with great signs of curiosity and admiration. He took up all my clothes in his pastern, one piece after another, and examined them diligently; he then stroked my body very gently and looked round me several times, after which he said, it was plain I must be a perfect yahoo; but that I differed very much from the rest of my species, in the softness, and whiteness, and smoothness of my skin, my want of hair in several parts of my body, the shape and shortness of my claws behind and before, and my affectation of walking continually on my two hinder feet. He desired to see no more, and gave me leave to put on my clothes again, for I was shuddering with cold.

I expressed my uneasiness at his giving me so often the appellation of *'yahoo'*, an odious animal, for which I had so utter an hatred and contempt; I begged he would forbear applying that word to me, and take the same order in his family, and among his friends whom he suffered to see me. I requested likewise, that the secret of my having a false covering to my body might be known to none but himself, at least as long as my present clothing should last; for as to what the sorrel nag his valet had observed, his Honour might command him to conceal it.

All this my master very graciously consented to, and thus the secret was kept till my clothes began to wear out, which I was forced to supply by several contrivances, that shall hereafter be mentioned. In the mean time, he desired I would go on with my utmost diligence to learn their language, because he was more astonished at my capacity for speech and reason than at the figure of my body, whether it were covered or no; adding, that he waited with some impatience to hear the wonders which I promised to tell him.

From thenceforwards he doubled the pains he had been at to instruct me; he brought me into all company, and made them treat me with civility, because, as he told them privately, this would put me into good humour, and make me more diverting.

Every day when I waited on him, beside the trouble he was at in teaching, he would ask me several questions concerning myself, which I answered as well as I could; and by these means he had already received some general ideas, though very imperfect. It would be tedious to relate the several steps by which I advanced to a more regular conversation: but the first account I gave of myself in any order and length, was to this purpose:

That I came from a very far country, as I already had attempted to tell him, with about fifty more of my own species; that we travelled upon the seas, in a great hollow vessel made of wood, and larger than his Honour's house. I described the ship to him in the best terms I could, and explained by the help of my handkerchief displayed, how it was driven forwards by the wind. That upon a quarrel among us, I was set on shore on this coast, where I walked forwards without knowing whither, till he delivered me from the persecution of those execrable yahoos. He asked me, who made the ship, and how it was possible that the Houyhnhnms of my country would leave it to the management of brutes? My answer was, that I durst proceed no farther in my relation, unless he would give me his word and honour that he would not be offended, and then I would tell him the wonders I had so often promised. He agreed; and I went on by assuring him, that the ship was made by creatures like myself, who in all the countries I had travelled, as well as in my own, were the only governing, rational animals; and that upon my arrival hither, I was as much astonished to see the Houyhnhnms act like rational beings, as he or his friends could be in finding some marks of reason in a creature he was pleased to call a yahoo, to which I owned my resemblance in every part, but could not account for their degenerate and brutal nature. I said farther, that if good fortune ever restored me to my native country, to relate my travels hither, as I resolved to do, every body would believe that I 'said the thing which was not'; that I invented the story out of my own head; and with all possible respect to himself, his family, and friends, and under his promise of not being offended, our countrymen would hardly think it probable, that a Houyhnhnm should be the presiding creature of a nation, and a yahoo the brute.

Chapter Four

The Houyhnhnms' notion of truth and falsehood. The author's discourse disapproved by his master. The author gives a more particular account of himself, and the accidents of his voyage.

Y MASTER HEARD ME WITH GREAT APPEARances of uneasiness in his countenance, because *doubting* or *not believing,* are so little known in this country, that the inhabitants cannot tell how to behave themselves under such circumstances. And I remember in frequent discourses with my master concerning the nature of manhood, in other parts of the world, having occasion to talk of 'lying' and 'false representation', it was with much difficulty that he comprehended what I meant, although he had otherwise a most acute judgment. For he argued thus; that the use of speech was to make us understand one another, and to receive information of facts; now if any one 'said the thing which was not', these ends were defeated; because I cannot properly be said to understand him, and I am so far from receiving information, that he leaves me worse than in ignorance, for I am led to believe a thing *black* when it is *white,* and *short* when it is *long.* And these were all the notions he had concerning that faculty of *lying,* so perfectly well understood among human creatures.

To return from this digression; when I asserted that the yahoos were the only governing animals in my country, which my master said was altogether past his conception, he desired to know, whether we had Houyhnhnms among us, and what was their employment: I told him, we had great numbers, that in summer they grazed in the fields, and in winter were kept in houses, with hay and oats, where yahoo servants were employed to rub their skins smooth, comb their manes, pick their feet, serve them with food, and make their beds. 'I understand you well', said my master, 'it is now very plain, from all you have spoken, that whatever share of reason the yahoos pretend to, the Houyhnhnms are your masters; I heartily wish our yahoos would be so tractable'. I begged his Honour would please to excuse me from proceeding any farther, because I was very certain that the account he expected from me would be highly displeasing. But he insisted in commanding me to let him know the best and the worst: I told him, he should be obeyed. I owned, that the Houyhnhnms among us, whom we called horses, were the most generous[1] and comely animal we had, that they excelled in strength and swiftness; and when they belonged to persons of quality, employed in travelling, racing, or drawing chariots, they were treated with much kindness and care, till they fell into diseases, or became foundered in the feet; and then they were sold, and used to all kind of drudgery till they died; after which their skins were stripped and sold for what they were worth, and their bodies left to be devoured by dogs and birds of prey. But the common race of horses had not so good fortune, being kept by farmers and carriers and other mean people, who put them to greater labour, and fed them worse. I described, as well as I could, our way of riding, the shape and use of a bridle, a saddle, a spur, and a whip, of harness and wheels. I added, that we fastened plates of a certain hard substance called 'iron' at the bottom of their feet, to preserve their hoofs from being broken by the stony ways on which we often travelled.

My master, after some expressions of great indignation, wondered how we dared to venture upon a Houyhnhnm's back, for he was sure that the weakest servant in his house would be able to shake off the strongest yahoo, or by lying down, and rolling on his back, squeeze

1. Noble.

the brute to death. I answered, that our horses were trained up from three or four years old to the several uses we intended them for; that if any of them proved intolerably vicious, they were employed for carriages; that they were severely beaten while they were young, for any mischievous tricks; that the males, designed for common use of riding or draught, were generally 'castrated' about two years after their birth, to take down their spirits, and make them more tame and gentle; that they were indeed sensible of rewards and punishments; but his Honour would please to consider, that they had not the least tincture of reason any more than the yahoos in this country.

It put me to the pains of many circumlocutions to give my master a right idea of what I spoke; for their language doth not abound in variety of words, because their wants and passions are fewer than among us. But it is impossible to represent his noble resentment at our savage treatment of the Houyhnhnm race, particularly after I had explained the manner and use of 'castrating' horses among us, to hinder them from propagating their kind, and to render them more servile. He said, if it were possible there could be any country where yahoos alone were endued with reason, they certainly must be the governing animal, because reason will in time always prevail against brutal strength. But, considering the frame of our bodies, and especially of mine, he thought no creature of equal bulk was so ill contrived for employing that reason in the common offices of life; whereupon he desired to know whether those among whom I lived resembled me or the yahoos of his country. I assured him, that I was as well shaped as most of my age: but the younger and the females were much more soft and tender, and the skins of the latter generally as white as milk. He said, I differed indeed from other yahoos, being much more cleanly, and not altogether so deformed, but in point of real advantage he thought I differed for the worse. That my nails were of no use either to my fore or hinder feet; as to my fore-feet, he could not properly call them by that name, for he never observed me to walk upon them; that they were too soft to bear the ground; that I generally went with them uncovered, neither was the covering I sometimes wore on them of the same shape or so strong as that on my feet behind. That I could not walk with any security, for if either of my hinder feet slipped, I must inevitably fall. He then began to find fault with other parts of my body, the flatness of my face, the prominence of my nose, my eyes placed directly in front, so that I could not look on either side without turning my head: that I was not able to feed myself without lifting one of my fore-feet to my mouth: and therefore nature had placed those joints to answer that necessity. He knew not what could be the use of those several clefts and divisions in my feet behind; that these were too soft to bear the hardness and sharpness of stones without a covering made from the skin of some other brute; that my whole body wanted a fence against heat and cold, which I was forced to put on and off every day with tediousness and trouble. And lastly, that he observed every animal in this country naturally to abhor the yahoos, whom the weaker avoided, and the stronger drove from them. So that supposing us to have the gift of reason, he could not see how it were possible to cure that natural antipathy which every creature discovered against us; nor consequently, how we could tame and render them serviceable. However, he would (as he said) debate that matter no farther, because he was more desirous to know my own story, the country where I was born, and the several actions and events of my life before I came hither.

I assured him how extremely desirous I was that he should be satisfied in every point; but I doubted much, whether it would be possible for me to explain myself on several subjects whereof his Honour could have no conception, because I saw nothing in his country to which I could resemble them. That however, I would do my best, and strive to express myself by similitudes, humbly desiring his assistance when I wanted proper words; which he was pleased to promise me.

I said, my birth was of honest parents, in an island called England, which was remote from this country as many days' journey as the strongest of his Honour's servants could travel in the annual course of the sun. That I was bred a surgeon, whose trade it is to cure wounds and hurts in the body, got by accident or violence; that my country was governed by a female man, whom we called a 'queen'. That I left it to get riches, whereby I might maintain myself and family when I should return. That in my last voyage I was commander of the ship, and had about fifty yahoos under me, many of which died at sea, and I was forced to supply them by others picked out from several nations. That our ship was twice in danger of being sunk; the first time by a great storm, and the second, by striking against a rock. Here my master interposed, by asking me, how I could persuade strangers out of different countries to venture with me, after the losses I had sustained, and the hazards I had run. I said, they were fellows of desperate fortunes, forced to fly from the places of their birth, on account of their poverty or their crimes. Some were undone by lawsuits; others spent all they had in drinking, whoring, and gaming; others fled for treason; many for murder, theft, poisoning, robbery, perjury, forgery, coining false money, for committing rapes or sodomy, for flying from their colours, or deserting to the enemy, and most of them had broken prison; none of these durst return to their native countries for fear of being hanged, or of starving in a jail; and therefore were under a necessity of seeking a livelihood in other places.

During this discourse, my master was pleased to interrupt me several times; I had made use of many circumlocutions in describing to him the nature of the several crimes, for which most of our crew had been forced to fly their country. This labour took up several days' conversation before he was able to comprehend me. He was wholly at a loss to know what could be the use or necessity of practising those vices. To clear up which I endeavoured to give him some ideas of the desire of power and riches, of the terrible effects of lust, intemperance, malice, and envy. All this I was forced to define and describe by putting of cases, and making of suppositions. After which, like one whose imagination was struck with something never seen or heard of before, he would lift up his eyes with amazement and indignation.

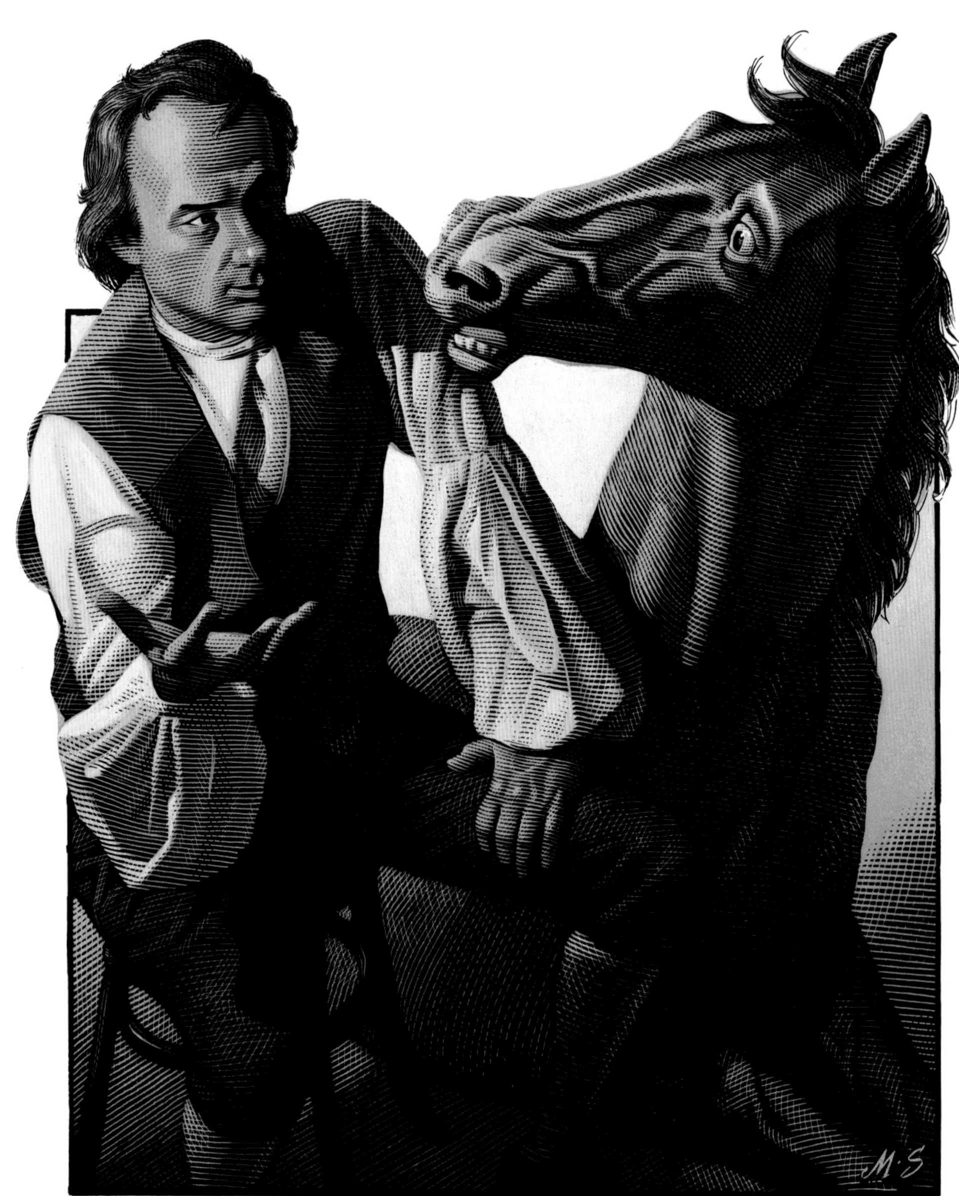
M·S

Every day when I waited on him,... he would ask me several questions concerning myself, which I answered as well as I could;...

PAGE 268

Power, government, war, law, punishment, and a thousand other things had no terms wherein that language could express them, which made the difficulty almost insuperable to give my master any conception of what I meant. But being of an excellent understanding, much improved by contemplation and converse, he at last arrived at a competent knowledge of what human nature in our parts of the world is capable to perform, and desired I would give him some particular account of that land which we call Europe, but especially of my own country.

Chapter Five

The author, at his master's commands, informs him of the state of England. The causes of war among the princes of Europe. The author begins to explain the English constitution.

HE READER MAY PLEASE TO OBSERVE, THAT THE following extract of many conversations I had with my master contains a summary of the most material points which were discoursed at several times for above two years; his Honour often desiring fuller satisfaction as I farther improved in the Houyhnhnm tongue. I laid before him, as well as I could, the whole state of Europe; I discoursed of trade and manufactures, of arts and sciences; and the answers I gave to all the questions he made, as they arose upon several subjects, were a fund of conversation not to be exhausted. But I shall here only set down the substance of what passed between us concerning my own country, reducing it into order as well as I can, without any regard to time or other circumstances, while I strictly adhere to truth. My only concern is, that I shall hardly be able to do justice to my master's arguments and expressions, which must needs suffer by my want of capacity, as well as by a translation into our barbarous English.

In obedience therefore to his Honour's commands, I related to him the Revolution under the Prince of Orange; the long war with France entered into by the said prince, and renewed by his successor the present queen, wherein the greatest powers of Christendom were engaged, and which still continued: I computed, at his request, that about a million of yahoos might have been killed in the whole progress of it, and perhaps a hundred or more cities taken, and thrice as many ships burnt or sunk.[1]

He asked me what were the usual causes or motives that made one country go to war with another. I answered they were innumerable, but I should only mention a few of the chief. Sometimes the ambition of princes, who never think they have land or people enough to govern: sometimes the corruption of ministers, who engage their master in a war in order to stifle or divert the clamour of the subjects against their evil administration. Difference in opinions hath cost many millions of lives: for instance, whether *flesh* be *bread,* or *bread* be *flesh;* whether the juice of a certain *berry* be *blood* or *wine;* whether *whistling* be a vice or a virtue; whether it be better to *kiss a post,* or throw it into the fire; what is the best colour for a *coat,* whether *black, white, red,* or *grey;* and whether it should be *long* or *short, narrow* or *wide, dirty* or *clean,*[2] with many more. Neither are any wars so furious and bloody, or of so long continuance, as those occasioned by difference in opinion, especially if it be in things indifferent.[3]

Sometimes the quarrel between two princes is to decide which of them shall dispossess a third of his dominions, where neither of them pretend to any right. Sometimes one prince quarrelleth with another, for fear the other should quarrel with him. Sometimes a war is entered upon, because the enemy is too *strong,* and sometimes because he is too *weak.* Sometimes our neighbours *want* the things which we *have,* or *have* the things which we *want;* and we both fight, till they take ours or give us theirs. It is a very justifiable cause of war to invade a country after the people have been wasted by famine, destroyed by pestilence, or embroiled by factions among themselves. It is justifiable

1. Swift exaggerates the losses in the War of the Spanish Succession.

2. The first two controversies were concerned with the doctrine of transubstantiation, the third with the use of music in church services, the fourth with the use of the crucifix, and the others with various quarrels about ecclesiastical vestments.

3. Unimportant.

to enter into war against our nearest ally, where one of his towns lies convenient for us, or a territory of land, that would render our dominions round and complete. If a prince sends forces into a nation where the people are poor and ignorant, he may lawfully put half of them to death, and make slaves of the rest, in order to civilise and reduce them from their barbarous way of living. It is a very kingly, honourable, and frequent practice, when one prince desires the assistance of another to secure him against an invasion, that the assistant, when he hath driven out the invader, should seize on the dominions himself, and kill, imprison or banish the prince he came to relieve. Alliance by blood or marriage is a sufficient cause of war between princes, and the nearer the kindred is, the greater is their disposition to quarrel: *poor* nations are *hungry,* and *rich* nations are *proud,* and pride and hunger will ever be at variance. For these reasons, the trade of a 'soldier' is held the most honourable of all others: because a 'soldier' is a yahoo hired to kill in cold blood as many of his own species, who have never offended him, as possibly he can.

There is likewise a kind of beggarly princes in Europe, not able to make war by themselves, who hire out their troops to richer nations, for so much a day to each man; of which they keep three fourths to themselves, and it is the best part of their maintenance; such are those in Germany and other northern parts of Europe.[4]

'What you have told me', said my master, 'upon the subject of war, does indeed discover most admirably the effects of that reason you pretend to: however, it is happy that the *shame* is greater than the *danger;* and that nature hath left you utterly uncapable of doing much mischief.

'For your mouths lying flat with your faces, you can hardly bite each other to any purpose, unless by consent. Then as to the claws upon your feet before and behind, they are so short and tender, that one of our yahoos would drive a dozen of yours before him. And therefore in

4. George I, as King of Hanover, had been involved in this traffic.

recounting the numbers of those who have been killed in battle, I cannot but think that you have "said the thing which is not".'

I could not forbear shaking my head and smiling a little at his ignorance. And being no stranger to the art of war, I gave him a description of cannons, culverins, muskets, carabines, pistols, bullets, powder, swords, bayonets, battles, sieges, retreats, attacks, undermines, countermines, bombardments, sea-fights; ships sunk with a thousand men, twenty thousand killed on each side; dying groans, limbs flying in the air, smoke, noise, confusion, trampling to death under horses' feet; flight, pursuit, victory; fields strewed with carcases left for food to dogs, and wolves, and birds of prey; plundering, stripping, ravishing, burning, and destroying. And to set forth the valour of my own dear countrymen, I assured him, that I had seen them blow up a hundred enemies at once in a siege, and as many in a ship, and beheld the dead bodies come down in pieces from the clouds, to the great diversion of the spectators.

I was going on to more particulars, when my master commanded me silence. He said, whoever understood the nature of yahoos might easily believe it possible for so vile an animal to be capable of every action I had named, if their strength and cunning equalled their malice. But as my discourse had encreased his abhorrence of the whole species, so he found it gave him a disturbance in his mind, to which he was wholly a stranger before. He thought his ears being used to such abominable words, might by degrees admit them with less detestation. That although he hated the yahoos of this country, yet he no more blamed them for their odious qualities, than he did a *gnnayh* (a bird of prey) for its cruelty, or a sharp stone for cutting his hoof. But when a creature pretending to reason could be capable of such enormities, he dreaded lest the corruption of that faculty might be worse than brutality itself. He seemed therefore confident, that instead of reason, we were only possessed of some quality fitted to encrease our natural vices; as the reflection from a troubled stream returns the image of an ill-shapen body, not only *larger,* but more *distorted.*

He added, that he had heard too much upon the subject of war, both in this and some former discourses. There was another point which a little perplexed him at present. I had informed him, that some of our crew left their country on account of being ruined by 'law'; that I had already explained the meaning of the word; but he was at a loss how it should come to pass, that the 'law' which was intended for *every* man's preservation, should be any man's ruin. Therefore he desired to be farther satisfied what I meant by 'law', and the dispensers thereof according to the present practice in my own country; because he thought nature and reason were sufficient guides for a reasonable animal, as we pretended to be, in showing us what we ought to do, and what to avoid.

I assured his Honour, that law was a science wherein I had not much conversed, further than by employing advocates in vain, upon some injustices that had been done me: however, I would give him all the satisfaction I was able.

I said, there was a society of men among us, bred up from their youth in the art of proving by words multiplied for the purpose, that white is black, and black is white, according as they are paid. To this society all the rest of the people are slaves. For example, if my neighbour hath a mind to my cow, he hires a lawyer to prove, that he ought to have my cow from me. I must then hire another to defend my right, it being against all rules of law that any man should be allowed to speak for himself. Now in this case, I who am the right owner lie under two great disadvantages. First, my lawyer, being practised almost from his cradle in defending falsehood, is quite out of his element when he would be an advocate for justice, which as an office unnatural, he always attempts with ill will. The second disadvantage is, that my lawyer must proceed with great caution, or else he will be reprimanded by the judges, and abhorred by his brethren, as one that would lessen the practice of the law. And therefore I have but two methods to preserve my cow. The first is to gain over my adversary's lawyer with a double fee, who will then betray his client by insinuating that he hath justice on his side. The second way is for my lawyer to make my cause appear as unjust as he can, by allowing the cow to belong to my adversary; and this, if it be skilfully done, will certainly bespeak the favour of the bench. Now, your Honour is to know that these judges are persons appointed to decide all controversies of property, as well as for the trial of criminals, and picked out from the most dextrous lawyers who are grown old or lazy, and, having been biassed all their lives against truth and equity, are under such a fatal necessity of favouring fraud, perjury, and oppression, that I have known several of them refuse a large bribe from the side where justice lay, rather than injure the faculty[5] by doing any thing unbecoming their nature or their office.

It is a maxim among these lawyers, that whatever hath been done before may legally be done again: and therefore they take special care to record all the decisions formerly made against common justice and the general reason of mankind. These, under the name of 'precedents', they produce as authorities, to justify the most iniquitous opinions; and the judges never fail of decreeing accordingly.

In pleading, they studiously avoid entering into the *merits* of the cause, but are loud, violent, and tedious in dwelling upon all *circumstances* which are not to the purpose. For instance, in the case already mentioned; they never desire to know what claim or title my adversary hath to my *cow,* but whether the said *cow* were red or black, her horns long or short; whether the field I graze her in be round or square, whether she was milked at home or abroad, what diseases she is subject to, and the like; after which they consult 'precedents', adjourn the cause from time to time, and in ten, twenty, or thirty years come to an issue.

It is likewise to be observed that this society hath a peculiar cant and jargon of their own, that no other mortal can understand, and wherein all their laws are written, which they take special care to

5. Profession.

multiply; whereby they have wholly confounded the very essence of truth and falsehood, of right and wrong; so that it will take thirty years to decide whether the field left me by my ancestors for six generations belongs to me or to a stranger three hundred miles off.

In the trial of persons accused for crimes against the state the method is much more short and commendable: the judge first sends to sound the disposition of those in power, after which he can easily hang or save the criminal, strictly preserving all due forms of law.

Here my master, interposing, said it was a pity, that creatures endowed with such prodigious abilities of mind as these lawyers, by the description I gave of them, must certainly be, were not rather encouraged to be instructors of others in wisdom and knowledge. In answer to which I assured his Honour, that in all points out of their own trade they were the most ignorant and stupid generation among us, the most despicable in common conversation, avowed enemies to all knowledge and learning, and equally disposed to pervert the general reason of mankind in every other subject of discourse, as in that of their own profession.

Chapter Six

A continuation of the state of England. The character of a first minister in the courts of Europe.

Y MASTER WAS YET WHOLLY AT A LOSS TO UNderstand what motives could incite this race of lawyers to perplex, disquiet, and weary themselves, and engage in a confederacy of injustice, merely for the sake of injuring their fellow-animals; neither could he comprehend what I meant in saying they did it for 'hire'. Whereupon I was at much pains to describe to him the use of 'money', the materials it was made of, and the value of the metals; that when a yahoo had got a great store of this precious substance, he was able to purchase whatever he had a mind to, the finest clothing, the noblest houses, great tracts of land, the most costly meats and drinks, and have his choice of the most beautiful females. Therefore since 'money' alone was able to perform all these feats, our yahoos thought they could never have enough of it to spend or to save, as they found themselves inclined from their natural bent either to profusion or avarice. That the rich man enjoyed the fruit of the poor man's labour, and the latter were a thousand to one in proportion to the former. That the bulk of our people were forced to live miserably, by labouring every day for small wages to make a few live plentifully. I enlarged myself much on these and many other particulars to the same purpose: but his Honour was still to seek,[1] for he went upon a supposition that all animals had a title to their share in the productions of the earth, and especially those who presided over the rest.[2] Therefore he desired I would let him know what these costly meats were, and how any of us happened to want[3] them. Whereupon I enumerated as many sorts as came into my head, with the various methods of dressing them, which could not be done without sending vessels by sea to every part of the world, as well for liquors to drink, as for sauces, and innumerable other conveniencies. I assured him, that this whole globe of earth must be at least three times gone round, before one of our better female yahoos could get her breakfast, or a cup to put it in. He said, that must needs be a miserable country which cannot furnish food for its own inhabitants. But what he chiefly wondered at was how such vast tracts of ground as I described should be wholly without *fresh water,* and the people put to the necessity of sending over the sea for drink. I replied, that England (the dear place of my nativity) was computed to produce three times the quantity of food more than its inhabitants are able to consume, as well as liquors extracted from grain, or pressed out of the fruit of certain trees, which made excellent drink, and the same proportion in every other convenience of life. But in order to feed the luxury and intemperance of the males, and the vanity of the females, we sent away the greatest part of our necessary things to other countries, from whence in return we brought the materials of diseases, folly, and vice, to spend among ourselves. Hence it follows of necessity that vast numbers of our people are compelled to seek their livelihood by begging, robbing, stealing, cheating, pimping, forswearing, flattering, suborning, forging, gaming, lying, fawning, hectoring, voting, scribbling, star-gazing, poisoning, whoring, canting, libelling, free-thinking, and the like occupations: every one of which terms, I was at much pains to make him understand.

1. At a loss to understand.
2. The meaning is 'especially that species which presided over the rest'.
3. Lack.

That 'wine' was not imported among us from foreign countries to supply the want of water or other drinks, but because it was a sort of liquid which made us merry, by putting us out of our senses; diverted all melancholy thoughts, begat wild extravagant imaginations in the brain, raised our hopes, and banished our fears, suspended every office of reason for a time, and deprived us of the use of our limbs, till we fell into a profound sleep; although it must be confessed, that we always awaked sick and dispirited, and that the use of this liquor filled us with diseases, which made our lives uncomfortable and short.

But beside all this, the bulk of our people supported themselves by furnishing the necessities or conveniencies of life to the rich, and to each other. For instance, when I am at home and dressed as I ought to be, I carry on my body the workmanship of an hundred tradesmen; the building and furniture of my house employ as many more, and five times the number to adorn my wife.

I was going on to tell him of another sort of people, who get their livelihood by attending the sick, having upon some occasions informed his Honour that many of my crew had died of diseases. But here it was with the utmost difficulty that I brought him to apprehend what I meant. He could easily conceive that a Houyhnhnm grew weak and heavy a few days before his death, or by some accident might hurt a limb. But that Nature, who works all things to perfection, should suffer any pains to breed in our bodies, he thought it impossible, and desired to know the reason of so unaccountable an evil. I told him, we fed on a thousand things which operated contrary to each other; that we eat when we were not hungry, and drank without the provocation of thirst; that we sate whole nights drinking strong liquors without eating a bit, which disposed us to sloth, enflamed our bodies, and precipitated or prevented digestion. That prostitute female yahoos acquired a certain malady, which bred rottenness in the bones of those who fell into their embraces; that this and many other diseases were propagated from father to son, so that great numbers come into the world with complicated maladies upon them; that it would be endless to give him a catalogue of all diseases incident to human bodies; for they could not be fewer than five or six hundred, spread over every limb and joint; in short, every part, external and intestine, having diseases appropriated to them. To remedy which, there was a sort of people bred up among us, in the profession or pretence of curing the sick. And because I had some skill in the faculty, I would, in gratitude to his Honour, let him know the whole mystery and method by which they proceed.

Their fundamental is, that all diseases arise from *repletion,* from whence they conclude that a great *evacuation* of the body is necessary, either through the natural passage, or upwards at the mouth. Their next business is, from herbs, minerals, gums, oils, shells, salts, juices, seaweed, excrements, barks of trees, serpents, toads, frogs, spiders, dead men's flesh and bones, birds, beasts and fishes, to form a composition for smell and taste the most abominable, nauseous, and detestable they can possibly contrive, which the stomach immediately rejects with loathing; and this they call a 'vomit'; or else from the same storehouse, with some other poisonous additions, they command us to take in at the orifice *above* or *below* (just as the physician then happens to be disposed) a medicine equally annoying and disgustful to the bowels, which, relaxing the belly, drives down all before it, and this they call a 'purge' or a 'glyster'. For nature (as the physicians allege) having intended the superior anterior orifice only for the intromission of solids and liquids, and the inferior posterior for ejection, these artists ingeniously considering that in all diseases Nature is forced out of her seat, therefore to replace her in it, the body must be treated in a manner directly contrary, by interchanging the use of each orifice, forcing solids and liquids in at the anus, and making evacuations at the mouth.

But besides real diseases we are subject to many that are only imaginary, for which the physicians have invented imaginary cures; these have their several names, and so have the drugs that are proper for them, and with these our female yahoos are always infested.

One great excellency in this tribe is their skill at 'prognostics', wherein they seldom fail; their predictions in real diseases, when they rise to any degree of malignity, generally portending *death,* which is always in their power, when recovery is not: and therefore, upon any unexpected signs of amendment, after they have pronounced their sentence, rather than be accused as false prophets, they know how to approve[4] their sagacity to the world by a seasonable dose.

They are likewise of special use to husbands and wives who are grown weary of their mates, to eldest sons, to great ministers of state, and often to princes.

I had formerly upon occasion discoursed with my master upon the nature of 'government' in general, and particularly of our own 'excellent constitution', deservedly the wonder and envy of the whole world. But having here accidentally mentioned a 'minister of state', he commanded me some time after to inform him, what species of yahoo I particularly meant by that appellation.

I told him that a 'first' or 'chief minister of state', who was the person I intended to describe, was a creature wholly exempt from joy and grief, love and hatred, pity and anger; at least made use of no other passions but a violent desire of wealth, power, and titles; that he applies his words to all uses, except to the indication of his mind; that he never tells a *truth,* but with an intent that you should take it for a *lie;* nor a *lie,* but with a design that you should take it for a *truth;* that those he speaks worst of behind their backs are in the surest way to preferment; and whenever he begins to praise you to others or to yourself, you are from that day forlorn. The worst mark you can receive is a *promise,* especially when it is confirmed with an oath; after which every wise man retires, and gives over all hopes.

There are three methods by which a man may rise to be chief minister: the first is, by knowing how with prudence to dispose of a wife, a daughter, or a sister: the second, by betraying or undermining

4. Prove.

his predecessor: and the third is, by a *furious zeal* in public assemblies against the corruptions of the court. But a wise prince would rather choose to employ those who practise the last of these methods; because such zealots prove always the most obsequious and subservient to the will and passions of their master. That these 'ministers' having all employments at their disposal, preserve themselves in power by bribing the majority of a senate or great council; and at last, by an expedient called an act of indemnity[5] (whereof I described the nature to him) they secured themselves from after reckonings, and retired from the public, laden with the spoils of the nation.

The palace of a 'chief minister' is a seminary to breed up others in his own trade: the pages, lackeys, and porter, by imitating their master, become 'ministers of state' in their several districts, and learn to excel in the three principal *ingredients,* of *insolence, lying,* and *bribery.* Accordingly, they have a *subaltern* court paid to them by persons of the best rank, and sometimes by the force of dexterity and impudence arrive through several gradations to be successors to their lord.

He is usually governed by a decayed wench or favourite footman, who are the tunnels through which all graces are conveyed, and may properly be called, *in the last resort,* the governors of the kingdom.

One day in discourse my master, having heard me mention the 'nobility' of my country, was pleased to make me a compliment which I could not pretend to deserve: that he was sure I must have been born of some noble family, because I far exceeded in shape, colour, and cleanliness, all the yahoos of his nation, although I seemed to fail in strength and agility, which must be imputed to my different way of living from those other brutes, and besides, I was not only endowed with the faculty of speech, but likewise with some rudiments of reason, to a degree that with all his acquaintance I passed for a prodigy.

He made me observe, that among the Houyhnhnms, the *white,* the

5. An act of this sort was usually passed at each session of Parliament, to protect holders of public office from the possible consequences of any official acts done illegally but in good faith.

sorrel, and the *iron-grey,* were not so exactly shaped as the *bay,* the *dapple-grey,* and the *black;* nor born with equal talents of the mind, or a capacity to improve them; and therefore continued always in the condition of servants, without ever aspiring to match out of their own race, which in that country would be reckoned monstrous and unnatural.

I made his Honour my most humble acknowledgements for the good opinion he was pleased to conceive of me; but assured him at the same time that my birth was of the lower sort, having been born of plain honest parents, who were just able to give me a tolerable education: that 'nobility' among us was altogether a different thing from the idea he had of it; that our young 'noblemen' are bred from their childhood in idleness and luxury; that as soon as years will permit, they consume their vigor and contract odious diseases among lewd females; and when their fortunes are almost ruined, they marry some woman of mean birth, disagreeable person, and unsound constitution, merely for the sake of money, whom they hate and despise. That the productions of such marriages are generally scrofulous, ricketty, or deformed children, by which means the family seldom continues above three generations, unless the wife takes care to provide a healthy father among her neighbours or domestics, in order to improve and continue the breed. That a weak diseased body, a meager countenance, and sallow complexion are the true marks of noble blood; and a healthy robust appearance is so disgraceful in a man of quality, that the world concludes his real father to have been a *groom,* or a *coachman.* The imperfections of his mind run parallel with those of his body, being a composition of spleen, dulness, ignorance, caprice, sensuality, and pride.

Without the consent of this *illustrious body* no law can be made, repealed, or altered, and these have the decision of all our possessions without appeal.

Chapter Seven

The author's great love of his native country. His master's observations upon the constitution and administration of England, as described by the author, with parallel cases and comparisons. His master's observations upon human nature.

HE READER MAY BE DISPOSED TO WONDER HOW I could prevail on myself to give so free a representation of my own species, among a race of mortals who were already too apt to conceive the vilest opinion of human kind from that entire congruity betwixt me and their yahoos. But I must freely confess, that the many virtues of those excellent *quadrupeds,* placed in opposite view to human corruptions, had so far opened my eyes and enlarged my understanding, that I began to view the actions and passions of man in a very different light, and to think the honour of my own kind not worth managing;[1] which, besides, it was impossible for me to do before a person of so acute a judgment as my master, who daily convinced me of a thousand faults in myself, whereof I had not the least perception before, and which among us would never be numbered even among human infirmities: I had likewise learned from his example an utter detestation of all falsehood or disguise; and *truth* appeared so amiable to me, that I determined upon sacrificing every thing to it.

Let me deal so candidly with the reader as to confess, that there was yet a much stronger motive for the freedom I took in my representation of things. I had not been a year in this country before I con-

1. Treating with care.

tracted such a love and veneration for the inhabitants, that I entered on a firm resolution never to return to human kind, but to pass the rest of my life among these admirable Houyhnhnms in the contemplation and practice of every virtue; where I could have no example or incitement to vice. But it was decreed by Fortune, my perpetual enemy, that so great a felicity should not fall to my share. However, it is now some comfort to reflect, that in what I said of my countrymen I *extenuated* their faults as much as I durst before so strict an examiner, and upon every article gave as *favourable* a turn as the matter would bear. For, indeed, who is there alive that will not be swayed by his bias and partiality to the place of his birth?

I have related the substance of several conversations I had with my master, during the greatest part of the time I had the honour to be in his service, but have indeed for brevity sake omitted much more than is here set down.

When I had answered all his questions, and his curiosity seemed to be fully satisfied, he sent for me one morning early, and commanding me to sit down at some distance (an honour which he had never before conferred upon me), he said, he had been very seriously considering my whole story, as far as it related both to myself and my country: that he looked upon us as a sort of animals to whose share, by what accident he could not conjecture, some small pittance of *reason* had fallen, whereof we made no other use than by its assistance to aggravate our *natural* corruptions, and to acquire new ones which Nature had not given us. That we disarmed ourselves of the few abilities she had bestowed, had been very successful in multiplying our original wants, and seemed to spend our whole lives in vain endeavours to supply them by our own inventions. That as to myself, it was manifest I had neither the strength or agility of a common yahoo, that I walked infirmly on my hinder feet, had found out a contrivance to make my claws of no use or defence, and to remove the hair from my chin, which was intended as a shelter from the sun and the weather. Lastly, that I could neither run with speed, nor climb trees like my 'brethren' (as he called them) the yahoos in this country.

That our institutions of 'government' and 'law' were plainly owing to our gross defects in *reason,* and by consequence, in *virtue;* because *reason* alone is sufficient to govern a *rational* creature; which was therefore a character we had no pretence to challenge, even from the account I had given of my own people, although he manifestly perceived, that in order to favour them I had concealed many particulars, and often 'said the thing which was not'.

He was the more confirmed in this opinion, because he observed, that as I agreed in every feature of my body with other yahoos, except where it was to my real disadvantage in point of strength, speed, and activity, the shortness of my claws, and some other particulars where nature had no part; so from the representation I had given him of our lives, our manners, and our actions, he found as near a resemblance in the disposition of our minds. He said the yahoos were known to hate one another more than they did any different species of animals; and the reason usually assigned was the odiousness of their own shapes, which all could see in the rest, but not in themselves. He had therefore begun to think it not unwise in us to *cover* our bodies, and, by that invention, conceal many of our own deformities from each other, which would else be hardly supportable. But he now found he had been mistaken, and that the dissensions of those brutes in his country were owing to the same cause with ours, as I had described them. 'For if', said he, 'you throw among five yahoos as much food as would be sufficient for fifty, they will, instead of eating peaceably, fall together by the ears, each single one impatient to *have all to itself';* and therefore a servant was usually employed to stand by while they were feeding abroad, and those kept at home were tied at a distance from each other; that if a cow died of age or accident, before a Houyhnhnm could secure it for his own yahoos, those in the neighbourhood would come in herds to seize it, and then would ensue such a battle as I had described, with terrible wounds made by their claws on both sides, although they seldom were able to kill one another, for want of such convenient instruments of death as we had invented. At other times the like battles have been fought between the yahoos of several neighbourhoods without any visible cause: those of one district watching all opportunities to surprise the next before they are prepared. But if they find their project hath miscarried, they return home, and, for want of enemies, engage in what I call a civil war among themselves.

That in some fields of his country there are certain *shining stones* of several colours, whereof the yahoos are violently fond, and when part of these *stones* is fixed in the earth, as it sometimes happeneth, they will dig with their claws for whole days to get them out, then carry them away, and hide them by heaps in their kennels; but still looking round with great caution, for fear their comrades should find out their treasure. My master said, he could never discover the reason of this unnatural appetite, or how these *stones* could be of any use to a yahoo; but now he believed it might proceed from the same principle of 'avarice' which I had ascribed to mankind; that he had once, by way of experiment, privately removed a heap of these *stones* from the place where one of his yahoos had buried it: whereupon the sordid animal, missing his treasure, by his loud lamenting brought the whole herd to the place, there miserably howled, then fell to biting and tearing the rest, began to pine away, would neither eat, nor sleep, nor work, till he ordered a servant privately to convey the *stones* into the same hole and hide them as before; which when his yahoo had found, he presently recovered his spirits and good humour, but took care to remove them to a better hiding-place, and hath ever since been a very serviceable brute.

My master farther assured me, which I also observed myself, that in the fields where these *shining stones* abound, the fiercest and most frequent battles are fought, occasioned by perpetual inroads of the neighbouring yahoos.

He said, it was common, when two yahoos discovered such a *stone*

in a field, and were contending which of them should be the proprietor, a third would take the advantage, and carry it away from them both; which my master would needs contend to have some kind of resemblance with our 'suits at law'; wherein I thought it for our credit not to undeceive him; since the decision he mentioned was much more equitable than many decrees among us: because the plaintiff and defendant there lost nothing beside the *stone* they contended for, whereas our *courts of equity* would never have dismissed the cause while either of them had any thing left.

My master, continuing his discourse, said, there was nothing that rendered the yahoos more odious than their undistinguishing appetite to devour every thing that came in their way, whether herbs, roots, berries, the corrupted flesh of animals, or all mingled together: and it was peculiar in their temper, that they were fonder of what they could get by rapine or stealth at a greater distance, than much better food provided for them at home. If their prey held out, they would eat till they were ready to burst, after which Nature had pointed out to them a certain *root* that gave them a general evacuation.

There was also another kind of *root* very *juicy,* but somewhat rare and difficult to be found, which the yahoos sought for with much eagerness, and would suck it with great delight; and it produced in them the same effects that wine hath upon us. It would make them sometimes hug, and sometimes tear one another; they would howl and grin, and chatter, and reel, and tumble, and then fall asleep in the dirt.

I did indeed observe, that the yahoos were the only animals in this country subject to any diseases; which, however, were much fewer than horses have among us, and contracted not by any ill treatment they meet with, but by the nastiness and greediness of that sordid brute. Neither has their language any more than a general appellation for those maladies, which is borrowed from the name of the beast, and called '*hnea-yahoo*', or the 'yahoo's evil', and the cure prescribed is a mixture of *their own dung* and *urine* forcibly put down the yahoo's throat. This I have since often known to have been taken with success, and do freely recommend it to my countrymen, for the public good, as an admirable specific against all diseases produced by repletion.

As to learning, government, arts, manufactures, and the like, my master confessed he could find little or no resemblance between the yahoos of that country and those in ours. For he only meant to observe what parity there was in our natures. He had heard indeed some curious Houyhnhnms observe, that in most herds there was a sort of ruling yahoo (as among us there is generally some leading or principal stag in a park), who was always more *deformed* in body, and *mischievous in disposition,* than any of the rest. That this *leader* had usually a favourite as *like himself* as he could get, whose employment was to *lick his master's feet and posteriors, and drive the female yahoos to his kennel;* for which he was now and then rewarded with a piece of ass's flesh. This 'favourite' is hated by the whole herd, and therefore, to protect himself, keeps always *near the person of his leader.* He usually continues in office till a worse can be found; but the very moment he is discarded, his successor, at the head of all the yahoos in that district, young and old, male and female, come in a body, and discharge their excrements upon him from head to foot. But how far this might be applicable to our 'courts' and 'favourites', and 'ministers of state', my master said I could best determine.

I durst make no return to this malicious insinuation, which debased human understanding below the sagacity of a common *hound,* who has judgment enough to distinguish and follow the cry of the *ablest dog in the pack,* without being ever mistaken.

My master told me, there were some qualities remarkable in the yahoos, which he had not observed me to mention, or at least very slightly, in the accounts I had given him of human kind; he said, those animals, like other brutes, had their females in common; but in this they differed, that the she-yahoo would admit the male while she was pregnant, and that the hees would quarrel and fight with the females as fiercely as with each other. Both which practices were such degrees of brutality, that no other sensitive creature ever arrived at.

Another thing he wondered at in the yahoos was their strange disposition to nastiness and dirt, whereas there appears to be a natural love of cleanliness in all other animals. As to the two former accusations, I was glad to let them pass without any reply, because I had not a word to offer upon them in defence of my species, which otherwise I certainly had done from my own inclinations. But I could have easily vindicated human kind from the imputation of singularity upon the last article, if there had been any *swine* in that country (as unluckily for me there were not), which, although it may be a *sweeter quadruped* than a yahoo, cannot, I humbly conceive, in justice pretend to more cleanliness; and so his Honour himself must have owned, if he had seen their filthy way of feeding, and their custom of wallowing and sleeping in the mud.

My master likewise mentioned another quality which his servants had discovered in several yahoos, and to him was wholly unaccountable. He said, a fancy would sometimes take a yahoo to retire into a corner, to lie down and howl, and groan, and spurn away all that came near him, although he were young and fat, wanted neither food nor water; nor did the servants imagine what could possibly ail him. And the only remedy they found was to set him to hard work, after which he would infallibly come to himself. To this I was silent out of partiality to my own kind; yet here I could plainly discover the true seeds of *spleen,*[2] which only seizeth on the *lazy,* the *luxurious,* and the *rich;* who, if they were forced to undergo the *same regimen,* I would undertake for the cure.

His Honour had farther observed, that a female yahoo would often stand behind a bank or a bush, to gaze on the young males passing by, and then appear, and hide, using many antic gestures and grimaces, at which time it was observed, that she had a most *offensive smell;* and

2. Hypochondria.

when any of the males advanced, would slowly retire, looking often back, and with a counterfeit show of fear, run off into some convenient place where she knew the male would follow her.

At other times if a female stranger came among them, three or four of her own sex would get about her, and stare and chatter, and grin, and smell her all over, and then turn off with gestures that seemed to express contempt and disdain.

Perhaps my master might refine a little in these speculations, which he had drawn from what he observed himself, or had been told him by others: however, I could not reflect without some amazement, and much sorrow, that the rudiments of *lewdness, coquetry, censure,* and *scandal,* should have place by instinct in womankind.

I expected every moment that my master would accuse the yahoos of those unnatural appetites in both sexes, so common among us. But Nature, it seems, hath not been so expert a schoolmistress; and these politer pleasures are entirely the productions of art and reason, on our side of the globe.

Chapter Eight

The author relates several particulars of the yahoos. The great virtues of the Houyhnhnms. The education and exercise of their youth. Their general assembly.

As I ought to have understood human nature much better than I supposed it possible for my master to do, so it was easy to apply the character he gave of the yahoos to myself and my countrymen, and I believed I could yet make farther discoveries from my own observation. I therefore often begged his favour to let me go among the herds of yahoos in the neighbourhood, to which he always very graciously consented, being perfectly convinced that the hatred I bore those brutes would never suffer me to be corrupted by them; and his Honour ordered one of his servants, a strong sorrel nag, very honest and good-natured, to be my guard, without whose protection I durst not undertake such adventures. For I have already told the reader how much I was pestered by those odious animals upon my first arrival. And I afterwards failed very narrowly three or four times of falling into their clutches, when I happened to stray at any distance without my hanger. And I have reason to believe they had some imagination that I was of their own species, which I often assisted myself, by stripping up my sleeves, and showing my naked arms and breast in their sight, when my protector was with me. At which times they would approach as near as they durst, and imitate my actions after the manner of monkeys, but ever with great signs of hatred, as a tame *jackdaw,* with cap and stockings, is always persecuted by the wild ones, when he happens to be got among them.

They are prodigiously nimble from their infancy; however, I once caught a young male of three years old, and endeavoured by all marks of tenderness to make it quiet; but the little imp fell a squalling, and scratching, and biting with such violence, that I was forced to let it go, and it was high time, for a whole troop of old ones came about us at the noise, but finding the cub was safe (for away it ran), and my sorrel nag being by, they durst not venture near us. I observed the young animal's flesh to smell very rank, and the stink was somewhat between a *weasel* and a *fox,* but much more disagreeable. I forgot another circumstance (and perhaps I might have the reader's pardon if it were wholly omitted) that while I held the odious vermin in my hands, it voided its filthy excrements of a yellow liquid substance, all over my clothes; but by good fortune there was a small brook hard by, where I washed myself as clean as I could, although I durst not come into my master's presence, until I were sufficiently aired.

By what I could discover, the yahoos appear to be the most unteachable of all animals, their capacities never reaching higher than to draw or carry burthens. Yet I am of opinion this defect ariseth chiefly from a perverse, restive disposition. For they are cunning, malicious, treacherous and revengeful. They are strong and hardy, but of a cowardly spirit, and by consequence insolent, abject, and cruel. It is observed, that the *red-haired* of both sexes are more libidinous and mischievous than the rest, whom yet they much exceed in strength and activity.

The Houyhnhnms keep the yahoos for present use in huts not far from the house; but the rest are sent abroad to certain fields, where they dig up roots, eat several kinds of herbs, and search about for carrion, or sometimes catch weasels and *luhimuhs* (a sort of wild rat), which they greedily devour. Nature hath taught them to dig deep holes with their nails on the side of a rising ground, wherein they lie by themselves, only the kennels of the females are larger, sufficient to hold two or three cubs.

They swim from their infancy like frogs, and are able to continue long under water, where they often take fish, which the females carry home to their young. And upon this occasion, I hope the reader will pardon my relating an odd adventure.

Being one day abroad with my protector the sorrel nag, and the weather exceeding hot, I intreated him to let me bathe in a river that was near. He consented, and I immediately stripped myself stark naked, and went down softly into the stream. It happened that a young female yahoo, standing behind a bank, saw the whole proceeding, and enflamed by desire, as the nag and I conjectured, came running with all speed, and leaped into the water within five yards of the place where I bathed. I was never in my life so terribly frighted; the nag was grazing at some distance, not suspecting any harm. She embraced me after a most fulsome manner; I roared as loud as I could, and the nag came galloping towards me, whereupon she quitted her grasp, with the utmost reluctancy, and leapt upon the opposite bank, where she stood gazing and howling all the time I was putting on my clothes.

This was matter of diversion to my master and his family, as well as of mortification to myself. For now I could no longer deny that I was a real yahoo in every limb and feature, since the females had a natural propensity to me as one of their own species: neither was the hair of this brute of a red colour (which might have been some excuse for an appetite a little irregular) but black as a sloe, and her countenance did not make an appearance altogether so hideous as the rest of the kind; for, I think, she could not be above eleven years old.

Having lived three years in this country, the reader I suppose will expect that I should, like other travellers, give him some account of the manners and customs of its inhabitants, which it was indeed my principal study to learn.

As these noble Houyhnhnms are endowed by nature with a general disposition to all virtues, and have no conceptions or ideas of what is

evil in a rational creature, so their grand maxim is, to cultivate *reason*, and to be wholly governed by it. Neither is *reason* among them a point problematical as with us, where men can argue with plausibility on both sides of a question; but strikes you with immediate conviction; as it must needs do where it is not mingled, obscured, or discoloured by passion and interest. I remember it was with extreme difficulty that I could bring my master to understand the meaning of the word 'opinion', or how a point could be disputable; because *reason* taught us to affirm or deny only where we are certain; and beyond our knowledge we cannot do either. So that controversies, wranglings, disputes, and positiveness in false or dubious propositions are evils unknown among the Houyhnhnms. In the like manner, when I used to explain to him our several systems of 'natural philosophy', he would laugh that a creature pretending to *reason* should value itself upon the knowledge of other people's conjectures, and in things where that knowledge, if it were certain, could be of no use. Wherein he agreed entirely with the sentiments of Socrates, as Plato delivers them;[1] which I mention as the highest honour I can do that prince of philosophers. I have often since reflected what destruction such a doctrine would make in the libraries of Europe, and how many paths to fame would be then shut up in the learned world.

Friendship and *benevolence* are the two principal virtues among the Houyhnhnms, and these not confined to particular objects, but universal to the whole race. For a stranger from the remotest part is equally treated with the nearest neighbour, and wherever he goes, looks upon himself as at home. They preserve *decency* and *civility* in the highest degrees, but are altogether ignorant of *ceremony*. They have no fondness[2] for their colts or foals, but the care they take in educating them proceeds entirely from the dictates of *reason*. And I observed my master to show the same affection to his neighbour's

1. The reference may be to the discussion at the end of the fifth book of the *Republic*.
2. Foolish tenderness.

issue that he had for his own. They will have it that *Nature* teaches them to love the whole species, and it is *reason* only that maketh a distinction of persons, where there is a superior degree of virtue.

When the matron Houyhnhnms have produced one of each sex, they no longer accompany with their consorts, except they lose one of their issue by some casualty, which very seldom happens: but in such a case they meet again, or when the like accident befalls a person whose wife is past bearing, some other couple bestow him one of their own colts, and then go together again till the mother is pregnant. This caution is necessary to prevent the country from being overburthened with numbers. But the race of inferior Houyhnhnms bred up to be servants is not so strictly limited upon this article; these are allowed to produce three of each sex, to be domestics in the noble families.

In their marriages they are exactly careful to choose such colours as will not make any disagreeable mixture in the breed. *Strength* is chiefly valued in the male, and *comeliness* in the female, not upon the account of *love,* but to preserve the race from degenerating; for where a female happens to excel in *strength,* a consort is chosen with regard to *comeliness.* Courtship, love, presents, jointures, settlements, have no place in their thoughts, or terms whereby to express them in their language. The young couple meet and are joined, merely because it is the determination of their parents and friends: it is what they see done every day, and they look upon it as one of the necessary actions of a rational being. But the violation of marriage, or any other unchastity, was never heard of: and the married pair pass their lives with the same friendship and mutual benevolence that they bear to all others of the same species who come in their way; without jealousy, fondness, quarrelling, or discontent.

In educating the youth of both sexes, their method is admirable, and highly deserves our imitation. These are not suffered to taste a grain of *oats,* except upon certain days, till eighteen years old; nor *milk,* but very rarely; and in summer they graze two hours in the morning, and as long in the evening, which their parents likewise observe, but the servants are not allowed above half that time, and a great part of their grass is brought home, which they eat at the most convenient hours, when they can be best spared from work.

Temperance, industry, exercise, and *cleanliness,* are the lessons equally enjoined to the young ones of both sexes: and my master thought it monstrous in us to give the females a different kind of education from the males, except in some articles of domestic management; whereby, as he truly observed, one half of our natives were good for nothing but bringing children into the world: and to trust the care of our children to such useless animals, he said, was yet a greater instance of brutality.

But the Houyhnhnms train up their youth to strength, speed, and hardiness, by exercising them in running races up and down steep hills, and over hard stony grounds, and when they are all in a sweat, they are ordered to leap over head and ears into a pond or a river. Four times a year the youth of a certain district meet to show their proficiency in running and leaping, and other feats of strength and agility, where the victor is rewarded with a song made in his or her praise. On this festival the servants drive a herd of yahoos into the field, laden with hay, and oats, and milk for a repast to the Houyhnhnms; after which these brutes are immediately driven back again, for fear of being noisome to the assembly.

Every fourth year, at the *vernal equinox,* there is a representative council of the whole nation, which meets in a plain about twenty miles from our house, and continues about five or six days. Here they enquire into the state and condition of the several districts; whether they abound or be deficient in hay or oats, or cows or yahoos. And wherever there is any want (which is but seldom) it is immediately supplied by unanimous consent and contribution. Here likewise the regulation of children is settled: as for instance, if a Houyhnhnm hath two males, he changeth one of them with another that hath two females: and when a child hath been lost by any casualty, where the mother is past breeding, it is determined what family in the district shall breed another to supply the loss.

Chapter Nine

A grand debate at the general assembly of the Houyhnhnms, and how it was determined. The learning of the Houyhnhnms. Their buildings. Their manner of burials. The defectiveness of their language.

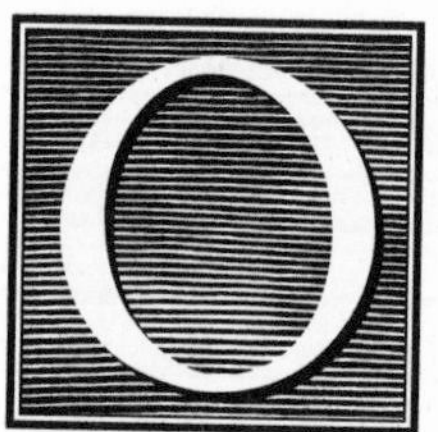

NE OF THESE GRAND ASSEMBLIES WAS HELD IN MY time, about three months before my departure, whither my master went as the representative of our district. In this council was resumed their old debate, and indeed, the only debate which ever happened in that country; whereof my master after his return gave me a very particular account.

The question to be debated was, whether the yahoos should be exterminated from the face of the earth. One of the members for the affirmative offered several arguments of great strength and weight, alleging, that as the yahoos were the most filthy, noisome, and deformed animal which nature ever produced, so they were the most restive and indocible, mischievous and malicious: they would privately suck the teats of the Houyhnhnms' cows, kill and devour their cats, trample down their oats and grass, if they were not continually watched, and commit a thousand other extravagancies. He took notice of a general tradition, that yahoos had not been always in that country: but that many ages ago two of these brutes appeared together upon a mountain, whether produced by the heat of the sun upon corrupted mud and slime, or from the ooze and froth of the sea, was never known. That these yahoos engendered, and their brood in a short time grew so numerous as to overrun and infest the whole nation. That the Houyhnhnms, to get rid of this evil, made a general hunting, and at last inclosed the whole herd; and destroying the elder, every Houyhnhnm kept two young ones in a kennel, and brought them to such a degree of tameness, as an animal so savage by nature can be capable of acquiring; using them for draught and carriage. That there seemed to be much truth in this tradition, and that those creatures could not be *ylnhniamshy* (or *aborigines* of the land) because of the violent hatred the Houyhnhnms, as well as all other animals, bore them; which although their evil disposition sufficiently deserved, could never have arrived at so high a degree, if they had been *aborigines,* or else they would have long since been rooted out. That the inhabitants taking a fancy to use the service of the yahoos, had very imprudently neglected to cultivate the breed of asses, which were a comely animal, easily kept, more tame and orderly, without any offensive smell, strong enough for labour, although they yield to the other in agility of body; and if their braying be no agreeable sound, it is far preferable to the horrible howlings of the yahoos.

Several others declared their sentiments to the same purpose, when my master proposed an expedient to the assembly, whereof he had indeed borrowed the hint from me. He approved of the tradition, mentioned by the 'honourable member' who spoke before, and affirmed, that the two yahoos said to be first seen among them had been driven thither over the sea; that coming to land, and being forsaken by their companions, they retired to the mountains, and degenerating by degrees, became in process of time much more savage than those of their own species in the country from whence these two originals came. The reason of his assertion was, that he had now in his possession a certain wonderful yahoo (meaning myself) which most of them had heard of, and many of them had seen. He then related to them how he first found me; that my body was all covered with an artificial composure of the skins and hairs of other animals: that I had a language of my own, and had thoroughly learned theirs: that I had related to him the accidents which brought me thither: that when he saw me without my covering, I was an exact yahoo in every part, only of a whiter colour, less hairy, and with shorter claws. He added, how I had endeavoured to persuade him, that in my own and other countries the yahoos acted as the governing, rational animal, and held the Houyhnhnms in servitude: that he observed in me all the qualities of a yahoo, only a little more civilised by some tincture of reason, which however was in a degree as far inferior to the Houyhnhnm race as the yahoos of their country were to me: that, among other things, I mentioned a custom we had of 'castrating' Houyhnhnms when they were young, in order to render them tame; that the operation was easy and safe; that it was no shame to learn wisdom from brutes, as industry is taught by the ant, and building by the swallow. (For so I translate the word *lyhannh,* although it be a much larger fowl.) That this invention might be practised upon the younger yahoos here, which, besides rendering them tractable and fitter for use, would in an age put an end to the whole species without destroying life. That in the mean time the Houyhnhnms should be *exhorted* to cultivate the breed of asses, which, as they are in all respects more valuable brutes, so they have this advantage, to be fit for service at five years old, which the others are not till twelve.

This was all my master thought fit to tell me at that time of what passed in the grand council. But he was pleased to conceal one particular, which related personally to myself, whereof I soon felt the unhappy effect, as the reader will know in its proper place, and from whence I date all the succeeding misfortunes of my life.

The Houyhnhnms have no letters, and consequently their knowledge is all traditional. But there happening few events of any moment among a people so well united, naturally disposed to every virtue, wholly governed by reason, and cut off from all commerce with other nations, the historical part is easily preserved without burthening their memories. I have already observed, that they are subject to no diseases, and therefore can have no need of physicians. However, they have excellent medicines composed of herbs, to cure accidental bruises

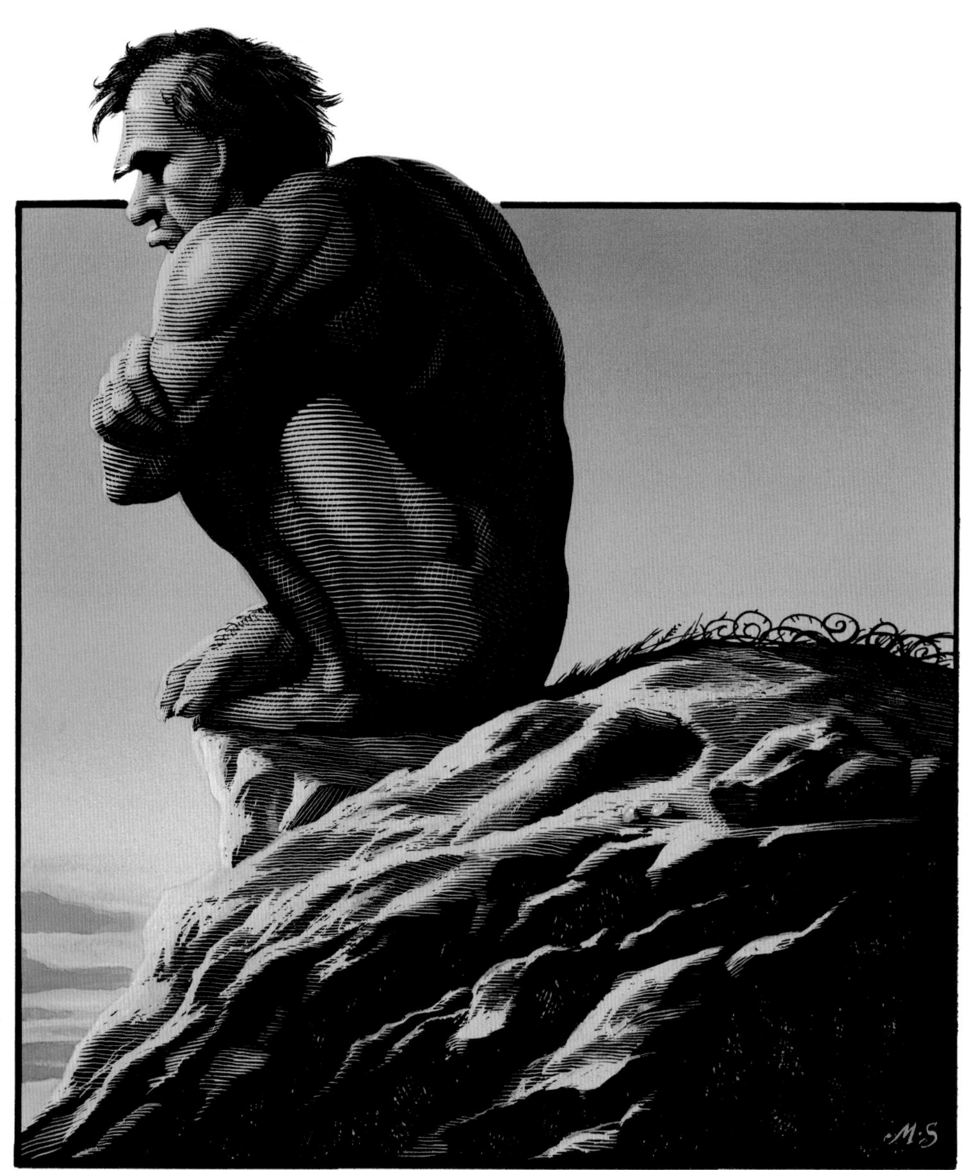
M·S

[T]he sordid animal, missing his treasure, . . . began to pine away, would neither eat, nor sleep, nor work, . . .

PAGE 293

and cuts in the pastern or frog of the foot by sharp stones, as well as other maims and hurts in the several parts of the body.

They calculate the year by the revolution of the sun and the moon, but use no subdivisions into weeks. They are well enough acquainted with the motions of those two luminaries, and understand the nature of *eclipses;* and this is the utmost progress of their *astronomy.*

In *poetry* they must be allowed to excel all other mortals; wherein the justness of their similes, and the minuteness, as well as exactness of their descriptions, are indeed inimitable. Their verses abound very much in both of these, and usually contain either some exalted notions of friendship and benevolence, or the praises of those who were victors in races and other bodily exercises. Their buildings, although very rude and simple, are not inconvenient, but well contrived to defend them from all injuries of cold and heat. They have a kind of tree, which at forty years old loosens in the root, and falls with the first storm; they grow very straight, and being pointed like stakes with a sharp stone (for the Houyhnhnms know not the use of iron), they stick them erect in the ground about ten inches asunder, and then weave in oat-straw, or sometimes wattles betwixt them. The roof is made after the same manner, and so are the doors.

The Houyhnhnms use the hollow part between the pastern and the hoof of their fore-feet as we do our hands, and this with greater dexterity than I could at first imagine. I have seen a white mare of our family thread a needle (which I lent her on purpose) with that joint. They milk their cows, reap their oats, and do all the work which requires hands, in the same manner. They have a kind of hard flints, which, by grinding against other stones, they form into instruments, that serve instead of wedges, axes, and hammers. With tools made of these flints they likewise cut their hay, and reap their oats, which there groweth naturally in several fields: the yahoos draw home the sheaves in carriages, and the servants tread them in certain covered huts, to get out the grain, which is kept in stores. They make a rude kind of earthen and wooden vessels, and bake the former in the sun.

If they can avoid casualties, they die only of old age, and are buried in the obscurest places that can be found, their friends and relations expressing neither joy nor grief at their departure; nor does the dying person discover the least regret that he is leaving the world, any more than if he were upon returning home from a visit to one of his neighbours; I remember my master having once made an appointment with a friend and his family to come to his house upon some affair of importance; on the day fixed, the mistress and her two children came very late; she made two excuses, first for her husband, who, as she said, happened that very morning to *shnuwnh.* The word is strongly expressive in their language, but not easily rendered into English; it signifies, 'to retire to his first mother'. Her excuse for not coming sooner was, that her husband dying late in the morning, she was a good while consulting her servants about a convenient place where his body should be laid; and I observed she behaved herself at our house as cheerfully as the rest, and died about three months after.

They live generally to seventy or seventy-five years, very seldom to fourscore: some weeks before their death they feel a gradual decay, but without pain. During this time they are much visited by their friends, because they cannot go abroad with their usual ease and satisfaction. However, about ten days before their death, which they seldom fail in computing, they return the visits that have been made them by those who are nearest in the neighbourhood, being carried in a convenient sledge drawn by yahoos, which vehicle they use, not only upon this occasion, but when they grow old, upon long journeys, or when they are lamed by any accident. And therefore when the dying Houyhnhnms return those visits, they take a solemn leave of their friends, as if they were going to some remote part of the country, where they designed to pass the rest of their lives.

I know not whether it may be worth observing, that the Houyhnhnms have no word in their language to express any thing that is *evil,* except what they borrow from the deformities or ill qualities of the yahoos. Thus they denote the folly of a servant, an omission of a child, a stone that cuts their feet, a continuance of foul or unseasonable weather, and the like, by adding to each the epithet of '*yahoo*'. For instance, '*hhnm yahoo*', '*whnaholm yahoo*', '*ynlhmndwihlma yahoo*', and an ill-contrived house '*ynholmhnmrohlnw yahoo*'.

I could with great pleasure enlarge farther upon the manners and virtues of this excellent people; but intending in a short time to publish a volume by itself expressly upon that subject, I refer the reader thither. And in the mean time, proceed to relate my own sad catastrophe.

Chapter Ten

The author's œconomy and happy life among the Houyhnhnms. His great improvement in virtue, by conversing with them. Their conversations. The author has notice given him by his master that he must depart from the country. He falls into a swoon for grief, but submits. He contrives and finishes a canoe, by the help of a fellow-servant, and puts to sea at a venture.

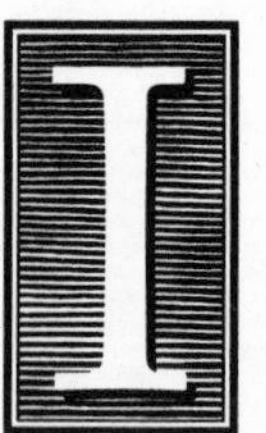

I HAD SETTLED MY LITTLE ŒCONOMY TO MY OWN HEART'S content. My master had ordered a room to be made for me after their manner, about six yards from the house, the sides and floors of which I plaistered with clay, and covered with rush mats of my own contriving; I had beaten hemp, which there grows wild, and made of it a sort of ticking: this I filled with the feathers of several birds I had taken with springes made of yahoos' hairs, and were excellent food. I had worked two chairs with my knife, the sorrel nag helping me in the grosser and more laborious part. When my clothes were worn to rags, I made myself others with the skins of rabbits, and of a certain beautiful animal about the same size, called *nnuhnoh,* the skin of which is covered with a fine down. Of these I likewise made very tolerable stockings. I soled my shoes with wood which I cut from a tree, and fitted to the upper leather, and when this was worn out, I supplied it with the skins of yahoos dried in the sun. I often got honey out of hollow trees, which I mingled with water, or eat with my bread. No man could more verify the truth of these two maxims, 'That nature is very easily satisfied'; and 'That necessity is the mother of invention'. I enjoyed perfect health of body and tranquillity of mind; I did not find the treachery or inconstancy of a friend, nor the injuries of a secret or open enemy. I had no occasion of bribing, flattering, or pimping to procure the favour of any great man or of his minion. I wanted no fence against fraud or oppression; here was neither physician to destroy my body, nor lawyer to ruin my fortune; no informer to watch my words and actions, or forge accusations against me for hire: here were no gibers, censurers, backbiters, pickpockets, highwaymen, housebreakers, attorneys, bawds, buffoons, gamesters, politicians, wits, splenetics, tedious talkers, controvertists, ravishers, murderers, robbers, virtuosos: no leaders or followers of party and faction: no encouragers to vice, by seducement or examples: no dungeon, axes, gibbets, whipping-posts, or pillories: no cheating shopkeepers or mechanics: no pride, vanity, or affectation: no fops, bullies, drunkards, strolling whores, or poxes: no ranting, lewd, expensive wives: no stupid, proud pedants: no importunate, overbearing, quarrelsome, noisy, roaring, empty, conceited, swearing companions: no scoundrels, raised from the dust for the sake of their vices, or nobility thrown into it on account of their virtues: no lords, fiddlers, judges, or dancing-masters.

I had the favour of being admitted to several Houyhnhnms, who came to visit or dine with my master; where his Honour graciously suffered me to wait in the room, and listen to their discourse. Both he and his company would often descend to ask me questions, and receive my answers. I had also sometimes the honour of attending my master in his visits to others. I never presumed to speak, except in answer to a question, and then I did it with inward regret, because it was a loss of so much time for improving myself: but I was infinitely delighted with the station of an humble auditor in such conversations, where nothing passed but what was useful, expressed in the fewest and most significant words: where the greatest *decency* was observed, without the least degree of ceremony; where no person spoke without being pleased himself, and pleasing his companions: where there was no interruption, tediousness, heat, or difference of sentiments. They have a notion, that when people are met together, a short silence doth much improve conversation: this I found to be true; for during those little intermissions of talk, new ideas would arise in their thoughts, which very much enlivened the discourse. Their subjects are generally on friendship and benevolence, or order and œconomy, sometimes upon the visible operations of nature, or ancient traditions, upon the bounds and limits of virtue, upon the unerring rules of reason, or upon some determinations to be taken at the next great assembly, and often upon the various excellencies of poetry. I may add without vanity, that my presence often gave them sufficient matter for discourse, because it afforded my master an occasion of letting his friends into the history of me and my country, upon which they were all pleased to descant in a manner not very advantageous to human kind; and for that reason I shall not repeat what they said: only I may be allowed to observe, that his Honour, to my great admiration, appeared to understand the nature of yahoos in all countries much better than myself. He went through all our vices and follies, and discovered many which I had never mentioned to him, by only supposing what qualities a yahoo of their country, with a small proportion of reason, might be capable of exerting; and concluded, with too much probability, how vile as well as miserable such a creature must be.

I freely confess, that all the little knowledge I have of any value was acquired by the lectures I received from my master, and from hearing the discourses of him and his friends; to which I should be prouder to listen, than to dictate to the greatest and wisest assembly in Europe. I admired the strength, comeliness, and speed of the inhabitants; and such a constellation of virtues in such amiable persons produced in me the highest veneration. At first, indeed, I did not feel that natural awe which the yahoos and all other animals bear towards them; but it grew upon me by degrees, much sooner than I imagined, and was mingled with a respectful love and gratitude, that they would condescend to distinguish me from the rest of my species.

When I thought of my family, my friends, my countrymen, or human race in general, I considered them as they really were, yahoos

in shape and disposition, only a little more civilised, and qualified with the gift of speech, but making no other use of reason than to improve and multiply those vices whereof their brethren in this country had only the share that nature allotted them. When I happened to behold the reflection of my own form in a lake or a fountain, I turned away my face in horror and detestation of myself, and could better endure the sight of a common yahoo, than of my own person. By conversing with the Houyhnhnms, and looking upon them with delight, I fell to imitate their gait and gesture, which is now grown into an habit, and my friends often tell me in a blunt way that I 'trot like a horse'; which, however, I take for a great compliment: neither shall I disown, that in speaking I am apt to fall into the voice and manner of the Houyhnhnms, and hear myself ridiculed on that account without the least mortification.

In the midst of all this happiness, and when I looked upon myself to be fully settled for life, my master sent for me one morning a little earlier than his usual hour. I observed by his countenance that he was in some perplexity, and at a loss how to begin what he had to speak. After a short silence, he told me, he did not know how I would take what he was going to say; that in the last general assembly, when the affair of the yahoos was entered upon, the representatives had taken offence at his keeping a yahoo (meaning myself) in his family more like a Houyhnhnm than a brute animal. That he was known frequently to converse with me, as if he could receive some advantage or pleasure in my company: that such a practice was not agreeable to reason or nature, nor a thing ever heard of before among them. The assembly did therefore *exhort* him, either to employ me like the rest of my species, or command me to swim back to the place from whence I came. That the first of these expedients was utterly rejected by all the Houyhnhnms who had ever seen me at his house or their own: for they alleged, that because I had some rudiments of reason, added to the natural pravity of those animals, it was to be feared, I might be able to seduce them into the woody and mountainous parts of the country, and bring them in troops by night to destroy the Houyhnhnms' cattle, as being naturally of the ravenous kind, and averse from labour.

My master added, that he was daily pressed by the Houyhnhnms of the neighbourhood to have the assembly's *exhortation* executed, which he could not put off much longer. He doubted it would be impossible for me to swim to another country, and therefore wished I would contrive some sort of vehicle resembling those I had described to him, that might carry me on the sea, in which work I should have the assistance of his own servants, as well as those of his neighbours. He concluded, that for his own part he could have been content to keep me in his service as long as I lived, because he found I had cured myself of some bad habits and dispositions, by endeavouring, as far as my inferior nature was capable, to imitate the Houyhnhnms.

I should here observe to the reader, that a decree of the general assembly in this country is expressed by the word *hnhloayn,* which signifies an 'exhortation', as near as I can render it: for they have no conception how a rational creature can be *compelled,* but only advised or *exhorted,* because no person can disobey reason, without giving up his claim to be a rational creature.

I was struck with the utmost grief and despair at my master's discourse, and being unable to support the agonies I was under, I fell into a swoon at his feet; when I came to myself he told me, that he concluded I had been dead. (For these people are subject to no such imbecilities of nature.) I answered, in a faint voice, that death would have been too great an happiness; that although I could not blame the assembly's *exhortation,* or the urgency of his friends, yet, in my weak and corrupt judgment, I thought it might consist with reason to have been less rigorous. That I could not swim a league, and probably the nearest land to theirs might be distant above an hundred; that many materials, necessary for making a small vessel to carry me off, were wholly wanting in this country, which, however, I would attempt in obedience and gratitude to his Honour, although I concluded the thing to be impossible, and therefore looked on myself as already devoted[1] to destruction. That the certain prospect of an unnatural death was the least of my evils: for, supposing I should escape with life by some strange adventure, how could I think with temper[2] of passing my days among yahoos, and relapsing into my old corruptions, for want of examples to lead and keep me within the paths of virtue? That I knew too well upon what solid reasons all the determinations of the wise Houyhnhnms were founded, not to be shaken by arguments of mine, a miserable yahoo; and therefore, after presenting him with my humble thanks for the offer of his servants' assistance in making a vessel, and desiring a reasonable time for so difficult a work, I told him I would endeavour to preserve a wretched being; and, if ever I returned to England, was not without hopes of being useful to my own species, by celebrating the praises of the renowned Houyhnhnms, and proposing their virtues to the imitation of mankind.

My master in a few words made me a very gracious reply, allowed me the space of two months to finish my boat; and ordered the sorrel nag, my fellow-servant (for so at this distance I may presume to call him) to follow my instructions, because I told my master, that his help would be sufficient, and I knew he had a tenderness for me.

In his company my first business was to go to that part of the coast where my rebellious crew had ordered me to be set on shore. I got upon a height, and looking on every side into the sea, fancied I saw a small island, towards the northeast: I took out my pocket-glass, and could then clearly distinguish it about five leagues off, as I computed; but it appeared to the sorrel nag to be only a blue cloud: for as he had no conception of any country beside his own, so he could not be as expert in distinguishing remote objects at sea as we who so much converse in that element.

1. Doomed.
2. Equanimity.

After I had discovered this island, I considered no farther; but resolved it should, if possible, be the first place of my banishment, leaving the consequence to fortune.

I returned home, and consulting with the sorrel nag, we went into a copse at some distance, where I with my knife, and he with a sharp flint fastened very artificially[3] after their manner, to a wooden handle, cut down several oak wattles about the thickness of a walking-staff, and some larger pieces. But I shall not trouble the reader with a particular description of my own mechanics; let it suffice to say that in six weeks' time, with the help of the sorrel nag, who performed the parts that required most labour, I finished a sort of Indian canoe, but much larger, covering it with the skins of yahoos well stitched together, with hempen threads of my own making. My sail was likewise composed of the skins of the same animal; but I made use of the youngest I could get, the older being too tough and thick, and I likewise provided myself with four paddles. I laid in a stock of boiled flesh, of rabbits and fowls, and took with me two vessels, one filled with milk, and the other with water.

I tried my canoe in a large pond near my master's house, and then corrected in it what was amiss; stopping all the chinks with yahoos' tallow, till I found it staunch, and able to bear me and my freight. And when it was as complete as I could possibly make it, I had it drawn on a carriage very gently by yahoos to the seaside, under the conduct of the sorrel nag and another servant.

When all was ready, and the day came for my departure, I took leave of my master and lady, and the whole family, my eyes flowing with tears, and my heart quite sunk with grief. But his Honour, out of curiosity, and perhaps (if I may speak it without vanity) partly out of kindness, was determined to see me in my canoe, and got several of his neighbouring friends to accompany him. I was forced to wait above an hour for the tide, and then observing the wind very fortu-

3. Ingeniously.

nately bearing towards the island, to which I intended to steer my course, I took a second leave of my master: but as I was going to prostrate myself to kiss his hoof, he did me the honour to raise it gently to my mouth. I am not ignorant how much I have been censured for mentioning this last particular. For my detractors are pleased to think it improbable, that so illustrious a person should descend to give so great a mark of distinction to a creature so inferior as I. Neither have I forgot how apt some travellers are to boast of extraordinary favours they have received. But if these censurers were better acquainted with the noble and courteous disposition of the Houyhnhnms, they would soon change their opinion.

I paid my respects to the rest of the Houyhnhnms in his Honour's company; then getting into my canoe, I pushed off from shore.

Chapter Eleven

The author's dangerous voyage. He arrives at New Holland, hoping to settle there. Is wounded with an arrow by one of the natives. Is seized and carried by force into a Portuguese ship. The great civilities of the captain. The author arrives at England.

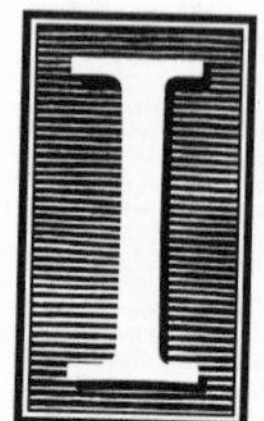

I began this desperate voyage on February 15, 1714–5, at 9 o'clock in the morning. The wind was very favourable; however, I made use at first only of my paddles, but considering I should soon be weary, and that the wind might chop about, I ventured to set up my little sail; and thus with the help of the tide I went at the rate of a league and an half an hour, as near as I could guess. My master and his friends continued on the shore till I was almost out of sight; and I often heard the sorrel nag (who always loved me) crying out, *'Hnuy illa nyha majah yahoo'*, 'Take care of thyself, gentle yahoo'.

My design was, if possible, to discover some small island uninhabited, yet sufficient by my labour to furnish me with the necessaries of life, which I would have thought a greater happiness than to be first minister in the politest court of Europe; so horrible was the idea I conceived of returning to live in the society and under the government of yahoos. For in such a solitude as I desired, I could at least enjoy my own thoughts, and reflect with delight on the virtues of those inimitable Houyhnhnms, without any opportunity of degenerating into the vices and corruptions of my own species.

The reader may remember what I related when my crew conspired against me, and confined me to my cabin. How I continued there

several weeks, without knowing what course we took, and when I was put ashore in the longboat, how the sailors told me with oaths, whether true or false, that they knew not in what part of the world we were. However, I did then believe us to be about ten degrees southwards of the Cape of Good Hope, or about 45 degrees southern latitude, as I gathered from some general words I overheard among them, being I supposed to the southeast in their intended voyage to Madagascar. And although this were but little better than conjecture, yet I resolved to steer my course eastwards, hoping to reach the southwest coast of New Holland, and perhaps some such island as I desired, lying westwards of it. The wind was full west, and by six in the evening I computed I had gone eastwards at least eighteen leagues, when I spied a very small island about half a league off, which I soon reached. It was nothing but a rock, with one creek, naturally arched by the force of tempests. Here I put in my canoe, and climbing up a part of the rock, I could plainly discover land to the east, extending from south to north. I lay all night in my canoe, and repeating my voyage early in the morning, I arrived in seven hours to the southeast point of New Holland. This confirmed me in the opinion I have long entertained, that the maps and charts place this country at least three degrees more to the east than it really is; which thought I communicated many years ago to my worthy friend Mr. Herman Moll[1] and gave him my reasons for it, although he hath rather chosen to follow other authors.

I saw no inhabitants in the place where I landed, and being unarmed, I was afraid of venturing far into the country. I found some shellfish on the shore, and eat them raw, not daring to kindle a fire, for fear of being discovered by the natives. I continued three days feeding on oysters and limpets, to save my own provisions, and I fortunately found a brook of excellent water, which gave me great relief.

1. A famous eighteenth-century mapmaker.

On the fourth day, venturing out early a little too far, I saw twenty or thirty natives upon a height, not above five hundred yards from me. They were stark naked, men, women, and children, round a fire, as I could discover by the smoke. One of them spied me, and gave notice to the rest; five of them advanced towards me, leaving the women and children at the fire. I made what haste I could to the shore, and getting into my canoe, shoved off: the savages observing me retreat, ran after me; and before I could get far enough into the sea, discharged an arrow, which wounded me deeply on the inside of my left knee (I shall carry the mark to my grave). I apprehended the arrow might be poisoned, and paddling out of the reach of their darts (being a calm day), I made a shift to suck the wound, and dress it as well as I could.

I was at a loss what to do, for I durst not return to the same landing-place, but stood to the north, and was forced to paddle; for the wind, though very gentle, was against me, blowing northwest. As I was looking about for a secure landing-place, I saw a sail to the north-northeast, which appearing every minute more visible, I was in some doubt, whether I should wait for them or no; but at last my detestation of the yahoo race prevailed, and turning my canoe, I sailed and paddled together to the south, and got into the same creek from whence I set out in the morning, choosing rather to trust myself among these barbarians, than live with European yahoos. I drew up my canoe as close as I could to the shore, and hid myself behind a stone by the little brook, which, as I have already said, was excellent water.

The ship came within an half a league of this creek, and sent out her longboat with vessels to take in fresh water (for the place it seems was very well known) but I did not observe it till the boat was almost on shore, and it was too late to seek another hiding-place. The seamen at their landing observed my canoe, and rummaging it all over, easily conjectured that the owner could not be far off. Four of them well armed searched every cranny and lurking-hole, till at last they found me flat on my face behind the stone. They gazed a while in admiration at my strange uncouth dress, my coat made of skins, my wooden-soled shoes, and my furred stockings; from whence, however, they concluded I was not a native of the place, who all go naked. One of the seamen in Portuguese bid me rise, and asked who I was. I understood that language very well, and getting upon my feet, said, I was a poor yahoo, banished from the Houyhnhnms, and desired they would please to let me depart. They admired to hear me answer them in their own tongue, and saw by my complexion I must be an European; but were at a loss to know what I meant by yahoos and Houyhnhnms, and at the same time fell a laughing at my strange tone in speaking, which resembled the neighing of a horse. I trembled all the while betwixt fear and hatred: I again desired leave to depart, and was gently moving to my canoe; but they laid hold on me, desiring to know, what country I was of, whence I came, with many other questions. I told them I was born in England, from whence I came about five years ago, and then their country and ours were at peace. I therefore hoped they would not treat me as an enemy, since I meant them no harm, but was a poor yahoo, seeking some desolate place where to pass the remainder of his unfortunate life.

When they began to talk, I thought I never heard or saw any thing so unnatural; for it appeared to me as monstrous as if a dog or a cow should speak in England, as a yahoo in Houyhnhnmland. The honest[2] Portuguese were equally amazed at my strange dress, and the odd manner of delivering my words, which however they understood very well. They spoke to me with great humanity, and said they were sure their captain would carry me *gratis* to Lisbon, from whence I might return to my own country; that two of the seamen would go back to the ship, inform the captain of what they had seen, and receive his orders; in the mean time, unless I would give my solemn oath not to fly, they would secure me by force. I thought it best to comply with

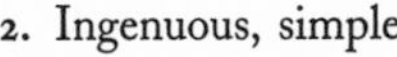

2. Ingenuous, simple.

their proposal. They were very curious to know my story, but I gave them very little satisfaction; and they all conjectured, that my misfortunes had impaired my reason. In two hours the boat, which went loaden with vessels of water, returned with the captain's commands to fetch me on board. I fell on my knees to preserve my liberty; but all was in vain, and the men having tied me with cords, heaved me into the boat, from whence I was taken into the ship, and from thence into the captain's cabin.

His name was Pedro de Mendez; he was a very courteous and generous person; he intreated me to give some account of myself, and desired to know what I would eat or drink; said, I should be used as well as himself, and spoke so many obliging things, that I wondered to find such civilities from a yahoo. However, I remained silent and sullen; I was ready to faint at the very smell of him and his men. At last I desired something to eat out of my own canoe; but he ordered me a chicken and some excellent wine, and then directed that I should be put to bed in a very clean cabin. I would not undress myself, but lay on the bed-clothes, and in half an hour stole out, when I thought the crew was at dinner, and getting to the side of the ship was going to leap into the sea, and swim for my life, rather than continue among yahoos. But one of the seamen prevented me, and having informed the captain, I was chained to my cabin.

After dinner Don Pedro came to me, and desired to know my reason for so desperate an attempt: assured me he only meant to do me all the service he was able, and spoke so very movingly, that at last I descended to treat him like an animal which had some little portion of reason. I gave him a very short relation of my voyage, of the conspiracy against me by my own men, of the country where they set me on shore, and of my three years' residence there. All which he looked upon as if it were a dream or a vision; whereat I took great offence; for I had quite forgot the faculty of lying, so peculiar to yahoos in all countries where they preside, and, consequently, the disposition of suspecting truth in others of their own species. I asked him, whether it were the custom in his country to 'say the thing that was not'. I assured him I had almost forgot what he meant by falsehood, and if I had lived a thousand years in Houyhnhnmland, I should never have heard a lie from the meanest servant; that I was altogether indifferent whether he believed me or no; but however, in return for his favours, I would give so much allowance to the corruption of his nature as to answer any objection he would please to make, and then he might easily discover the truth.

The captain, a wise man, after many endeavours to catch me tripping in some part of my story, at last began to have a better opinion of my veracity, and the rather because he confessed, he met with a Dutch skipper, who pretended to have landed with five others of his crew upon a certain island or continent south of New Holland, where they went for fresh water, and observed a horse driving before him several animals exactly resembling those I described under the name of yahoos, with some other particulars, which the captain said he had forgot; because he then concluded them all to be lies. But he added, that since I professed so inviolable an attachment to truth, I must give him my word of honour to bear him company in this voyage without attempting any thing against my life, or else he would continue me a prisoner till we arrived in Lisbon. I gave him the promise he required; but at the same time protested that I would suffer the greatest hardships rather than return to live among yahoos.

Our voyage passed without any considerable accident. In gratitude to the captain I sometimes sate with him at his earnest request, and strove to conceal my antipathy to human kind, although it often broke out, which he suffered to pass without observation. But the greatest part of the day, I confined myself to my cabin, to avoid seeing any of the crew. The captain had often intreated me to strip myself of my savage dress, and offered to lend me the best suit of clothes he had. This I would not be prevailed on to accept, abhorring to cover myself with any thing that had been on the back of a yahoo. I only desired he would lend me two clean shirts, which having been washed since he wore them, I believed would not so much defile me. These I changed every second day, and washed them myself.

We arrived at Lisbon, Nov. 5, 1715. At our landing the captain forced me to cover myself with his cloak, to prevent the rabble from crowding about me. I was conveyed to his own house, and, at my earnest request, he led me up to the highest room backwards.[3] I conjured him to conceal from all persons what I had told him of the Houyhnhnms, because the least hint of such a story would not only draw numbers of people to see me, but probably put me in danger of being imprisoned, or burnt by the Inquisition. The captain persuaded me to accept a suit of clothes newly made, but I would not suffer the tailor to take my measure; however, Don Pedro being almost of my size, they fitted me well enough. He accoutred me with other necessaries all new, which I aired for twenty-four hours before I would use them.

The captain had no wife, nor above three servants, none of which were suffered to attend at meals, and his whole deportment was so obliging, added to very good *human* understanding, that I really began to tolerate his company. He gained so far upon me, that I ventured to look out of the back window. By degrees I was brought into another room, from whence I peeped into the street, but drew my head back in a fright. In a week's time he seduced me down to the door. I found my terror gradually lessened, but my hatred and contempt seemed to encrease. I was at last bold enough to walk the street in his company, but kept my nose well stopped with rue, or sometimes with tobacco.

In ten days Don Pedro, to whom I had given some account of my domestic affairs, put it upon me as a matter of honour and conscience, that I ought to return to my native country, and live at home with my wife and children. He told me, there was an English ship in the port just ready to sail, and he would furnish me with all things necessary. It

3. At the rear of the house.

would be tedious to repeat his arguments, and my contradictions. He said it was altogether impossible to find such a solitary island as I had desired to live in; but I might command in my own house, and pass my time in a manner as recluse as I pleased.

I complied at last, finding I could not do better. I left Lisbon the 24th day of November, in an English merchantman, but who was the master I never enquired. Don Pedro accompanied me to the ship, and lent me twenty pounds. He took kind leave of me, and embraced me at parting, which I bore as well as I could. During the last voyage I had no commerce with the master or any of his men, but pretending I was sick kept close in my cabin. On the fifth of December, 1715, we cast anchor in the Downs about nine in the morning, and at three in the afternoon I got safe to my house at Rotherhith.

My wife and family received me with great surprise and joy, because they concluded me certainly dead; but I must freely confess the sight of them filled me only with hatred, disgust, and contempt, and the more by reflecting on the near alliance I had to them. For although, since my unfortunate exile from the Houyhnhnm country, I had compelled myself to tolerate the sight of yahoos, and to converse with Don Pedro de Mendez, yet my memory and imaginations were perpetually filled with the virtues and ideas of those exalted Houyhnhnms. And when I began to consider, that by copulating with one of the yahoo species I had become a parent of more, it struck me with the utmost shame, confusion, and horror.

As soon as I entered the house, my wife took me in her arms, and kissed me, at which, having not been used to the touch of that odious animal for so many years, I fell in a swoon for almost an hour. At the time I am writing it is five years since my last return to England: during the first year I could not endure my wife or children in my presence, the very smell of them was intolerable, much less could I suffer them to eat in the same room. To this hour they dare not presume to touch my bread, or drink out of the same cup, neither was I ever able to let one of them take me by the hand. The first money I laid out was to buy two young stone-horses,[4] which I keep in a good stable, and next to them the groom is my greatest favourite; for I feel my spirits revived by the smell he contracts in the stable. My horses understand me tolerably well; I converse with them at least four hours every day. They are strangers to bridle or saddle; they live in great amity with me, and friendship to each other.

4. Stallions.

Chapter Twelve

The author's veracity. His design in publishing this work. His censure of those travellers who swerve from the truth. The author clears himself from any sinister ends in writing. An objection answered. The method of planting colonies. His native country commended. The right of the crown to those countries described by the author is justified. The difficulty of conquering them. The author takes his last leave of the reader, proposeth his manner of living for the future, gives good advice, and concludes.

HUS, GENTLE READER, I HAVE GIVEN THEE A FAITHful history of my travels for sixteen years, and above seven months, wherein I have not been so studious of ornament as truth. I could perhaps like others have astonished thee with strange improbable tales; but I rather chose to relate plain matter of fact in the simplest manner and style, because my principal design was to inform, and not to amuse thee.

It is easy for us who travel into remote countries, which are seldom visited by Englishmen or other Europeans, to form descriptions of wonderful animals both at sea and land. Whereas a traveller's chief aim should be to make men wiser and better, and to improve their minds by the bad as well as good example of what they deliver concerning foreign places.

I could heartily wish a law was enacted, that every traveller, before he were permitted to publish his voyages, should be obliged to make oath before the Lord High Chancellor that all he intended to print was absolutely true to the best of his knowledge; for then the world would no longer be deceived as it usually is, while some writers, to make their works pass the better upon the public, impose the grossest falsities on the unwary reader. I have perused several books of travels with great delight in my younger days; but having since gone over most parts of the globe, and been able to contradict many fabulous accounts from my own observation, it hath given me a great disgust against this part of reading, and some indignation to see the credulity of mankind so impudently abused. Therefore since my acquaintance were pleased to think my poor endeavours might not be unacceptable to my country, I imposed on myself as a maxim, never to be swerved from, that I would *strictly adhere to truth;* neither indeed can I be ever under the least temptation to vary from it, while I retain in my mind the lectures and example of my noble master, and the other illustrious Houyhnhnms, of whom I had so long the honour to be an humble hearer.

——Nec si miserum Fortuna Sinonem
Finxit, vanum etiam mendacemque improba finget.[1]

I know very well how little reputation is to be got by writings which require neither genius nor learning, nor indeed any other talent, except a good memory or an exact journal. I know likewise, that writers of travels, like *dictionary-makers,* are sunk into oblivion by the weight and bulk of those who come after, and therefore lie uppermost. And it is highly probable, that such travellers who shall hereafter visit the countries described in this work of mine, may, be detecting my errors (if there be any), and adding many new discoveries of their own, justle me out of vogue, and stand in my place, making the world forget that I was ever an author. This indeed would be too great a mortification if I wrote for fame: but, as my sole intention was the PUBLIC GOOD, I

1. Nor has Fortune, although she has created Sinon an unfortunate man, been so harsh as to fashion him untrustworthy and lying as well.
Virgil, *Æneid,* 2.79, 80

cannot be altogether disappointed. For who can read of the virtues I have mentioned in the glorious Houyhnhnms, without being ashamed of his own vices, when he considers himself as the reasoning, governing animal of his country? I shall say nothing of those remote nations where yahoos preside, amongst which the least corrupted are the Brobdingnagians, whose wise maxims in morality and government it would be our happiness to observe. But I forbear descanting farther, and rather leave the judicious reader to his own remarks and applications.

I am not a little pleased that this work of mine can possibly meet with no censurers: for what objections can be made against a writer who relates only plain facts that happened in such distant countries, where we have not the least interest with respect either to trade or negotiations? I have carefully avoided every fault with which common writers of travels are often too justly charged. Besides, I meddle not the least with any *party,* but write without passion, prejudice, or ill will against any man or number of men whatsoever. I write for the noblest end, to inform and instruct mankind, over whom I may, without breach of modesty, pretend to some superiority from the advantages I received by conversing so long among the most accomplished Houyhnhnms. I write without any view towards profit or praise. I never suffer a word to pass that may look like reflection, or possibly give the least offence even to those who are most ready to take it. So that I hope I may with justice pronounce myself an author perfectly blameless, against whom the tribe of answerers, considerers, observers, reflecters, detecters, remarkers, will never be able to find matter for exercising their talents.

I confess, it was whispered to me that I was bound in duty, as a subject of England, to have given in a memorial to a secretary of state, at my first coming over; because, whatever lands are discovered by a subject belong to the crown. But I doubt whether our conquests in the countries I treat of would be as easy as those of Ferdinando Cortez over the naked Americans. The Lilliputians, I think, are hardly worth the charge of a fleet and army to reduce them, and I question whether it might be prudent or safe to attempt the Brobdingnagians. Or whether an English army would be much at their ease with the Flying Island over their heads. The Houyhnhnms, indeed, appear not to be so well prepared for war, a science to which they are perfect strangers, and especially against missive weapons. However, supposing myself to be a minister of state, I could never give my advice for invading them. Their prudence, unanimity, unacquaintedness with fear, and their love of their country would amply supply all defects in the military art. Imagine twenty thousand of them breaking into the midst of an European army, confounding the ranks, overturning the carriages, battering the warriors' faces into mummy,[2] by terrible yerks[3] from their hinder hoofs. For they would well deserve the character given to Augustus; *'Recalcitrat undique tutus'*.[4] But instead of proposals for conquering that magnanimous nation, I rather wish they were in a capacity or disposition to send a sufficient number of their inhabitants for civilising Europe, by teaching us the first principles of honour, justice, truth, temperance, public spirit, fortitude, chastity, friendship, benevolence, and fidelity. The *names* of all which virtues are still retained among us in most languages, and are to be met with in modern as well as ancient authors; which I am able to assert from my own small reading.

But I had another reason which made me less forward to enlarge his Majesty's dominions by my discoveries. To say the truth, I had conceived a few scruples with relation to the distributive justice of princes upon those occasions. For instance, a crew of pirates are driven by a storm they know not whither, at length a boy discovers land from the topmast, they go on shore to rob and plunder, they see an harmless people, are entertained with kindness, they give the country a new

2. Pulpy mass.
3. Kicks.
4. He kicks backward, invulnerable on every side.
Horace, *Satires,* 2.1.20

name, they take formal possession of it for their king, they set up a rotten plank or a stone for a memorial, they murder two or three dozen of the natives, bring away a couple more by force for a sample, return home, and get their pardon. Here commences a new dominion acquired with a title by *divine right.* Ships are sent with the first opportunity, the natives driven out or destroyed, their princes tortured to discover their gold, a free licence given to all acts of inhumanity and lust, the earth reeking with the blood of its inhabitants: and this execrable crew of butchers employed in so pious an expedition, is a *modern colony* sent to convert and civilise an idolatrous and barbarous people.

But this description, I confess, doth by no means affect the British nation, who may be an example to the whole world for their wisdom, care, and justice in planting colonies; their liberal endowments for the advancement of religion and learning; their choice of devout and able pastors to propagate Christianity; their caution in stocking their provinces with people of sober lives and conversations from this the mother kingdom; their strict regard to the distribution of justice, in supplying the civil administration through all their colonies with officers of the greatest abilities, utter strangers to corruption; and to crown all, by sending the most vigilant and virtuous governors, who have no other views than the happiness of the people over whom they preside, and the honour of the king their master.

But, as those countries which I have described do not appear to have any desire of being conquered, and enslaved, murdered or driven out by colonies, nor abound either in gold, silver, sugar, or tobacco; I did humbly conceive they were by no means proper objects of our zeal, our valour, or our interest. However, if those whom it more concerns think fit to be of another opinion, I am ready to depose, when I shall be lawfully called, that no European did ever visit these countries before me. I mean, if the inhabitants ought to be believed; unless a dispute may arise about the two yahoos, said to have been seen many ages ago on a mountain in Houyhnhnmland, from whence the opinion is, that the race of those brutes hath descended; and these, for any thing I know, may have been English, which indeed I was apt to suspect from the lineaments of their posterity's countenances, although very much defaced. But, how far that will go to make out a title, I leave to the learned in colony-law.

But as to the formality of taking possession in my sovereign's name, it never came once into my thoughts; and if it had, yet as my affairs then stood, I should perhaps, in point of prudence and self-preservation, have put it off to a better opportunity.

Having thus answered the only objection that can ever be raised against me as a traveller, I here take a final leave of all my courteous readers, and return to enjoy my own speculations in my little garden at Redriff, to apply those excellent lessons of virtue which I learned among the Houyhnhnms, to instruct the yahoos of my own family as far as I shall find them docible animals, to behold my figure often in a glass, and thus if possible habituate myself by time to tolerate the sight of a human creature: to lament the brutality of Houyhnhnms in my own country, but always treat their persons with respect, for the sake of my noble master, his family, his friends, and the whole Houyhnhnm race, whom these of ours have the honour to resemble in all their lineaments, however their intellectuals came to degenerate.

I began last week to permit my wife to sit at dinner with me, at the farthest end of a long table, and to answer (but with the utmost brevity) the few questions I ask her. Yet the smell of a yahoo continuing very offensive, I always keep my nose well stopped with rue, lavender, or tobacco leaves. And although it be hard for a man late in life to remove old habits, I am not altogether out of hopes in some time to suffer a neighbour yahoo in my company without the apprehensions I am yet under of his teeth or his claws.

My reconcilement to the yahoo-kind in general might not be so difficult if they would be content with those vices and follies only which nature hath intitled them to. I am not in the least provoked at the sight of a lawyer, a pickpocket, a colonel, a fool, a lord, a gamester, a politician, a whoremaster, a physician, an evidence, a suborner, an attorney, a traitor, or the like; this is all according to the due course of things: but when I behold a lump of deformity and diseases both in body and mind, smitten with *pride,* it immediately breaks all the measures of my patience; neither shall I be ever able to comprehend how such an animal and such a vice could tally together. The wise and virtuous Houyhnhnms, who abound in all excellencies that can adorn a rational creature, have no name for this vice in their language, which hath no terms to express any thing that is evil, except those whereby they describe the detestable qualities of their yahoos, among which they were not able to distinguish this of pride, for want of thoroughly understanding human nature, as it showeth itself in other countries, where that animal presides. But I, who had more experience, could plainly observe some rudiments of it among the wild yahoos.

But the Houyhnhnms, who live under the government of reason, are no more proud of the good qualities they possess, than I should be for not wanting a leg or an arm, which no man in his wits would boast of, although he must be miserable without them. I dwell the longer upon this subject from the desire I have to make the society of an English yahoo by any means not insupportable, and therefore I here intreat those who have any tincture of this absurd vice, that they will not presume to come in my sight.

FINIS

Appendices

APPENDIX A

Background and Sources

Supplementary Notes

Commentary

Supplementary Notes*

Historical Notes

78. 12. A considerable person at court. Harley and St. John had been hostile to the Duke of Marlborough and his prosecution of the war with France after their exclusion from the cabinet in 1708, and had been the principal instruments of his downfall a few years later. Nevertheless, when Bolingbroke found himself threatened with prosecution for treason in 1715 he turned to Marlborough, his old patron, for advice. The latter took a belated revenge by professing to have private information concerning the severe punishments which the Whigs meant to visit upon the important Tories: he played on Bolingbroke's fears to such an extent that the latter fled to France, and thus appeared to confess the justice of the charges against him.

79. 12. Limtoc, Lalcon, Balmuff. Stanhope, Devonshire and Cowper were all members of the Whig cabinet and of the Committee of Secrecy, and all of them attacked the late Tory administration in speeches at the opening of Parliament in 1715. The most dubious identification is that of Lalcon, since there was a Lord Chamberlain in the British cabinet of 1715, the Duke of Shrewsbury. This nobleman, however, was a moderate man who did not join the outcry against the Tories.

229. 33. One person whose case appeared a little singular. The Earl of Peterborough and General Webb were two military leaders in the War of the Spanish Succession who were thought to have been unfairly treated by the Whig government of 1708–10, and who were consequently hailed by the Tories as martyrs. Swift was very friendly with Peterborough, and had written verses in his praise. The most striking similarities between Peterborough's career and that of the anonymous Roman hero are that Peterborough had been a successful naval commander, that his son had been fatally wounded in a sea-fight at which the father was present, that the Earl, after his successes, had been removed from his command, that he had been unable to secure reinstatement in a responsible military post, and that he had eventually retired in disgust to his country estate.

* Adapted from the "Supplementary Notes" and "Commentary" to *Gulliver's Travels* by Jonathan Swift, ed. Arthur E. Case (New York: The Ronald Press Company, 1938), pp. 331–57.

Textual Notes

These emendations do not depend upon any 'authority': they are merely attempts to correct obvious blunders which make nonsense of the passages in which they occur or of some other part of the book. Most of these changes were made in early editions, presumably by alert compositors who observed the discrepancies: a few have been made by Arthur E. Case.

Table of contents and heading of Part III. All early editions interchange 'Glubbdubdrib' and 'Luggnagg' in the list of countries visited by Gulliver. This was due to the original compositor's desire to avoid dividing 'Glubbdubdrib' between two lines in the heading of Part III. The table of contents copied the heading, and the error remained unnoticed in later editions.

25. 6. 'Northeast' has been substituted by Case for 'northwest'.

26. 4.; 28. 16.; 163. 30. The first edition consistently printed 'mine' instead of 'my' in the phrases 'mine eyes' and 'mine ears'. Ford systematically corrected 'mine' to 'my', but failed to note these three instances, which have been emended in accord with the general practice.

51. 19; 52. 6.; 52. 12. '1724', the reading of the first edition, should presumably be '1728' (the cube of twelve). The emendation, although it was not one of those suggested by Ford in his letter to Motte, appears in the fourth octavo, either because the original manuscript had been consulted or, more probably, because someone had pointed out the mathematical error to the printer.

97. 2. The statement that Gulliver remained ten months in England conflicted with other statements in **93. 14, 93. 29** and **97. 4**. The correction (though not in Ford's list) was made in the fourth octavo.

97. 16. The date '19th' of April is inconsistent with the assertion that the storm which began on that date lasted for twenty days and was over by the second of May. The easiest way to account for the error is to assume that the compositor, carrying a long phrase in his memory, set up '19th' for the correct '9th'.

174. 4. The greatest discrepancy in dates in this voyage can most easily be cured by altering the year in which Gulliver reached Fort St. George from 1707 to 1708.

180. 6. The first edition reads 'two or three more persons': this undoubted error has usually been corrected by deleting 'three'. It seems more likely that this is a case of the transposition of words by the compositor, and that the proper reading is 'two, three, or more': this is supported by the phrase 'him or them' immediately below.

189. 13, 14. 'This declivity' should, obviously, be 'The declivity', since no declivity has previously been mentioned. Faulkner's 1735 edition made the necessary correction.

208. 10. 'Companions' should be 'companion', since Gulliver was attended by a single guide.

209. 2. 'Projector' should, of course, be changed to the plural, as it was in Faulkner's edition of 1735.

210. 10. 'Emptied', the reading of Faulkner's 1735 edition, is the most plausible emendation for the incorrect 'employed' which was carelessly repeated by the original compositor from the line above.

233. 16. 'Invited' seems inconsistent with the statement that Gulliver was confined to his house and garden. The emendation 'visited', which has been universally accepted, was made in Faulkner's edition of 1759.

243. 18. 'Deprived', clearly an error, was changed in a pirated Dublin edition of 1726 to 'despised'. This correction, which was adopted by Motte and Faulkner, has since become a part of the standard text.

248. 18. The first edition reads '16th' of April: the emendation to '6th', in order to avoid a conflict with the date given five lines below, is in accord with the similar emendation in **97. 16.**

248. 25. The reading of all early editions is 'after an absence of five years and six months complete.' This would carry the date of Gulliver's departure from England back to October 1704, at which time he was still in Brobdingnag. The elapsed time between the dates given for his departure (August 5, 1706) and his return (April 10, 1710) is just over three years and eight months: the text has been emended accordingly. If these numbers were written in figures in the manuscript it is easy to see how 3 and 8 might have been read as 5 and 6; but it cannot be said with any certainty that this is the explanation of the mistake, which may well have been the result of careless revision of the complicated scheme of the voyage.

251. 2. The alteration from 'five' to 'four' months is the simplest way of resolving the slight conflict in dates.

Commentary*

Jonathan Swift

Jonathan Swift was born in Dublin on November 30, 1667. His father, Jonathan Swift senior, and his mother, both of English stock, had removed to Ireland some ten years earlier, and there the father died after a not too successful career in the law. His namesake and only son was born eight months after his death. Young Jonathan was brought up under the general supervision of his paternal uncle Godwin, his mother electing, at some unknown date during her son's childhood, to return to her family in Leicestershire. Jonathan's education, which was that of the better-class Anglo-Irish, was largely the gift of his uncle: Swift, however, expressed little gratitude for this in later life, possibly because he felt that he should have been educated in England, or because the bounty had been given in a way which galled his pride. He attended Kilkenny School, where he met William Congreve, and subsequently Trinity College, Dublin, in which, during a residence of seven years, he had an undistinguished academic record, except in classical literature. His progress toward the degree of Master of Arts was cut short by the disturbances in Ireland which accompanied the 'Glorious Revolution' in 1688–89: the spring of the latter year found him in England, occupying a secretarial post in the household of a distant maternal relative, Sir William Temple, who had retired to his country estate of Moor Park after a long and distinguished political career. In these surroundings Swift spent the next ten years, save for two intervals of life in Ireland. The first visit, in 1691–92, was made in the hope that it might benefit the young secretary's health; the second was the result of a disagreement between Temple and Swift, who seems to have felt that his relative should have put him in the way of political preferment. During this second absence from England Swift was ordained in the Church of Ireland (i.e., the Irish branch of the Church of England): for more than a year he led the life of a country vicar. In the final period of his residence at Moor Park (1696–99) he wrote his first great book, *A Tale of a Tub*, which, however, was not published for several years.

* Adapted from the "Commentary" to *Gulliver's Travels* by Jonathan Swift, ed. Arthur E. Case (New York: The Ronald Press Company, 1938), pp. 337–57.

After Temple's death in 1699 Swift returned to Ireland with a new patron, Lord Berkeley, who had been appointed one of the Lords Justices. Through the influence of this nobleman Swift soon received appointments in the Irish Church, in which he rapidly became a person of some importance. His experience in England made him the best ambassador the church could select to negotiate for certain concessions from the English government, and he was sent to London upon several such missions. Here he made numerous acquaintances in the literary and political world, among them Addison, Steele, Prior, Gay, Arbuthnot, Pope, Harley and St. John; here also, in 1704, his *Tale of a Tub* was published, anonymously, and perhaps without his consent. The book made him famous in the world of letters, but its jocose attitude toward religion militated against his future advancement in the church.

During his visits to England in the early part of the century Swift occasionally tried his hand at political pamphleteering. At first his affiliations were with the Whigs, but he found, as time went on, that the English Whigs were less sympathetic with his views about ecclesiastical affairs than the English Tories. To Swift this was a matter of vital importance, and accordingly, about 1710, he transferred his allegiance to the Tory party. In the next four years he wrote a large number of political pamphlets, becoming not only the best writer for his side, but probably the greatest political pamphleteer that England has ever known. As a reward for his services he anticipated that the Tories would grant the concessions he had asked for the Irish Church, and also provide him with some important post in the Church of England. But in this latter hope he was disappointed: Queen Anne, who had been offended by the tone of *A Tale of a Tub,* was hostile, and the best that his friends could secure for him was the position of Dean of St. Patrick's Cathedral in Dublin. Swift, by this time, had come to regard life in Ireland as virtual exile. He managed, for over a year, to spend most of his time in London, on leave of absence from his new charge. But in the summer of 1714 Queen Anne died, and was succeeded by her distant cousin, King George of Hanover: at the same time the Tories fell from power and were succeeded by the Whigs, the supporters of the new dynasty. Disappointed and embittered, Swift retired to Dublin, his political hopes and those of his friends destroyed forever.

For the next six years Swift busied himself with the duties of his ecclesiastical office, writing almost nothing. These years witnessed the growth of difficulties in his private life. At the time of his residence in Moor Park he had been the tutor of a child, Esther Johnson, who was, like himself, a distant relative and protégé of Sir William Temple, and whom, as she grew older, he came to love.

Temple's will left her a small income, hardly sufficient for a comfortable existence in England, and in 1701, on Swift's advice, she and her companion, Mrs. Dingley, removed to Dublin, where she spent the remainder of her life, save for brief visits to her native country. The precise relationship between Swift and Esther (or Stella, as he called her) has never been established: it is more than possible that they went through a ceremony of marriage in 1716, although it is certain that the marriage, if it took place, was a mere form. One undisputed fact is that Stella was the only great love of Swift's life. He was, however, fond of feminine companionship; during his missions to London he met a young girl named Hester Vanhomrigh (Vanessa) who became infatuated with him and pursued him to Ireland, where she carried on a prolonged campaign to secure from him an admission of affection. This affair was to reach a climax some years later, when Swift was in the midst of the composition of *Gulliver's Travels.*

Before that time came, however, Swift was moved to take up his pen once more by his increasing anger at the activities of the Whig government in England, especially the continuation of the policy of exploiting Ireland for the benefit of the English. In 1720 he published a pamphlet urging the Irish to retaliate by purchasing goods of their own manufacture rather than those imported from England. At about the same time he began the composition of *Gulliver's Travels.* This occupied him for more than five years, in the course of which his work was interrupted by pressing affairs both public and private. In 1723 Vanessa, having determined to force the issue, wrote to ask Stella whether she was married to Swift. Swift, upon learning of this, withdrew even his friendship from Vanessa, who died shortly afterward, leaving a will which charged Swift with cruel neglect of her. Her death, and the notoriety resulting from the publication of her will and of certain verses that Swift had written to her, affected Swift deeply. It may have been, in part, a desire to wrest his mind from the contemplation of this affair that led him to throw himself with such fervor into the controversy over 'Wood's halfpence'—a conflict which had been brewing since 1722. Briefly, the English government had authorized the minting of a large number of copper coins for Ireland: the patent for this work had been given, by a piece of political jobbery, to an English ironmonger named Wood. Irish opposition to the scheme grew by degrees, and was finally raised to its height in 1724 by Swift's famous pamphlets, written in the assumed character of a Dublin tradesman, 'M. B., Drapier'. In the end the English government was forced to abandon its project, largely because these *Drapier's Letters* had solidified the resistance of the Irish; and Swift became the great Irish hero.

Early in 1726 Swift completed the final revision of the manuscript of *Gulliver's Travels*, and in the spring he journeyed to London for the first time in twelve years, to visit old friends and to arrange for the publication of his book. This last design was surrounded by secrecy, and had not yet been accomplished when Swift returned to Ireland in August. Two and a half months later the *Travels* were published by Benjamin Motte, and became immediately the sensation of the day. In the following spring Swift visited England again, and enjoyed in person some of the acclaim which had greeted the book of which he was well known to be the author. Two months after his arrival in England George I died, and the Tories had a momentary gleam of hope that they might regain power. This gleam was extinguished almost at once by the triumph of Walpole and his reappointment as prime minister by George II, who, as Prince of Wales, had been his avowed enemy. Swift returned once more to Ireland, which he was never to leave again.

He was now sixty years of age, oppressed by ailments which had harassed him during most of his life, and made still more melancholy by the mortal illness of Stella. After her death, in 1728, there was little in life to interest him. He turned his attention to his ecclesiastical duties and other Irish affairs. Although he began to complain, not only of ill-health, but of failing memory, it was some years before his mental powers showed any perceptible lessening: to this period belong some of his most vigorous compositions, among them such poems as *On Poetry: a Rhapsody, The Legion Club,* and *On the Death of Dr. Swift.* But age and illness pressed relentlessly on; Swift lost, one by one, the few close friends who lived near enough at hand to be of comfort to him; at length his memory became so bad that he could not trust it in the common affairs of daily life. By his seventy-third year his deepening melancholy made it impossible for him to engage in ordinary social intercourse, and his mental condition grew steadily worse until it was necessary to put his affairs into the hands of guardians. Still he lingered until almost the end of his seventy-eighth year. By his will nearly all his estate was bequeathed to charity, to which he had given a large proportion of his income during his life. His body was buried in the cathedral where he had been dean for so long, and where now, in the words of the epitaph he had written for himself, 'fierce indignation could no longer tear his heart'.

•

The Theme of Gulliver's Travels

The theme of *Gulliver's Travels* is that of Swift's earlier great work, *A Tale of a Tub,* worked out more clearly, more concretely, and more universally: it is the effect of folly upon the fate of humanity. Yet the genesis of the book did not promise a result of so wide a scope. Early in 1714 the chief Tory wits formed a club, the purpose of which was to write the memoirs of an imaginary pedant, one 'Martinus Scriblerus'. The most important members of this group were Swift, Pope, Arbuthnot, Gay and Thomas Parnell, an Irish protégé of Swift. Each member of the club was to be held responsible for the exposure of pedantry in one or more fields of intellectual endeavor—literature, philology, archaeology, exploration, science, medicine, law—while the group as a whole was to discuss the material contributed, arrange the results, and write the memoirs. Before the scheme had progressed very far the political crisis of 1714 intervened, dispersed the club, and put an end to the plan, although some of the more sanguine members cherished for a time a hope that it might be resumed. Finally, in 1741, Pope published the fragmentary work of the Scriblerus Club in an edition of his own works.

At least a part of Swift's allotted share in this project seems to have been a burlesque of the literature of exploration and travel, which had enjoyed increasing popularity since William Dampier, in 1697, had begun to publish accounts of his voyages in the South Seas and elsewhere. How much Swift accomplished in 1714 we have no means of knowing. Years afterward Pope told Joseph Spence, 'It was from a part of those memoirs [of Scriblerus] that Dr. Swift took his first hints for *Gulliver.* There were pigmies in Schreibler's *Travels;* and the projects of Laputa'. This may mean no more than that Swift had begun to collect ideas in 1714. There is no evidence that he wrote any part of the *Travels* at this time, or, if he did, that he incorporated what he wrote in the finished work. The resumption of his abandoned plan in 1720, the year in which he wrote his pamphlet urging the Irish to use their own manufactures rather than those brought from England, suggests that he had seen in the old project of Scriblerus a medium through which to expound an idea of far greater importance than the absurdity of pedantic scholarship. This idea was the demonstration of the effects of folly in the life of man, in all its manifestations, but especially with regard to man as a social being. Swift's intense interest in politics and government during the most active part of his career had strongly affected the bent of his genius. It is true, of course, that he criticizes many of the individual vices of man in *Gulliver's Travels,* but he is even more deeply concerned with the institutions which man has created for himself, their wisdom or unwisdom, their efficacy, their decay: conversely he is interested in the effect of these institutions upon their servants, and in the regrettable fact that men who in themselves are virtuous and amiable may, when they act as members of a class, be foolish, hard-hearted and vicious.

Swift's method of achieving his end is novel in its combination of literary genres. Other writers, to convey their philosophic creeds, have described the customs of imaginary countries: Swift gives the expression of his beliefs an imaginative framework planned and written after the manner of contemporary travel books, and thereby produces an illusion of reality which goes far toward putting the reader in a receptive mood toward the more important part of the *Travels.* Within the narrative framework Swift urges his views by two methods, ridicule of vice and praise of virtue. These he employs alternately, for purposes of contrast and relief, interspersing also, especially in the first two voyages, interludes of pure imagination for the reader's enjoyment and his own. The desire to provide contrast results, once or twice, in apparent inconsistencies: the central portion of the sixth chapter of the first voyage, for example, has been objected to as out of keeping with the rest, because it makes some of the laws of Lilliput Utopian. It should be noted, however, that Swift does not proceed to extremes in the first two voyages: Lilliput is not altogether bad, nor is Brobdingnag altogether admirable. On the whole, the *Travels* are unified and ordered. Especially noteworthy is the deepening tone as the story progresses: to create this Swift has been careful even of the minor details, one or two of which may be cited as examples. The accidents by which Gulliver arrives in the several countries which he visits are varied not only for the sake of novelty, but to keep pace with his growing realization of the defects in human nature. When he is cast ashore in Lilliput the worst fault contributing to the disaster is lack of vigilance on the part of the lookout. In Brobdingnag he is abandoned by his shipmates because of cowardice (not altogether inexcusable). In the third voyage the violence of pirates is responsible for Gulliver's predicament, and in the last he suffers through that most hateful of human vices, treachery. Parallel with this progression is the development of Gulliver's character from that of an average intelligent Englishman, with an uncritical acceptance of the customs of his country and a good-natured contempt for the odd behavior of foreigners, to that of a humbled admirer of the virtues of a superior race, the Houyhnhnms. In the first and third voyages Swift's method is chiefly satiric, and beneath the general commentary upon life there lie references to particular characters and events in eighteenth-century England which serve as texts. Between these two voyages intervenes a description of Brobdingnag, which may be called a modified Utopia

—not an ideal civilization, but a better one in many ways than that which Europe knew, and not so far advanced as to be out of reach of Swift's contemporaries, if they could but be brought to realize its superiority. The fourth voyage, which was Swift's goal from the beginning, and which is perhaps his greatest literary achievement, is a Utopia of another sort, in which the ideal virtue of the Houyhnhnms is heightened by contrasting it with the degradation of the yahoos. Critics do scant honor to Swift when they suggest that the descriptions of these subhuman creatures are satiric portraits of the native Irish, drawn by the hand of an embittered exile from England. Swift himself gives the answer to any such interpretation in a letter which he wrote to the Abbé Desfontaines, the translator of the *Travels* into French, who had explained to Swift that he had altered or omitted passages in the book which had no application to France. Swift replied, 'If the volumes of Gulliver were designed only for the British Isles, that traveler ought to pass for a very contemptible writer. The same vices and the same follies reign everywhere; at least in the civilized countries of Europe: and the author who writes only for one city, one province, one kingdom, or even one age, does not deserve to be read, let alone translated'.

Mention of the voyage to the country of the Houyhnhnms inevitably leads to a discussion of Swift's feelings about humanity, and to the quotation of a famous passage from a letter which he wrote to Pope in 1725:

> The chief end I propose to myself in all my labours is to vex the world rather than divert it, and if I could compass that design without hurting my own person or fortune, I would be the most indefatigable writer you have ever seen. . . . When you think of the world give it one lash the more at my request. I have ever hated all nations, professions, and communities, and all my love is toward individuals; for instance, I hate the tribe of lawyers, but I love Counsellor Such-a-one and Judge Such-a-one; so with physicians—I will not speak of my own trade—soldiers, English, Scotch, French, and the rest. But principally I hate and detest that animal called man, although I heartily love John, Peter, Thomas, and so forth. This is the system upon which I have governed myself many years, but do not tell, and so I shall go on till I have done with them. I have got materials toward a treatise proving the falsity of that definition *animal rationale,* and to show it should be only *rationis capax* [capable of reason]. Upon this great foundation of misanthropy, though not in Timon's manner, the whole building of my *Travels* is erected; and I never will have peace of mind, till all honest men are of my opinion.

It is chiefly upon this letter that those critics rely who charge Swift with misanthropy: but the charge is refuted by the very source which gave it birth. What Swift meant by 'misanthropy' was a hatred of the vices of men, especially as manifested by their actions in groups, rather than as individuals. He did not identify the yahoos with mankind, although to enforce a partial likeness he sometimes allowed Gulliver to speak of himself and other 'civilized' men as yahoos. Yahoos and Houyhnhnms are, in fact, the symbols of the opposite ends of a scale, the one totally without reason, and consequently, according to Swift's theory, utterly brutish and evil; the other perfectly reasonable and therefore of necessity perfectly good, requiring no government from without. The very Houyhnhnms recognized the great difference between the yahoos and Gulliver, who was only slightly above the average European in mental and moral qualities: had it not been so, Gulliver's master would never have treated him as he did. Swift undoubtedly wished to indicate that man as he is is nearer to the lower than to the upper end of the scale, but he did not imply that man will ever attain the height or sink to the depth. Swift believed, in common with most of his contemporaries, that man has degenerated from a higher state: it was his wish to induce man to reverse his downward trend and to aim once more at the excellencies which he could never reach, but toward which he might strive. The great difference between man and the yahoo was that man was capable of reason, and herein lay his hope. There were times when Swift, in an agony of bitterness at the folly of mankind, and their refusal to listen to his voice, declared his whole project of reforming humanity chimerical, and man incapable of redemption. But these moods are no more indicative of real misanthropy than are the desponding utterances of the Hebrew prophets. Swift's constant preoccupation, throughout his life, with one reform or another is the clearest refutation of any real misanthropy in his nature. More than most men he depended upon human society and friendship. And although in his "A Letter from Capt. Gulliver to his cousin Sympson", he denounced all schemes for the reformation of mankind as visionary, his real feelings were more truly expressed in his poem, *On the Death of Dr. Swift,* written some years earlier, in which he described prophetically his own death and its effect upon the world in which he had lived.

> Suppose me dead; and then suppose
> A club assembled at the Rose; . . .
> One, quite indifferent in the cause,
> My character impartial draws: . . .
> 'Perhaps I may allow the Dean
> Had too much satire in his vein;

And seemed determined not to starve it,
Because no age could more deserve it.
Yet malice never was his aim;
He lashed the vice, but spared the name; . . .
His satire points at no defect,
But what all mortals may correct; . . .
And since you dread no farther lashes,
Methinks you may forgive his ashes'.

Two elements in *Gulliver's Travels* have repelled many readers—the occasional grossness of its language, and the relentlessness of its attack upon human vice and folly. Concerning the former, one can only repeat what has so often been said: that Swift's coarseness is never suggestive, and that in the *Travels*, at least, it always has a definite purpose, whether it be to burlesque the travel-writer's preoccupation with inconsequential details, as at the end of the first chapter of the second voyage, or, more frequently, to deflate human pride by emphasizing the undignified nature of the bodily processes in which man must recognize his kinship with the brute creation. As for the element of 'ferocity', it is necessary to remember that Swift thought of men as beings capable of reason, and that his early failure to reform mankind by gentler means led him, as time passed, to employ increasing violence of expression, in the hope that he might succeed by shocking the audience he had been unable to persuade. It is possible that this course partially defeated its own ends. But the modern reader (for whom the shock of *Gulliver's Travels* is often the greater because he read it first in expurgated form as a nursery tale) should not pronounce final judgment at once. He will do well to imitate Gulliver, who at first found himself deafened by the speech of the Brobdingnagians, but who finally discovered, in the philosophy of their king, a wisdom greater than his own.

Geography and Chronology

It has been remarked that the narrative portions of *Gulliver's Travels* serve both as a satire upon travel literature and as a framework for the ideas which Swift meant to convey to his readers. The term 'framework' might, perhaps, be reserved for application to those parts of the tale which describe Gulliver's journeys to and from the fabulous countries which he visits. Swift took a great deal of pains to make these sections of the narrative as plausible and circumstantial as possible. In the beginning of the eighteenth century the Indian and the Pacific Oceans were still largely unexplored, save for the coast of Asia, which was charted as far north as Japan. New discoveries were constantly being reported by adventurous sea-captains, but as the accounts of these men were inexact, fragmentary and often mutually inconsistent, the maps of rival cartographers showed disagreements which left the author of travels a good deal of liberty. Swift placed his imaginary countries in the borderland of the unexplored parts of the globe—far enough from well-known lands to avoid conflict with universally accepted geographical data, but near enough to established trade-routes to make Gulliver's eventual rescues not too implausible. The smaller countries, Lilliput, Blefuscu, and Houyhnhnmland, were located not far from Australia; the larger, Brobdingnag and Balnibarbi, in the North Pacific. Swift was bold enough to supply fairly exact data concerning the positions of these countries, although two errors (in the first chapter of the first voyage and the first chapter of the third voyage) and an insufficiently detailed paragraph in the next to the last chapter of the fourth voyage have led to some misunderstanding as to the whereabouts of Lilliput, Blefuscu, Laputa, and Houyhnhnmland. Had a contemporary of Swift sought in his atlas for Lilliput in the region northwest of Tasmania and in latitude 30° 2′ S., he would have found that it lay, not in the ocean, but well inland in Australia. The cause of this discrepancy, which has puzzled commentators ever since, appears to be the compass-direction: Swift meant to place the island northeast of Tasmania, in the relatively unexplored seas between Australia and New Zealand. If this initial error is corrected all the rest of the geographical data which have caused confusion fall neatly into place. The map-maker for the first edition, who obviously did not have the benefit of Swift's guidance, followed the original description, and was forced to move Tasmania far to the west of its actual position in an attempt to surmount his difficulties. He had a still greater problem in drawing the map of Laputa and its neighboring countries—a problem he might have solved had he made use of all the data supplied in the third voyage. The error here is the position (46° N. 177° W.) given in the first chapter of the voyage. The continent must, as a matter of fact, lie far to the southeast of this spot. The map-maker was more fortunate in interpreting the geographical data of the last voyage. Modern editors have suggested that Gulliver, on his return from Houyhnhnmland, must have touched at the southwest point of Australia, rather than the southeast. This, however, is not the case. Gulliver at first fancied himself to have been marooned on an island west of Australia, but subsequently found that Houyhnhnmland was slightly south of the eastern part of the continent. The eastern coast of Australia, as the eighteenth century had already discovered, projects farther south than the western: Gulliver was lucky enough to strike the southeast point (or perhaps the

southeastern point of Tasmania) by sailing due east. After he escaped the savages he rounded the point and sailed north along the uncharted east coast: it was here that he sighted the ship coming from the north-northeast—an impossible position for the vessel had Gulliver been in the neighborhood of the southwest point of Australia.

The chronology of Gulliver's voyages, like the geography, was carefully worked out, although once again a few slips on the part of either Swift or the printer have led to some inconsistency and confusion. The chronology of the first voyage presents no difficulties if one supposes a period of about four months to be occupied by Gulliver's preparations to capture the Blefuscudian fleet. The time-schedule of the second voyage is extremely simple: so is that of the fourth, if one keeps in mind Swift's preference for round numbers: Gulliver's three years and nine months in the country of the Houyhnhnms are spoken of as three years, and his absence from England of five years and four months as five years. The third voyage has several discrepancies, which may be due either to the failure of the author to make necessary alterations in dates during the revision of his manuscript, or to mistakes of the printer, a solution strongly suggested in the letter to Sympson. An entire year is unaccounted for—a loss that can be most easily remedied by supposing that Gulliver reached Fort St. George in 1708, rather than 1707, the date given in all early editions. The inconsistency resulting from Gulliver's statement that he spent three months in Luggnagg, although he gives the dates of his arrival and departure as April 21 and May 6, respectively, can only be laid to an oversight on the part of the author; the error of a few days in one or the other of the two dates in the last two paragraphs of the voyage may safely be laid at the door of the printer.

Several attempts have been made to discover political or personal references in the dates of Gulliver's departures and arrivals, but so far no one has proposed any convincing or even likely theories, and it seems probable that the chronology may be taken at its face value.

The Text

The first edition of *Gulliver's Travels* was published in London on October 28, 1726. The circumstances attending its publication made it impracticable for the author to correct the press. Nevertheless the publisher, Benjamin Motte, directed the work carefully and conscientiously, even canceling two leaves in order to correct errors. He did, however, omit or alter a few passages which he feared might lay him open to prosecution, and he added at least one passage not written by Swift. The latter protested these changes through the agency of his friend Charles Ford, who wrote a letter to Motte, not only specifying the major alterations in the text, but furnishing a list of minor errata. These last the printer corrected in the fourth octavo edition of 1727 (called on its title-page the second edition), but he allowed the more important corrupt passages to stand, either because he still feared arrest, or because he had lost or destroyed the manuscript from which the first edition had been set.

In 1732 a Dublin printer named Faulkner informed Swift of a design to print a four-volume edition of his works. Swift at first protested, but finding that Faulkner meant to proceed with or without permission, he so far fell in with him as to secure for him from Ford a list of corrections for *Gulliver's Travels.* He also undertook some oversight of the proof, but from the evidence now available it appears that this was perfunctory, and that he delegated much of the duty to friends. The resulting text, published in 1735, restored nearly, but not quite all, of the suppressed and mutilated passages to something approaching their original state; it also made numerous verbal alterations, many of which were obviously intended to eliminate infelicities caused by repetitions. A number of the changes which affect the sense, however, are distinctly for the worse: they indicate that the reviser, whether Swift or another, either misunderstood or had forgotten the reasons underlying the original passages. In view of this, the best text seems to be that of Charles Ford's copy of the first edition, which contains corrections copied from the original manuscript.

The text of the present edition is based on the Huntington Library's common paper copy of the first edition (HL106606), collated with the large paper copy (HL106645), and corrected by photographic reproductions of Charles Ford's letter to Motte and his manuscript notes in his large paper copy of the *Travels,* both of which are now in the Victoria and Albert Museum.

There are only a few instances in which the text of the present edition deviates from the basis described above: they have been indicated in the footnotes and are listed in the Supplementary Notes (pp. 339–41).

In spelling, punctuation and typography the present text has been partially modernized. The spelling of the basic text has been retained wherever it is sanctioned by modern authorities, although no longer preferred; and even obsolete spellings have been kept if a change would have resulted in a change in pronunciation. Names coined by the author are always given in their most usual form.

In dealing with the punctuation the aim has been to change only those practices of the original printer which might hamper or mislead the modern reader.

For example, in phrases such as 'But, I could not tell . . .' (which occur frequently) the comma has been omitted. Again, in the following sentence, '. . . we came to a long kind of building, made of timber, stuck in the ground, and wattled across . . .', the misleading comma after 'timber' has been deleted.

The typography has undergone the most frequent emendation. Quotation marks (not used in the first edition) have been introduced in the appropriate places. Capitalization follows the modern practice. Italics have been variously dealt with as the occasion required: where the first edition used them to designate proper names they have been altered to roman; where it employed them to indicate a foreign language, or to give emphasis, they have been retained. In a few instances in which they seemed pointless, and were probably used by mistake, they have been normalized to accord with modern usage.

APPENDIX B

Perspectives on *Gulliver's Travels*

GULLIVER'S TRAVELS*

Maynard Mack

That Swift's greatest satire, *Gulliver's Travels,* is sometimes relegated to the nursery can be explained in part by the fact that most adults are unwilling to face the truth about themselves.

Gulliver, who is Swift's *persona* in this work, is more complex and more complexly used than the assumed identities we have met in the *Argument* and the *Modest Proposal.* He is, first of all, a stolid, unemotional, but candid and reliable observer. In this respect, his account has been made to resemble those of the authentic voyagers of Swift's time, whose narratives of distant lands (it was the last great age of exploration) were devoured by Augustan readers. Voyages, both authentic and imaginary, were in fact one of the prominent literary genres. The intent of the imaginary voyages was almost always to satirize the existing European order, and it did so by playing up the innocence, manliness, and high ethical standards of the untutored peoples whom the voyager claimed to have met. But the real voyages also, even those recounted by missionaries and priests, pointed to the same conclusion. Reflecting, without realizing it, the general modern rehabilitation of "nature" (in contrast to the older view of nature as fallen and in need of redemption), all these voyages tended alike to stress the goodness of unspoiled primitive man. The human nature presented in such accounts (and in a substantial tradition of other writings ranging from Montaigne to Rousseau) did not appear to be morally unreliable, or controllable only by the disciplines of civilization. On the contrary, it was evidently instinctively good, and had been corrupted by civilization; if these corrupting influences could be removed, there was practically no limit to its perfectibility.

Swift, whose aim in *Gulliver* is (among other things) to show the fatuity of this creed, deliberately adopts the voyage genre of the enemy and turns it to his own ends. Wherever Gulliver goes among his fantastic aborigines, he is always encountering, instead of handsome and noble savages, aspects of man as he perennially is, whether in civilized society or in nature. Among the Lilliputians,

* From Maynard Mack, *English Masterpieces V, The Augustans,* 2d ed. © 1961, pp. 14–16. Reprinted by permission of Prentice-Hall, Inc., Englewood Cliffs, NJ.

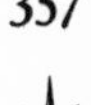

it is human pettiness, especially moral pettiness, and the triviality of many of the forms, titles, customs, pretenses, and "points of honour" by which men assert their dignity and about which they conduct their quarrels. Characteristically, the devices Gulliver meets with in this country are those of little men: pomposity, intrigue, and malice. Among the Brobdingnagians, on the other hand, it is the physical grossness of the human species, its callous indifference to what it flings aside or tramples underfoot: "For I apprehended every moment that he would dash me against the ground, as we usually do any hateful little animal which we have in mind to destroy." In this country, Gulliver is constantly being appalled by circumstances of coarseness: the nurse's monstrous breast, the linen "coarser than sackcloth," the Queen crunching "the wing of a lark, bones and all, between her teeth," and drinking "above a hogshead at a draught"—or else of calloused contempt: the schoolboy's hazelnut, the farmer's indifference to Gulliver's fatigue, the pet lamb promised to Glumdalclitch but casually dispatched to the butcher. At the same time (for in this voyage the satire cuts two ways), Gulliver's conversations with the King throw a frightful light on man as civilized European.

The fourth voyage brings us the Yahoos and the animal nastiness that is also one aspect of the human situation. The Yahoos are Swift's climactic answer to the contemporary infatuation with noble "natural" men; and the language used of them becomes especially vulgar and anatomical to indicate the repulsiveness of "unspoiled" nature, either physical or moral. But the Yahoos are also something more. We may see embodied in them that extreme view of man as hopelessly irrational, decadent, and depraved, which extreme Puritanism fostered in religious terms, and which had been exemplified in nonreligious terms by Hobbes's portrait of life in a state of nature as "nasty, brutish, and short." This view, it will be observed, Swift embodies in the Yahoos only to reject it. Though Gulliver makes the error of identifying himself and other human beings completely with the Yahoos, we and Swift do not. Nor do we take the ideal life for man, as Gulliver does, to be the tepid rationality of the horses. Reacting against the Yahoos because he mistakes the animal part of human nature which they represent for the whole, Gulliver goes to the other extreme and worships pure rationality in the Houyhnhnms, which is likewise only a part of the whole. Neither extreme answers to the actual human situation, and Swift, despite the persistence with which this voyage has been misinterpreted, is careful to show us this. That Gulliver's self-identification with the Yahoos is mistaken, we realize (if we have not realized it long before) as soon as we see Gulliver insisting that his wife and children are Yahoos, and preferring to live in the stable. Similarly, we see the mistakenness of his desire to be like the Houyhnhnms as soon as we pause to reflect that they are horses: Swift has used *animals* as his symbols here in order to make it quite plain that pure rationality is not available to *man*—would make us as absurd, monstrous, and tedious as the Houyhnhnms. For the truth, as we are meant to realize, is that man is neither irrational physicality like the Yahoos nor passionless rationality like the Houyhnhnms; neither (to paraphrase Swift's own terms in a famous letter to Pope) *animal implume bipes* nor *animal rationale,* but *animal rationis capax.*

And now, if we look back again at the voyages, we can see that this middle view has been the theme from the very beginning. In Lilliput, the vices and trivialities of the little people are seen against the normal humanity and benevolence of Gulliver. In Brobdingnag, over against Gulliver's unconscious brutality in recommending gunpowder and the description of Europeans as "the most pernicious race of little odious vermin that nature ever suffered to crawl upon the face of the earth," Swift shows us the magnanimity of the King and the tenderness of Glumdalclitch. Even in the last and darkest voyage, we are never allowed to suppose (witness the Portuguese sea-captain) that real human beings are the detestable creatures Gulliver supposes them. Man is fallen so far as Swift is concerned, and the new notions of natural goodness and infinite perfectibility are nonsense; but man is also—to put it in the nonreligious terms that Swift has chosen for his parable—capable of regeneration: *rationis capax.*

Swift's instrument in this blending of light and shadow is the assumed identity, Gulliver. Through Gulliver, Swift is able to deliver the most powerful indictment of man's inhumanity ever written in prose, and at the same time to distinguish his own realistic view of man's nature from the misanthropy of which he has sometimes been accused. While Gulliver is still naïve, mainly in the first two voyages, satire can be uttered through him, he himself remaining unaware of it. Later, when he begins to fall into misanthropy, still more corrosive satire can be uttered by him. But in the end, satire is uttered of him, and we see his mistake. For we discover, if we look closely, that all through the fourth voyage Gulliver is represented as becoming more and more like a horse—learning to neigh, to walk with an equine gait, to cherish the ammoniac smell. He is represented, in other words, as isolating himself from mankind, and it is only this isolation in its climactic form that we see in his treatment of his family and his residence in the stables at the close. To suppose, as many careless critics have done, that Swift is recommending this as an *ideal* for man is the consequence of the fatal error mentioned earlier—of identifying the author of an Augustan work with its *persona.*

Key to the Language of the Houyhnhnms in *Gulliver's Travels**

Marjorie W. Buckley

For more than two centuries scholars have pondered the question of significant satire in the names *Houyhnhnm* and *Yahoo* in Swift's 'A Voyage to the Houyhnhnms'. At last it seems possible that the question may be answered. The key appears to be phonetic and it may be applied to all the Houyhnhnm words in the fourth book of *Gulliver.* The first section of the paper will set forth a brief explanation of the key's basic form. The second will offer supporting evidence proving that the key is valid, and finally the study will demonstrate the detailed working of the key in the text of 'A Voyage to the Houyhnhnms'.

The word *Yahoo* spoken phonetically in the eighteenth century would be pronounced 'Yay who', which, correctly spelt, would be 'Ye who'. *Houyhnhnm* pronounced phonetically with the final *mn* transposed becomes 'Who inhuman'. Transposition is found elsewhere in Swift, notably in the title of his poem 'Cadenus and Vanessa', 'Cadenus' being taken from the Latin, *decanus,* 'a dean'. *Yahoo* is used as 'Ye who' in the sense of an indictment: 'Ye who behave thus.' *Houyhnhnm* is used as an indictment, also, in the sense of 'You who, inhuman, behave thus.' The word 'inhuman' has a vastly different connotation from 'unhuman' previously applied to the satiric significance of Swift's horses. It will be seen, therefore, that in the phonetic interpretation of the words *Yahoo* and *Houyhnhnm* lies the secret of a deeper level of satire than hitherto realised.

Swift provides many clues in his text in support of the view that he intended to demonstrate the Houyhnhnms' behaviour as inhuman. Many pertinent passages occur in chapter iii. In Ricardo Quintana's edition, pp. 190–1, we read of the Houyhnhnms: 'To help my Memory, I formed all I learned into the *English* Alphabet, and writ the Words down with the Translations. This last, after some time, I ventured to do in my Master's Presence. It cost me much Trouble to explain to him what I was doing; for the Inhabitants have not the least Idea

* From *Fair Liberty Was All His Cry: A Tercentenary Tribute to Jonathan Swift,* ed. A. Norman Jeffares (London: Macmillan & Co. Ltd., 1967), pp. 270–78.

of Books or Literature.'[1] It seems clear that Swift is telling us that the Houyhnhnms are without the gift of creativity. They have no means of communicating by the written word therefore no means of preserving ideas in a lasting and communicable form. An idea communicated only by speech could not retain its original form beyond a very short time. Swift is recording, therefore, that the Houyhnhnms lack the human quality of wishing to record their history and ideas, a quality common to all communities where human intelligence exists. We must be careful to recognise that Swift does not deny his horses' intelligence, it is the human quality that is missing.

On p. 191 we read: 'The Word *Houyhnhnm*, in their Tongue, signifies a *Horse;* and in its Etymology, *the Perfection of Nature.'* But, as we know, the perfection of nature has nothing to do with humanity. And on p. 193 Gulliver describes the ship which brought him to the land of the Houyhnhnms. His Honour was mystified that a ship could be made and managed by Yahoos, and had never before heard of a ship although he lived on an island. Thus again Swift demonstrates the lack of creativity in his horses. The same deficiency is clear again on pp. 196–7 in the passage: 'He said, I differed indeed from other Yahoos . . . but in point of real Advantage, he thought I differed for the worse. That my Nails were of no Use either to my fore or hinder Feet: As to my fore Feet, he could not properly call them by that Name, for he never observed me to walk upon them; that they were too soft to bear the Ground; that I generally went with them uncovered, neither was the Covering I sometimes wore on them, of the same Shape, or so strong as that on my Feet behind.' His Honour was unable to realise the need for creative manual work.

The chief Houyhnhnm expressed great indignation on hearing that in Gulliver's country horses were used as beasts of burden. Gulliver says: 'I described as well as I could, our Way of Riding; the Shape and use of a Bridle, a Saddle, a Spur, and a Whip . . .' His Honour replied that he 'wondered how we dared to venture upon a Houyhnhnm's Back . . . that the meanest Servant in his House would be able to shake off the strongest *Yahoo;* or by lying down, and rouling upon his Back, squeeze the Brute to Death'. Yet on p. 196 comes the antithetical statement that 'if it were possible there could be any Country where *Yahoos* alone were endowed with Reason, they certainly must be the governing Animal, because Reason will in Time always prevail against Brutal Strength. But, considering the Frame of our Bodies, and especially of mine, he thought no Creature of equal Bulk was so ill-contrived, for employing that Reason in the common Offices of Life . . .' Thus Swift shows us that whilst paying lip-service to

1. *Gulliver's Travels and other writings* (New York, 1958). Reference throughout the study will be to Quintana's edition.

reason His Honour is expressing the negation of reason. Therefore if reason is a human quality then it is not conspicuous in the Houyhnhnms. It seems incredible that they have been credited with a high standard of reasoning power for over two hundred years.

Evidence of inhuman characteristics in lack of emotion occur throughout the text. On page 219 we read: 'They have no Fondness for their Colts or Foles; but the care they take in educating them proceedeth entirely from the Dictates of *Reason*. . . . In their Marriages they are exactly careful to chuse such Colours as will not make any disagreeable Mixture in the Breed.' Another example of extreme placidity appears on p. 224: 'I remember, my Master having once made an Appointment with a Friend and his Family to come to his House upon some Affair of Importance; on the Day fixed, the Mistress and her two Children came very late . . . Her excuse for not coming sooner, was, that her Husband dying late in the Morning, she was a good while consulting her Servants about a convenient Place where his Body should be laid.' There are other examples of absence of emotion in the Houyhnhnms, but it is unnecessary to cite them for the purposes of our study. We have established that Swift appears to have provided his horses deliberately with a lack of human qualities, often disguised as an advantageous lack. It seems to be clear from the text therefore, irrespective of the phonetic qualities of the word *Houyhnhnm,* that the correct interpretation is 'Who inhuman'.

We must consider now the term *Yahoo*—the ostensible object of scorn in the book. It seems plain that Swift had no intention of offering praise of the Yahoos, but our study sets out to prove that he is bent on holding them up for inspection, that their true condition may be known, pitied, and possibly improved. In order to carry out such a project Swift must therefore have given us evidence that the Yahoos exhibited an essential humanity beyond the inhuman Houyhnhnms' comprehension.

Let us examine three quotations from Swift's text where evidences exist in the Yahoos of the three human characteristics we studied in the passages on the Houyhnhnms. The qualities are creativity, reason, and emotion. Swift cloaks the human qualities in a disguise of filth and depravity for the purposes of his satire. Under the disguises we find vestiges of creativity on p. 212, where we read of the neighbourhood battles of the Yahoos: 'Those of the District watching all Opportunities to surprise the next before they are prepared.' And on p. 215 Swift gives us a description of emotion in a Yahoo, accompanied, incidentally, by a description of His Honour's inability to understand the condition. The passage reads: 'My Master likewise mentioned another Quality, which his Servants had discovered in several *Yahoos,* to retire into a Corner, to lie down and howl, and groan, and spurn away all that came near him, although he were young and fat, and wanted neither Food nor Water; nor did the Servants imagine what could possibly ail him. And the only Remedy they found was to set him to hard Work, after which he would infallibly come to himself.'

In spite of constant avowals from the Houyhnhnms that the Yahoos are completely devoid of reason,[2] we read on p. 212: 'That, if a Cow died of Age or Accident, before a *Houyhnhnm* could secure it for his own *Yahoos*, those in the Neighbourhood would come in Herds to seize it.' Again, we read on p. 217: 'the *Yahoos* appear to be the most unteachable of all Animals, their Capacities never reaching higher than to draw or carry Burthens. Yet I am of Opinion this Defect ariseth chiefly from a perverse, restive Disposition. For they are cunning, malicious, treacherous and revengeful.' Both the passages quoted above display understandable emotional reactions and reasoning power in the Yahoos under the treatment accorded them by the Houyhnhnms.

Having established for the purpose of our study that Swift uses the behaviour of both Houyhnhnms and Yahoos as material for indictment, our phonetic interpretations of both names as phrases of indictment 'Who inhuman' and 'Ye who' apply perfectly as the key phrases in the meaning of the satire.

Applying the phonetic key, the reader may unlock Swift's meaning with relative ease. The method is simple. Between the letters of each Houyhnhnm word, unwritten vowel sounds occur in speech. Many of the speech-inserted diphthongs are varied by Swift between similar letters in the text according to the sound he wishes to produce. The sounds implied coincide with the meaning of the word or phrase, thus giving added fascination to Swift's puzzles. He uses also the usual alternative sounds for letters in the text of the Houyhnhnm words, i.e. *Y* is used as in 'sky' or as in 'you' exactly as in ordinary writing. Unlike some previously suggested interpretations of Swift's invented language,[3] there are no anagrams in the language of the Houyhnhnms. Nor are there any transpositions apart from the final *nm* in *Houyhnhnm.* The phonetic spelling is accurate in the text and the interpretation of the spelling is straightforward, requiring no rearrangement.

Evidence of an exactly similar technique used by Swift occurs in his letters to Sheridan where he writes 'IstmuaDt' for 'I esteem you a Deity'.[4] Further support for the phonetic interpretation comes from the *Journal to Stella* (7 March

2. Quintana, pp. 190, 191, 196, 211.
3. H. D. Kelling, 'Some Significant Names in Gulliver's Travels', in *SP*, vol. XLVIII, no. 4 (Oct. 1951).
4. F. E. Ball (ed.), *The Correspondence of Jonathan Swift, D.D.* (London, 1910–14), vol. V, p. 436.

1710–11), where he says, 'When I am writing in our language, I make up my mouth just as if I was speaking it.'[5]

In order to facilitate phonetic interpretation a list of similar letters with different pronunciations must be applied to the study of the Houyhnhnm words. The key to the different sounds of similar letters is:

A	Pronounced as in *lay.*
A	Pronounced as in *hernia.*
A	Pronounced as in *hand.*
H	May be silent as in *doh.*
HN	May develop an intervening vowel *er* as in h*er*nia.
HN	May develop an intervening vowel as in h*oo*f.
HN	A diphthong forms when N is pronounced as *en,* the sound becoming *hoo-en,* which becomes 'when'.
HN	May develop an intervening vowel sound of *er, oo,* or 'when' as described above. The N may be followed by the vowel sound *o* as in *no;* thereby producing a phrase (when the intervening vowel is *oo*) *hoo-no,* which becomes 'who know'. The other combinations are obvious.
L	May be pronounced unvoiced as an initial letter, thus becoming 'ill'.
L	May be pronounced *ell.*
U	May be pronounced as in *nun.*
U	May be pronounced as in *you.*
Y	May be pronounced as in *you.*
Y	May be pronounced as in *shy.*
Y	May be unvoiced as in *layn* 'lane'.
Y	May be pronounced as in *tin.*

Let us examine a Houyhnhnm word after applying our key. On pp. 213–14 we read: 'Neither has their language any more than a general Appellation for those Maladies; which is borrowed from the Name of the Beast, and called *Hnea Yahoo,* or the *Yahoo's-Evil.'* Applying our key we find that *HN* produces an intervening vowel sound *er* and the disease is shown in the word 'hernia'. As the general name for disease in the Yahoos, hernia is an excellent choice. It comes from strain in bearing burdens heavier than the body should bear. As the Houyhnhnms found it expedient to employ the Yahoos mainly as beasts of burden the disease is appropriate, particularly as in man's environment horses, as beasts of burden, often contract hernia.

5. Kelling, p. 766.

Another simple example of the efficacy of this phonetic key occurs in the word *Hnhloayn,* which appears on p. 229 in the following context: 'I should here observe to the Reader, that a Decree of the general Assembly in this Country, is expressed by the Word *Hnhloayn,* which signifies an *Exhortation.'*

We discover that between *H* and *n* the spoken vowel is *oo.* Therefore the first syllable becomes 'Who'. Between *n* and *h* the voiced vowel is *o* and the sound becomes *noh* producing 'know'. Between *h* and *l* the interposed vowel is *a.* The last five letters *loayn* are spoken as 'lone'. Adding together the four syllables we find the 'Decree' to be 'Who-know-alone'. It is decreed among the Houyhnhnms that the members of the Assembly are those 'Who-know-alone'. It is a type of decree which has been popular among many legislative assemblies.

On p. 225 we find an interesting list of Houyhnhnm words. Studying them in context we read: 'I know not whether it may be worth observing, that the *Houyhnhnms* have no Word in their Language to express any thing that is *evil,* except what they borrow from the Deformities or ill Qualities of the *Yahoos.* Thus they denote the Folly of a Servant, an Omission of a Child, a Stone that cuts their Feet, a Continuance of foul or unseasonable Weather, and the like, by adding to each the Epithet of *Yahoo.* For Instance, *Hhnm Yahoo, Whnholm Yahoo, Ynlhmnawihlma Yahoo,* and an ill-contrived House, *Ynholmhnmrohlnw Yahoo.'*

Possibly as an added hurdle Swift has given us four clues and only three Houyhnhnm phrases, for the last item on the list carries its own free interpretation. Bearing in mind the information in the text and regarding Yahoo as a derogatory adjective, we shall decipher each phrase in turn. It would seem that we must discard 'a Stone that cuts their Feet' as the extra phrase.

The first item, *Hhnm Yahoo,* meaning 'the Folly of a Servant', is simply *Houyhnhnm Yahoo,* the spelling *Hhnm* being an alternative form of *Houyhnhnm.* The twist must have appealed to its wry author!

The second phrase, *Whnaholm Yahoo,* meaning 'an Omission of a Child', develops the vowel sound *ee* between *W* and *h* thus producing the syllable *Wee.* The other letters in the word, *hnaholm,* form yet another spelling of *Houyhnhnm.* Thus *Whnaholm* becomes *Wee Houyhnhnm.* After adding our derogatory adjective *Yahoo* we find that the erring child has been described adequately as 'Wee Houyhnhnm Yahoo'. The variation in spelling must have been devised to make the puzzle doubly baffling, for the list is a direct invitation to interpreters.

The third phrase, *Ynlhmnawihlma Yahoo,* meaning a 'Continuance of foul or unseasonable Weather', uses *Y* as in *you* developing the vowel sound *oo* between *Y* and *n.* Thus the first syllable becomes 'You'. Between *n* and *l* the voiced vowel is *o* as in *no.* The vowel *o* shades into the unvoiced consonant *w* before *l* produc-

ing the sound *no-well* which becomes 'know well'. Between *h* and *m* the sound developed is *i* producing the syllable *in.* The remainder of the word *awihlma* reads quite simply as 'a while may'. Therefore when we assemble our syllables we produce the result 'You-know-well-home-in-a-while-may'. The following adjective *Yahoo* gives the 'evil' connotation to the phrase. Swift says in the passage quoted above: 'The Houyhnhnms have no Word in their Language to express any thing that is *evil.*' Therefore the foul weather over a long period must be described by its effect. And its effect is to keep the Houyhnhnms at home.

The last phrase, *Ynholmhnmrohlnw Yahoo,* meaning an 'ill-contrived House', uses the initial letter *Y* with *n* as *in. Holm* becomes 'home'. *Hnm* is another spelling of *Houyhnhnm. Rohl* is 'roll'. Between *n* and *w* the vowel sound *ow* occurs, thus the final syllable becomes 'now'. Therefore, assembling our syllables once more, we find that the phrase becomes 'In-home-Houyhnhnm-roll-now Yahoo'. Analysing the description we find that the Houyhnhnms, being horses, roll in their homes. The phrase indicates one particular home as Swift uses the singular of *Houyhnhnm.* Therefore with the added stigma of *Yahoo* the home becomes 'an ill-contrived House'.

One more example will serve to demonstrate our key. On p. 221 we read: 'That those Creatures [Yahoos] could not be *Ylnhniamshy* (or *Aborigines* of the Land) because of the violent Hatred the *Houyhnhnms* as well as all other Animals, bore them: which although their evil Disposition sufficiently deserved, could never have arrived at so high a Degree, if they had been *Aborigines,* or else they would have long since been rooted out.' Reading the word *Ylnhniamshy* in Swift's phonetic key we find that between *Y* and *l* is developed the vowel sound *oo* merging into 'well' before *l,* thus forming the two words 'You well'. Between *n* and *h* the vowel sound *o* occurs, producing the syllable *noh,* which becomes 'know'. Between *h* and *n* the sound 'when' develops, and the end of the word *iamshy* reads just as it is written: 'I am shy.' Adding together our syllables we find the phrase is 'You-well-know-when-I-am-shy,' which fits into the context admirably in describing an aborigine.

It is superfluous to offer other examples of elucidation. Once the key is grasped the rest is easy. Swift's brilliance in adapting so closely his invented language to the natural sounds made by the horses, has helped materially in obscuring the key for so long. We must credit him with having invented a device which has occupied scholars with his text almost from the date when it was published. Thus his work, designed 'to vex the world rather than to divert it', has had more close attention than even Swift could have hoped for.

The Frailty of Lemuel Gulliver*

Paul Fussell, Jr.

"... I was bred a Surgeon, whose Trade it is to cure Wounds and Hurts in the Body, got by Accident or Violence."

Because it provides its age with a lively image of a representative man, Gulliver's *Travels into Several Remote Nations of the World* is at once both the *Hamlet* and the *Faust* of its time. And like these analogous humanist masterpieces that precede and follow it, it has been found perplexing both in theme and in method. As with *Hamlet* or *Faust,* no single, exclusive interpretative procedure can render an account of *Gulliver's Travels* at all adequate to its rich complications. But by employing one necessarily limited analytical procedure at a time, we can unravel and detach for examination certain important techniques and themes. I should like to begin, therefore, by disregarding the rest of the book for a moment in order to observe closely Gulliver the man and the sailor. This pathetically diminished Enlightenment Odysseus is, after all, the one constant in the four voyages: he is forever before us. Although the satire and the polemic and the intellectual comedy wax and wane, we constantly hear Gulliver's voice and feel his postures and gestures. We are always aware of both his present action as narrator and his past action as protagonist. And he is, we find, equally an object of pity in each role.

Gulliver can be considered a sort of post-Renaissance New Man, and to compare him to Robinson Crusoe is to perceive at once a part of his meaning. Crusoe the Dissenter is a personification of religious awareness, however coarse. He is concerned with conscience; he experiences visions; he devotes himself to Bible study, to Christian good works in the conversion of Friday, to prayer and divine meditation. He is conscious of an "invisible world," a world of spirits. He recognizes the psychological inadequacy of a purely mechanical explanation of phenomena, and the word "Providence" is often on his lips. But when we bring Gulliver next to Crusoe, not to mention other loquacious sailors like Odysseus, Coleridge's Mariner, Melville's Ishmael, or Conrad's Marlow, nothing is more striking than Gulliver's complacent materialism, his lack of a critical sense, his

* From *Essays in Literary History*, Rudolf Kirk and C. F. Main, eds. (New Brunswick, NJ: Rutgers University Press, 1960), pp. 113–25, copyright © 1960 by Rutgers, the State University. Reprinted by permission of Rutgers University Press.

naïve absence of interest in any other kind of experience than that in which he is immersed by his senses. Unlike Crusoe, Gulliver appears as a personification of religious unawareness. He is an eighteenth-century rationalistic naturalist with an incurable itch for mere exploration, inquiry, and reportage. Had he been conceived a century later, he would have joined with enthusiasm the team of Bouvard and Pécuchet. He embodies the very spirit of the Royal Society; he is a figure whose choices are motivated by that violent and rapid reaction against medieval and Renaissance values known as the scientific revolution. And his sufferings, I suggest, constitute in large part a passionate, almost Burkean critique of that earlier revolution.

II

During his four voyages, Gulliver undergoes countless profound intellectual and psychological humiliations, from the cumulative impact of which his morose, self-righteous, self-pitying state of mind at the end of the fourth voyage is an almost predictable result. The man who, devoted now to merely intellectual "systems," finally comes to prefer the company of two young stallions and their groom to the presence of his own human family is a man whose initial conviction of rational self-sufficiency has been gravely injured, and a man who has been left without means for the restoration of his dignity but outrageous expressions of a mad (and, to a humanist, sublimely comical) self-regard.

Although *Gulliver's Travels* is a series of variations on the theme of intellectual and psychological pride, the expression of this theme (as we see when we focus on the physical Gulliver) is accomplished less by direct revelation of Gulliver's mental attitudes than by a characteristically Swiftian employment of particularized physical emblems and correlatives. Throughout his career Swift makes it clear that he is uninterested in merely describing and reacting to the states of mind which he is anatomizing: instead, he thrusts into the reader's face some concrete physical emblem of a corrupted mind or psyche. The squalor of Chloe's mind, for example, finds its emblem in filthy towels; the Æolists express their meager, gaseous intellectual matter by belching through their noses; the spider emits his self-manufactured nastiness from his own behind. And in *Gulliver's Travels,* Swift's method of inventing vivid physical correlatives for moral circumstances results in an important recurring motif of physical injury, damage, pain, and loss. This motif is expressive of extreme physical frailty and vulnerability, of the pathetic likelihood of damage to weak and unassisted things, whether minds, eyes, limbs, or even hats and breeches. The physical damage which Gulliver either undergoes or fears becomes, through concrete, muscular rendering, a uniquely naturalistic emblem of the damage wrought by experience on Gulliver's presumably self-sufficient mind. It is this motif of physical injury, damage, and loss that I now wish to explore in an attempt to point to an important theme in *Gulliver's Travels,* and, at the same time, in an attempt to define Swift's most characteristic method of imagination.

III

From the beginning to the end of his travels (with time out now and then, of course, for standard touristic inquiries), Gulliver generally suffers rather than acts. Crusoe, once cast away, acts, and he acts with great vigor and stubbornness, but Gulliver is the archetypal victim. He anticipates the modern victim-protagonist in the work of Kafka or in the early works of Hemingway, the man whom things are done to. Most obviously, Gulliver is cast away four times, and each time in a more outrageous manner than the last. Even though, as a surgeon, he is more likely than most to dwell obsessively on his own physical injuries, and even though his commitment to the scientific ideals of the Royal Society impels him to deliver his narrative with a comically detailed circumstantiality, he records a really startling number of hurts. In the voyage to Lilliput, for example, his hair is painfully pulled, and his hands and face are blistered by needle-like arrows. During his visit among the people of Brobdingnag, Gulliver is battered so badly that we are tempted to regard him as strangely accident-prone: his flesh is punctured by wheat beards; twice his sides are painfully crushed; he is shaken up and bruised in a box; his nose and forehead are grievously stung by flies the size of larks; he suffers painful contusions from a shower of gigantic hailstones; he "breaks" his shin on a snailshell; and he is pummeled about the head and body by a linnet's wings.

In the third voyage Gulliver is given a respite: his experiences here are primarily intellectual, and he is permitted for a brief period to behave as curious tourist rather than universal sufferer. But the final voyage, the voyage to the land of the Houyhnhnms, brings Gulliver again into dire physical jeopardy. His last series of physical ordeals begins as his hand is painfully squeezed by a horse. And finally, as he leaves Houyhnhnmland to return to England, he is made to suffer a serious and wholly gratuitous arrow wound on the inside of his left knee ("I shall carry the Mark to my Grave"). Looking back on the whole extent of Gulliver's foreign experiences before his final return to his own country, we are hardly surprised that Gulliver's intellectuals have come unhinged: for years his body has been beaten, dropped, squeezed, lacerated, and punctured. When all is said, his transforming experiences have been as largely physical as intellectual and psychological. So powerfully does Swift reveal Gulliver's purely mental difficulties at the end of the fourth voyage that we tend to forget that Gulliver has also been made to undergo the sorest physical trials: during the four voyages he has been hurt so badly that, although he is normally a taciturn, unemotional, "Roman" kind of person, he has wept three times; so severely has he been injured at various times that at least twenty-four of his total traveling days he has been forced to spend recuperating in bed.

In addition to these actual emblematic injuries which Gulliver endures, he also experiences a large number of narrow escapes, potential injuries, and pathetic fears of physical hurt. In Lilliput, the vulnerability of his eyes is unremittingly insisted upon: an arrow barely misses his left eye, and only his spectacles prevent the loss of both his eyes as he works on the Blefuscan fleet. Furthermore, one of the Lilliputian punishments decreed for Quinbus Flestrin is that his eyes be put out.

And in the voyage to Brobdingnag, Gulliver's experience is one of an almost continuous narrow escape. He almost falls from the hand of the farmer and off the edge of the table. Stumbling over a crust, he falls flat on his face, barely escaping injury. After being held in a child's mouth, he is dropped, and he is saved only by being almost miraculously caught in a woman's apron. He is tossed into a bowl of cream, knocked down but not badly hurt by a shower of falling apples, and clutched dangerously between a spaniel's teeth. He is lucky to escape serious injury during a nasty fall into a mole hill. An agonizing fall of forty feet seems to bode ill for Gulliver, but no—his breeches catch on the point of a pin, and again he is wonderfully saved from destruction. In the same way, during the sojourn at Laputa, Gulliver is afraid of some "hurt" befalling him during the episode of the magician. And likewise in the fourth voyage Gulliver is frequently conscious of potential injury.

But Gulliver, this physically vulnerable ur-Boswell on the Grand Tour, is not the only one in the book who suffers or who fears injury: the creatures he is thrown among also endure strange catastrophes of pain and damage, often peculiarly particularized by Swift. Thus, in Lilliput, two or three of the rope-dancing practitioners break their limbs in falls. A horse, falling part way through Gulliver's handkerchief, strains a shoulder. The grandfather of the Lilliputian monarch, it is reported, as a result of breaking his egg upon the larger end suffered a cut finger. In the same way, the fourth voyage is full of what seem to be gratuitous images of injury and pain: for example, Gulliver carefully tells us that an elderly Houyhnhnm "of Quality" alighted from his Yahoo-drawn sledge "with his Hind-feet forward, having by Accident got a Hurt in his Left Fore-foot."

Nor are all these injuries confined to the bodies of Gulliver and his hosts. Gulliver's clothing and personal property are perpetually suffering damage, and, when they are not actually being damaged, Gulliver is worrying that, at any moment, they may be. Of course, mindful of Crusoe's pathetic situation, we are not surprised that a shipwrecked mariner suffers damage to his clothing and personal effects. But we may be surprised to hear Gulliver go out of his way to call careful attention to the damages and losses he suffers. In the first voyage, for example, Gulliver circumstantially lets us know that his scimitar has rusted, that his hat has been sorely damaged by being hauled through the dust all the way from the sea to the capital, and that his breeches have suffered an embarrassing rent. The boat in which Gulliver escapes to Blefuscu is, we are carefully told, "but little damaged." Once off the islands and, we might suppose, secure from losses and accidents until his next voyage, Gulliver loses one of his tiny souvenir sheep—it is destroyed by a rat aboard ship.

Presumably outfitted anew, Gulliver arrives ashore in Brobdingnag with his effects intact, but the old familiar process of damage and deterioration now begins all over again. Wheat beards rip his clothes; a fall into a bowl of milk utterly spoils Gulliver's suit; his stockings and breeches are soiled when he is thrust into the marrow bone which the queen has been enjoying at dinner; his clothes are again damaged by his tumble into the mole hill; and his suit (what's left of it) is further ruined by being daubed by frog slime and "bemired" with cow dung. Likewise, in the third voyage, our attention is called to the fact that Gulliver's hat has again worn out, and in the fourth voyage we are informed yet again by Gulliver that his clothes are "in a declining Condition."

At times, in fact, Gulliver's clothes and personal effects seem to be Gulliver himself: this is the apparent state of things which fascinates the observing Houyhnhnm before whom Gulliver undresses, and this ironic suggestion of an equation between Gulliver and his clothing, reminding us of the ironic "clothes philosophy" of Section II of *A Tale of a Tub,* Swift exploits to emphasize that damage to Gulliver's naturalistic garments is really damage to the naturalistic Gulliver. The vulnerability of Gulliver's clothing, that is, is a symbol three degrees removed from what it signifies: damage to Gulliver's clothes is symbolic of damage to Gulliver's body, which, in turn, is emblematic of damage to Gulliver's self-esteem.

These incidents of injury and destruction are thus pervasive in Gulliver's travels, as one is reminded by the recurrence, very striking when one is attuned to it, of words such as "hurt," "injury," "damage," "accident," "mischief," "misfortune," and "spoiled." Once his attention is aroused to what is going on physically in *Gulliver's Travels,* the reader senses the oblique appearance of this pervading vulnerability motif even in passages which really focus on something quite different. For example: "His Majesty [the Emperor of Blefuscu] presented me . . . with his Picture at full length, which I put immediately into one of my Gloves, to keep it from being hurt." In *Gulliver's Travels* Swift never allows us to forget that there is a pathetic fragility in his objects, both animate and inanimate. Swift's conception of Gulliver reminds us of Pope's sense of the vulnerability of the china jar which is Belinda's virtue. The Augustan mind in one of its most significant moods senses man thus as a little delicate cage of bones and skin constantly, if not always consciously, trembling before the likelihood of accidental damage or destruction. This is an image which we encounter increasingly following the impact of the philosophic naturalism of the Renaissance. Sir John Davies, still writing early enough to retain a feeling for man's essential dignity, expresses the idea this way:

> I know I am one of Nature's little Kings,
> Yet to the least and vilest things am thrall.

Pope in his more formal, oratorical moments is similarly possessed by a sense that, although man is the "Great Lord of all things," he is yet paradoxically "a prey to all" because, like Gulliver fearing for his eyes in Lilliput and for his body in Brobdingnag, he is "so weak, so little, and so blind." Even John Gay, satirizing a lady's passion for old china, moralizes in the same strain:

> If all that's frail we must despise,
> No human view or scheme is wise.

This conservative consciousness of the limitations of man persists in the eighteenth century up through serious humanists like Johnson and Burke. Johnson, for all his massive insistence on the freedom of the will and for all his own passionate personal incarnation of the Promethean spirit, reminds Boswell that "There is nothing . . . too little for so little a creature as man." And Burke insists on the necessity to human life of "superadded ideas" (ideas of an hereditary nobility, for example) "to cover the defects of our naked, shivering nature." Burke's figure reminds us of the image of Gulliver stripped and thus forlorn before the puzzled Houyhnhnm. The repeated variations on this theme of the

inadequacy of secularized man throughout that body of eighteenth-century literature which derives its primary vision most clearly from Renaissance humanism (I am speaking mainly of the work of Pope, Swift, Johnson, Burke, and Gibbon) present us with the eighteenth-century version of Shakespeare's consciousness, as expressed in *King Lear,* of the vast spiritual embarrassment implicit in the idea of a wholly naturalistic, "unaccommodated" man. And yet, participating also in a Newtonian, Lockian, naturalistic view of things (Swift, for one, constantly betrays his predicament by his instinctively materialistic images, which suggest his debt to Newtonian physics and optics), none of these major humanists of the English eighteenth century is able to find a wholly satisfactory principle for redeeming, or even ameliorating, human vulnerability. Hence, perhaps, the violence of the aged Swift, the masochistic spiritual agonizings of the aged Johnson. Gulliver's pride is mocked by the liability of his own frail person to the degradation of injury. Gulliver's intellectual vainglory becomes the more ironically empty the more his body, which is regarded as intimately allied to his almost material soul, reveals its fragility.

IV

Swift seems to have provided within the text of *Gulliver's Travels* materials for some further speculations about these pervasive concrete reminders of the vulnerability of man and the fragility of the physical objects with which he is fond of associating himself. In the voyage of Brobdingnag, we are told in a voice which sounds perhaps more Swiftian than Gulliverian of a "little old Treatise" treasured now only by elderly women and the more credulous vulgar, a copy of which Glumdalclitch has been given by her governess. The burden of this mysterious little book, we are told, is precisely the theme of the physical vulnerability of man: the book shows "how diminutive, contemptible, and helpless an Animal . . . [is] Man in his own Nature." It emphasizes, like Johnson's version of Juvenal in *London,* man's inability to defend himself against the accidents of injury, and argues that "the very Laws of Nature absolutely required we should have been made in the Beginning, of a Size more large and robust, not so liable to Destruction from every little Accident of a Tile falling from an House, or a Stone cast from the Hand of a Boy, or of being drowned in a little Brook." Here we might say that Swift avails himself of the humanist myth of The Decay of Nature just because the traditional formulation of The Fall no longer impels instinctive acceptance. In other words, Swift is making philosophic use of the myth of The Decay of Nature as a surrogate for a Christian explanation of human frailty which is no longer, in Swift's age, artistically employable. Although, as Miss Kathleen Williams reminds us, Godfrey Goodman's *The Fall of Man, or the Corruption of Nature* (1616) is perhaps the kind of "little old Treatise" Swift has in mind, I think we shall not go far wrong if we associate (even though we do not identify) Glumdalclitch's conservative little book with the Bible itself.

In the fourth voyage Swift returns to the theme expressed in this "little old Treatise" and characteristically again embodies it in the most physical, even fleshly terms: Gulliver proudly strips himself to demonstrate to the Houyhnhnm master the wonders of human clothing, and then hastens to dress again, for, as he explains, "I was shuddering with Cold." The naked but nevertheless warm and comfortable horse, in the following chapter, emphasizes the permanent flaw in the human situation by commenting that something must be gravely wrong with Gulliver's body, which requires "a Fence against Heat and Cold, which [Gulliver says] I was forced to put on and off every Day with Tediousness and Trouble." One way for the conviction of a deep, permanent flaw in human nature to find expression is through myths of The Fall; another way for the same conviction to find expression is through these Swiftian myths of The Decay of Nature and the consequent physical vulnerability of man. Swift's choice of this physical imagery suggests his profound artistic awareness of the inaccessibility to his largely secularized audience of traditional Christian symbols and modes of thought. Earlier in his career, in the allegory of the three brothers and their clothing (like Gulliver's, subject to shocking damage), Swift had demonstrated that his favorite literary action was the articulation of late seventeenth-century Church of England commonplaces with a new physical immediacy which the Lockian age demanded. He is doing just this in his most notorious poems. And in *Gulliver's Travels* we see him doing the same sort of thing as in *A Tale of a Tub* and poems like "The Progress of Beauty," and doing it still by means of the same fundamental method. The happy physical violence of the imagery in *A Tale of a Tub,* the obvious glee with which Swift depicts coats being ripped and Jack crashing into posts: these destructive physical immediacies anticipate the meaty empirical destructions of *Gulliver's Travels,* the images of painful abrasions, shocking contusions, blisters and arrow wounds, ruined hats and coats and breeches. These are the concrete particulars of fiction, not the abstractions and constructions of exhortation and polemic, and it is here that we can see most clearly that Swift was only secondarily a satirist: he was primarily a maker of fiction.

The vulnerability motif, then, realized by this empirical, emblematic method, is Swift's way of incarnating Gulliver's spiritual embarrassment. By these means

Swift realizes in *Gulliver's Travels* his quasi-Christian theme: the theme of the inadequacy of an unassisted self-esteem in redeeming Everyman from his own essential frailties. By these means Swift treats Gulliver the naturalist from a traditional Christian-Humanist point of view: what is done to Gulliver physically during his voyages constitutes Swift's major assault on progressivist naturalism.

But Swift finds that he cannot bruise and wound Gulliver without suffering himself some of Gulliver's agonies, and a suggestion of the sympathetic pain which Swift experiences lies in the pathos of many of these injuries. What we discover when we probe into some of the means by which *Gulliver's Travels* creates the illusion of life is what we are now learning to recognize in everything Swift wrote—his quick sympathetic humanity.

Mary Gulliver to Captain Lemuel Gulliver

Alexander Pope

ARGUMENT. *The Captain, some Time after his Return, being retired to Mr.* Sympson's *in the Country, Mrs. Gulliver, apprehending from his late Behaviour some Estrangement of his Affections, writes him the following expostulating, soothing, and tenderly-complaining Epistle.*

Welcome, thrice welcome to thy native Place!
—What, touch me not? what, shun a Wife's Embrace?
Have I for this thy tedious Absence born,
And wak'd and wish'd whole Nights for thy Return?
In five long Years I took no second Spouse;
What *Redriff* Wife so long hath kept her Vows?
Your Eyes, your Nose, Inconstancy betray;
Your Nose you stop, your Eyes you turn away.
'Tis said, that thou shouldst cleave unto thy Wife;
Once *thou* didst cleave, and *I* could cleave for Life.
Hear and relent! hark, how thy Children moan;
Be kind at least to these, they are thy own:
Behold, and count them all; secure to find
The honest Number that you left behind.
See how they pat thee with their pretty Paws:
Why start you? are they Snakes? or have they Claws?
Thy Christian Seed, our mutual Flesh and Bone:
Be kind at least to these, they are thy own.

Biddel, like thee, might farthest *India* rove;
He chang'd his Country, but retain'd his Love.
There's Captain *Pennel,* absent half his Life,
Comes back, and is the kinder to his Wife.
Yet *Pennel's* Wife is brown, compar'd to me;
And Mistress *Biddel* sure is Fifty three.

Not touch me! never Neighbour call'd me Slut!
Was *Flimnap's* Dame more sweet in *Lilliput*?
I've no red Hair to breathe an odious Fume;
At least thy Consort's cleaner than thy *Groom.*
Why then that dirty Stable-boy thy Care?
What mean those Visits to the *Sorrel Mare*?
Say, by what Witchcraft, or what Daemon led,
Preferr'st thou *Litter* to the Marriage Bed?

Some say the Dev'l himself is in that *Mare*:
If so, our *Dean* shall drive him forth by Pray'r.
Some think you mad, some think you are possest
That *Bedlam* and clean Straw will suit you best:
Vain Means, alas, this Frenzy to appease!
That *Straw,* that *Straw* would heighten the Disease.

My Bed, (the Scene of all our former Joys,
Witness two lovely Girls, two lovely Boys)
Alone I press; in Dreams I call my Dear,
I stretch my Hand, no *Gulliver* is there!
I wake, I rise, and shiv'ring with the Frost,
Search all the House; my *Gulliver* is lost!
Forth in the Street I rush with frantick Cries:
The Windows open; all the Neighbours rise:
Where sleeps my Gulliver*? O tell me where?*
The Neighbours answer, *With the Sorrel Mare.*

At early Morn, I to the Market haste,
(Studious in ev'ry Thing to please thy Taste)
A curious *Fowl* and *Sparagrass* I chose,
(For I remember you were fond of those,)
Three Shillings cost the first, the last sev'n Groats;
Sullen you turn from both, and call for *Oats.*

Others bring Goods and Treasure to their Houses,
Something to deck their pretty Babes and Spouses;
My *only* Token was a Cup like Horn,
That's made of nothing but a Lady's *Corn.*

'Tis not for that I grieve; no, 'tis to see
The *Groom* and *Sorrel Mare* preferr'd to me!

These, for some Monuments when you deign to quit,
And (at due distance) sweet Discourse admit,
'Tis all my Pleasure thy past Toil to know,
For pleas'd Remembrance builds Delight on Woe.
At ev'ry Danger pants thy Consort's Breast,
And gaping Infants squawle to hear the rest.
How did I tremble, when by thousands bound
I saw thee stretch'd on *Lilliputian* Ground;
When scaling Armies climb'd up ev'ry Part,
Each Step they trod, I felt upon my Heart.
But when thy Torrent quench'd the dreadful Blaze,
King, Queen and Nation, staring with Amaze,
Full in my View how all my Husband came,
And what extinguish'd theirs, encreas'd my Flame.
Those *Spectacles,* ordain'd thine Eyes to save,
Were once my Present; *Love* that Armour gave.
How did I mourn at *Bolgolam's* Decree!
For when he sign'd thy Death, he sentenc'd me.

When folks might see thee all the Country round
For Six-pence, I'd have giv'n a thousand Pound.
Lord! when the *Giant-Babe* that Head of thine
Got in his Mouth, my Heart was up in mine!
When in the *Marrow-Bone* I see thee ramm'd;
Or on the House-top by the *Monkey* cramm'd;
The Piteous Images renew my Pain,
And all thy Dangers I weep o'er again!
But on the *Maiden's Nipple* when you rid,
Pray Heav'n, 'twas all a wanton Maiden did!
Glumdalclitch too!—with thee I mourn her Case.
Heav'n guard the gentle Girl from all Disgrace!
O may the King that one Neglect forgive,
And pardon her the Fault by which I live!
Was there no other Way to set him free?
My Life, alas! I fear prov'd Death to Thee!

O teach me, Dear, new Words to speak my Flame;
Teach me to wooe thee by thy best-lov'd Name!
Whether the Style of *Grildrig* please thee most,
So call'd on *Brobdingnag's* stupendous Coast,
When on the Monarch's ample Hand you sate,
And hollow'd in his Ear Intrigues of State:
Or *Quinbus Flestrin* more Endearment brings,
When like a Mountain you look'd down on Kings:
If Ducal *Nardac, Lilliputian* Peer,
Or *Glumglum's* humbler Title sooth thy Ear:
Nay, wou'd kind *Jove* my Organs so dispose,
To hymn harmonious *Houyhnhnm* thro' the Nose,
I'd call thee *Houyhnhnm,* that high sounding Name,
Thy Children's Noses all should twang the same.
So might I find my loving Spouse of course
Endu'd with all the *Virtues* of a *Horse.*

APPENDIX C

Perspectives on Jonathan Swift

Chronology: The Author and His Times

	Jonathan Swift	*Historical Context*
1667	Jonathan Swift is born in Dublin on November 30. His father, an English-born solicitor, died earlier in the year, leaving his family impoverished.	England's Second Dutch War ends in a stalemate. An inquiry into the navy brings discredit to the Lord High Admiral—the future James II.
1668		Sir William Temple, the English ambassador to the Hague, scores a diplomatic triumph by arranging an alliance of England, the United Provinces (the Dutch), and Sweden to frustrate the expansionist policies of Louis XIV of France.
1674	Swift enters Kilkenny College. At age forty he will recall "confinement ten hours a day to nouns and verbs, the terror of the rod, the bloody noses, and broken shins."	
1685	Trinity College grants Swift his bachelor's degree *speciali gratia*—because of his private absorption in history and poetry his scholarship has been merely adequate. He stays on for master's studies, and over the next three years is frequently disciplined for absences from school and for missing lectures and chapel.	Charles II dies and is followed on the throne by his brother as James II. An avowed Catholic, he is regarded with trepidation by most adherents of the Church of England. A rebellion in June and struggles with Parliament over the treatment of Catholics give a taste of troubles to come.
1688		On the invitation of English nobles hostile to James, William of Orange, a Protestant, lands in England to make a bid for the throne.
1689	Because of the imminent entry of King James into Dublin, Swift leaves Trinity College for England. At the end of the year he becomes secretary to Sir William Temple, who will become his mentor, and befriends Temple's protégé, the eight-year-old Hester Johnson.	In February, William of Orange becomes King of England as William III. By March, all Ireland outside of Ulster is in the hands of Catholics supporting James II.
1690	Swift returns to Ireland, where he writes an ode to the victorious King William III.	The victory of William's forces at Boyne puts Dublin into his hands. James II flees to France. Temple publishes his *Essay on Ancient and Modern Learning.* John Locke publishes his *Essay Concerning Human Understanding.* Part Four of *Gulliver's Travels* will reflect the *Essay*'s distrust of general classifications.

Jonathan Swift	*Historical Context*	
Swift returns to the service of Sir William Temple.		1691
Contemplating a career in the Church, Swift takes his M.A. degree at Oxford.	The English and Dutch defeat the French in a naval battle at La Hogue, frustrating the hopes of James II.	1692
Swift pays tribute in verse to his friend William Congreve, whom he first met when they were both students at Trinity.	Congreve's comedy *The Old Bachelor* is produced in London with great success.	1693
Feeling unappreciated by Sir William Temple, Swift again leaves his service and returns to Ireland.		1694
Swift is ordained a priest of the Established Church and takes up parish duties in Kilroot, Ireland.		1695
Miss Jane Waring ("Varina"), whom Swift has been courting for months, declines his final offer of marriage.	A plot by supporters of James II (Jacobites) to kill King William is foiled.	1696
Swift returns to Temple's service as editor of his manuscripts and his designated literary executor.		1698
Swift publishes two volumes of the letters of Sir William Temple, who died the previous year.	Charles II of Spain dies, having bequeathed his kingdom to Philip, the Duke of Anjou. The threat posed by the combination of Spanish and French power alarms the rest of Europe. John Dryden dies. The former Poet Laureate, a relative of Swift, reportedly once told him: "Cousin Swift, you will never be a poet." Swift will attack Dryden in *The Battle of the Books.*	1700
Swift's first original book, *A Discourse of the Contests and Dissensions between the Nobles and the Commons in Athens and Rome,* appears anonymously because he is uncertain of its prospects. The book deplores the recent impeachment by the Commons of the four most powerful Whig lords as an example of the tyranny of the many over the few.	The Act of Settlement vests the ultimate succession to the English throne in the House of Hanover, but specifies that the new monarchs must become members of the Church of England. Death puts an end to James II's quest for his lost throne. His claim is inherited by his son James Edward, known as James III, or the Old Pretender.	1701

	Jonathan Swift	*Historical Context*
1701 (cont'd)	Swift returns to Ireland accompanied by Hester Johnson, who with his help establishes herself in Dublin.	
1702	Taking his divinity degree at Trinity, Swift becomes Doctor Swift. Returning to England and finding that the *Contests* has been well received, Swift acknowledges it as his own ("the vanity of a young man prevailed with me," he will later explain). Two of the impeached lords defended in the book commend him.	King William, having involved England in the War of the Spanish Succession earlier in the year, dies and is followed on the throne by Anne, a daughter of James II but a Protestant, pledged to uphold the Established Church. England's first partisan periodical, *The Observator,* is launched by the Whigs.
1704	Swift makes the acquaintance of two of the foremost wits and writers of England, John Addison and Richard Steele. Again using anonymity, Swift publishes his first masterpiece, *A Tale of a Tub,* whose irreverence will impede his clerical career after his authorship becomes known. *The Battle of the Books,* a subsidiary part of the volume, spoofs the theme of Temple's *Essay on Ancient and Modern Learning.* Swift returns to Ireland, where he will remain for the next three and a half years, enjoying the company of Hester Johnson and performing his duties as vicar of Laracor.	The English capture Gibraltar and win an impressive victory under the Duke of Marlborough at Blenheim. Two more partisan periodicals appear: *Review,* edited by Daniel Defoe and subsidized by the government, and the ultra-Tory *Rehearsal.*
1707	Archbishop King sends Swift to England on a mission for the Irish Church. In England, Swift befriends the affluent, socially well-connected Vanhomrigh family—including the eldest daughter, Esther, then nineteen.	The Queen and the Whigs quarrel over appointments to some empty episcopal sees, and the emboldened Whigs manage to have Parliament resolve not to end the war until Philip of Anjou is tossed off the Spanish throne. The Act of Union abolishes the Scottish parliament and joins England and Scotland.
1708	In anticipation of April Fool's Day, Swift publishes *Predictions for the Year 1708,* by "Isaac Bickerstaff." This burlesque almanac, absurdly laying down the true principles of astrology and predicting the death of a famous astrologer, becomes a runaway bestseller.	

Jonathan Swift	*Historical Context*	
Swift writes *An Argument Against Abolishing Christianity,* which contends that such a measure is not needed to suppress Christian virtue, already long dead, and that the pretense of religion is better than none at all.		**1708 (cont'd)**
One of Swift's finest poems, "A Description of the Morning," appears in *The Tatler,* No. 9. Swift publishes Part III of Temple's *Memoirs,* which contains revelations painful to the author's sister and her best friend Lady Essex. A feud with the Temple family results.	Malplaquet, the bloodiest battle of the eighteenth century, leaves the nation war-weary. Steele launches a new literary periodical, *The Tatler.* In the first issue, he uses a pen-name guaranteed to boost his readership: Isaac Bickerstaff.	**1709**
Swift suffers the first onslaughts of the vertigo that will plague him for the rest of his life. In May, Swift receives news of the death of his mother the previous month. "I have now lost my barrier between me and death." In September, Swift begins a series of diaristic letters to Hester Johnson, which he will continue until mid-1713. Ranging in content between comment on crucial political events of the day and tender solicitousness for Hester, expressed in a highly inventive "baby talk," the letters will become famous as the *Journal to Stella.* In October, the leading government minister, Robert Harley, the Earl of Oxford, puts the Tory periodical *The Examiner* into the hands of Swift.	On March 1 and 2, rioters calling for the release of an imprisoned anti-Whig preacher and for peace sweep London, even menacing the Bank of England. In the autumn, Robert Harley initiates top-secret preliminary peace talks with Louis XIV's foreign minister.	**1710**
Swift publishes "A Hue and Cry After Dismal," a broadside ridiculing Whig uneasiness at peace prospects.	The French defeat an army of England's German and Dutch allies at Demain in Flanders. During the battle the Elector of Hanover, who will become king of England, is almost killed.	**1712**
His long quest for church preferment finally bearing fruit, Swift is installed as Dean of St. Patrick's Cathedral in Dublin. In his poem "Cadenus and Vanessa," Swift describes his reluctance in the face of Esther Vanhomrigh's avowal of passionate love for him.	The Treaty of Utrecht ends the War of the Spanish Succession. The prerequisite for peace specified by Parliament in 1707 is not met: Philip V still rules in Spain. George Berkeley publishes his *Dialogues Between Hylas and Philonous,* in which he writes ". . . what you can hardly discern, will to another extremely minute animal appear as some huge mountain."	 **1713**

	Jonathan Swift	*Historical Context*
1713 (cont'd)	Swift, Pope, John Gay, and John Arbuthnot form a literary club, which will center around a collaborative satire featuring the absurdly learned character Martinus Scriblerus.	The *Dialogues* may help move Swift toward *Gulliver's Travels.*
1714	Crossing swords with his former friend Steele, who has just published the staunchly pro-Whig volume *The Crisis,* Swift anonymously publishes *The Publick Spirit of the Whigs,* the deftest—and most venomous—of all his partisan tracts.	The Queen offers a reward to anyone who will divulge the name of the author of a pamphlet entitled *The Publick Spirit of the Whigs,* which defends Tory efforts to break up the Union with Scotland and abuses the Scottish lords sitting in Parliament.
	Swift returns to Dublin, where he takes up his duties as Dean of St. Patrick's.	The Queen dies and is succeeded by the Elector of Hanover, who becomes George I.
		Pope publishes a new version of *The Rape of the Lock,* now an elaborate mock-epic in five cantos. *The Rape* will strongly influence Swift's 1729 poem "Journal of a Modern Lady."
1715		With the Whigs now ascendant, Harley's former colleague Bolingbroke flees England in disguise, and later in the year Harley is sent to the Tower on charges of treason. Desperate Tories lead uprisings on behalf of the divine right of James III. The Jacobites hold Scotland for a while but their main forces are defeated at Preston and Sherrifmuir.
1716	Possibly Swift and Hester Johnson are secretly married some time this year. Whether they are or not, their passionate mutual love probably remained unconsummated.	
1717	Remaining loyal to Harley, Swift begins writing Part Two of his *Enquiry into the Behaviour of the Queen's Late Ministry,* which attempts to clear his old friend of charges of conniving to bring in James III.	The Drury Lane theater in London offers *Three Hours After Marriage,* a collaboration by Pope, Gay, and Arbuthnot that echoes the Scriblerus Club's ridicule of pedantry.
1719	In the first of a series of birthday poems for Hester Johnson, Swift for the first time addresses her as Stella—probably in half-humorous reference to Sir Philip Sidney's poem *Astrophel and Stella.*	Daniel Defoe publishes *Robinson Crusoe,* which will perhaps help stimulate Swift to write *Gulliver's Travels.*
1720	Swift publishes anonymously *A Proposal for the Universal Use of Irish Manufacture,* advocating an	Parliament passes the Declaratory Act, establishing its absolute right to make law for Ireland

Jonathan Swift	*Historical Context*	
Irish boycott of English goods and indicting British oppression and Irish landlords. The printer of the pamphlet is prosecuted. The following year Bolingbroke, writing to Swift about the *Proposal,* will chide him for trying "to talk sense or to do good to the rabble."	and reducing the Irish Parliament to virtual impotence. Britain assigns its entire national debt to the South Sea Company, whose shares skyrocket in value, spurring widespread reckless speculations. Panic and widespread bankruptcies follow.	**1720 (cont'd)**
Swift publishes his poem "The Bubble"—fifty-seven stanzas denouncing the perpetrators and deriding the victims of the South Sea fiasco.		**1720**
Perhaps using sketches from his Scriblerus Club days, Swift begins writing *Gulliver's Travels.*		**1721**
	William Wood obtains a patent to coin copper half-pence and farthings for Ireland.	**1722**
Esther Vanhomrigh dies after nine years of largely unreciprocated passion for Swift. She has saved their correspondence—didactic and guardedly tender on his side, piquant and yearningly amorous on hers.	Bolingbroke returns from exile. Swift's friend Bishop Atterbury is exiled for conspiring to put James III on the throne. *Gulliver's Travels* will satirize the government's case in a passage on cryptograms.	**1723**
Under the pseudonym M.[arcus] B.[rutus] Drapier, Swift publishes five successive letters calling for the boycott of Wood's coins. Widely known to be the actual author in spite of his guise of a patriotic tradesman, Swift becomes the hero of broad (joint Catholic and Protestant) resistance to British misrule.	The Dublin government, having no solid evidence against Swift, arrests John Harding, the printer of Drapier's inflammatory attacks, who refuses in jail to name the author.	**1724**
The first collected edition of *The Drapier's Letters* appears: *Fraud Detected: or, The Hibernian Patriot.*		**1725**
Swift publishes *Gulliver's Travels.* "The whole impression sold in a week," Pope and Gay report. However, the cautious printer Motte has considerably emasculated Swift's original text.	Crop failures lead to famine in Ireland, which will continue into 1729.	**1726**
Swift is presented to George II.	George I dies and is succeeded by his son as George II. *Gulliver's Travels* appears in French, German, and Dutch translations.	**1727**

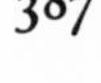

	Jonathan Swift	*Historical Context*
1727 (cont'd)		Sir Isaac Newton dies. In 1724, while heading the Royal Mint, the great scientist had assayed Wood's coins and pronounced them excellent.
1728	The death of Hester Johnson deprives Swift of the closest relationship of his life. In his eulogy of her he writes: "Neither was it easy to find a more proper or impartial judge, whose advice an author might better rely on. . . ." Her will specifies that she is to be buried under the great aisle of St. Patrick's—where Swift can lie beside her.	Gay's *The Beggar's Opera* enjoys a run that sets a new record for the London stage. Pope publishes *The Dunciad.* In a note to the text he credits Swift with having snatched the first sketches from the fire.
1729	Responding to continued famine in Ireland, Swift publishes one of the most disturbing satires of his career, *A Modest Proposal.*	
1731	The supposition of his own death in "Verses on the Death of Doctor Swift," intended for posthumous publication, gives Swift a pretext for filling the poem with lavish self-praise. In another poem, "A Beautiful Young Nymph Going to Bed," written in or around this year but not published until 1734, Swift exhibits his growing misogyny.	
1732	Receiving a letter from Pope and Arbuthnot, Swift does not open it for five days, "by an impulse foreboding some misfortune." It turns out to be news of the death of Gay.	The funeral of John Gay is held in Westminster Abbey "as though he had been a peer of the realm" (Arbuthnot).
1733	Swift publishes "The Life and Genuine Character of Doctor Swift," which again uses the premise of his own death, but provides a more balanced self-appraisal.	
1735	George Faulkner begins publication of Swift's complete works. Volume III of the initial set of four volumes introduces the public to the most authentic *Gulliver's Travels* to date, with the passages rewritten by Motte replaced with their originals and all but one of the passages he suppressed restored.	George Berkeley begins publication of his journal *The Querist,* devoted to the problems of Irish peasants and landowners. The death of Arbuthnot deprives Swift of one of his warmest and most admiring friends, who perhaps served as the model for the "courteous and generous" Pedro de Mendez in *Gulliver's Travels.*

Jonathan Swift	*Historical Context*	
In his poem "A Character, Panegyric, and Description of the Legion Club," Swift lashes the Irish Commons for exempting graziers from church tithes.		1736
To a friend Swift writes: "I have entirely lost my memory except when it is roused by perpetual subjects of vexation."		1738
Swift makes his will, which includes his epitaph, a bequest for the foundation and maintenance of a hospital for the insane, and some whimsical bequests to friends.		1740
	Pope publishes his joint correspondence with Swift in Volume II of his collected prose works, and later in the year the *Memoirs of Martinus Scriblerus.*	1741
After arguing violently with an applicant for the position of subdean in his cathedral, Swift is assigned a committee of guardians.		1742
	With a Jacobite invasion of England expected, the government reactivates a law forbidding Catholics to live in or within ten miles of London. In February, Pope, a lifelong Catholic, avoids the capital in order not to be "imprudent and thought insolent." In May, he dies at his villa in Twickenham, where in 1726 Swift had stayed with him while seeing *Gulliver's Travels* through the press.	1744
Swift dies on October 19: "expires a driv'ler and a show," Samuel Johnson will cynically write. He is buried in St. Patrick's Cathedral, beneath the Latin epitaph he wrote for himself. Its last line refers to him as "one who never failed to defend liberty to the utmost of his strength."	The eldest son of the titular James III, Prince Charles Edward, lands in Scotland, takes Edinburgh, and invades England, reaching Darby in December. The defeat of his army at Culloden the following year will finish Jacobitism as a potent political force.	1745

Dr. Swift's Will

In the Name of God, *Amen.* I Jonathan Swift, Doctor in Divinity, and Dean of the Cathedral Church of St. *Patrick, Dublin,* being at this Present of sound Mind, although weak in Body, do here make my last Will and Testament, hereby revoking all my former Wills.

Imprimis: I bequeath my Soul to God, (in humble Hopes of his Mercy through Jesus Christ) and my Body to the Earth. And, I desire that my Body may be buried in the great Isle of the said Cathedral, on the South Side, under the Pillar next to the Monument of Primate *Narcissus Marsh,* three Days after my Decease, as privately as possible, and at Twelve o'Clock at Night: And, that a Black Marble of Feet square, and seven Feet from the Ground, fixed to the Wall, may be erected, with the following Inscription in large Letters, deeply cut, and strongly gilded. HIC DEPOSITUM EST CORPUS *JONATHAN SWIFT,* S.T.D. HUJUS ECCLESIÆ CATHEDRALIS DECANI, UBI SÆVA INDIGNATIO ULTERIUS COR LACERARE NEQUIT. ABI VIATOR, ET IMITARE, SI POTERIS, STRENUUM PRO VIRILI LIBERTATIS VINDICATOREM. OBIIT ANNO (1745) MENSIS (OCTOBRIS) DIE (19) ÆTATIS ANNO (78).

Item: I give and bequeath to my Executors all my worldly Substance, of what Nature or Kind soever (excepting such Part thereof as is herein after particularly devised) for the following Uses and Purposes, that is to say, to the Intent that they, or the Survivors or Survivor of them, their Executors, or Administrators, as soon as conveniently may be after my Death, shall turn it all into ready Money, and lay out the same in purchasing Lands of Inheritance in Fee-simple, situate in any Province of *Ireland,* except *Connaught,* but as near to the City of *Dublin,* as conveniently can be found, and not incumbered with, or subject to any Leases for Lives renewable, or any Terms for Years longer than Thirty-one: And I desire that a yearly Annuity of Twenty Pounds *Sterling,* out of the annual Profits of such Lands when purchased, and out of the yearly Income of my said Fortune, devised to my Executors as aforesaid, until such Purchase shall be made, shall be paid to *Rebecca Dingley* of the City of *Dublin,* Spinster, during her Life, by two equal half-yearly Payments, on the Feasts of *All-Saints,* and St.

Philip and St. *Jacob,* the first Payment to be made on such of the said Feasts as shall happen next after my Death. And that the Residue of the yearly Profits of the said Lands when purchased, and until such Purchase be made, the Residue of the yearly Income and Interest of my said Fortune devised as aforesaid to my Executors, shall be laid out in purchasing a Piece of Land, situate near Dr. *Steven*'s Hospital, or if it cannot be there had, somewhere in or near the City of *Dublin,* large enough for the Purposes herein after mentioned, and in building thereon an Hospital large enough for the Reception of as many Idiots and Lunaticks as the annual Income of the said Lands and worldly Substance shall be sufficient to maintain: And, I desire that the said Hospital may be called St. *Patrick*'s Hospital, and may be built in such a manner, that another Building may be added unto it, in case the Endowment thereof should be enlarged; so that the additional Building may make the whole Edifice regular and compleat. And my further Will and Desire is, that when the said Hospital shall be built, the whole yearly Income of the said Lands and Estate, shall, for ever after, be laid out in providing Victuals, Cloathing, Medicines, Attendance, and all other Necessaries for such Idiots and Lunaticks, as shall be received into the same; and in repairing and enlarging the Building, from Time to Time, as there may be Occasion. And, if a sufficient Number of Idiots and Lunaticks cannot readily be found, I desire that Incurables may be taken into the said Hospital to supply such Deficiency: But that no Person shall be admitted into it, that laboureth under any infectious Disease: And that all such Idiots, Lunaticks and Incurables, as shall be received into the said Hospital, shall constantly live and reside therein, as well in the Night as in the Day; and that the Salaries of Agents, Receivers, Officers, Servants, and Attendants, to be employed in the Business of the said Hospital, shall not in the Whole exceed one Fifth Part of the clear yearly Income, or Revenue thereof. And, I further desire that my Executors, the Survivors or Survivor of them, or the Heirs of such, shall not have Power to demise any Part of the said Lands so to be purchased as aforesaid, but with Consent of the Lord Primate, the Lord High Chancellor, the Lord Archbishop of *Dublin,* the Dean of *Christ-Church,* the Dean of St. *Patrick*'s, the Physician to the State, and the Surgeon-General, all for the Time being, or the greater Part of them, under their Hands in Writing; and that no Leases of any Part of the said Lands, shall ever be made other than Leases for Years not exceeding Thirty-one, in Possession, and not in Reversion or Remainder, and not dispunishable of Waste, whereon shall be reserved the best and most improved Rents, that can reasonably and moderately, without racking the Tenants, be gotten for the same, without Fine. Provided always, and it is my Will and earnest Desire, that no Lease of any Part of the

said Lands, so to be purchased as aforesaid, shall ever be made to, or in Trust for any Person any way concerned in the Execution of this Trust, or to, or in Trust for any Person any way related or allied, either by Consanguinity or Affinity, to any of the Persons who shall at that Time be concerned in the Execution of this Trust: And, that if any Leases shall happen to be made contrary to my Intention above expressed, the same shall be utterly void and of no Effect. And I further desire, until the Charter herein after mentioned be obtained, my Executors, or the Survivors or Survivor of them, his Heirs, Executors, or Administrators, shall not act in the Execution of this Trust, but with the Consent and Approbation of the said seven additional Trustees, or the greater Part of them, under their Hands in Writing, and shall, with such Consent and Approbation, as aforesaid, have Power, from time to time, to make Rules, Orders, and Regulations for the Government and Direction of the said Hospital. And, I make it my Request to my said Executors, that they may in convenient Time apply to his Majesty for a Charter to incorporate them, or such of them as shall be then living, and the said additional Trustees, for the better Management and Conduct of this Charity, with a Power to purchase Lands; and to supply by Election such Vacancies happening in the Corporation, as shall not be supplied by Succession, and such other Powers as may be thought expedient for the due Execution of this Trust, according to my Intention herein before expressed. And when such Charter shall be obtained, I desire that my Executors, or the Survivors or Survivor of them, or the Heirs of such Survivor, may convey to the Use of such Corporation in Fee-simple for the Purposes aforesaid, all such Lands and Tenements, as shall be purchased in manner above mentioned. Provided always, and it is my Will and Intention, that my Executors, until the said Charter, and afterwards the Corporation to be hereby incorporated, shall out of the yearly Profits of the said Lands when purchased, and out of the yearly Income of my said Fortune devised to my Executors as aforesaid, until such Purchase be made, have Power to reimburse themselves for all such Sums of their own Money, as they shall necessarily expend in the Execution of this Trust. And that until the said Charter be obtained, all Acts which shall at any Time be done in Execution of this Trust by the greater Part of my Executors then living, with the Consent of the greater Part of the said additional Trustees, under their Hands in Writing, shall be as valid and effectual, as if all my Executors had concurred in the same.

Item: Whereas I purchased the Inheritance of the Tythes of the Parish of *Effernock* near *Trim* in the County of *Meath,* for Two Hundred and Sixty Pounds *Sterling;* I bequeath the said Tythes to the Vicars of *Laracor* for the Time being, that is to say, so long as the present Episcopal Religion shall

continue to be the National Established Faith and Profession in this Kingdom: But whenever any other Form of Christian Religion shall become the Established Faith in this Kingdom, I leave the said Tythes of *Effernock* to be bestowed, as the Profits come in, to the Poor of the said Parish of *Laracor*, by a weekly Proportion, and by such Officers as may then have the Power of distributing Charities to the Poor of the said Parish, while Christianity under any Shape shall be tolerated among us, still excepting professed *Jews, Atheists* and *Infidels.*

Item: Whereas I have some Leases of certain Houses in St. *Kevin's-street*, near the Deanry-House, built upon the Dean's Ground, and one other House now inhabited by *Henry Land*, in *Deanry-lane* alias *Mitre-alley*, some of which Leases are let for forty-one Years, or forty at least, and not yet half expired, I bequeath to Mrs. *Martha Whiteway* my Lease or Leases of the said Houses; I also bequeath to the said *Martha*, my Lease of forty Years of *Goodman*'s Holding, for which I receive Ten Pounds *per Annum;* which are two Houses, or more lately built; I bequeath also to the said *Martha* the Sum of Three Hundred Pounds *Sterling*, to be paid her by my Executors out of my ready Money, or Bank Bills, immediately after my Death, as soon as the Executors meet. I leave, moreover, to the said *Martha*, my repeating Gold Watch, my yellow Tortoise Shell Snuff Box, and her Choice of four Gold Rings, out of seven which I now possess.

Item: I bequeath to Mrs. *Mary Swift* alias *Harrison*, Daughter of the said *Martha*, my plain Gold Watch made by *Quare*, to whom also I give my *Japan* Writing Desk, bestowed to me by my Lady *Worseley*, my square Tortoise Shell Snuff Box, richly lined and inlaid with Gold, given to me by the Right Honourable *Henrietta* now Countess of *Oxford*, and the Seal with a *Pegasus*, given to me by the Countess of *Granville.*

Item: I bequeath to Mr. *Ffolliot Whiteway*, eldest son of the aforesaid *Martha*, who is bred to be an Attorney, the Sum of Sixty Pounds, as also Five Pounds to be laid out in the Purchase of such Law Books as the Honourable Mr. Justice *Lyndsay*, Mr. *Stannard*, or Mr. *McAullay* shall judge proper for him.

Item: I bequeath to Mr. *John Whiteway*, youngest Son of the said *Martha*, who is to be brought up a Surgeon, the Sum of One Hundred Pounds, in order to qualify him for a Surgeon, but under the Direction of his Mother; which said Sum of One Hundred Pounds is to be paid to Mrs. *Whiteway*, in Behalf of her said Son *John*, out of the Arrears which shall be due to me from my Church Livings, (except those of the Deanry Tythes, which are now let to the Reverend Doctor *Wilson*) as soon as the said Arrears can be paid to my Executors. I also

leave the said *John* Five Pounds to be laid out in buying such Physical or Chirurgical Books as Doctor *Grattan* and Mr. *Nichols* shall think fit for him.

Item: I bequeath to Mrs. *Anne Ridgeway,* now in my Family, the Profits of the Lease of two Houses let to *John Cownly,* for forty Years, of which only eight or nine are expired, for which the said *Cownly* payeth me Nine Pounds *Sterling* for Rent yearly. I also bequeath to the said *Anne,* the Sum of One Hundred Pounds *Sterling,* to be paid her by my Executors in six Weeks after my Decease, out of whatever Money or Bank Bills I may possess when I die: As also three Gold Rings, the Remainder of the seven above mentioned, after Mrs. *Whiteway* hath made her Choice of four; and all my small Pieces of Plate, not exceeding in Weight one Ounce and one third Part of an Ounce.

Item: I bequeath to my dearest Friend *Alexander Pope* of *Twittenham,* Esq; my Picture in Miniature, drawn by *Zinck,* of *Robert* late Earl of *Oxford.*

Item: I leave to *Edward* now Earl of *Oxford,* my Seal of *Julius Cæsar,* as also another Seal, supposed to be a young *Hercules,* both very choice Antiques, and set in Gold: Both which I chuse to bestow to the said Earl, because they belonged to her late Most Excellent Majesty Queen *Anne,* of ever Glorious, Immortal, and truly Pious Memory, the real Nursing Mother of all her Kingdoms.

Item: I leave to the Reverend Mr. *James Stopford,* Vicar of *Finglass,* my Picture of King *Charles* the First, drawn by *Vandike,* which was given to me by the said *James;* as also my large Picture of Birds, which was given to me by *Thomas* Earl of *Pembroke.*

Item: I bequeath to the Reverend Mr. *Robert Grattan,* Prebendary of St. *Audeon*'s, my Gold Bottle Screw, which he gave me, and my strong Box, on Condition of his giving the sole Use of the said Box to his Brother Dr. *James Grattan,* during the Life of the said Doctor, who hath more Occasion for it, and the second best Beaver Hat I shall die possessed of.

Item: I bequeath to Mr. *John Grattan,* Prebendary of *Clonmethan,* my Silver Box in which the Freedom of the City of *Cork* was presented to me; in which I desire the said *John* to keep the Tobacco he usually cheweth, called Pigtail.

Item: I bequeath all my Horses and Mares to the Reverend Mr. *John Jackson,* Vicar of *Santry,* together with all my Horse Furniture: Lamenting that I had not Credit enough with any Chief Governor (since the Change of Times) to get some additional Church Preferment for so virtuous and worthy a Gentleman. I also leave him my third best Beaver Hat.

Item: I bequeath to the Reverend Doctor *Francis Wilson,* the Works of *Plato* in three Folio Volumes, the Earl of *Clarendon*'s History in three Folio Volumes, and my best Bible; together with thirteen small *Persian* Pictures in the Drawing

Room, and the small Silver Tankard given to me by the Contribution of some Friends, whose Names are engraved at the Bottom of the said Tankard.

Item: I bequeath to the Earl of *Orrery* the enamelled Silver Plates to distinguish Bottles of Wine by, given to me by his excellent Lady, and the Half-length Picture of the late Countess of *Orkney* in the Drawing Room.

Item: I bequeath to *Alexander McAullay,* Esq; the Gold Box in which the Freedom of the City of *Dublin* was presented to me, as a Testimony of the Esteem and Love I have for him, on Account of his great Learning, fine natural Parts, unaffected Piety and Benevolence, and his truly honourable Zeal in Defence of the legal Rights of the Clergy, in Opposition to all their unprovoked Oppressors.

Item: I bequeath to *Deane Swift,* Esq; my large Silver Standish, consisting of a large Silver Plate, an Ink Pot, a Sand Box and Bell of the same Mettal.

Item: I bequeath to Mrs. *Mary Barber* the Medal of Queen *Anne* and Prince *George,* which she formerly gave me.

Item: I leave to the Reverend Mr. *John Worral* my best Beaver Hat.

Item: I bequeath to the Reverend Doctor *Patrick Delany* my Medal of Queen *Anne* in Silver, and on the Reverse the Bishops of *England* kneeling before her Most Sacred Majesty.

Item: I bequeath to the Reverend Mr. *James King,* Prebendary of *Tipper,* my large gilded Medal of King *Charles* the First, and on the Reverse a Crown of Martyrdom, with other Devices. My Will, nevertheless, is, that if any of the above named Legatees should die before me, that then, and in that Case, the respective Legacies to them bequeathed, shall revert to myself, and become again subject to my Disposal.

Item: Whereas I have the Lease of a Field in Trust for me, commonly called the *Vineyard,* let to the Reverend Doctor *Francis Corbet,* and the Trust declared by the said Doctor; the said Field, with some Land on this Side of the Road, making in all about three Acres, for which I pay yearly to the Dean and Chapter of St. *Patrick*'s * * *.

Whereas I have built a strong Wall round the said Piece of Ground, eight or nine Feet high, faced to the South Aspect with Brick, which cost me above Six Hundred Pounds *Sterling:* And likewise another Piece of Ground as aforesaid, of half an Acre, adjoining to the Burial Place called the *Cabbage-Garden,* now tenanted by *William White,* Gardener: My Will is, that the Ground inclosed by the great Wall, may be sold for the Remainder of the Lease, at the highest Price my Executors can get for it, in Belief and Hopes, that the said Price will exceed Three Hundred Pounds at the lowest Value: For which my Successor in the

Deanry shall have the first Refusal: and it is my earnest Desire, that the succeeding Deans and Chapters may preserve the said *Vineyard* and Piece of Land adjoining, where the said *White* now liveth, so as to be always in the Hands of the succeeding Deans during their Office, by each Dean lessening One Fourth of the Purchase Money to each succeeding Dean, and for no more than the present Rent.

And I appoint the Honourable *Robert Lyndsay,* one of the Judges of the Court of Common-Pleas: *Henry Singleton,* Esq.; Prime-Sergeant to his Majesty: the Reverend Doctor *Patrick Delany,* Chancellor of St. Patrick's; the Reverend Doctor *Francis Wilson,* Prebendary of *Kilmactolway; Eaton Stannard,* Esq; Recorder of the City of *Dublin;* the Reverend Mr. *Robert Grattan,* Prebendary of St. *Audeon*'s; the Reverend Mr. *John Grattan,* Prebendary of *Clonmethan;* the Reverend Mr. *James Stopford,* Vicar of *Finglass;* the Reverend Mr. *James King,* Prebendary of *Tipper;* and *Alexander McAullay,* Esq; my Executors.

In Witness whereof, I have hereunto set my Hand and Seal, and published and declared this as my last Will and Testament, this third Day of May, 1740.

JONATHAN SWIFT

Signed, sealed, and published by the above named JONATHAN SWIFT, *in Presence of Us, who have subscribed our Names in his Presence,*

JO. WYNNE,
JO. ROCHFORT,
WILLIAM DUNKIN.

Codicil to the Will of Dr. Swift

In the name of God Amen. I *Jonathan Swift,* Doctor in Divinity, and Dean of the Cathedral Church of St. *Patrick*'s *Dublin,* being weak in Body but sound in Mind, do make this codicil Part of my last Will and Testament, and do appoint this Writing to have the same Force and Effect thereof.

Whereas the Right Honourable *Theophilus,* Lord *Newtown,* deceased, did, by his last Will and Testament, bequeath unto *Anne Brent* a legacy of Twenty Pounds *Sterling* a Year during her Life, in Consideration of the long and faithful Service of her the said Anne: And wheras the said *Anne,* since the Death of the said Lord *Newtown,* did intermarry with *Anthony Ridgeway,* of the City of *Dublin,* Cabinet-Maker; and that the said *Anthony Ridgeway* and *Anne* his Wife, for valuable Considerations, did Grant and Assign unto me, the said Dr. *Swift,* the said Annuity or Rent Charge of Twenty Pounds *sterling, per annum,* to hold

to me, my Executors, and Administrators, during the Life of the said *Anne;* and the said *Anthony Ridgeway* being since dead; Now I the said Dr. *Swift,* do hereby devise and bequeath unto the Rev. Dr. *John Wynne,* Chanter of St. *Patrick*'s *Dublin,* the Rev. Mr. *James King,* Curate of St. *Bridget*'s, *Dublin,* and the Rev. Dr. *Francis Willson,* Prebendary of Kilmactolway, and the Survivor or Survivors of them, their Heirs, Executors, and Administrators, the said Annuity or yearly Rent Charge of Twenty Pounds *Sterling, per annum;* devised by the said Lord *Newtown* to the said *Anne,* to have, receive, and enjoy the same during the Life of the said *Anne,* to the Uses, Intents, and Purposes herein after specified; that is to say, it is my Will, that my said Trustees, and the Survivor or Survivors of them, his, and their Heirs, Executors and Administrators, shall, (so soon after as they shall have received the Annuity, or any Part thereof, as conveniently as they can,) Pay or cause to be paid unto the said *Anne Ridgeway,* the said Annuity of Twenty Pounds *Sterling, per annum,* during her Life. In Witness whereof, I, the said Dr. *Jonathan Swift,* have hereunto set my Hand and Seal, and published this Codicil, as Part of my last Will and Testament, this Fifth Day of May, 1740.

JONATHAN SWIFT

Signed, sealed and published in Presence of us, who witnessed this Codicil, in presence of the said Testator.

JOHN LYON,
WILLIAM DUNKIN,
ROGER KENDRICK.

THE "WILL OF 1745": A DOUBTFUL CASE

Paul Montazzoli

An apocryphal successor to the authentic will of 1740 was published in 1745 as a pamphlet entitled *An Authentic Copy of the Last Will and Testament of the Reverend Dr. Swift.* Caveat emptor! Swift himself had perpetrated such hoaxes: his *Predictions for the Year 1708* had carried the name of the fictional astrologer Isaac Bickerstaff as its author, his *Travels* that of their narrator Lemuel Gulliver. Now an impersonation by an anonymous wit carried the name of Swift—and displayed enough of his style and spirit for at least some readers to have taken it as genuine. Yet like Swift's own hoaxes this one was probably meant to be seen through. Though it follows the correct legal form for wills, it is blatantly a *mock*-will, showing the Dean clowning and jibing at death's door, rather than responsibly settling his estate. The document is dated August 24, 1745: in reality Swift by that time was incapable of sustained effort of any kind. Readers who found, while scrutinizing the pamphlet, that they had fallen for yet another eighteenth-century marketing snare need not have felt cheated: This uncanny imitation of the great satirist, patriot, and curmudgeon was worth far more than the sixpence it cost.

The chief surprise of the piece is offered early on: Swift's full contrition over his poem "On the Words 'Brother Protestants and Fellow Christians' "—intended, he confesses here, "to foment and encrease the uncharitable Differences betwixt the Church of *England,* and her dissenting Brethren." This new ecumenical and humble Swift then yields the stage to the familiar misogynist and enragé:

> Whether the Soul has any Communication with the Grave, or ever visits its old Tenement the Body, is, I believe, what no Man in this Life can certainly know: However, to guard against the Worst, I desire that I may not be buried too near the Body of any gaming, gossiping married Woman, any malicious or affected old Maid, or any prudish, coquetish [sic], or slatternly young One; or any rigid calvinist Teacher; or any High-church Jacobite Clergyman; or any dull or Worldly-minded Bishop; any High-titled Knave . . . or, in fine, any Rascal, Blockhead, Coxcomb, or silly Female, whom I

> have justly exposed in my satirical Writings: Because I would not run the Hazard of being tormented by their Company, or lying within reach of their Resentment.

This persona now exits, and Swift the rebellious patriot strides on to the boards, appointing as executors of the will those members of the Irish Parliament who are "zealous Defenders of that small Stock of National Liberty and Property, which the good natur'd English have generously left us"; if at least six such legislators cannot be found, other provisions are to be made. (The pamphlet was first printed in Dublin; its author seems to have been an Irishman as patriotic as Swift.)

The will then proceeds to make a series of preposterous bequests: Any person or persons able to convince the English to cease oppressing Ireland is to receive £500,000; any person or persons able to convince the tradesmen of Ireland's cities to live according to their means and dress according to their station is to receive £15,000; the writer of "the finest and most pompous Panegyrick upon the Wisdom and Honesty of the *British* Ministers of State" is to receive "one Shilling and nine Pence, which I have sealed up in a Paper for this Purpose"; the writer of "the most lofty and sublime Ode, on the success of the *British* Arms on the *European* Continent" is to receive "three Gallons of excellent, high-spirited Bottled Small-Beer." More bequests—equally barbed—follow, along with a recommendation that Swift's works be republished according to the method of Alexander Pope, who acquired "great Profits and Gains . . . by vamping and vending, in various Manners and Forms, [of] most of his original Pieces over and over again."

The whole performance concludes with the bequest of all of Swift's remaining assets to the poor of Dublin—but only if a certain stipulation concerning an obscure and bothersome literary controversy has not been met. What a contrast this nihilistic fooling about misery makes with the hospital bequest in the authentic will of 1740 previously cited!

Further Reading

Brady, Frank, comp., *Twentieth Century Interpretations of Gulliver's Travels* (Englewood Cliffs, NJ: Prentice-Hall, 1968).

Case, Arthur E., *Four Essays on Gulliver's Travels* (Gloucester, MA: Peter Smith, 1958).

Donoghue, Denis, *Jonathan Swift: A Critical Introduction* (London: Cambridge University Press, 1969).

Ehrenpreis, Irvin, *The Personality of Jonathan Swift* (London: Methuen, 1958).

Ehrenpreis, Irvin, *Swift: The Man, His Works, and the Age,* 3 vols. (London: Methuen, 1962, 1967, 1983).

Fussell, Paul, *The Rhetorical World of Augustan Humanism* (Oxford: Clarendon Press, 1965).

Johnson, Samuel, *Lives of the English Poets,* 3 vols. (New York: Octagon Books, 1967).

Landa, Louis, *Swift and the Church of Ireland* (Oxford: Clarendon Press, 1954).

Murry, John Middleton, *Jonathan Swift* (New York: Farrar, Straus, and Giroux, 1955).

Quintana, Ricardo, *The Mind and Art of Jonathan Swift* (Gloucester, MA: Peter Smith, 1965).

Quintana, Ricardo, *Swift: An Introduction* (London: Oxford University Press, 1955).

Scott, Sir Walter, *Memoirs of Jonathan Swift, D.D.* (Vol. 2 of *The Miscellaneous Prose Works of Sir Walter Scott*) (Boston: Wells and Lilly, 1829).

Thackeray, William Makepeace, *The English Humorists of the Eighteenth Century* (New York: Harper and Brothers, 1854).

Van Doren, Carl, *Swift* (New York: The Viking Press, 1930).

Vickers, Brian, ed., *The World of Jonathan Swift* (Cambridge, MA: Harvard University Press, 1968).

Swift's Epitaph

Written by himself

HIC DEPOSITVM EST CORPVS

JONATHAN SWIFT, S.T.D.

HVIVS ECCLESIAE CATHEDRALIS

DECANI,

VBI SAEVA INDIGNATIO

VLTERIVS COR LACERARE NEQUIT.

ABI, VIATOR,

ET IMITARE, SI POTERIS,

STRENVVM PRO VIRILI LIBER-

TATIS VINDICEM.

OBIIT ANNO MDCCXLV

MENSIS OCTOBRIS DIE 19

AETATIS ANNO LXXVIII

The body of Jonathan Swift, Doctor of Theology, Dean of this cathedral church, is laid to rest here, where violent indignation can no longer torment his heart. Go, wayfarer, and imitate, if you can, one who never failed to defend liberty to the utmost of his strength.

Colophon

The text of this edition of *Gulliver's Travels* is based upon that of the Ronald Press, including notes and commentary by Arthur E. Case. It is set in 11 ½ point Adobe Caslon, 14 point leaded. Designed by Carol Twombly in 1990, this is a digitized version of the popular face introduced by William Caslon in the early eighteenth century.

This volume was composed by Digital Composition of Berryville, Virginia, and printed and bound by Quebecor Printing Book Group. The color illustrations were printed by Disc Graphics. The text stock is Bellbrook Laid. It is acid free for archival durability, and it meets or exceeds all guidelines set forth by the U.S. Environmental Protection Agency for recycled content and use of post-consumer waste. The binding is Holliston's Linen Finish Roxite and the jacket is made from Chartham Natural Translucent. The jacket was printed by Phoenix Color Corp.

Mark Summers's scratchboard and watercolor illustrations were film-set by Oceanic Graphics Printing, Inc. The typography and binding design are by Charles J. Ziga of Ziga Design.

LAND OF
St James Bay
Robbin I
IESSO
Salmon B
C Canal
Sea of Corea
C Patience
Straits of the Vries
Companys
Land
Stats I
Sando I
Torpui
Toy
Red Pt
Inaba
Meoco
Iedo
Bosho Pt
Osacca
Surungo
Barnevelts
Tonsa I
Ongeluckig I
Bungo I
South I
Dimeris Strats
I Tanaxima
Sialo
Glangurn
Traldragdubh
Maldonada
Clamrgnig
I Deserta
Glubdrubdrib
Urac
Timal

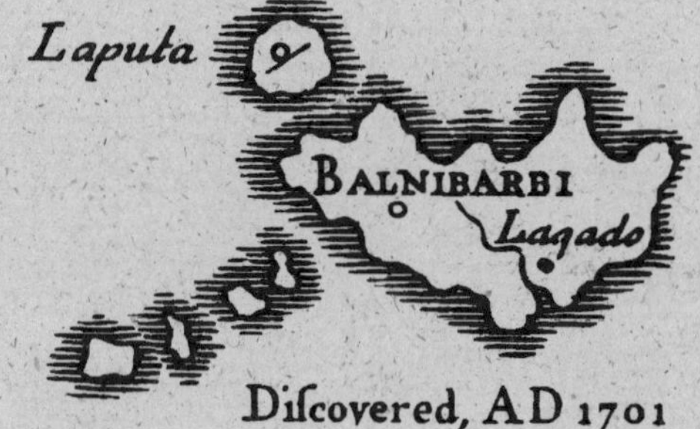

Laputa
BALNIBARBI
Lagado
Discovered, AD 1701